BLOODFALL ARENA

BLOODFALL ARENA

THE BLOOD MAGIC SERIES, BOOK 1

J.A. LUDWIG

BABYLON
BOOKS

For my family, who saw many versions of this story and pushed me to publish

And the amazing group of women who inspire me every day, the Princess Cottage

I

PEACE BROKEN

CHAPTER ONE

Pounding. Loud pounding reverberates inside her head and right leg, making her foot spasm.

Aya opens her eyes, damp with sweat.

A breeze through an open window makes her shiver. She reaches for her blanket but can't find it. Sitting up, her eyes search the small room, wincing at the morning light. A corner of the blanket has spilled onto the floor. She grabs the heavy cloth and pulls it up.

Thump, thump, thump, thump, thump.

Wrapping the soothing blanket around her, she tries to remember why she's awake. She had a strange dream...frighteningly realistic. Fragments of it flash in her mind.

She'd been climbing a tree. Not a full-grown tree, but it still stood tall. She remembers reaching for a branch, but the one beneath her feet cracked. She fell, the world rushing by, and when she hit the ground...intense pain from her right leg. She still feels it, her leg twitching even more at the thought.

Thump, thump, thump. Thump, thump, thump, thump, thump.

She stares at the front door, realizing the pounding is not in her head but real. Someone is at her door. Listening carefully, she hears a faint voice.

"Aya! Please, wake up!"

She moves to the edge of her bed and stands. Her right leg locks uncomfortably, tingling. She takes in a sharp breath.

"Just a dream." She throws her blanket onto the bed and rubs her leg, the numbness fading. Taking a few careful steps to ensure her leg is able to support her weight, she struggles to the door.

Thump, thump, thump, thump. Thump, thump, thump, thump, thump. Thump, thump, th– Grabbing the handle, she opens the door mid-pound, startling the one responsible.

"Aya! Thank the gods!" The young man at the door breathes quickly, sweat rolling down his forehead. He must have run from the village, a decent distance.

"What is it, Lane?" Aya's voice comes out harsher than she intends.

Lane's eyes don't focus on any one thing. He shifts his weight from side to side constantly. "You're needed in the village. Elder Mircien sent me."

"Why?"

"I'm not sure."

Aya leans against the doorframe, her right leg's numbness turning to aching. "Do I have time to put clothes on? I'm a little underdressed."

Lane eyes her nightgown, the sweat causing the cloth to cling to her body and leave little to the imagination. He quickly looks away and nods. "They need you immediately, but I think you have time to dress."

"It won't take long. Wait for me here." She prepares to close the door but hesitates. "And no peeking."

"Right," he says as she closes the door. "But you aren't going to take long, are you?"

Aya doesn't answer. She pulls off the sweaty nightgown and throws it into a basket of varied clothes.

Why is Elder Mircien calling her? Her mind races with scenarios, ranging from simple to dramatic. *It couldn't be some-*

4

thing small, she would've fetched me herself. Something urgent enough to send Lane.

Why her and not someone else? Unless they needed her to—

"You promised you wouldn't call me for that anymore," Aya says to herself, as though Elder Mircien were here.

She wipes a wet towel over her body to remove the sweat and stink. She grabs a clean pair of trousers and a shirt. Over the shirt she puts on a short tunic, tying it tight. She pulls her hair back, pinning it out of her way.

Pulling her boots on, she stops at a small table by the door. Sitting on top is a small drawing of three figures, her mother and father holding a young Aya between them. A gift from an artist who passed through the village many years past.

Smiling, Aya touches the picture with the tips of her fingers. Hanging on the corner of the portrait is a woven bracelet made of four different colored silks—green for the earth, blue for the sea, white for the sky, and red for the sun. It was the last gift her parents gave her before they died, a treasure they'd brought from their homeland when they settled here.

Another treasure sits on the table in front of the portrait. A dagger made of black metal, a gift her father gave her in case she ever needed protection. She rarely wears it out of the house, but today she feels the need to hide it in her boot.

"Aya, we should be going," Lane calls through the door. "Elder Mircien may send someone else if we don't get to the village soon."

Grabbing the silk bracelet, Aya ties it securely to her wrist and opens the door. "All right, all right. I'm ready."

Shutting the door behind her, Aya takes a deep breath of the morning air. Lane is already walking away, eager to return to the village.

Light from the risen sun sparkles off the dew-covered leaves and grass. Birds fly happily from tree to tree, their songs filling the air. Smaller animals scurry across the ground, including a family of lidae. The mother hurries her young pups with her long tail, gently

5

pushing them into the brush. They go about their business, stopping only as the two walk past. Aya follows Lane down the small path.

"Why did Mircien send for me? Couldn't she find anyone else in the village for whatever she needs?"

"I don't know. All she said was she needed you."

"But why? What happened?"

"I don't know. She approached me at the village center and ordered me to fetch you."

Aya raises an eyebrow. "Ordered you?"

"Asked me. She asked me to fetch you." Lane keeps his eyes ahead, never looking at Aya or meeting her eyes.

Her suspicions grow, as well as the ache in her right leg. The path makes a sharp descent and the tops of houses appear through the trees.

Oula Village comes into full sight, resting at the bottom of Foula Valley. The valley stretches for many days in both directions and provides the little village ample protection from the lands beyond the surrounding mountains. Wildflowers bloom amongst the trees, covering the forest floor in a wild cache of colors. Insects fly greedily from one promising bloom to the next and the scent of flowers fill the air.

To the north of the village flows the river Garen, a great source of fish and fresh water. Since the village is half a day's walk from the river, most villagers draw their water from wells spread throughout.

Aya's house is outside the village, a choice she'd made after her mother and father died. She stayed with Elder Mircien until she could take care of herself. The villagers have always been kind to her. She appreciated their warmth after her parents' deaths but couldn't stand to see their faces fill with pity for her.

Aya and Lane enter the village and pass the houses quickly. Villagers doing their morning chores glance up at the two passing by. When they see Aya, their eyes widen. She purposefully avoids the gazes, knowing how she'll be greeted.

"Aya! Lane!" The village elder, Mircien Alluvia, bustles towards them. Her short, gray hair is barely visible poking from under the braided cloth wound around her head. Her gray eyes are sunken, and a dark spot is visible on her cheek. A slight hunch makes her appear shorter than she actually is but doesn't diminish her graceful elegance.

"Good morning, Elder Mircien." Aya gives her a slight nod, but her smile falters.

"I hate bothering you so early this morning with unpleasant things, but we need your help." She waves away Lane, who eagerly accepts the dismissal. He disappears among the homes as Mircien places a hand on Aya's arm and leads her into the village.

With Lane gone, Aya drops the formalities and pulls away from Mircien. "You need my help or my *kind* of help?"

"I specifically sent Lane to fetch you because he didn't see the…unpleasantness. His lack of knowledge was the only way to get you here."

So, this is exactly what Aya feared. "I hope it isn't *too* unpleasant. I didn't sleep well last night."

"It's about one of the children, Petri. A group of them were playing by a growing sapling. Petri climbed it and fell when one of the larger branches broke beneath him."

Aya's dream flashes before her eyes and her right leg aches. "Truly?"

"His mother believes he may have broken his leg."

Aya plays with the silk bracelet on her wrist. "I've never dealt with anything more complicated than a finger. Have you had Iria look at him?"

"Petri's mother specifically asked for you, my dear. We should hurry. We've wasted too much time." Mircien gently pulls her forward.

Aya's mind races. Her nightmare had to be a coincidence…right?

"Did you have the nightmares again?" Mircien's voice breaks her thoughts. "The ones with the...what do you call them?"

"Ever-watching shadows." She swallows a lump in her throat. "No. I had a different nightmare last night. It felt too real."

Mircien shakes her head. "I don't understand why you won't accept Iria's sleeping balm. I assure you it works quite well, speaking as one who uses it for the nights Iria's snoring becomes unbearable."

"Falling asleep isn't the issue. It's the dreams." She wants to tell her about this morning's dream but can't bring herself to speak the words.

They pass two houses built close together, revealing a gathering of villagers beyond. Loud cries of pain reach Aya's ears and she prepares herself for whatever horror waits for her.

CHAPTER TWO

CLEARING A PATH THROUGH THE SMALL CROWD, MIRCIEN KEEPS AYA close. The villagers watch her, the pitying look she hates filling their eyes. She avoids the stares, instead focusing on a group of children standing off to the side. Most have their hands in their pockets, while one has hers in her mouth. Her eyes are red, and tears dry on her cheeks.

They stare with wide eyes at the boy cradled in his mother's arms. The woman holds her son tightly, being extra careful not to touch his right leg. It's bent at an odd angle at the knee, aiming to the right. Swelling around the knee and several cuts discolor the skin, a nasty bruise growing.

Aya grabs Mircien's shoulder and leans close to her ear. "You told me you *thought* it was broken. It's almost twisted off!"

She places a hand on hers. "If I told you what it looked like, you might not have come."

Lowering her voice so only the elder can hear, Aya whispers, "You wanted to get me in front of a crowd so I couldn't refuse. I don't know if I can do anything to help."

"If anyone can help the boy now, it's you. It definitely wouldn't have been Iria. He may have taught you all he knew, but he simply doesn't have your gift."

Taking a deep, calming breath, Aya kneels beside the mother and child, her right leg tingling, reminding her of the dream. The villagers move closer to get a better look as she reaches for Petri's leg. Her hand stops above, and she locks eyes with the boy's mother.

"Please hold him tightly, Zuri. I can't do anything with the leg bent in the wrong position. This will hurt."

Petri's mother nods and squeezes her son. His cries are muffled, but Aya knows it'll only last for a moment. She returns her attention to the injury and places her shaking hands on the leg. Taking a deep breath, she grips the leg tightly.

Memories flood her. She remembers Iria, the village's true healer, spending hours, sometimes even days, teaching Aya everything he knew about natural healing. She remembers visiting those with broken bones and helping reset the bones while Iria explained how they connected at joints. Lessons Mircien encouraged due to Aya's gift.

Releasing her breath, Aya forcibly twists Petri's leg back into the normal position. Feeling the bones beneath her hands sends a small wave of nausea through her, but Aya is able to keep her expression steady. A trick, Iria assured her, that would only be needed until the hundredth time.

Zuri has trouble holding Petri completely still and his strong leg kicks at Aya. It makes contact with the side of her abdomen and she's knocked back, gasping in shock. His shrieks of pain intensify, sending an audible gasp rippling through those standing around.

"I need him to stay as still as possible while I heal him," Aya says, surprised at how calm her voice sounds.

Zuri nods again, unable to speak as tears roll down her cheeks. She strokes her son's hair, whispering soothing words, but when Aya moves closer the boy's struggles intensify. Petri's father, Ervine, kneels down and helps hold Petri steady. His clenched jaw shows the pain he feels at seeing his son this way, but he keeps a firm grip to show his trust in Aya.

Placing both hands on the broken leg, Aya closes her eyes and does her best to block the world out. Petri's cries of pain and fear fade as she reaches deep inside. A calming sensation fills her as she taps into her gift, the magic she inherited from her parents. The magic only she holds, no one else.

Warmth gathers in her chest and she concentrates on it. She imagines it moving down her arms and into Petri's leg, feeling it move inside him.

Images fill her mind.

Petri's leg appears clearly, even with her eyes closed. The boy's clothes and skin fade away, revealing the injury. Bones are broken but resetting the position of the leg has placed them where they need to be. Muscles are bruised, and two are detached from the bone. Tendons are torn and the knee is still dislocated.

She remembers Iria's lessons, the hand-drawn diagrams of what people look like beneath the skin. She remembers the old skeleton in Iria's home and learning every bone on it. She remembers dark nights after an older villager passed on, secretly watching Iria carefully pull the skin away and display the muscles, tendons, veins, arteries, organs, and nerves.

Pain shoots up her arms and into her chest, bringing her back to the task before her. The pain is normal. She's learned that it only means her magic is working. As she heals Petri, the pain from the injury transfers to her briefly. She focuses on the pain, forcing it away. Once it fades, the person she's working on no longer feels it.

Aya concentrates on one issue at a time. Repair the bone before reattaching the muscle. The dislocated knee is next, moving it back into its proper position before she fixes the tendons. Blood flow returns to normal and she searches for anything she may have overlooked, but she's confident she won't find anything.

An ice-cold feeling rises amongst the warmth in her chest.

She recognizes it and knows she must finish quickly. Her magic is done; if she pushes any further...

She pulls her magic from Petri's leg and feels it quickly disperse inside her, sending the coldness away. Opening her eyes, Aya winces at the now blinding sunlight. Her eyes are always highly sensitive and her head foggy after using her magic. She blinks a few times until her eyesight returns to normal, stabilizing herself. Her mind clears and she carefully turns her head.

She isn't sure when the boy stopped crying, but Petri's eyes are now filled with wonder. He sits up, his parents releasing him, and stares at his leg. Aya smiles with relief.

The leg is fully healed, not even a bruise left behind. Aya sits back on her heels, removing her hands from Petri. The young boy moves carefully, amazement filling him.

Zuri moves quickly, grabbing Aya's hands before she moves too far away. The tears are much heavier now, tears of joy. "Thank you, Healer! Thank you." Petri's mother gasps between heavy sobs and places her forehead on Aya's hands.

Ervine moves closer to his son and pulls both him and Zuri into a tight hug, allowing Aya to pull her hands free. His eyes meet hers, full of gratitude and something else. Something that scares her.

The villagers huddle closer; sounds of awe and echoes of Zuri's words of thanks fill the air. The children rush forward, investigating Petri's leg.

Aya knows if she meets every pair of eyes of those around her, she'll see the same look in Ervine's eyes.

A look of utter and total devotion.

CHAPTER THREE

STANDING, AYA SMILES DOWN AT THE SMALL FAMILY. "NO MORE climbing trees for a while, Petri. I may not always be around to help."

Petri's head nods against his mother and father, wiping away his tears.

A young girl in the group of children turns to Aya. "But you'll never leave us, will you?"

Aya feels the weight of every eye on her. Everyone waits for her answer, but a sudden wave of lightheadedness surges through her. Mircien is there to steady her before the rest notice.

"Enough, everyone. We've bothered Aya with unpleasantness enough for one day. Return to your mornings." Mircien pulls Aya away before those closest can bother her.

They walk back past the homes towards the center of the village where there is more space from the crowd and to breathe. Mircien leads her to a large well, helps her sit on the edge, and brings her a cup of water. The wave of lightheadedness passes and the dizzy, dancing spots of light fade from her vision.

"Thank you," she says, implying both the cup of water and the escape from villagers.

"I should be thanking you." Mircien sits next to her. "I know the looks in their eyes can be...overwhelming. But your magic is a great gift. You have a natural talent for it."

"As natural as going in blind can be," Aya scolds between gulps.

"You were not completely blind. Iria saw to that." Mircien pats her, sensing the discomfort. "Your parents would be proud."

"I like to believe they would." She stares at the cool liquid. Her thoughts darken as she thinks about her parents. She remembers the illness that took them from her when she was seven, three years before her own magic manifested. They were the village healers; no one had been able to heal them as their magic ate them from inside.

Mircien places a comforting hand on her shoulder. "I know they would. And they would never want you to blame yourself for what happened. The illness that took them was borne of their magic. Even if you'd had your gift, you could have done nothing."

"We'll never know that for sure."

"They knew it." Smiling weakly, the elder takes a deep breath. "Though I'm not sure they'd understand why you choose to live so far from the village."

"I appreciate everything everyone has done for me since my parents passed, but they already treated us differently because mother and father were Healers. Once my own magic became evident, it felt as though I became a stranger to them." She turns, staring into Mircien's eyes. "I'll never forget how you and Iria took me in and treated me like your own daughter. But living outside the village...I feel less like a rarity for everyone to ogle at."

"You are as much a part of this village as anyone else," Mircien says. "They treat you differently because they respect you as a Healer. Before your parents settled down here, there hadn't been a magic user in this village for many generations.

We felt blessed they chose our small village as home. They believe you carry on their good luck."

"The looks in their eyes say otherwise," Aya says, turning away and finishing her water. She spies a figure sitting against the well, almost hidden by a bush. "Iria?"

The figure jumps at his name and slowly stands. "Aya…Mircien."

The two elders meet each other's gaze and a silent understanding passes between them. Aya remembers the look from her years living with the two.

"I must be going," Mircien says, locking eyes with Iria. "Tell her. I know it weighs on you." She leaves, hugging Aya before heading towards her home.

Aya places the cup on the edge of the well. "Should I ask what she meant?"

Iria avoids her eyes, an expression of shame clear on his face. He lowers himself onto the wall beside her. "I'm sorry, Aya. I forced Mircien to send for you."

"I nearly passed out from the strain." Anger tints her voice.

"I know, but—"

"The coldness of death came back."

"I understand—"

"If I'd needed even a speck more magic to heal him…"

Iria places a finger to her lips. "I'm sorry. When I saw the extent of his injury, I knew the only thing I could do was force it back into place. There was too high a risk of doing more damage and laming his leg permanently." Iria removes his finger and clasps his hands in his lap. "I couldn't do that to a child."

Aya hesitates, trying to find the strength to stay angry at him. But she feels his anguish and stays silent.

"You healed him?" he asks. "Fully?"

"Yes."

Iria's shoulders relax and a shaky, relieved breath escapes his lips. "Amazing. Your magic is growing."

15

Lowering her eyes to the ground, Aya kicks a rock between her feet. "I dreamed about Petri's fall."

"When?"

"Last night...or maybe this morning? I fell out of the same tree and broke the same leg as Petri. I felt the pain and while I was healing him...it was the same pain." She turns to Iria, her eyes wide with fear and a little excitement. "I knew I could heal him. I knew because of my dream I'd be able to heal him."

He searches Aya's face for something, but she can't tell what. Perhaps wondering if she's gone mad. "The same as Ollie?"

She nods. Several years past, Aya dreamed of her finger breaking during a home repair. The next day she went with Iria to visit Ollie who'd broken his finger in a similar accident as in her dream. She managed to heal his finger even though before the incident the only things she could heal were cuts. When she told Iria about the dream, he wondered if her magic had been telling her she was ready to try mending bone.

"Mircien would be furious with me if she knew I was about to tell you this," Iria says, moving closer to Aya on the well. "She doesn't want to believe it, but I understand the resignation you have about the villagers. She doesn't truly see the way they look at you. But I do."

Standing, Aya shakes her head. "Don't say it."

"They idolize you. To the point of near blasphemy to the gods." Aya tries to walk away, but Iria moves quickly, grasping her wrists. "And the illness that took your parents...you still fear it will come for you if you continue to heal others."

"Iria, please."

"You shouldn't be a captive in your home or in your heart, Aya. Remember this, the fear inside is what creates the illness." Iria pulls her close to him. "And the nightmares feed the fear."

Aya stares at the sweet, sentimental old man, feeling the fear rise. "Why are you saying this?"

Realization crosses Iria's face and he releases her. "Mircien refuses to speak of these things. I just—I needed to get them out. Please, forgive me."

"I have to go." She walks away, then stops and turns back to Iria. "I haven't had the nightmares in several weeks...but I have seen the looks in their eyes. Maybe...it would better if I left the village altogether."

Before Iria can respond, Aya leaves, moving quickly. She heads east, avoiding most of the villagers, and spies two small shacks used to store food for winter and mark the edge of the village. Beyond them, a single path leads into the forest. She follows it a short distance before checking if anyone is following. Confirming she's alone, she turns sharply into the forest, the village behind her slowly disappearing amongst the trees.

The forest grows dense as she moves away from Oula Village, escaping the feeling of being trapped. Her path grows steadily steeper as she approaches the base of the surrounding mountains. She climbs uphill with an ease that comes from years of practice, though her clothes still occasionally catch on low branches and thick bushes.

There hasn't been much human interaction in this area. No clear paths are visible, but Aya knows her way. A sharper incline forces her to use her hands to maintain balance, and she grabs large rocks embedded in the earth to pull herself forward.

She reaches a rock wall, a minor cliff she uses to guide her way. Aya follows the wall around until she finds boulders larger than herself and uses these massive stones to climb higher. Reaching the top of the cliff, she rests a moment to catch her breath and glances around the open area.

Thick bushes grow where the forest continues higher up the mountain, but on one side of the clearing a waterfall flows, creating a small pond surrounded by ash trees.

Aya walks to the edge of the cliff. Foula Valley is bright green from the rains, and clusters of wildflowers add delicate splashes of color. Farther out in the valley, the Garen River cuts through the mountains. Other villages dot the distance.

She's spent her whole life in the valley, never going beyond the mountains towering high above. Her parents weren't from Foula Valley and rarely spoke about their homeland. Aya didn't know the name of their village or town. She didn't even know if they came from a village or town. When they did speak of their past, it was always with an air of caution and little to no details. They spoke of the dangers of bandits or, worse, slave traders, citing these warnings as the reason they left to find a more peaceful home.

The farthest Aya's ever been from Oula Village is a larger village, Goro, almost a day's walk away. She remembers staying at an inn and the innkeeper, a warm man who spoke with Mircien like an old friend. He asked Aya many questions, eager to learn about the Elder of Oula Village's little protégé. She remembers asking him what that meant, but the innkeeper only laughed.

She went with Mircien a short time after her parents died. The elder thought it would help take Aya's mind off her sorrow. It worked, but only because there had been travelers in the village from beyond the valley.

She remembers wondering if they'd come from her parents' homeland, but she didn't know enough to ask. Instead, she asked about those with gifts like hers, other magic users. They told her of the variety of magic beyond the valley and how there were many rumors of those with power enough to destroy the stars. And rumors of those who used their magic for evil things.

Mircien dragged her away, claiming the travelers were exaggerating, trying to frighten her.

It never frightened her. It made her yearn for other magic users to talk with.

She tries to visualize the lands beyond the mountains, based on what she's heard from the travelers, wondering if she'll ever see great mountains disappear into the sky, vast seas continuing into the horizon for eternity, or fantastic creatures only imagined in dreams. Her argument with Iria wasn't the first time she'd mentioned leaving the village. But it is the first time she'd left an argument without smoothing things over.

The smell of wildflowers surrounds her as a warm breeze rises from the valley. She smiles and sits next to the rippling water of the pond. She traces the cool water with her hand. The sound of the waterfall soothes her, and Aya notices small, white fish swimming close to the center. She picks a red berry from a nearby bush and throws it to the fish. They quickly devour it, leaving behind a spot of red in the water.

The red in the water sends a chill up her spine. It reminds her of the recurring nightmares she's been having since she was a child. Especially the nightmare from two nights ago.

CHAPTER FOUR

I KNOW THE LIGHT CAN'T CHASE THEM AWAY. THEY ARE HERE, always here, always watching. Standing still as statues and always watching...me.

Shadows. So many shadows looking at me as I move among them.

No features distinguish them, at least, none I can see. They're only shadows. What defines them is where and how they stand. Most cluster together, stretching far into the distance, making an ocean of shadows. Some tall, some short, some oddly shaped, and others—appear almost human.

Walking through the endless rows, I hear whispers, indistinguishable. Occasionally a solitary word rings clear, but I can never recall it. Where there are no whispers, breathing or laughter follow me, sending chills through my body.

But two always stand above the others, oblivious to me. Oblivious to everything around. They're the closest in shape to men and, unlike the indefinable shadows surrounding me, they have eyes.

One's eyes burn with a white flame. The other's are so black they stand out even against the dark of its body.

I know this place, these shadows. I've been here many times.

20

But this time there's something new. Symbols appear above each figure, each familiar, yet unfamiliar, composed of different entities.

One close to me is made of ice, vapor rising around it. Another burns, the flames dancing. Curiosity outweighs any discomfort and I move closer to these figures, feeling nothing from the symbols. No heat, no cold.

Exploring these additions to the familiar shadows, I discover one made of metal, another of leaves. One made of light, another of darkness. And so on, and so on, and so on. Thousands upon thousands, stretching far beyond my sight.

The world shakes, drawing my attention to the two above. The two who remain oblivious to all. They don't have symbols. But before them, standing in the distance, four figures appear. All have symbols floating above their heads.

One figure before White Eyes has a symbol made of a strange light. It pulses oddly, moving forward and in reverse. The symbol grows and shrinks as though breathing with the sound of wind.

The second figure has a symbol made of the four elements: earth, water, air, and fire mixing together as though living things. But the fire is the strongest, swallowing the other elements when they move too close.

I'm drawn to the beauty of the mixing elements, sensing the sadness and pain within the figure feeding the symbol.

The feeling disperses quickly when I see the symbols of those on the other side.

Chains slither up and around the figures standing before Black Eyes. The chains connect the figures not only to Black Eyes, but also the symbols above them. One figure has a symbol made of black shadows and smoke.

But it's the second figure's symbol, made of a dark liquid, that sends a chill through me. Spikes on the chain tear into the figure, drawing blood that rises to the symbol, mixing with the liquid.

Red droplets fall to the ground around me. I notice the others moving away from the blood. I feel something, too. Fear. Growing dread. This shadow with chains and blood is unnatural. This entity shouldn't exist.

The dark spots grow at my feet, the tiny droplets expanding to create a small stream. The stream grows, becoming a red river, blood rising. It separates me from the other shadows, trapping me with the six figures above.

I feel eyes on me and stare up at the figure with chains, the figure with shadows, and Black Eyes watching me. The chained figures raise their hands, reaching for me. The chains fly through the air towards me, blood dripping from the metal.

Then I wake up.

THE WATER from the waterfall stops; silence fills the clearing on the cliff and Aya snaps out of her reverie. She looks at the waterfall, the boulders still wet from the water. Confused, her eyes are drawn to the red spot on the water from the berry, steadily growing larger.

The water of the pond turns red and murky, making it impossible to see beyond the surface. Even the fish are hidden from view. She pulls her hands from the pond, her eyes locked on the fluid now rolling down her arms. The red liquid is thick, and a metallic smell fills her nostrils.

Her breathing quickens. She tries wiping the familiar liquid onto the grass around her. Aya knows this smell. She knows it from the many injuries she's witnessed with Iria.

Blood.

A faint sound echoes across the clearing, coming from the pond itself. She searches the surface of the water, trying to see beneath the dark liquid. The center of the pond bubbles as through someone were releasing air beneath the thick red liquid.

Something moves beneath the surface, creating small ripples in the blood.

The sound of chains rattling fills the air and her heart pounds loudly in her chest. Terror roots her to the spot, the movement in the blood slowly inching towards the edge of the pond, towards Aya.

She wants to back away, but her body refuses to move. She doesn't want to know what's beneath the surface. She wants to escape. She needs to run.

Then the surface stills, whatever is beneath seeming to disappear deeper in the pond as the rattling of chains stops.

The muttering sound of the breeze rises, but she doesn't feel any wind. As it intensifies, she realizes the sound is actually whispers. Hundreds, maybe thousands, of whispers so low they blend together. But she almost hears a clear pattern of words, repeating over and over.

She leans forward, angling her head so her ear is close to the surface.

I've found you.

A hand explodes from the blood, sending a wave of red splashing onto the grass, spattering the bushes. Aya screams, throwing herself back as the hand grabs the empty air where she'd been. The shock fills her with energy, and she scrambles to her feet.

The sound of rattling chains precedes the feeling of something cold and sharp grabbing her legs. Aya falls to the ground and rolls onto her back. Blood-soaked chains wrap around her ankles, steadily climbing higher up her legs. Spikes dig into her skin, adding her own blood to the living metal.

She cries out in pain and reaches down to the chains, trying to free herself. The pain fills her body, her senses screaming at her to escape.

The chains tighten and pull her towards the pond where a form crawls from the bloody surface. A trail of red follows the figure as it moves closer to her. When near enough, the creature grabs her legs and roughly pulls her closer.

"No. You can't be here. You aren't real," Aya pleads, trying desperately to convince herself she's dreaming.

But the pain feels very real.

The agony of the spiked chains biting into her legs fades as she stares into the blood-covered face, or where the face should be. She throws her hands at the figure, trying to shove it off her, but more chains appear and wrap around her wrists, pulling her arms to the ground. She screams as new spikes puncture her skin.

The figure's long-fingered hands reach for her and she struggles beneath it like a trapped animal.

The cold hands close around her throat.

CHAPTER FIVE

A LARGE SPLASH OF WATER HITS AYA'S FACE. SHE JUMPS, FALLING back from the pond. A small branch floats on the surface of the clear water and the waterfall trickles as if nothing had happened. Looking around, Aya realizes she never moved from the side of the pond.

A dream? Or a vision conjured from memories?

Cautiously moving up to the edge of the pond, Aya peers into the disturbed water. The water is clear. She can see the bottom. The waterfall pushes the branch that fell towards the edge.

There's no blood, no chains, no figure. Only frightened white fish reemerging from the rocks.

"Felt real," Aya whispers to herself, rubbing her legs. She still feels the spikes in her skin, but there are no marks. It reminds her of how she still felt the pain of Petri's broken leg after waking from her dream that morning. Are these dreams, or visions, part of her magic? Or something else?

She looks away from the pond, unable to stare at her reflection anymore. She notices the air is unusually warm, and a smell overpowers the wildflowers. Slowly standing, Aya realizes the birds are silent.

25

Everything seems to have stopped in the forest.

Aya's heart grows cold. She walks towards the edge of the cliff, her eyes locked on the smoke now filling the sky. She forces her eyes to lower and her hands cover her mouth in shock.

Flames tear into homes on the northern edge of Oula Village, sending black plumes into the sky.

Villagers run from the flames, clinging to each other as strange men in black armor herd them towards the center of the village. Their screams are loud enough to reach the cliff. Men not gathering villagers move building to building, breaking the doors down and looting.

Squinting through the smoke, she makes out Elder Mircien, Iria, and many others being forced together by the very well she'd sat on almost an hour before.

Aya runs to the edge of the slope where she climbed up. She nearly falls down the side of the mountain, moving faster than ever before. As she moves lower, the smoke thickens and darkens the air. It burns Aya's eyes and lungs, and she coughs. The pain blurs her vision and forces her to slow her pace.

No. No more death.

She can't lose any more people she loves. Not when she can save them. Her magic may not be strong, but...if she can heal, she must be able to harm as well.

The dark thought fills Aya with anger. She pauses to grab the dagger from her boot. The heavy metal feels strange in her hand, but she keeps running.

A sudden blur of fur runs across her path, nearly tripping her. She grabs a nearby tree to keep from falling as animals flee the fire.

Once the wave of terrified animals passes, she continues her approach, reaching the eastern rim of the village. The homes burn, collapsing as the fire eats away at the wood. Sparks fly into the air, threatening to set the surrounding forest ablaze.

The usual path into the village is blocked with men in armor.

Aya decides to circle around and try to enter near where she healed Petri.

She carefully makes her way, keeping an eye on the flames as she goes. About to cross the small path leading up to her house, Aya hears a scream. She drops to the ground.

Heavy footsteps and angry voices grow in volume ahead of her. She quickly creeps into a group of bushes between two trees, pulling the dagger from her boot and gripping it tightly. Her heart pounds loudly in her chest, her thoughts filling with prayers to the gods to keep her hidden.

Three men in black armor appear out of a nearby home. One of the men drags an unconscious male villager behind him. Blood covers the villager's head and Aya's breath catches in her throat.

"See where this path leads. There may be stragglers," the man dragging the villager orders, then heads off towards the center of the village.

The other two head up the path, their eyes glancing into the surrounding trees. After they move past Aya's hiding place, she crosses to the opposite side of the path. She hesitates only a moment, deciding whether to follow the men, but she knows she can't stop them from doing whatever they plan to her home.

Aya doesn't know how many attackers there are and doesn't care. She only cares about the villager's safety. She runs between two homes, staying close to the ground. When she reaches the edge, she peers around the corner.

Five men run by, carrying large jars. Aya hears liquid sloshing inside and wonders what they could be for. Pressing herself against the wall of the house, she hopes they don't notice her. Once they pass, she hurries to the next house. She follows the wall of the house quickly, nearly running into two more men blocking her path.

Aya curses silently and circles back. Finally making her way to the back of Mircien's house, she follows the wall around to the left side. A tall pile of cut wood towers on one side. Aya moves behind the pile and peeks through a gap in the logs.

She can now see the center of the village, the familiar well at its center. Huddled together, the villagers are clustered on the left side of the clearing from Aya's hiding spot. Many weep or pray softly. Petri clings to his mother, his father forming a wall in front of the two.

Aya searches the faces and spots Iria sitting at the front of the gathered mob. His eyes are focused across the well to the right side of the clearing. Mircien stands between two men in armor. A third walks in front of her.

This third man is different. Aya can tell by how he stands: confident, commanding, hands on hips as if surveying good work.

More men in black armor enter the clearing from between homes, including the five carrying the jars. Placing the jars around the well, the men join the rest in blocking any possible escape routes. She counts thirteen in all, a few carrying burning torches. One man moves in front of the pile of wood where Aya is hiding but doesn't quite block her view.

The man in front of Mircien stops as two men approach, increasing the total number to fifteen. Aya recognizes them as the ones sent to her house, marveling at how quickly they returned.

"There's one house outside the village but no one inside. From what we saw, only one person lives there. Should we burn it down?"

Aya's heart leaps into her throat. She squeezes the dagger in her hand. Why even suggest such a thing if they didn't do it already? She understands looting, but why burning?

A hand grabs her arm and she turns quickly, raising her dagger. She stops as the familiar face sends a wave of relief through her. "Lane!"

The frightened man whimpers in response, his wide eyes

28

bouncing from the blade to Aya. "I was told to find you. I'm supposed to get you out of the village and away from here."

"We can't leave! We have to help."

"There's nothing we can do. We're outnumbered." He pulls on her arm, attempting to drag her away.

Aya aggressively pulls her arm free. "I'm not leaving. There has to be something I can do."

She spies through the logs once more. The man in front of Mircien, whose armor is more elegant and has seen more action than that of the others, shakes his head and waves the man away. He turns to face Mircien, giving Aya her first look at the man responsible for this attack.

His black hair is shaggy, and his eyes are bright blue lanterns within the dark skin of his face. He smiles almost pleasantly and leans close to Mircien. The elder leans away, but the two men on either side grab her by the shoulders to keep her still.

Aya barely hears the question the man asks.

"Where is the magic user?"

CHAPTER SIX

"WE KNOW YOU'RE HIDING A MAGIC USER HERE. TELL US WHO HE IS, and we'll spare the rest of you," the blue-eyed man says.

Aya presses close to the woodpile. These men are here for her. All of this is her fault.

Mircien eyes the villagers, pausing on Iria's worried expression. Sweat rolls down the side of her face, but her voice is calm when she speaks. "There haven't been magic users in this part of the valley in many generations."

Blue Eyes' smile falters for a moment. He locks eyes with both men holding Mircien and nods. They release him and move away. Before the elder can react, Blue Eyes punches her hard in the face. Mircien stumbles back and the two men catch her before she hits the ground. Her eyes widen and blood rolls down her chin. The villagers scream in shock and huddle closer together. Iria tries to stand, but one of the villagers holds him back.

Blue Eyes grabs Mircien's throat and pulls her close to him. "You've seen men like me before. I can see it in your eyes. You know why we're here."

Mircien licks the cut on her lip. Her voice is no longer calm, shaking with fear and anger. "You're slave traders. You're collecting slaves for the Arena."

Arena? Aya doesn't remember ever hearing about an Arena. She knew about slave traders, but she never thought about what happened to those who became slaves.

"Very good. If we don't find the magic user, we'll take the others. All of them. Tell me where he is and no one else will be taken."

Mircien swallows, having difficulty with the man's hand at her throat. She spits blood into Blue Eyes' face. "Go back to your murderous land and leave us in peace. We are poor people who only wish to be left alone."

Blue Eyes sighs and wipes the blood from his face. He steps forward, thrusting his knee into the old woman's gut, driving her to the ground. He enunciates each word through gritted teeth. "Where is the magic user?"

Struggling to her knees, Mircien's wandering eyes lock on Aya in her hiding spot behind the pile of logs. Aya's eyes widen and she tries to stand. *They're only here because of me. I can stop this.*

She starts to rise. Lane grabs her arms and pulls. "We must go."

"Let me go, Lane. I can stop this right now!"

Mircien smiles sadly before turning to meet Iria's eyes. She touches her chest with her hand, placing her fist over her heart. Iria's eyes widen and he struggles against the villager holding him.

"I'll only ask one more time. Where is the magic user?"

Looking up at Blue Eyes, Mircien leans back on her heels. "Leave us in peace." Mircien closes her eyes and speaks a prayer under her breath

Slowly nodding, Blue Eyes steps back from Mircien. "Very well." He points to the man standing to Mircien's right. "Silence her."

The man draws the axe from behind his back, and in one

31

quick movement, the blade slices cleanly through Mircien's neck, beheading her. The braided cloth on her head flies off, landing in front of the villagers.

Aya screams. Lane's hand quickly clasps over her mouth. Luckily, her screams aren't heard over the cries of the villagers.

Mircien's body stays kneeling upright for longer than Aya thought possible before slumping to the ground. The man with the axe cleans his blade on Mircien's clothes.

The villagers scream in terror and a few try to shove their way through the surrounding men, but the armored men easily force them back to the center. Some even draw their weapons and wave deadly metal in front of the villagers, laughing at the fear in their eyes.

Aya squeezes the hilt of the dagger in her hand tightly. Why? Why did Mircien have to die? Why didn't she tell them she was here? She isn't worth anyone else's life. Mircien shouldn't have protected her.

Again she stands, but Lane grabs her around the waist and falls back, dragging her to the ground with him.

Blue Eyes storms forward and rips the axe from his man's hand. "I said *silence* her. Not kill her." He slams the handle of the axe into the other man's stomach. When the man doubles over, Blue Eyes knees him in the face then throws the axe to the ground in disgust.

Iria stares at Mircien's body in shock, unmoving. His eyes lower to the bloody cloth on the ground in front of him. He reaches for it with a shaking hand and pulls it to his chest, the blood staining his hands.

The man with blue eyes moves towards the group, not even glancing at the body lying at his feet. "We've heard tales from the other villages about the magic user that lives here. Bring him forth." Staring down at Iria's frozen form, the man's eyes narrow. "Or take your chances in the Arena."

"Let go, Lane!" Aya fights to free herself. "Now."

"No! I promised Mircien I'd get you out of here!" He tightens his hold on her. "Come with me, for her sake!"

"For her sake…" Aya pauses, still gazing on the scene.

The villagers stare at the man in fear, but none speak. Aya sees Zuri holding Petri so he's facing away from the still body, blood pooling on the ground. Ervine is sitting beside them, his arm protectively around his wife and son.

Frustrated, Blue Eyes gazes at the men surrounding the clearing and waves his hand. The men close in on the group, drawing their weapons. They each grab a single villager and pull them from the large group. Other villagers try to keep hold of those being separated, but the men kick them back or threaten them with their weapons.

Petri is ripped from Zuri and Ervine's arms by the same man who beheaded Mircien, but his father tries to fight the man off. "No!" she cries at the same time as Ervine. A second man hits Ervine with the butt of his sword, knocking him to the ground. The man dragging Petri from his family returns to a position in front of Aya's hiding spot, blocking her view for a moment.

Aya's heart pounds louder and louder in her head. They wouldn't kill a child…would they? They couldn't possibly. She fights against Lane, but he's surprisingly strong.

Blue Eyes grabs Iria and drags him to his feet. He draws a dagger and holds the blade to the unresponsive man's throat. The other men follow suit, preparing to kill the ones they hold.

"No, no, no, don't do this," Aya whispers, the dagger shaking in her hand. "Don't protect me."

"Where is the magic user?" Blue Eyes asks. She can tell from his tone that he is finished asking.

She wipes the tears from her cheeks and grips a log tightly, splinters burying into her palm, as the villagers remain silent. For her sake.

Blue Eyes meets his men's eager expressions and takes a deep breath. The man holding Petri tightens his grip on the small boy, his hand holding the blade tensing with anticipation.

33

"No!"

Aya elbows Lane low in his gut. His arms loosen around her and she breaks free. She throws one of the logs at the man holding Petri. The heavy wood hits him in the back of the head. The shock causes him to drop his axe, but he holds firmly onto the boy. She stands and crashes into the man, using her dagger to slice the hand holding the frightened boy.

Yelling, the man releases Petri, swinging his free arm at her. Aya quickly pulls Petri to the ground, dodging the strike. She kicks the man in the knee and, feeling a small shock of magic shoot through her leg, dislocates it. She hesitates a moment, realizing her magic ensured the man would be seriously hurt.

Petri scrambles to his feet and scrambles to his mother and father, passing the man with blue eyes. He watches his man collapse to the ground, screaming and holding his leg in excruciating pain.

Aya stands, holding her dagger in front of her and stares at Blue Eyes, anger filling her. He returns her look, his expression calm.

When Iria sees Aya, life returns to him. He struggles against Blue Eyes, clutching Mircien's cloth close to him. "Aya, get out of here! Leave now!"

"I'm the magic user," Aya announces. "Don't hurt any more people."

The man rolling on the ground grabs for her. She kicks him in the side and another shock of magic shoots through her. She feels the man's rib break. He curses and grabs his side. A wave of exhaustion rushes through her. She knows it's from the sudden uses of her magic. If she needs to use it again...she may pass out.

Blue Eyes shoves Iria away, knocking the older man to the ground, and waves for his men to do the same. His men release their captives and sheathe their weapons, somewhat reluctantly. Two run to the wounded man and pull him away as Blue Eyes walks towards Aya, stopping an arm's length from her.

She struggles to keep her breath steady as exhaustion threatens to take over.

The villagers find their voices and speak all at once.

"I'm the magic user!"

"I'm the magic user."

"No, I am!"

"Run! What are you doing?" Iria hisses as he crawls towards her.

The men standing around the villagers silence their cries with threats of dismemberment or immolation. None seem to view Iria as any threat as he moves across the ground. Ervine runs to him and holds him back.

The leader's gaze moves up and down Aya's unsteady frame before eyeing his injured man. Satisfied the man's injury is not life threatening, his eyes lock on the knife in her shaky hand. "What's your name?"

"Aya Flandeen."

"And it's true? You're the magic user?"

"Yes."

The man steps closer to her, easily moving her hand with the knife away. His blue eyes take in her face, curiosity making them almost shine. "What did you do to him?"

Unable to tear her eyes from him, Aya lowers her arm. "I don't know."

He faces the villagers, sheathing his dagger. His eyes move to Mircien's body before rising to his men. "Burn the village to the ground. We'll take them all to the Arena."

CHAPTER SEVEN

SEVERAL OF BLUE EYES' MEN CHEER AND RUSH TO THE JARS SITTING by the well. They open them and throw the contents on the closest houses. An acrid smell fills the air and men carry burning torches towards the drenched houses. The villagers plead for mercy and some try to stop the men. But others in armor close in on the large group, pulling shackles from their belts.

They grab the women and children first, attacking any men who try to stop them. One waves his flame at the villagers, threatening to set them alight. Lane is dragged from behind the log pile.

Another man kicks Mircien's severed head into the crowded villagers, creating an explosion of screams. The head lands in front of Iria and many of the armored men laugh. Iria stares at the head sitting before him, his body freezing.

"No!" Aya grabs Blue Eyes' arm. "Please! I said I'd go with you! Spare them, please!"

Blue Eyes holds his hand up, slowing the men with torches. They watch their leader, awaiting the order to continue. The others keep shackling villagers, excitedly mocking them.

"Why should I? They had their chance to save themselves,

but they chose to remain silent." He leans close to her ear. "And you seriously injured one of my men. I can't allow that to pass without proper restitution."

"You killed the head of our village."

"Yes. But now that man you injured is a liability to my men and, by extension, my business. I'll need more bodies to sell to make up for it."

"If you touch them, I won't go with you."

Blue Eyes grabs both of her arms, tightly, and pulls her closer. "And how will you stop me?"

Anger rushes through her and she tries to pull away. She feels her magic answer her rage and flow from her arms into his. Blue Eyes quickly releases her, taking two quick steps back.

Aya raises her dagger, the tip of the blade aimed at the man. "I'll kill you."

Hesitating, Blue Eyes glances down at his hands. He opens and closes them, smiling. "I highly doubt that."

"I injured your man."

"You caught him by surprise. And you didn't kill him."

Aya quickly glances at Iria. He's now picked up the head and wrapped it in the bloody cloth. He cradles it with tears in his eyes, heartbroken.

Returning her gaze to Blue Eyes, she places the blade at her throat. "Then I'll kill myself."

Several villagers protest loudly, moving towards Aya. Blue Eyes silences them with a glare then turns back to her. "You're bluffing."

She presses the blade against her throat, drawing blood. "Can you afford to lose a magic user you threatened an entire village for?" Her lip quivers before adding, "And killed for?"

Blue Eyes' hesitation answers her. He orders his men to stop, but several don't hear him. Two mock Iria's crying, trying to take Mircien's head from his arms.

Storming up to the two men, Blue Eyes grabs one by the

37

collar and throws him at the other, knocking both to the ground. "I ordered you to stop!"

The two men stare at him confused. They quickly climb back to their feet and move away from their leader.

"Enough!" Blue Eyes' booming voice freezes the rest of his men. "We're leaving."

The armored men shout angrily in disagreement.

"Now!" Blue Eyes grabs one of the now empty jars and throws it at the thickest gathering of his men. The shattering jar silences them. They grumble as they throw the burning torches down the well and unshackle the villagers.

Aya lowers the dagger from her throat and Blue Eyes grabs it forcefully from her hand. He ties it to his belt, grabs her arm, and drags her behind him. "No goodbyes."

They pass the two men carrying the wounded man. He's fallen unconscious from the pain of his broken rib and dislocated knee. Blood drips from the gouge in his hand to the ground.

"Leave him," Blue Eyes orders.

The two men gape at him, and one readies to argue. Seeing their hesitation, Blue Eyes steps in front of them. Faster than Aya can see, he draws his sword and stabs the wounded man in the chest. He jerks before falling limp, blood pouring from the fresh wound as Blue Eyes pulls his blade free.

"I said leave him. He's weak." Blue Eyes waves his sword at the two men. "Are you two weak as well?"

The two immediately drop the body to the ground and follow the rest of the armored men. Blue Eyes sheathes his sword and continues leading Aya away.

As the men in black armor leave, the villagers come to life. Most rush to douse the last of the fires engulfing their homes while a few gather around Mircien's body. Iria slowly stands, still holding the elder's head in his arms. He turns away from those who try to help him, and disappears into Mircien's house.

The men of the village grab the body of the dead man and

pull it out of sight, many throwing stones or kicking the body as it passes. Others weep over Mircien's body, waiting for the men to take it away.

The children, including Petri, gather together and watch as she's taken away, tears in their eyes.

CHAPTER EIGHT

"TAKE HER." BLUE EYES PASSES AYA TO THE NEAREST MAN, quickening his pace to reach the head of the group and lead them out of the village.

The man pulls out shackles, the chains echoing in Aya's ears. Flashes of her vision fill her and her heart pounds loudly in her chest. She resists the urge to push the man away as the cold metal is secured to her wrists.

As the group travels north, three more men join them from hiding spots inside the trees. Judging from the light leather armor and the bows and arrows slung on their backs, Aya guesses they were scouts or back-up in case her village proved too much for the fifteen men.

The air cools and Aya tastes dampness in the air. The sound of rushing water precedes the Garen River's appearance through the trees, blocking their path. The group changes course, following the water upriver. Some of the men stop to drink, then quickly catch up to the group without causing a delay.

Aya refuses to look at the man holding her, keeping her eyes to the ground or watching the rushing water next to them.

The sound of the water is comforting, reminding Aya of times she visited the river, swimming for hours, until the sun set, and she rushed home in the dark to be scolded by her parents. After their death, she'd use the river to escape from depressing thoughts. Only to then rush home and be scolded by Mircien or Iria.

Her chest aches. Mircien's dead body lies still fresh in her mind. She thinks about the man she injured, attempting to distract herself. She knows her magic somehow helped. It understood her anger and desire to stop the man. It flowed through her and guided her leg to where it would cause the most damage.

She concentrates on her arm being held by the man in armor and tries to repeat the feeling, but nothing happens. She doesn't feel her magic flare up and move into him, like it did with Blue Eyes. It hides deep within her, waiting to be called.

The man in armor notices her gaze on his hand. He pulls her close, the foul stench from his breath making her own breath catch in her throat. "Don't think of trying anything. We may need you alive, but it doesn't mean you gotta be in one piece."

She turns away, refusing to acknowledge him. She catches sight of Blue Eyes walking ahead, her dagger on his belt. Anger fills her. Is he going to keep it? Is there a way she can convince him to return it?

Perhaps sensing her eyes on him, Blue Eyes places a hand on the hilt of her dagger. He draws it and stares at the black metal of the blade. He traces its edges with his thumb before waving one of the archers close. They speak in whispers before the man nods and slows his pace.

"Where's the sheath for the dagger?" the archer asks, moving next to Aya.

She stares at him with what she hopes is a blank stare, fearing the pounding of her heart will give her away.

The Archer grabs her free arm tightly. "You can either hand it over or we can search you."

The grip of the man with foul breath tightens with excitement and a disgusting chuckle from behind makes her skin crawl.

41

"Left boot."

He quickly bends down and slides his fingers into her boot. She stiffens at the sudden touch, but the archer easily grabs the sheath, only slowing her pace for a moment.

Without another word, the man walks back to Blue Eyes and hands the sheath to him. Blue Eyes takes it and slides the black dagger in before tying it to his belt.

They continue following the river until the sun disappears behind the mountains. The sound of the forest changes as darkness approaches. Birds fall silent and nocturnal insects begin their serenades.

Blue Eyes stops the group by turning around. "We'll sleep here and meet the caravan tomorrow. Spread out and keep guard in case any villagers decide to be *heroes*."

The group spreads out and sets up a small perimeter. They cut foliage away to make a clearing and a few gather kindling for a fire.

The man with foul breath holds Aya, waiting patiently for his orders, and soon Blue Eyes approaches. He waves Foul Breath away, takes her by the arm and leads her to the center of the small camp. He forces her to the ground and sits across from her, leaning back against a tree. His blue eyes look her up and down as though only truly seeing her for the first time.

"I know I'm probably the last person you want to speak to right now, but you deserve an apology."

Aya jerks her head up, staring at him in shock. "You're right. I don't want to speak to you." She turns her head away from him and they sit in silence.

Was this a trick? Was he trying to lower her guard? How dare he apologize now, after all the things he's done? Did he truly feel remorse for any of it?

Still, her curiosity convinces her to eye him cautiously. "Why are you apologizing?"

"For the death of that old woman—"

"Mircien. Her name was Mircien," she interrupts angrily.

He glances at her with a shrug, but his eyes narrow slightly. "I couldn't have known that, so watch your tone. And for burning down a nice chunk of your village. Do you not want an apology?"

"Of course, I do," she says softly. *But I didn't expect one,* she wants to say. The image of Mircien's head in Iria's arms fills her with an unforgivable rage. "Murderers tend not to apologize right after the fact. Or ever, actually."

Leaning forward, Blue Eyes speaks low, so his words don't reach the men around them. "I didn't order the killing. Our caravan has recently gained new members and they were a little excited. I haven't allowed them a chance to really cut loose, and unfortunately your village released their more...*fiery* spirits. Normally, we send a small group ahead to attempt negotiations. Less people get hurt that way. But we're on a strict time limit now."

Aya's face flushes with anger. "And Elder Mircien?"

"My order was to *silence her.* I was hoping to stop the annoying prayer she was spouting, knock her unconscious. The idiot with the axe chose to misinterpret the command. Don't misunderstand, I'm quite capable of killing, but only as a last resort."

"All of this for me. Why?"

"Magic users bring in higher pay, for one. For another, I needed to remind the new members I'm in charge. You'd be surprised how many caravan leaders are killed by their own men. In that, you actually helped me out."

She won't give him the satisfaction of answering. But he continues, regardless.

"That man you injured was giving me trouble. You saw how poorly he followed my orders. He probably would've killed that little boy even if I'd ordered him to stop. You gave me an excuse to get rid of him." He leans back against the tree, his head angled to the side. "Though truthfully, it's our own fault. Slave traders hire thugs and killers on purpose, so in the end we get what we deserve."

Aya realizes she's almost laughing, and quickly frowns. She hates herself for allowing him to make her feel at ease, even for a glimmer of a moment. There's something about him she cannot help but find...likable. But how much of it is his true face?

"Jaxon Parth," he says, suddenly. "Since you'll be traveling with us, you should at least know my name." His eyes darken and the smile disappears. "But don't think you'll be treated any differently than the other slaves. I tell every one of them my name. It's a courtesy, should they ever choose to seek revenge. You're not the only magic user we've collected. You're nothing more than a *thing* for me to sell."

Swallowing a large lump in her throat, she finds it strange he can flip so easily from kindness to ruthlessness.

"What is the Arena?" she asks, afraid of the answer. She remembers Mircien's shaking voice when she mentioned it.

His eyebrow raises inquisitively, an amused laugh following. "It's where the King entertains himself with games."

"Why?"

"*Why?*" Jaxon sighs and notices the men in armor close by grimace, two spit on the ground. "Because he is king, and his decree is law."

"I didn't know there was a king. Where does he rule?"

"You've been fortunate. This valley is outside of his self-proclaimed realm—for now. But valuable fighters have been harvested for many years. Your village has always been too poor and far away to merit his notice, but the stories about your magic attracted attention."

She wonders about his odd description: *self-proclaimed*. "My magic isn't strong. Perhaps the stories you were told were about my parents."

"It's possible. Word takes a long time to travel to us. But I did find you. And if you inherited your magic from them, it will only grow stronger. Sometimes the potential in a magic user is worth more than their current power."

Aya lowers her eyes to the ground. Potential? Inside of her? The only thing she can imagine is the illness waiting to grow. That was why Elder Mircien allowed her to learn traditional healing with Iria. So that, if it ever came to that, she might be able to heal herself.

"The other villages of your valley have been visited by slave traders a number of times. Not enough to fully deplete the supply of magic users, but enough that word spread through the village elders. Including to your own. She knew the risk of keeping you in the village. But apparently, she was ready to die to protect you. Possibly as a promise to your parents?" Jaxon prods.

Her eyes widen. Mircien knew that her magic put the village in danger? Was that why she worried about Aya living so far away? She couldn't keep an eye on her magic user?

Jaxon crosses his arms across his chest and leans his head against the tree. "Get some rest. We'll join up with the rest of our caravan tomorrow."

He closes his eyes, but Aya knows he's not sleeping. She hears it in the way he breathes. Another odd behavior, feigning sleep to make her comfortable enough to drift off, herself.

Exhaustion fills her as she carefully lies down on the hard ground, the shackles on her wrists a new, strange feeling. Images of Iria cradling Mircien's head flash before her closed eyes, bleeding into nightmares replaying the elder's death.

CHAPTER NINE

ROUGH VOICES WAKE HER. SHE PANICS, FORGETTING WHERE SHE IS. The cold air and hard ground refresh her memory. The sky barely lights as men put out small campfires and gather their belongings.

Jaxon stands nearby, still leaning against the same tree. He watches his men with angry eyes. The archer who took Aya's sheath walks up to him and whispers to him. He hands Jaxon a small bag, the clinking of coins barely heard over the men's voices and the breaking down of the small camp. Men bury fires with dirt and toss unused foliage across the clearing, blending the camp back into the forest.

Nodding, the anger fades from his eyes and he turns to face Aya when he hears her stir from sleep. "We're leaving. The caravan is waiting for us a few hours' walk from here." He forcefully pulls her to her feet.

The men gather at the center of the clearing, waiting for Jaxon. Pulling Aya to the front of the group, he surveys the area. "Good work. Let's move."

They follow the river for a couple of hours before entering the forest heading west. A creeping familiarity overtakes her as the path the group is heading reminds her of one she and Mircien took many years ago.

A village appears amongst the trees, much larger than Aya's. The houses are spread further apart, the trees of the forest naturally growing between them. Villagers mill about their homes; fowl peck at the earth for worms. A familiar building sits at the center: a two-story inn—the same that she and Mircien stayed in the last time she'd been to this village.

Villagers clear a path for the men in armor, some disappearing into their homes while others watch them pass with a mixture of fear and sadness in their expressions. Parents clutch their children, quickly guiding them away.

A man stands outside the inn, washing the windows. He's the owner; Aya remembers his large nose and white hair. Hearing the group approach, he turns with a practiced smile on his face. But it evaporates when he spots Aya with Jaxon's hand gripping her arm. His face pales, and shame fills his eyes as he turns his head away from her.

We've heard tales from the other villages about the magic user that lives here.

Your village has always been too poor and far away to merit attention, but the stories about your magic added incentive.

This man, someone Elder Mircien trusted, told Jaxon about Aya. It's obvious in the way he can't bear to look at her.

"Your stories were true," Jaxon calls to the man, tossing the small bag of coins at the innkeeper. "Though it seems some of the facts were I'm sure...*innocently* forgotten."

The innkeeper stares at the bag of coins in his hand, his eyes nearly burning a hole into the leather. "Thank you, sir," he mumbles, softly.

"You told them." Aya's voice trembles as her anger grows. "You led them to Oula Village. You're the reason Mircien is dead, and now you can't even muster the decency of looking me in the face!"

Tearing herself away from Jaxon, Aya runs towards the man.

47

The innkeeper glances up as she raises her arm. She hits him hard across the face with her fist. "You killed her. Elder Mircien is dead because of you!"

An arm grabs her around the waist, lifting her off the ground. She kicks at the stunned innkeeper before she's dragged away. Her feet miss him, but catch his hand holding the bag of coins. The bag falls to the ground, coins pouring onto the dirt.

She struggles to break free. Her magic swirls inside of her with her anger. She wants to hurt him. She wants him to feel the pain she's feeling even, if it's only physical.

The expression of horror and realization on the innkeeper's face brings her little satisfaction, but the tears escaping his eyes give her pause. He finally meets her eyes and his lip quivers.

"It was you or my family." The words are soft, barely a whisper. "I had no choice." He leaves, retreating to his inn without the bag of coins on the ground.

The man holding Aya throws her onto the ground before casually grabbing the bag and collecting the loose coins. It's the archer who took her sheath.

Jaxon glares at her, his hand dancing above his sword. "You pull that again, I'll cut your feet off and make you walk on the stubs."

Her anger returns and she gets back on her feet. "I'll heal myself."

A crooked smile forms on his lips. "Don't encourage me to cut your hands off, too." Jaxon grabs her and Aya's magic reaches out. He quickly draws his knife and holds it to her throat. "You better control yourself. My men may not be able to feel your magic, but I can."

She forces her magic back down deep inside her. Jaxon sheathes his knife and leads her around the side of the inn towards the back.

Men's voices echo ahead of them and the group arrives at a makeshift camp built behind the inn. Several men are relaxing until they notice Jaxon approaching. Their eyes give Aya a once-over before they return to their tasks. One man pulls feathers off a dead fowl. Others sit in a circle, drinking and playing a game with bone dice. Others either sleep or throw stones at small animals hiding in the brush.

At the center of the gathering are two large cages on wheels full of people, more chained behind, sitting on the ground. Some of the men in armor walk by and snap at those on the ground or rattle sticks on the bars of the cages. Large boxes and barrels are tied to the roofs.

Four large animals are tied to trees at the outskirts of the camp, drinking greedily from oversized troughs. They're thick creatures she's never seen before, legs short but strong. Two horns jut forward from their overhanging brows. Another shorter horn is on their chin. As she watches, one of the beasts buries the horn in the ground, pulling and tearing roots from the earth. Twitching their short, stubby tails, they make low sounds, which rumble through their entire bodies.

Aya stares at the large beasts in awe. They're the largest animals she's ever seen. Some of Jaxon's men throw large piles of grass and hay on either side of the troughs and their huge maws inhale great mouthfuls, except the one digging in the ground. It eats the roots it reveals using its horn, chewing on the thick wood.

"Stay far from those beasts. A grodun wouldn't think twice about crushing you beneath its powerful legs. The epirs over there aren't as bad,"

A whinnying from the other side of the camp catches Aya's attention. Smaller animals tied on either side of two long fences attached to the inn drink from large troughs of water. They're large enough for two men to ride, but there are enough animals for most of the men to ride alone. The epirs have long, lean legs. Strong muscles ripple under thick, furred skin Their necks stretch out with long, curly hair hanging down.

Jaxon leads Aya towards one of the cages. Those on the

ground shrink away from him. Her eyes dart down to the dagger on his belt, the one he took from her.

Noticing her look, Jaxon twists his grip on her arm. "If you're thinking of using your magic in some way to escape, stop. The metal of these chains and cages were made with magic. You can't use your gift while bound." He chains her wrists to the line of people behind the cage. "And I'll say one last time, don't try to run. The first time we'll break your legs. The second time, we'll kill you."

"Kill the prize you strove so hard for?" She meets his eyes and straightens her back, not letting the weight of the metal on her wrists pull her down. "I have no intention of running."

"Good choice. I'm afraid you'll have to walk. We ran out of room in the cages several days ago." He makes sure she hears what he says next. "Your village was a surprise stop, but the story that man told us was too tempting to dismiss. There are a few stops until we reach our destination. But if someone dies in the cage, you can take their place."

"I would rather walk than be caged like an animal."

"We'll see how you feel after the first day."

"How long is it going to take?"

He laughs. "Better you don't know. It'll make the journey seem shorter than it actually is. You should *enjoy* the scenery while you can still see clearly."

A large man, larger than any of the others, walks up to Jaxon and speaks quietly in his ear.

"I'll take care of it, Aldur," Jaxon responds softly and the larger man nods. Aldur walks around the camp, ordering the men to clean up.

Jaxon takes a few steps away before stopping. He turns to her again. "Rest as much as you can. We leave as soon as I've finished dealing with a little issue." He leaves, heading for the front of the inn.

Aya is alone with the other prisoners, who glance at their new companion briefly before returning their eyes to the ground.

Several cling to one another, others stretch the chains to their full lengths to remain separate.

Glancing down the line, Aya discovers most are men or young boys, but the number of women is higher than she expects. Though she has no experience to judge by.

She sits down on the ground and stares at those in the cages. Several appear thin and sickly. They're cramped close together and are as dirty as those forced to walk. By the hopelessness in their expressions, she guesses they were the first collected. They look defeated in spirit.

Little over an hour passes before the men in armor finish clearing the camp. They attach the groduns to the front of the cages and two men climb on top of each, holding the reins and long sticks to control the large beasts' movements.

The rest of the men force Aya and the other slaves to their feet. The cages move forward away from the inn before stopping. The large man who spoke to Jaxon orders the men into formation and they untie the epirs. They move into position. One group behind the caravan, one group on either side, and a smaller group in front.

The larger man holds one epir, waiting for Jaxon.

Jaxon appears around the side of the inn, tying a small bag onto his belt. He climbs onto his epir and takes the reins. He nudges the animal forward to the front.

"Let's move," he orders.

He receives an answer in the form of hoots and hollers from his men and the caravan begins the long journey to the Arena.

CHAPTER TEN

THE CARAVAN MOVES SLOWLY THROUGH THE FOREST, BUT THE TREES and thick bushes create obstacles for the groduns pulling the cages. Not used to being surrounded by trees, the beasts require extra urging and prodding from Jaxon's men.

The sound of the long stick slapping the thick hides makes Aya wince. She wonders if the large beasts feel pain or only annoyance. They bray with deep, rumbling sounds but continue moving forward.

The caravan passes other villages, too far away from Oula for Mircien to have taken Aya there when she was younger. The villagers don't even give the group a passing glance. Perhaps they remember the slave traders and fear that if any take notice, the rough men will halt and enslave them, too.

The distance between each village grows until they enter a part of the forest with little evidence of human life. Ruins of abandoned villages blend among the trees and grass. All that remain are foundations and broken statues, with plant life slowly regaining its stronghold.

Jaxon's words come back to her as her feet become sore and blisters form. Her shoes provide little comfort and the shackles around her wrists rub her skin raw. She's tempted to test whether the metal truly keeps her from her magic. But as she watches the others walking in front of her, she realizes the pain she's feeling is nothing compared to theirs.

Barely the first day and I'm already thinking of discomfort? Aya scolds herself.

Her stomach growls, reminding her she hasn't eaten in two days. The almost constant rush of adrenaline and fear is finally ebbing, giving way to her other senses.

Aren't they going to feed us? Aya eyes the other slaves and their tiny bellies. *It isn't looking very likely.*

A call moves down the line as several men move down the line of slaves, offering a single ladle of water to each. It's sloppily done, and more water slops to the ground than the parched, gaping mouths. They sound of the rushing river makes it even more torturous when full ladles are purposely dumped to the cage floor and the men laugh at the slaves trying to scoop muddy water into their mouths.

Aya drinks her share greedily, making sure to hold the ladle so the man serving her can't spill it. She's thankful for the cool feeling in her belly, but still wishes for food to stop the hunger pains.

Torches are lit as night darkens the forest around them. The sparse evening breeze does little to comfort those walking. Strange sounds in the trees frighten many of the slaves. Occasional screams echo down the line. The men respond with harsh orders, and the culprits are roughly silenced.

Aya tries to keep her mind from her painful feet by surveying the forest. She recognizes many of the strange sounds and laughs to herself. *If they knew the things making those sounds are no bigger than my hand, they'd feel silly.* She thinks of telling them this, but one look convinces her they may not welcome the knowledge. The night sounds and songs of the insects dredges up memories she's not thought of in years.

Her parents sat behind their house when she still lived within the village. She sat on her father's lap, listening to the noises of

53

the forest. She remembers feeling fear, as some of the slaves do now. Her mother walked into the dark forest and returned with something in her hand. Aya clung tightly to her father as her mother held her hands out. Sitting in her palm was a small animal covered in dirt. It stared at Aya with wide, green eyes before making one of the sounds reverberating through the dark forest. The small animal shook in her mother's hand, terrified for having been pulled from its earthen sanctuary. Her mother explained that sometimes the things that frighten us most are only scary because people choose to believe their imaginations instead of satisfying their curiosity. If they followed their curiosity, they'd find the scary thing is usually just as frightened of them.

I want to go home. I wish I were still in my soft bed. I wish I could eat dinner with Mircien and Iria one last time. Aya fights the tears in her eyes, her thoughts doing little to help. *I wish my last words to Iria weren't during a fight. I wasn't even allowed to say goodbye or check on Iria. Is he going to be all right?*

The following two days are the same: constant motion. They once again meet the river and follow it south. They stop only when fallen trees block the path or the dirt paths are flooded. These stops provide little rest and, occasionally, small amounts of food. But Aya realizes that, since she will not ride in the cages, they're the only opportunities for her to sleep and nurse her feet until they reach the first planned rest stop.

None of the men speak to her when she asks how much longer they must walk. But she catches bits and pieces of conversations.

"Oi, Vol," a man riding close to Aya says to another, "you ever notice he never sleeps?"

"Who?" Vol grumbles.

"Fearless leader."

"Of course, he sleeps, Kit. You moron."

"When have you ever seen him sleep?"

"I don't know. It ain't part of my job to watch him sleep." He cuffs his friend and laughs.

A third man rides up to the two. "He's awake all day and night. Even the guys who've been with him for years say he never sleeps."

"I'm telling you...he doesn't," Kit affirms.

"Shut up. *Both* of you." Vol glares at the two before riding his epir away from them.

Aya has seen many of the men catching naps on the back of their epirs while others hold the reins and lead. But Jaxon is always wide awake, alert to the forest around him.

On the fifth day, the caravan crosses a stone bridge over the river to head southwest. They're near the end of the valley, a concept foreign to Aya. *I knew the valley ended, but I never thought I would see it.* Aya gapes in wonder at the end of the mountains in the distance.

After several more hours of travel, Jaxon orders the caravan to stop. His men build a camp and a scouting team moves off to hunt or take food from a nearby village, whichever they can find. The slaves are allowed to bathe in the river, small groups at a time.

Aya takes the moment to assess the damage to her feet. Large, ruptured blisters turn her skin red and she removes rocks that found their way into her shoes. She winces as the cold water rushes over the blisters. Her shoes are slowly falling apart, holes already worn in the soles. She dreads the possibility of walking barefoot the rest of the way, as many of the other slaves already are.

Jaxon's men who remained in camp now hand out rations of dried food they keep in pouches. It's not enough to satisfy her empty stomach, but more than the tiny scraps they were given over the past week. Water is passed more generously and carefully.

Sleep comes quickly and, much to Aya's relief, she has no dreams.

Screams jar her from the blackness of sleep. She sits up. The moon, high in the sky, casts light through an opening in the trees. But it still takes a moment for her eyes to adjust.

The screams ring out again and she turns her attention to the second cage. Those chained to the back gather around two figures halfway down the line. Those in the cage glare through the bars.

Aya moves towards the huddled group, but her chains prevent her from moving too close. When she tries to move closer, the man she's attached to roughly tugs back, nearly pulling her over.

The small huddled group opens a little, revealing one woman holding a second in her arms. She's screaming and tears pour down her cheeks. The second woman's eyes are empty, staring at nothing.

Aya doesn't understand what's happening, but she recognizes the look in the second woman's eyes. It's the same one her parents had before they died.

CHAPTER ELEVEN

"HER SISTER IS SICK," JAXON SAYS.

Aya jumps.

He's sitting against a tree close to her, watching. "She's been ill since we picked them up. She wouldn't let us take her sister unless we took her, too. There's nothing to be done."

She stares at the group huddled around the two women. "Why didn't anyone heal her?"

"One so close to death? None of the magic users we've collected wield that kind of power."

Her eyes meet the sister of the dying woman. Her eyes plead with Aya for help. How many times has she seen such expressions aimed at her? But those times had only been for a mild illness, a small cut or bruise...or Petri's broken leg. She didn't think she could do anything then, either.

But this woman is dying.

Those pleading eyes bore their way into her mind. Her magic dances within her, eager to please the desire rising inside her.

"Let me try," she says, turning to Jaxon. "I'm a healer. Let me try."

He leans forward. "She'll be dead in a few minutes. You can do nothing."

57

I'm sorry, Aya. There's nothing to be done. The words Iria spoke to her so many years ago. The words he spoke the moment before her parents died.

She didn't have her magic then, but she had it now.

"Please. I have to try. If I could save even one life...."

Jaxon's blue eyes flash between Aya and the group. He stands and unchains her from the line of slaves. She waits for him to grab her, but he only waves his hand towards the women. She hurries to the second line of slaves and forces her way to the two women. She swallows as she takes in the pale face of the dying woman.

"She's dying," the healthy sister says. "It's my fault. She wouldn't let me be taken alone. She had to come with me. This endless walking is killing her."

Aya drops to her knees, looks into the healthy sister's eyes, and gently strokes her cheek. "It's not your fault. She knows it isn't your fault." She wipes several tears away and gives her a comforting smile.

Turning her attention to the dying sister, Aya places a hand on the woman's forehead. Aya flinches. The woman is cold to the touch. Leaning down, she places her ear on the woman's chest. Hidden beneath ragged breaths, Aya hears a very faint heartbeat.

Aya places both hands on the woman's chest. She closes her eyes and takes a deep, calming breath. She's never tried to bring someone so close to death back before. Without Iria or Mircien with her, there's no one to help her should she need it.

Illnesses in children are simple, but this is something beyond her experience.

The familiar warmth grows inside her chest. But as she concentrates, she feels something else. She feels the woman's warmth. It's so faint, Aya isn't sure she's truly feeling it. She moves her magic down her arms and into the woman. A strange sound echoes in her head. It takes her a moment to realize what it is.

It's her heartbeat, but it sounds strange. It doesn't sound the way a heart should. The pattern is uneven.

The woman appears in Aya's mind, just as though her eyes were open, and she imagines she can look right through the woman's clothes and skin. She delves deep until the heart appears. There's a strange lump disfiguring one side of the weakened muscle. She's never seen anything like it before, but she knows it's causing the illness.

If I know what it is, I can get rid of it.

She pushes her magic into the lump, trying to see what it's made of. She knows she doesn't have much time, but rushing will only lead to a quicker death.

As far as her magic can tell her, the lump seems to be made of living tissue. She wonders what caused it, but pushes the thought away and encourages the tissue to disperse. It's a strange feeling, her magic filling the lump and slowly eating it away.

Once it's gone, the beating of the heart grows stronger. She feels the blood easily moving through the muscle and spreading throughout the woman's body.

She searches where the lump grew and wonders if she should encourage the tissue in the wall to shed in case any more of the strange lump is still present. She doesn't know how long the woman's heart will stay this way. Could the lump grow back?

"By the Great Goddess!" one of the gathered slaves says in awe.

The sudden interruption snaps her from her questions, and she feels an icy coldness in her chest. *I used my magic too long.* Aya pulls it out of the woman and opens her eyes.

Her vision is blurry, and a sudden rush of light-headedness causes her to fall back. A hand catches her, and she falls against someone's chest. She takes a deep breath, heart racing.

The stricken woman sits up, color returning to her cheeks. She touches her chest and turns to her sister, tears filling her eyes.

59

"Rava!" Her sister cries and wraps her arm around her.

"It's gone," she says in disbelief. "The illness is gone, Mava."

The sisters hug tightly and those standing around them open the circle wider as all eyes fall on Aya. They speak words of praise, wonder, and fear. Mava and Rava stare at Aya with large smiles and bow their heads.

"Thank you. You are gifted by the Great Goddess," Rava says, squeezing her sister tighter.

"They said your village held a talented magic user, but they never suggested you were a Life Healer," Jaxon says in Aya's ear. She looks up, realizing he's the one holding her.

"Life Healer?" She tries to sit up. Her head is still woozy, and she feels drained.

"That healing you did is rare magic. You pulled that woman's soul back from near death. You might even be able to bring someone all the way back from death one day."

"And am I to be killed for such a power?"

Jaxon smiles, but his eyes fill with sadness. "You're to be treated better than these lesser slaves. You'll fetch me a very high price at the Arena. The people love slaves who wield such rare power."

She wonders how on earth her powers will be put on display for death games.

He lifts her to her feet. Although she stumbles, he easily supports her weight. She raises a hand to her forehead, focusing on her breathing.

"Is that silk?" he asks, grabbing her wrist and stroking her bracelet.

Aya's eyes widen and she tries to pull her wrist free, but his grip is too strong. "Why?"

"Good for trading." He pulls the soft cloth from her wrist and it disappears into a pocket in his armor.

"No! Give that back," she panics. She can't let him take another thing from her. Especially not the only other gift from her parents. "Give it back!"

He takes her to the cage she'd been attached to and orders three of his men to empty the cage. Only then does she realize most of the men in armor had witnessed her healing the woman, Rava. They stare at her with new expressions; ones she never imagined would be aimed at her...as though she weren't human.

"Did you not hear my order? Empty it," Jaxon barks at the men still standing, their eyes locked on Aya.

They quickly unlock the door and force those inside out. Many cry in panic, some claiming to be too weak to walk the whole distance. The men ignore them and chain them to the back of the cages, hitting any who try to fight them.

Realizing what's happening, Aya grabs Jaxon's arm. "No, please. Don't do this. Let them ride. They're weaker than I."

The slaves continue to plead as the men finish shackling the last of them. Jaxon forces Aya into the cage, throwing her roughly onto the metal floor. She immediately feels her magic cut off, adding to her panic. He slams the door shut behind her and locks it.

She quickly stands, having to lean over to keep her head from hitting the top, and runs to the door. She tries to force it open, but the metal is too thick, and the lock too well-made.

Leaning on the bars, Jaxon whistles. "You're to be well-treated. They only pay more for rare ones if they're healthy. They can put you in the games sooner."

One of his men approaches, the archer who took the sheath from Aya many days ago, and awaits orders.

"At least allow the weakest ones to ride with me," Aya protests.

Jaxon ignores her, whispering an order to the man before heading for his epir. "Everybody up! We leave now. We have a schedule to keep." He meets Aya's eyes once before mounting his epir and heading for the front of the caravan.

Aya inspects the cage. It's much larger with only one person inside, but the bars feel like they're closing in around her. She feels the eyes of those now forced to walk glaring at her.

The cage jerks forward as the groduns are forced to move. Aya falls to the floor, but instead of sitting up, she pulls her knees to her chest and rubs her wrist where her bracelet used to be. Tears roll down her cheeks.

Curse my magic. And curse me.

CHAPTER TWELVE

THE CARAVAN LEAVES THE VALLEY WELL BEFORE SUNRISE. THE valley shimmers dark blue in the scant light, and the slender trees now mix with thicker ones that block out most of the sky. Even after the sun rises, the forest is so dark that nocturnal animals continue their chorus.

Aya raises her head, watching the trees pass by. She moves to the front of the cage to escape the angry looks of those behind. The men patrolling the caravan pause to peer in at her. She avoids their gazes and peeks out at the new forest in awe.

The thick trees are darker in color with bark like fingers tracing long lines through the wood. The smell is new to her. She can almost feel the rough bark with each breath.

The rising sun finally reaches sufficient height for its rays to pierce the trees, revealing more of the forest floor. Strange plants cover the ground. Beautiful ferns grow vibrantly, tall fans of green. Oddly shaped flowers bloom at all heights from the earth or from the sides of the great trees. Sunlight is green, filtered by the leaves from above, giving the forest a dreamlike quality.

A bird lands inside the bars of the cage and casts curious glances at Aya with its golden eyes. Its sleek body is pitch-black, with a long tail curling up at the end. She reaches out her hand,

and feathers rise on the bird's head, displaying a beautiful shock of colors: red, blue, and green. As it flies away, she tries to follow its path but loses sight of it quickly.

Every hour provides strange new sights and sounds. Aya almost forgets she's travelling to be sold as a slave until one of the men brings her daily bowl of water and pathetic amount of food.

Every day the same man comes, the archer who took the sheath from her those many days ago. She can reckon, now, that Jaxon ordered the man to keep an eye on her.

By the fourth day, the trees space farther apart again. With each passing hour they become fewer and the ground cover lowers. Eventually the trees end and a great plain of tall, brown grass stretches before them. Wind blows the tall blades, creating beautiful waves.

The forest fades behind, leaving only the plains in view. For two more days there is nothing but the brown waves of grass. The few wild animals Aya spots are long, lean beasts. Their fur or scaled bodies are warm colors of tan and brown, making them blend with the grass.

When Archer slams her usual bowl and plate on the floor of her moving cell, she's forcibly reminded of the dozens of weaker slaves made to walk so she can ride. She observes the world passing by while they struggle to remain standing. Through the nights she cries for them and for herself, acutely aware of her growing loneliness. But not hopelessness. They haven't taken hope from her. Not yet.

Green grass mixes with the brown on the morning of the fifth day. By the sixth day, the green grass completely overtakes the brown. Hills are lower and rarer. Solitary trees appear, separated by great distances. The tops are flat and the bark twists into amazing shapes.

Aya takes to watching those behind her cage. Noting the varying ages and sizes, she wonders how those without magic are chosen to be taken. Jaxon briefly mentioned the sisters refusing to be separated, but why had he only chosen one to begin with? Was there more to these people? Were they threats to the so-called Blood King? She still has so many questions, but unsure who—or how—to ask.

Immense herds of great beasts move slowly in the distance, appearing at first to be stains on the earth. As the herds move, individual beasts stop to graze on the lush grass or, for taller animals, leaves on the occasional trees. Birds pick at bugs that land on the beasts, and a few birds hop beneath the animals for more insects. One young animal hops around its parents, only to be knocked over when the mother turns her head suddenly.

Aya fights the excitement of all she's seeing, guilty for enjoying it while others suffer around her. Her dreams of new lands and amazing beasts is coming to life around her, even if she must enjoy it from within a cage. She can't keep the wide smile from her lips.

"Is it like you imagined?" Jaxon asks, surprising her. "I'm sure you've listened to many stories from travelers." His eyes scan the great stretch of plains, stopping for a split second on each herd of beasts.

"Travelers rarely came to our village. It's too far for many to risk the journey, as you said." Aya erases the smile from her face and looks away from him and the sights around her. She rubs her wrist. "My parents weren't from Oula Village, but they never spoke of their homeland. They were afraid I'd want to leave. But Elder Mircien shared stories her mother told her as a child. She spoke of many different kinds of lands, unimaginable beasts, sights that could only be described in dreams."

Jaxon urges his epir closer to the cage. "Your valley is normal for you and a number of these slaves. But to my men it's strange and beautiful. The way you see this land is how they first viewed your own. Where we come from trees are sparse and barren and the ground is dry and cracked." He leans forward on his saddle. "It isn't shameful to be awed by the new even during times of hardship. You don't have to hide your excitement."

"I don't think it's appropriate for me to smile while the ones walking behind me are dying."

He glances behind. "Those who die are the lucky ones. They won't have to face the Arena or its cruel practices. Don't feel pity for them. Feel pity for the ones who survive this journey."

Shaking her head, Aya's brow furrows in confusion. "Do you feel nothing for those you capture?"

"If I did, I wouldn't be very good at my work."

"And this *king* of yours, does he feel nothing, too?"

Jaxon hesitates, a shadow crossing his face. "To him, those who do not honor him are not worth having a feeling for. They are simply to be used to tighten his reign."

"You know him personally, then?"

"Personally, no. I've had my run-ins with him. Brief though they were, there's no denying what that man's motivations are. Hope you never meet him." He kicks the side of his epir and returns to the front of the caravan.

Aya watches him until he's out of sight, then faces those walking behind her cage. Their eyes are downcast. They don't have the energy to look up and see the sights around them. Those few who do only enjoy it for a short time before the pain in their feet and bodies reminds them of their fate.

CHAPTER THIRTEEN

THESE PLAINS NEVER END.

Three more days pass before any change comes to the terrain. Jaxon leads the caravan onto a small road appearing through waves of grass. The rough, stone road causes several slaves to fall to the ground. Men move their epirs close to those who've fallen and yell for them to get back on their feet.

The slaves struggle to reclaim their footing, but one, a teenage boy, remains on the ground. The pull of the chains drags him slowly. One of the armored men (Aya remembers his name is Vol) climbs down from his epir and forces the boy to his feet. Vol whispers a threat into the boy's ear and the boy cries. The slave chained in front of the boy takes him by the arm, pulling him away from Vol, who climbs back onto his mount.

The other slave comforts the boy. She wonders if the two know each other, or if this is the first time they've interacted. The slave comforting the boy sneaks hidden food to him. Catching Aya watching, he flinches, but she smiles.

A bustling town along the road grows closer and Jaxon stops the caravan outside its borders. He orders five of his men to purchase or trade for supplies, then orders others to hand out food and water.

The slaves collapse in an agony of relief when they hear they will be fed. Some fall asleep, trying desperately to gather as much strength as possible. The slavers hand out bread and dried strips of meat as well as multiple buckets of water to be shared by every group of ten slaves. New life fills them. This meager offering is the most they've been given in weeks.

Archer brings Aya's share. He places the larger plate and bowl through the bars, but she doesn't fetch them. Instead she pushes them back towards the man.

"You should try to eat and drink. Our next stop isn't for four days," he says. His voice is cold, emotionless. The only reason he even cares about feeding her is because he's ordered to do it. Aya laughs at the false interest in her wellbeing and lies down on the metal floor. "You need to at least have water."

She remains silent, rolling onto her side so her back is to the man.

Jaxon walks up next to Archer. "What's the matter?"

Archer steps back, making room. "She won't eat or drink."

"You won't get another sip until we reach our next stop no matter how long it takes us," Jaxon says to Aya's back.

"The people walking need it more than I do. Give it to them," she says, angrily. It's a small gesture, she knows, but it's the only thing she can do. She wishes she could trade places with all of them.

Jaxon nods his head to Archer. The other man grabs the water and food, taking it to those who still haven't been fed. Jaxon leans through the bars to place his arms on the floor of the cage. "Starving yourself won't change anything. We'll force the food down your throat if we have to."

"Or you won't receive the highest price for me, right?"

"That's right. You'll learn quickly men will do anything to ensure they receive the payment they're due."

Rolling onto her back, Aya glares at him. "I'll eat after the others have finished."

He nods his head, his eyes smiling, but his lips neutral. "I'll make sure of it." He walks away and surveys the other slaves.

The last of the slaves eat and drink greedily, but not enough to keep all from receiving their fair share. Aya is amazed at how grace shines from these people who are starving. They have banded together to be certain all have enough.

While the men in armor collect empty buckets, Archer returns to Aya's cage and places a smaller plate of food and bowl of water in front of her. He stands with his arms crossed and watches her, unblinking.

"You don't have to watch me. I said I would eat."

"Jaxon ordered me to make sure you eat every piece and drink every drop. If you don't, I'm to force you." He shakes the bangle of keys in his hand.

She hesitates before grabbing the plate, wondering if he would actually follow through. He definitely has the look of someone who would enjoy it, and probably hopes she'll refuse. She eats the meager meal and drinks the water in two gulps. She makes sure to clean the bowl and plate with her tongue before throwing them to Archer. He takes them and leaves without a word.

When the group sent into town return with bags of supplies, the slaves are roused from their rest. The caravan skirts the edge of the town and continues across the plains. As the hours pass, the hills of the plains flatten in front of the caravan. The sky seems to touch the earth and a strange, dark line appears on the horizon. As the line grows closer, great birds fly overhead. They gather in large flocks and move in swirling, dizzying patterns.

The smell of water floats through the air, but it's a different smell from the river. Climbing to her knees, Aya can't place the new scent. She crawls to the side of the cage and tries to catch sight of what's ahead. A roaring sound echoes from in front of the caravan, reminding her of thunder, but there aren't any storm clouds in sight.

The caravan turns to run parallel to what she realizes isn't a line in the horizon, but a place where the plains abruptly fall away from tall cliffs bordering an endless stretch of water. The thunderous roars are the sound of giant waves crashing into rocks and boulders at the bottom of the cliff.

She remembers Mircien's stories and a word comes to her. *The sea. It's the sea!* She stares in awe at the sun's reflection on the distant waves.

The large birds dive down the cliffs towards the water. Several pull up at the last moment to fly out to sea above the waves. Others dive into the water and emerge with fish in their beaks. Great sprays of white water threaten to wash over the cliffs to the caravan, but only light mists make it.

Aya tastes the water in the air, and realizes the scent of the sea is salt. Water on her skin and hair from the mists dry, leaving behind small salt crystals. After so long starving, it tastes amazing on her lips.

The cliffs level out revealing rocks battered by the merciless waves. On the second day travelling along these cliffs, large leathery beasts appear resting on long, flattened rocks. They roll onto their backs or stomachs, warming themselves with the sun. The waves crash over them, but they're so large the water can't move them, and great mists of air shoot from the snouts of the animals.

"If you only look one way, you'll miss everything else," Aldur tells her, pulling alongside on his mount.

She jumps at his voice. This is the first time he's spoken to her during the entire journey. She knew his name from passing conversations and she noticed he'd been staying close to her cage the past few days. She wonders if Jaxon ordered him to, or if he's curious about her.

"When I first saw the Great Sea, I was as enamored with its size and ferocious nature as you. It took me several travels across these plains before I ever noticed those mountains far off in the opposite direction." He points to the other side of the cage.

She turns and her eyes take in an amazing view. In the

70

distance, filling the skies are mountains. They're completely white, covered in snow. She can't see where the bottoms rise from the hills of the plains, but she can tell they're a great distance away. They stand as a great testament to the power of the earth. She can only guess when they began their climb to the heavens. She was so transfixed by the size of the Great Sea she didn't think to look away or imagine anything could compare.

"Those mountains are the highest in this world. The snow remains on them all year round, and none have ever made it to the top. At least, none have survived to make it back. Many bodies found their final resting place at the gods' feet."

She tears her eyes away from the sight. "Why do you travel so far across this land? There must be closer towns and villages you can collect slaves?"

He laughs. "You come from peaceful lands, separate from the rest of the world. The other lands, closer to where we're from, are too dangerous to venture through with our small group. We'd lose more of our collection not because of the journey, but because of bandits."

"So, you take slaves from the peaceful lands because it's easier. You travel a circuit around, just to avoid your neighbors?"

He reaches through fast as a snake to grab her arm and he pulls her, hard, against the bars. She cries out in surprise and pain, grabbing the bars with her hands. He lets go, looking over the head of his mount.

"You misunderstand, girl." His voice is dangerously low. "The peace in your land has blinded you and these other slaves. You've all been living privileged lives, especially you magic users. Other lands have cities full of magic users. They don't use their powers to help each other. They're warriors. Things hide in the darkness, waiting for someone to wander into the shadows. There are places no man will travel through." He tightens his grip on her arm and she winces. "Things in this world you could never imagine would fill your sleep with such nightmares you'd fear to close your eyes."

"Stop it," Aya pleads, scooting back into the cage.

"Don't be fooled by this perceived peace you grew up know-ing. This land and its people will kill you if you wander too far." Two slaves start fighting behind the cage, and he slows his epir, ordering men nearby to stop the fight.

Aya moves to the front of the cage and leans against the metal wall. She looks over at the mountains. The awe she felt when she first saw them fades away. Now they're menacing giants, warning all to stay away.

Or daring any brave enough to try to conquer them.

CHAPTER FOURTEEN

TWO MORE DAYS THE CARAVAN TRAVELS ALONGSIDE THE CLIFFS before moving inland. The Great Sea fades into the horizon. The salty air turns dry. The grass browns with great patches of barren earth appearing more frequently. The ground is harder. Cracks explode through the earth and scream for moisture. Animals running from the caravan travel alone, unlike the great herds from the plains. Their thick skins reflect the dry earth.

When the grass disappears completely, the heat from the sun beats down on the caravan. Slaves beg for water or rest. Their feet, as cracked as the earth they tread, swell and bleed.

Aya feels their pain and tries, again in vain, to convince Jaxon's men to allow some of the weakest slaves to ride with her.

When the sun sets on their second day in the dry land, the caravan comes to a stop. Not waiting to hear if they'll be stopped long, the slaves collapse and weep, devoid of tears, as they don't have any liquid to spare.

Barrels are removed from the roof of Aya's cage, liquid sloshing loudly within. The water within passes through the caravan. To the slaves' surprise and relief, they're given large buckets, enough for everyone to get a good-sized helping. Food is still handed out in small, meager portions. But those who are walking are delighted just to have water.

Jaxon leads his epir to the center of the caravan. "Drink as much as you can. Rest as long as you're able. We'll rest for one day and then move out."

Jaxon passes Aya's cage with no sign of stopping. She expects him to look at her, but he turns his epir away and rides off with a small group into the dry land. She watches until the small group is out of sight.

Aldur shouts orders at the men in Jaxon's place. They set up a small, temporary camp, fires built from the wood of empty boxes.

Archer passes Aya's helping of food and water through the bars. The sudden noise makes her jump. He's waited for the rest of the slaves to be given their rations before even trying to give Aya hers. She thanks him, and he moves back a short distance from the bars, watching her.

She eats and drinks without argument. Sleep comes easily and her limbs are heavy; she knows nothing will wake her.

Although the next day is dedicated to rest, the sun beats down on the cracked earth and slaves without mercy. With so few trees, and those few barren of leaves, shade can't be found. Those at the front of the lines manage to find some comfort in the shadows of the cages. But the rest face the full wrath of the sun. Exposed skin glows red and painful blisters erupt.

A hot wind blows across the land and each breeze whips them with dust. Eyes burn and the camp fills with harsh coughing.

Jaxon's men distribute water sparingly, the sand making it difficult to drink it cleanly. A barrel of water is left open to the elements and a layer of mud builds on top of the clear liquid. Men scrape the muck away before closing the barrel up.

Jaxon and the group he left with the day before haven't returned, but Aldur seems unconcerned. The sun sets, but the heat is slow to fade. Food is handed out with the next round of water and sleep comes easily for most. Aya never ceases wishing she could help the others. She's tried multiple times to connect to her magic, but the metal of her cage excludes all magic.

At the same time, the feeling of having no magic is oddly relieving. She hates admitting it, yet the moment of being a normal person is a rare sensation for her. She barely remembers how she felt before her magic blossomed.

A loud cough reminds her she'll never be normal ever again, and she stares at the group asleep before her. Some have grown so thin their skin resembles parchment stretched over bone. She glances down at her own thinning frame and wonders how they'll be treated when they finally reach the Arena. Will they be fed well or kept near starvation? Will they be allowed rest? And what will the Arena be like? She forces her thoughts away.

"You should rest." Jaxon walks up to the cage, his epir straggling behind. He ties his beast to the cage and leans on it, holding one bar with his hand.

"Where did you go?" Aya asks.

"Did you worry about me?" He smirks. "Did you miss me?"

Her cheeks flush hot and she bows her head, hoping he won't see.

"We had a couple of troublemaker bandits following us, stealing food when no one was looking. I had to deal with them," he explains.

"You mean you killed them."

"I had two of the bandits' comrades do it. Now, they joined my caravan."

"What if they'd refused to kill their companions?"

"Then I would've killed them all."

She stares into his eyes holds his gaze. "Why do you do this?"

He raises an eyebrow. "You mean collect people and sell them to the Arena?"

She nods.

"To survive. Aldur told me about your little talk a few days ago. His words are true. You were living a carefree, privileged life in your valley. All of these people were the same. You were all protected from the life outside."

"Not protected enough."

Jaxon laughs and turns, leaning his back against the cage. The sudden movement scares his epir and it stomps its hoofed feet. "True, but the Blood King's influence hadn't reached you. Doing what needs to be done to see the light of the next day rules all our lives."

"Including stealing from your prisoners," Aya says.

"Still angry about the bracelet? If it's any consolation, it helped pay for the food you're eating. The dagger I think I'll hang onto for a little while longer."

Fighting back tears, she turns away. "They were the final gifts from my parents. They died after giving them to me." She takes a shaky breath and quickly changes the subject. "How much longer are you going to force the others to suffer? How much longer until you sell us?"

A slight pause precedes a loud sigh. "We're entering the Karrion Desert. We'll need to cross it to reach the Arena. It's a ten-day journey without stops." Jaxon turns his head to her, his smile gone. "But to not stop would be suicidal. There's an oasis town located about four days in. We'll stop to restock our supplies for the final trek. After Karrion it'll take about seven days to reach our destination."

She looks at those sleeping on the hard ground. "Why don't you help them? They can't bring you much money if they're half-dead."

"And where are the supplies meant to come from, eh? We collect large numbers because those who survive will provide enough money for all of my men to live a few moon cycles more."

"And once we reach the Arena, you'll sell us and return to the world looking for more slaves."

"You speak so ill of me, but you fail to grasp the truth of the world."

"At least let me help them a little before we enter the desert," she begs.

He takes a step back. "You don't have enough power to heal them all. You're as weak as they are."

"Please, I've already done more than I thought myself capable of. Let me make it easier for them, if only a little while. It's the only mercy they will receive."

Jaxon eyes the ground. His hand lowers to the hilt of her dagger.

"It could give you the chance to make more money," she adds.

His head shoots up and his expression surprises her. It's a mixture of anger and hurt, but as soon as she sees it, he wipes it away, leaving his usual, uncaring expression behind.

He unlocks the door of the cage and steps back. She quickly crawls to the opening and climbs out. She falls to her knees, weak from not standing for weeks.

A blade rests against her throat, her own dagger's black blade. She raises her head to Jaxon. He holds the dagger tightly in one hand. With his free hand he helps her to her feet. "We'll walk together. We'll move from one slave to the other together. If you try to move ahead or behind me, I'll kill you."

Aya nods.

He takes her to the first sleeping slave. She slowly leans down over him and looks at his feet. The cuts are still bleeding even while he sleeps, dirt turning to mud as the blood mixes with it. She places her hands on the side of his leg and closes her eyes.

It takes the entire night for Aya to heal the slaves. She heals the bruises and cuts quickly. To limit further damage, she thickens the skin on their feet to provide a little more padding. It takes her a couple of tries at first, an experiment in the beginning, but soon she does it as quickly as healing. She finds some worse than others, a few with broken toes or sprained ankles, and as the night drags on she feels her energy and strength dwindle.

By the time the sun shines its light over the earth, Aya finishes. Jaxon leads her back to the cage, the dagger safely sheathed. She stumbles, every step harder to make. They're still several feet away from the cage when her legs give out. Jaxon effortlessly lifts her in his arms and carries her the rest of the way. The door is still open, and he gently lays her inside.

He locks the door and unties his epir. He stares at her through the bars. "We're going to be heading out. Get some sleep while we start crossing the desert. This will be the hardest part of the journey, even for those not forced to travel on foot." He climbs onto his epir. "And...I'm sorry about your bracelet."

He shouts orders and his men in armor walk down the lines of slaves, waking those still asleep. The small camp is dismantled quickly and soon the caravan is ready to move.

Aya watches Jaxon at the front of the caravan as he speaks with Aldur. Her eyes droop, but she fights to stay awake. She remembers the conversations she heard so long ago about the leader of the caravan never sleeping. Even on the rest day, he went out to handle business about the caravan. Now he rides at the front, showing no sign of needing rest. But Aldur sleeps at night, as does Archer.

Maybe he's a magic user, she thinks, too tired to explore the idea any further. She laughs at the thought.

He glances back at her as though her thoughts reached him, and she catches the smile on his lips as her eyes close.

CHAPTER FIFTEEN

HEAT. THE KIND OF HEAT THAT SITS ON A BODY LIKE A BLANKET. Instead of providing relief, the hot, dry wind only brings more. Sweat rolls down her forehead, and the metal of the cage intensifies the heat onto her skin. She opens her eyes but is blinded by the sun reflecting off of the surrounding land. Great dunes of golden sand span the Karrion Desert, some so huge they tower above the caravan.

There's no escape from the sun. The dry air has stolen all the moisture from Aya's lips. She wonders how long she's been asleep. Her foot hits something cool, and she looks to the other side of the cage. A jug of water is sitting next to her.

"A thank-you from the other slaves," Aldur says from behind the cage. "They're grateful to you for healing them. They requested half their share of water go to you when you woke."

"How long have I been asleep?" Aya asks. Her voice rough, the dry air making her cough.

"A day and a half."

Aya looks at the slaves walking behind. They're dragging their feet through the hot sand, but at least the skin of their feet is unbroken now. Sweat covers their bodies and falls from their

79

chins like raindrops. Those in her line of vision smile at her, weakly.

"It's a shame they want to waste their precious water on you. This is where we usually lose most of our collection. This is where you would've probably died if you had been forced to walk," Aldur says, bluntly.

She doesn't respond. Her throat burns and sand blows into her eyes. She drinks from the jug eagerly. When half is gone, she locks eyes with Aldur. She holds it to him.

"What?"

"Give the rest back to them. I healed them so they'd have a fighting chance. If they kill themselves from dehydration, it'll have been for nothing."

Aldur takes the jug without argument and smiles. "You're trying so hard to keep them alive. Don't forget where this journey ends. When you reach the Arena, you may wish you'd died here. We'll see how many will be thankful to you for their lives, then." He hands the jug to one of the other men and orders him to pass it around.

Hours pass and Aya's throat burns again from lack of moisture. Sand irritates her nose and eyes. Every time she wipes away the sand, more is blown into them by the hot wind. The nights provide little comfort from the heat. By the time the air cools enough to be bearable, the sun is already rising. How can Jaxon and his men stand the constant motion in their black armor? She wonders.

On the fourth day since they stopped to rest, a strange sight rises in the distance. A single tree appears floating above the sand in the middle of the desert. Many rub their eyes, even with gritty hands, to be sure it's not a mirage. Other trees and floating buildings fade into view, as if by magic, around the tall tree. The men in armor eagerly push the caravan faster and soon Aya realizes the buildings and trees aren't floating. There is water in the air, making the earth shimmer.

They've reached the oasis town Jaxon spoke of days before.

The caravan enters the middle of the town. People look out windows and doors. They've seen caravans of slaves many times before, but it's been a long time since one stopped with so many still alive.

The more curious townsfolk walk past the caravan and glance over each slave. When their eyes land on Jaxon and his men dressed in black armor, they whisper to each other excitedly. Aya overhears two women walking by. All she can make out from their fast-paced conversation are two words.

Black Caravan.

The caravan comes to rest by a large well sitting underneath the large tree at the center of the town. The shade is welcome, even though the hot wind still causes most to sweat.

Buckets plunge into the cool water and pass around the slaves. Several of Jaxon's men venture through the town to restock supplies, mainly food.

A sudden shout comes from the back of the caravan. Aya rushes to the back of the cage and peers through the bars. Jaxon, Aldur, and three of his men run.

One of Jaxon's men lies dead on the ground, his blood staining the sandy earth. The culprit is an escaped slave, the keys he stole from the dead man lying forgotten next to his discarded chains. He speeds through the caravan, avoiding the men in armor by dodging underneath animals and cages. He passes Aya, meeting her eyes for only a moment, and then sprints out of the town.

Jaxon, Aldur, and his three men rush after him, but Jaxon stops them when he realizes where the slave is headed. "Let him go. He'll die out there alone."

They return to preparing the caravan for the next trek of the journey. The three men clear away their comrade's body, dragging it out of view, while Jaxon and Aldur speak in confidence.

But Aya squints, following the escaped slave until he can no longer be seen. Across the well, three men dressed head to toe in light clothing watch Jaxon's men. The man standing in the middle wears a red scarf covering his mouth and nose. His eyes are filled with a strange light, and she feels a chill run through her body. He turns his eyes on her and, even with the cloth covering his mouth, she can tell he's smiling.

A group of Jaxon's men lead their epirs in front of her and when they pass, the strange men are gone.

"We've lost four of our own, now," one of Jaxon's men whispers to the two others with him. "And not one of the slaves. It's uncanny, I tell you."

The group stops at the front of the cage and Aya carefully moves to sit within earshot.

"No wonder they're always needing new members. This pathetic leader can't keep anyone alive," a second man says.

"Why're you complaining, Hart? That means a larger share for us once we unload this lot."

"I say once we finish this trip, we procure this caravan for ourselves," Hart says, leaning closer to the other two. "I got some friends at the Arena who'd help out with a little accidental death of our fearless leader."

Aya's eyes widen and she wants to speak.

Aldur beats her to it. "You three! Quit talking and get back to work."

The men jump at the large man's appearance and their expressions fill with worry. Were they overheard? They quickly split up and finish preparing for departure.

If Aldur overheard their conversation, he doesn't show it.

As the sun sets, the caravan is ready to leave. Food has been restocked for the rest of the journey, and water is passed around one final time. Once each slave has his or her fill, the caravan heads back out into the desert.

Travel at night is easier. Many slaves appear more energized, but with the rising of the sun the newfound energy fades.

On the third day out from the town, the caravan stops briefly when they come across the dehydrated body of the slave who escaped, half-buried in the sand. Men search the corpse for anything of value. They pull the dried husk from the sand, showing small pieces of flesh missing, most likely having fed small lizards or insects. Finding nothing, the men drop the body in the sand and the caravan moves on.

Aya gazes back at the body, remembering the look in the slave's eyes as he passed her. There'd been such a look of gratitude...and devotion. The same looks she came to loathe in the villagers from her home. She'd given this man the strength to attempt an escape, and now he was dead.

She wants to cry for him, but the tears won't come.

CHAPTER SIXTEEN

THE DUNES FADE AWAY OVER THE NEXT THREE DAYS, ALLOWING THE hard earth below to show through. Tall mounds of rocks and distant canyons appear. Dry, thorny plants cover the ground. The heat level falls, no longer reflecting off the endless, dead sea of sand. Large birds of prey circle in the sky, searching for food with their powerful eyes.

The caravan enters a small canyon of rocks on the fourth day. The partial shade is a welcome reprieve from the sun. Small, scaled animals hide in the shadows of large rocks and trees. Large thorns cover the bark of the trees which grow from the walls of the canyon.

The air stills, putting the men on high alert. The groduns pulling the cages make strange sounds and move oddly, as though spooked. The slaves huddle closer together, sensing the unease.

Jaxon stops the caravan and climbs down from his epir. "Damn it. What is this?"

Aya strains to look around the large beasts pulling the cage. The canyon is blocked. Large boulders block the only path through. Jaxon glances from the block to the back of the caravan.

"What do we do?" Aldur asks.

Cursing, Jaxon kicks at the blockage. "We can't go back. The only other way is too long. We'll run out of food."

"Clear it, then?"

Before Jaxon answers, a spear flies through the air and into the neck of one of the groduns pulling the cage holding Aya. The beast rears back, frightening the other grodun. The cage lurches. The animals pull away from each other, breaking their restraints. The riders are thrown off, landing hard on the ground and Aya's cage is flung onto the ground. She screams as several of the metal bars break and one stabs into her arm.

The slaves connected to Aya's cage are thrown with the cage. Those farther from the cage lurch but are able to stay standing. Slaves and men in armor panic as the wounded grodun runs at them. Those who can't move out of the way are trampled or knocked to the side. A second spear flies into the large beast and kills it. The men in armor circle the caravan with their weapons drawn, some herding the slaves to the center.

"See to the healer!" Jaxon roars at Aldur.

Aldur runs to Aya's cage and forces the door open. He struggles at first with the bent lock but manages to break more of the loosened bars with a surge of strength. He climbs inside and eyes Aya's arm. The bar piercing her arm is still connected to the cage but bent upwards. A large rock beneath the cage bends bars like teeth between her and Aldur.

The large man quickly, but carefully, makes his way towards her. Locking eyes with her, he takes a deep breath. "I'm going to have to pull you off."

He doesn't need to say the words. It's clear from his face. It's going to hurt.

Aya nods and closes her eyes. He grabs her and roughly pulls her up. As her arm pulls free of the bar, she bites back a scream. Dark liquid rolls down the metal and small pieces of her flesh stick to the bar. Nausea overcomes her and she leans to the side,

85

the meager contents of her stomach splattering to the ground. The fact it was her own flesh, her own blood, was far more nauseating than tending others' wounds.

Aldur waits until she's finished before tearing a long strip from her shirt and dressing her arm. "This will have to do until you can heal it. Stay with me."

She glances around at the panicked slaves. Those who were trampled by the wounded grodun lie still, blood pooling on the ground. Those knocked to the sides are screaming for help, blood staining their clothes.

The second grodun that pulled her cage manages to escape and runs back the way the caravan came. Several of Jaxon's men, including the two who'd been thrown from the groduns, run after the loose beast with thick ropes.

Aya looks at Aldur with terror filled eyes. "What's going on? What's happened?"

He draws his sword. "Bandits."

Men appear from the walls around the caravan. A larger group stands atop the blockage in front of Jaxon. The bandits outnumber the caravan's men and Aya recognizes the one at the center of the group as the strange man from the oasis town.

The leader draws one of the two swords on his belt, aiming the point at Jaxon. "Black Caravan. We've heard many stories about you. We're here for your supplies and," his eyes shoot to Aya, "the Rare Kind you're transporting."

Aya's body runs cold, her heart pounding in her chest. Flashes of Jaxon's attack on Oula Village crosses her vision. Again, someone is after her and others are being killed because of it.

Aldur tightens his grip around her waist. "Stay with me, girl."

"Why should I?"

"These men have worse plans for you than the Arena."

The men of the caravan prepare to attack, but Jaxon holds up

86

a hand. They move back, and he walks towards the bandit leader, who stands atop the boulders. "You know of the Black Caravan and yet you still attack. You obviously didn't listen to the rest of the stories. Clear a path or be destroyed."

"You must not have heard me, slave trader. We want the Rare Kind. We outnumber your men. You can't win."

Jaxon draws his sword. "You misunderstand my threat."

He gives a shrill whistle and the men of the caravan sheathe their weapons and move closer together, tightening the circle around the slaves.

Aldur pulls Aya away from the fallen cage. But, faint though she is from loss of blood, she struggles to remain within eyesight of Jaxon. "He can't fight them alone!"

Aldur stays silent, moving them so they have a clear view of Jaxon and the bandits. He keeps his arm around her waist, ensuring she can't run off.

The bandit leader's eyes move over each of Jaxon's men and he laughs. He turns to his men and raises his hands in front of him. "Do you see this? He believes he can fight all of us alone!" The bandits laugh.

Jaxon eyes the fallen grodun and walks to it. He pulls the first spear from the thick flesh and eyes the bandits on the walls. He stops on one and in a flash throws the spear. It slams into one of the bandits sitting in one of the trees growing from the canyon's walls. The man falls to the ground and half the bandits disappear in puffs of smoke.

The laughter stops and the bandits remaining, the real bandits, number barely over a dozen.

Jaxon holds his hands out to each side. "I don't think it will be too difficult now."

The leader faces Jaxon, anger filling his eyes. "Cocky bastard. Let's see how you fair against us. Kill him!"

Four men run at Jaxon. Aya stares at Aldur in shock. "Why aren't you helping him?"

"I'd only get in his way."

The first bandit reaches Jaxon, raises his sword, and brings it down toward Jaxon's head. Jaxon easily steps to the side then forward, raising his sword. He stabs the man in the chest and pushes him back into the two behind.

The men grab their dying comrade, then throw him to the ground, moving to either side of Jaxon as a third bandit faces him. They swing their blades, but Jaxon blocks the attacks with his sword while dodging. The men move closer, limiting Jaxon's maneuvering room.

Jaxon side-steps a down-swing and stomps his foot on the man's sword, metal hidden in his boot keeping the blade from cutting through his shoe. The man tries to pull his blade free, but Jaxon kicks him. The man drops his sword and Jaxon spins to kick another man in the head. The two men collapse to the ground.

The third man grabs his dead comrade's sword and tries to stab Jaxon. Jaxon grabs the man's arm, twisting it and forcing the man to drop the blade. He draws Aya's dagger and stabs the man under the chin, twisting the blade before releasing him. The man falls to the ground dead and Jaxon sheathes the dagger after wiping it clean in the sand.

The other two men manage to climb back to their feet. They attack him simultaneously, one aiming for Jaxon's head and the other going for his stomach.

Blocking the first sword with his own, Jaxon moves closer to the two men. The second man hits Jaxon's stomach with his arm, not the blade. He tries to pull back to slice Jaxon's side, but Jaxon grabs his companion's wrist and brings down both swords on the man's arm. Both blades hit and he screams as his arm is detached.

Jaxon punches the man with the sword in the nose. The bandit stumbles back, releasing his sword. Jaxon grips the man's sword tightly and spins, slicing the blades into one man's neck and the other's side.

Throwing the dead man's sword away, Jaxon faces the rest of the bandits as the two behind him collapse to the ground. "I hope those weren't your best."

The bandit leader glares. He snaps at a second group and five men surround Jaxon.

Jaxon sighs and raises his sword, spreading his legs to lower his center of gravity. The bandits attack in a flurry of steel, but when Jaxon swings his sword it makes contact with steel or with a bandit every time. He quickly dispatches the second wave and faces the bandit leader again.

The bandit leader sends the rest of his men in one large wave. They circle Jaxon and attack him all at once. He keeps their swords from hitting him but has trouble keeping his back clear from sneak attacks.

His sword moves quickly from one blade to another, blocking those he can't dodge. Those he can dodge miss him by mere inches and some hit bandits too slow to avoid their comrades' blades.

Jaxon maneuvers the remaining bandits in front of him. He moves in close to those at the front, his sword precisely slicing to do the most damage. He grabs the nearest dying man rams the body into one bandit; a whoosh of foul air escapes the man's lips. While the man is stunned, Jaxon stabs him under the arm and slices, blood spraying to the ground.

The last four bandits charge Jaxon directly, to skewer him. He blocks two with the body in his hand, the blades making a meaty thud as they bury into the thick flesh. Jaxon blocks the third with his blade, a loud clang echoing in the air. The fourth bandit slips on the bloody sand, his blade missing Jaxon and throwing him off balance.

Sensing his chance, Jaxon kicks the fourth bandit, slices the throat of the third bandit, and shoves the last two. Releasing the body he'd been using as a shield, the two bandits fall to the earth, the body landing on top of them and knocking the air from their lungs. Pulling out Aya's dagger, Jaxon spins, stabbing the fourth bandit in the head. Pulling the blade free, he steps on the dead body holding the remaining two bandits down.

He stabs each in the heart with his sword and turns his full attention to the leader.

CHAPTER SEVENTEEN

THE BANDIT LEADER RUNS AT JAXON, SWINGING HIS BLADES, preventing Jaxon from dodging to either side or swinging at the man. He moves backwards, the only available path.

The leader kicks Jaxon in the stomach. Jaxon doubles over but attempts to slice the leader's leg with the black dagger. The leader pulls his foot away before Jaxon's blade makes contact and swings his blades down. Jaxon rolls to the side, trying to clear the blades, but misjudges the timing. He winces as one of the blades slices his arm. He moves away, but his back is forced against the dead grodun.

The bandit leader thrusts both swords forward, aiming to run Jaxon through. Jaxon drops to the ground, and the leader's swords dig into the dead beast. Jaxon slips his sword into the small opening between the other two blades, inches from the leader's face.

The two men freeze.

Jaxon holds his blade still, standing beside the leader. The leader breathes heavily, staring at the blade. He swallows and tries to pull his blades free, but they're stuck too deep into the beast's corpse.

He snatches a fallen knife from the sand and turns to slice

Jaxon's throat. In one quick move, Jaxon slices the leader from the base of his neck to under his armpit. Blood sprays into the air and Jaxon moves away. When the body hits the sand, he cleans his blade on the leader's scarfed head. The body lies slumped against the dead grodun.

Jaxon sheathes his sword and dagger, walking towards Aya. "How's her arm?"

"It was run through, but no major damage I think," Aldur says, emotionless. Aya guesses he had seen this sort of action many times in his life. He motions towards the dead bandits. "Always gotta show off, don't you?"

"Don't want to get rusty." Jaxon looks at her. "Can you heal it?"

She nods slowly, too stunned to speak.

"Good." He turns to his men. "Check all the slaves for injuries. We're going to need to clear this canyon before we can move on. But we now have more meat." He motions to the dead grodun.

Most of the men in black armor cheer and do as ordered, clearing the slaves to the sides of the canyon. Others, more than likely the newer members, stare at Jaxon in amazed fear. The older members shove them to get them to work. They check each slave and move those who were chained to Aya's bars to the next cage.

"Let's get you away," Aldur says. "Let you rest."

Aya shakes her head, staring at those injured. "I can help. I can heal anyone who's hurt."

"Worry about healing yourself first, girl."

"Let her heal the slaves," Jaxon says, passing by. "We've lost a grodun and a cage. I refuse to lose money on our haul." Jaxon walks away before the larger man can speak. Reluctantly, Aldur leads Aya to the closest slaves. But she passes by most, who are only bruised or scratched, to get to those who were trampled by the fleeing grodun. They are bleeding and their bones are broken, but Aya finds it easier to knit them than before. Her work is quicker and less exhausting now, even without the use of her wounded arm.

The men who ran after the second grodun return with it in tow. They quickly put the animal to work pulling larger rocks from the blocked canyon. Slaves strong enough to lift are put to work on the smaller rocks.

When Aya finishes healing the last of the slaves, Aldur sits her down on a boulder next to the canyon wall so she can lean back.

She places her hand over her wounded arm. Calming her nerves, she concentrates on healing the injury. Unlike when she heals others, the pain doesn't go away. She feels every muscle reform, her skin knitting back together. Finishing, Aya moves her arm around, testing it, to make sure it healed correctly.

She spies Jaxon walking through the caravan, double-checking the slaves. He orders four men to take the broken cage apart. Broken parts are thrown to the side, while useable parts are moved to a barrel in the last wagon. Jaxon orders two more of his men to move the dead slaves' bodies away and bury them. They're buried in the hard, dry earth close to the wall of the canyon.

Five others drag the dead bandits by the arms and legs, leaving trails of blood in the sand. After collecting valuables from the corpses, they toss them with sickening thuds into a large pile far from the caravan. Topping the morbid pile with the bandit leader's body, the slavers stack wood around the bottom and set fire to the pile. Black smoke fills the sky, but the wind blowing through the canyon sends the smoke—and the smell—away from the caravan.

"He hates that name," Aldur says. "The Black Caravan."

Aya turns to him. "What?"

He nods his head at Jaxon.

"Isn't it because of the black armor you wear?" she asks.

Aldur shakes his head. "People at the Arena believe Jaxon's blood is black."

Black blood? Like the stories? Aya thinks, remembering the stories her parents used to tell her about the gods.

MORDA, the mother God, and Velan, the God of Death, created the brother Gods, Ogrin and Kellot. Ogrin of the red blood was peaceful by nature, but his temper could be quick. Kellot of the black blood was weaker but made a great sport of playing tricks and angering Ogrin.

One day, the two brothers were walking through the lands of the earth, their favorite playground. Kellot decided to make Ogrin angry so that he would fight him. But no matter how Kellot tried, he couldn't make his brother angry. Kellot, in his rage, took Ogrin's blade and cut off his own hand. His black blood fell to the earth and created the beasts of this world. Ogrin, furious at his brother for his rash act, opened a vein and spilled his red blood to create mankind to control the beasts.

Jealous of his brother's creation, Kellot spilled his blood a second time to bring night to the earth. Mankind became fearful of the dark and its ability to hide the beasts of the world. They cried out to Ogrin for help. Ogrin spilled his blood again and gave men the gift of fire, his rage at his brother's cruel trickery.

Kellot, furiously jealous, and furious with his brother's blood's ability to thwart his plans, concocted a terrible trick. While Ogrin slept, Kellot stole some of his blood. He mixed his black blood with the red blood of his brother and poured the mixture onto the earth. From the blood came the first magic users. Kellot, excited to show off his new creation, awoke Ogrin and claimed the magic users came from his blood. But Ogrin refused to believe such beings could come from his brother's black blood. To prove it, Ogrin cut the creations. Only pure red blood flowed forth.

In Kellot's shocked rage over the red-blooded magic users, he spilled his blood a fourth and final time. From this blood came a new breed of mankind: a gifted, cruel breed that could not be killed. Mankind became fearful of this new breed they called Brüdel, or black-blooded, and imprisoned them. Magic users joined their powers together and sundered the Brüdel. Some they buried deep in the earth, some they sank to the bottom of the seas, and the last they threw into the very fires of the earth itself. The few Brüdel who escaped or survived went into hiding, but stories of men who could not be killed or even injured spread across the land.

∾

JAXON STOPS in front of Aldur and Aya. "All healed?"

Aya notices the cut on Jaxon's arm. "You're bleeding."

He glances at his arm. "Ah, yes. That bastard got me." He presses the skin around the wound. Red blood rolls down his arm and he wipes it with his fingers. He holds his hand up. "No, the rumors aren't true. Since we've lost your cage, you're going to have to make do with riding with the others in the second cage. It's not much farther to our destination."

Aya nods, filled with a new understanding of how powerful Jaxon truly is. She stares at his sheathed sword and remembers the attack on her village. He could've killed all of them alone, could've invaded the village by himself if he wanted.

"You killed all of them."

Jaxon's eyebrows furrow. "They threw off our schedule and were going to steal my prized cargo. They'll be a warning to other bandits who think they can take on the Black Caravan."

"I thought you hated that name."

He says nothing.

She notes how he refers to them as cargo, but she gazes from the buried slaves to the still-burning pile of bandits. He made sure to keep them separate, even if it would've been faster to burn all of them. She's seeing something in him she hadn't expected. He has a strong sense of honor and a hidden kindness, even for those he claims as slaves.

"How can they be a warning if they're all dead?" she asks.

"Their charred corpses will be enough. This is a well-traveled route. The message will make it to those who need to hear it." Jaxon heads towards the men pulling the boulders out of the canyon.

Aya is loaded into the second cage. In a space so cramped she can barely sit down, the others in the cage make room for her. Many emotions cross the faces of those around her. Anger, annoyance, sadness, but beneath them all is exhaustion.

"Great, even less room," a heavier man says, sweat rolling down his face.

A woman next to him snorts. "Wait a few days, I'm sure there'll be more room soon."

"What do you mean?"

"That one isn't going to last much longer." The woman motions to an old man lying limp against others at the center of the cage.

Aya remembers the night she healed the slaves, realizing she never thought to help those in the cages. She imagined since they weren't forced to walk, they didn't need help. But they were captured the same as those walking. Some more than likely had fought the slavers, sustaining injuries in the process, or already suffered from pre-existing illnesses.

The slaves are prepared for the last of the journey, with water and food passed around generously. Meat from the dead grodun is divided. Half is separated, cut into smaller pieces, and placed in jars of salt, saved for later. The other half is split again into two equal parts. The first is hung as jerky as the final pounds of meat are cooked and handed out, but even in near-starvation many find it hard to eat with still-smoking bodies close by.

It takes a whole day for the canyon to be cleared, but once ready, it doesn't take long to restart the journey. Jaxon and Aldur stay at the front, sending men ahead to make sure no more bandits are hiding in wait.

The silence throughout the caravan is different than before. The men in black armor who hadn't seen Jaxon fight before are more fearful of him. The slaves who still thought there was a chance of escape give up the idea. Four days pass in the newfound silence and fierce heat. It doesn't reach the same intensity as the sand dunes, but still bears down on the caravan mercilessly.

Aya tries to wet her tongue, but no moisture remains in her mouth. She needs water. She looks at those walking behind and her heart cries out. They barely resemble the vital humans they once were.

The final two days of the journey are brutal. No water is passed down the caravan, no food handed out, and no one rests. Slaves fall to the earth and the men in armor yell at them to stand. If the slaves don't stand fast enough, they're beaten. If the slaves can't stand at all, the men in armor pull out knives and cut the slave's hand free from the chained line. They're left behind to die in the intense heat and provide food to any creatures that dare call the land home.

They lose five slaves over the course of days, including the old man. But Aya stops noticing those disappearing behind the cage and even the screams of pain and thirst from those around her.

All she feels is heat and a growing numbness inside her.

This must be what it feels like to die.

CHAPTER EIGHTEEN

BIZARRE, SHARP-EDGED ROCK FORMATIONS STRETCH FOR MILES around the caravan. In the distance, low, dark mountains peek in the distance.

Aya looks around the crowded cage. Those who can, sleep, while others stare at the floor. Are they thinking of their homes? The loved ones they were torn from?

"The Arena is ahead."

She jumps at Jaxon's voice. He hasn't spoken to her since they left the canyon. A black cloth is wrapped around his arm, covering the cut he wouldn't let her heal.

"It's surrounded by the city of Bloodfall," he continues.

"Bloodfall?"

"A name many have come to call the city since the Blood King made it the site of his games. Whenever he comes to the city, it is inevitable that blood will fall. The true name of the city is Cortridge, but only those born long before the Blood King took over the city remember it."

"And where did he come from? This Blood King?"

Jaxon shakes his head and purses his lips.

Slaves with enough energy lift their heads, gasping at the

98

sight ahead. Aya understands their shock as the mirage among the rocks becomes clear. The mountains that seemed so far away appear as dry and barren as the land around them, providing a fitting background for the enormous building at their base.

The city is large, far larger than any town Aya has seen. Buildings on the edge are smaller and built with dried mud. The buildings become larger and more substantial the further from the wall they're built, reaching three stories in height.

The Arena towers over Bloodfall. Long tapestries flow down the outer walls, made entirely of stone. Emblems cover the red cloth and Aya's eyes widen as she realizes they're the symbols from her dreams.

"What are those symbols?" She grips the bars of the cage tightly.

Glancing ahead, Jaxon shrugs his shoulders. "They're from a dead language. Very few know it, but what I've heard is some denote magic, some represent different lands, and others are words for mythical beasts. Rumors say the Blood King is one of the few who can read it, but I doubt that."

Aya prods again, "You know him."

"You should move away from the bars. The locals like to touch fresh flesh."

"Fresh flesh?"

"New slaves. The locals like to fondle the women and beat the men. They think it's a proper welcoming for those forced to risk their lives in the Arena. Keep out of reach, or they may grab more than your clothing."

Aya jerks back and pulls her knees to her chest. Those around her who heard Jaxon do the same. Others, too weak to even lift their heads, stay still. Those walking push forward, moving as close to the cage as possible, but without the bars the only thing keeping the people from them are the slavers.

A low stone wall circles Bloodfall, an old defense, judging by the cracks in the rock. Guards walk along the top, watching the caravan as it approaches. After they pass through the open gate, the guards ignore them.

Wind blows sand and dust everywhere, caking everything in a gritty layer of filth. Those who live this close to the wall must not even try to sweep it away, knowing it's a losing battle.

Shops sell goods mostly outside, with a few located inside the homes of the owners. Merchandise is displayed on long tables while the more valuable oddities are kept behind locked, glass-covered cases.

The caravan moves slowly through the city; the buildings change from dried mud to stone as they reach those with more wealth. People follow the caravan with curious eyes, eager to see the fresh flesh for the Arena. Some walk along the cage or line of slaves, the men in black armor allowing them to get close.

A child kicks one of the slaves, causing him to trip and fall. One of Jaxon's men chases the child away, but others take his place. Some use long sticks to poke at those inside the cage until Aldur grabs the tools and snaps them in two.

Men poke their hands through the bars of the cage, grabbing for the women inside and making lewd remarks. If any of the men inside the cage try to stop them, men outside the cage throw rocks or punch them in the face. One heavy male slave drips blood from a broken nose.

Aya tries to force a man away from one of the weaker women whose dress is being torn from her. He hits her hard, knocking her back. A second man tries to grab her, barely missing her hair. She moves away, as close to the center of the cage as possible, but she feels eyes glaring at her.

Those following the caravan fall back as they enter a new section of the city. Buildings stand up to three stories, the facades covered in marble. Balconies on the upper floors hold curious people, eager to see the new commodities.

The wheels of the cage vibrate as the dirt gives way to stone-paved road. The rattling and creaking of the cage as it bounds along the stone echoes off the marble facades. The roads are wide enough to allow carts or wagons to pass the caravan, though it is close. The epirs stumble as their hooves adjust to the new ground beneath their feet, whinnying in discomfort. But they soon calm, and the clopping of their hooves joins in the city noise.

Branching roads stretch into the distance, giving Aya the idea the city is far larger than she first assumed. Children run through the streets, playing with wooden swords or playing hide and seek. Unlike the children in the poorer sections, they show no interest in the caravan above their play and the other carts rolling down the roads.

Citizens gawk at the caravan in a disgusted fashion. Mutterings from those passing on the raised walkways are low, but a few of the slavers kick at those too close. Aya assumes it's due to whatever the citizens whispered.

Armed men walk along the walkways, more guards of Bloodfall. They chase any of the remaining poorer residents away. They ignore the caravan, though occasionally one glares at Jaxon's men in disgust. Aya can't be certain if it's disgust for slave traders, or all these dirty bodies in the cleaner section of the city.

Rising above the buildings, filling almost the entire rear of section of the city, is the Arena. Large entrances fill with people selling food, animals, and trinkets. Families with small children ogle the varied assortment. The joy of the children is a stark contrast to the screams rising from inside the Arena.

Standing beneath a large banner, men flex their muscles and swing weapons in show of power. A smaller man standing at the end of the line of fighters collects coins from audience members betting on the day's victors.

The Arena boasts five levels in total. People mill through large openings in the walls on four of the levels. The top floor has larger openings, widely spaced. Fewer people are on that level, but it isn't difficult to see why. It is made entirely of marble and plants decorate the edges. It is the space reserved for the wealthy.

Cheers erupt from inside the Arena, thundering and bouncing off the mountains behind. Other, stranger sounds mix with the yells, like the lowing of beasts.

The caravan comes to an abrupt halt, sending a confused murmur through the men in black armor. A wall of men blocks their way. Their armor, unlike the guards of the city, are heavy and dyed blood-red. Many of the people who live in the city quickly gather in front of the caravan, trying to catch glimpses of what will happen.

A large carriage crosses behind the line of men. It's painted black with red lining along the edges. Thick curtains cover the windows so no one can see inside. Four epirs, draped in silk and with plumes of red feathers on their heads, pull the large vehicle and the crowd whispers excitedly.

Aya watches the vehicle pass, but a feeling deep inside of her slowly rises. Fear, but a different fear than she's ever felt before. The curtain covering the window pulls slightly away from the glass and a shadow appears. A feeling of dread overwhelms her and she turns away, senselessly terrified that the shadow will see her—recognize her.

She sees Jaxon turn away. He avoids her look by lowering his gaze to the ground.

The sound of the carriage passes, and the line of men follows after. The people of the city talk quickly and head for the Arena. The caravan continues moving forward, the opposite direction from the carriage. Aya still feels her heart pounding, and places one hand to her chest.

Following the wall of the Arena around to the back, the side closest to the mountains, the caravan slows its pace. Fewer people surround them, now, and the shadows of the mountains provide much-needed relief from the blazing sun.

A large entrance, larger than any of the others, leads down into the earth below the Arena. The caravan enters, the temperature of the air immediately dropping, and descends a ramp before reaching an empty room. The shade is a welcome reprieve from the heat outside. Even the smell of the damp earth is welcome, moisture in the air a strange feeling after so long in the desert.

The room is large enough for the caravan, including the three groduns, to easily stand with space for others walking by. Along the walls are long wooden poles for tying animals to, and long troughs filled with water. The smell of the water brings moans from the slaves, chains rattling as many attempt to venture closer to the life-saving liquid.

Jaxon signals his men to dismount. They tie their epirs to the poles before returning to their positions, shoving the slaves back into line. Young men run to the animals, carrying large pails of feed. They place a pail between every pair of epirs.

Across from the entrance is an opening leading further into the Arena. Men stand guard on either side of the opening, preventing curious spectators from entering.

The men in black armor remove the chains from the slaves and gather them into a large group. Opening the cage, the men order those within out. Aya is the last out, hesitating as she takes in the strange Arena. Free of the cage, she feels her magic uncurl inside her, moving through her body as though missing her. It fills her, and she feels comfort at the connection being restored.

The men of the caravan order the slaves to move and they head past the guards without a glance. The heat fades completely as they go even farther down under the Arena.

Hundreds of men fill these rooms. Some carry weapons. Some pull cages of wild animals across the dirt floor. Some operate strange machinery, their muscles bulging as they work. Some even use magic to assist others. Most are muscular, and all of them wear thick leather chest pieces with the same circular symbol carved on the right breast. Members of an even smaller group carry bags of money and talk amongst each other, looking at papers with numbers written across them.

Then there are those who wear torn, battered clothes hanging from their bodies like chains. Blood stains some, but most are covered in dirt. These men and women watch the caravan walk by with pity in their eyes.

Aya grasps that she and her fellow slaves are staring into their future.

CHAPTER NINETEEN

THE LINE OF SLAVES FINALLY COMES TO A STOP. THEY FALL TO THE cool earth, weeping with both tears of joy and sorrow. Joy they no longer have to walk great distances, but sorrow for reaching their destination.

Arena workers hand off buckets of water to the men in black armor. They in turn carry the buckets around and ladle out the life-giving liquid. The slaves drink greedily. Aya takes the opportunity to look around.

At first glance, the workings of the Arena seem chaotic. But all move with purpose and skill, seamless through the crowd and machinery. Even the arrival of the caravan doesn't slow the workers.

Aldur walks to Aya with a ladle of water.

"Where's the man who usually brings me water and food?" she asks, realizing she hasn't seen Archer in many days.

"Busy. Here you are, girl. Drink up, restore your strength."

She accepts the ladle and closes her eyes as the cool liquid pours down her throat. She feels it all the way to her stomach, drinking without taking a breath until her lungs scream for air. She gasps and catches her breath before drinking again.

A loud crack from behind makes her jump. She and the other

slaves turn to see a woman with scars on her arms and face standing with Jaxon. Her clothes are separate pieces of leather showing off her muscular body. Two large men stand behind her, standing a full head taller than Jaxon.

She winds her whip up and ties it to her belt. She walks through the group of slaves, looking each over carefully. She grabs some by the chin and others by the arm to pull them to their feet. She pokes and prods, making occasional grunts or interested sounds.

Jaxon follows close behind her, followed in turn by the two large men. He waves away any of his men who get too close to the woman but, otherwise, doesn't interfere with her examination of the slaves.

"You've brought me fewer magic users than last time, but more appeared to have survived the trip," the woman says, her voice deep and coarse, matching her appearance. "Which one is the rare creature you want to sell me for such a fortune?"

Jaxon leads her to Aya and Aldur, waving the other man away. The woman steps in front of Aya and looks her up and down.

"She's a Life Healer, Seera," Jaxon explains.

"We'll see what she is. Come closer, slave."

Aya notes how the woman refuses to refer to her as a person. She hesitates, then walks closer. Seera grabs her and inspects her as she did with the others. At one point, she grabs Aya's breasts, sending a shock through her. She instinctively throws her arms up, slapping the woman's hands away. She freezes, then, fully understanding what she did.

Laughing, Seera nods to one of her men. He steps around Jaxon and in front of Aya. He grabs her arms and holds her still as Seera walks behind her. She places her hands around Aya's waist, poking her stomach and moving to her back. She slaps Aya's buttocks once and makes an interested grunt.

"She seems like any other magic user to me," Seera finally says, waving her hand at the large man. He releases Aya and moves back to stand beside the other. She circles Aya and stops in front of her. "Though she still has a bit more energy in her than those you usually bring."

Jaxon takes a step forward, his eyes filled with an irritated glow. The two men behind him mimic his movement. "I saw her bring one of the others back from near death."

Seera grabs Aya's chin and turns her head one way, then the other. She touches Aya's hair with her free hand and smiles. She releases her and turns to Jaxon. "Let's see if she can do it again." She looks at one of the men behind Jaxon, carrying a thick blade, and nods.

The man bows and unsheathes his blade. He stabs Jaxon in the back, the tip of the weapon appearing through his chest. He screams out in shock and pain. Blood spatters Aya's face.

Jaxon's men all draw their weapons and move toward the scene. Except for four, the four she remembers talking about conspiring back in the oasis town. She remembers one mentioning he knew people in the Arena that could help with an *accidental death*. However, the look of shock filling their eyes makes her think they weren't involved…at least, not with this.

Seera raises a hand and the man pulls his large, thick blade out of Jaxon and holds it up. Aldur holds up a hand to stop the caravan men, but they keep their weapons drawn.

Jaxon collapses to his knees. Grasping at the hole in his chest, Jaxon glares up at Seera. He tries to speak, but his eyes glaze over and he falls forward onto the ground. Blood darkens the ground beneath him.

Seera turns to Aya, arms behind her back. "Heal him."

Aya's wide eyes stare at Jaxon's unmoving form. The reaction comes far too slowly. She screams and her hands go to her mouth. "How could you?"

"I said heal him."

Aya is unable to think or move. Her legs shake, but shock and fear arrest her movements.

Sighing angrily, Seera grabs Aya by the hair and throws her

to the ground next to Jaxon. "If you don't hurry, he'll die. I estimate, judging from the blood loss, he has less than ten seconds."

Aya shakes her head furiously at Seera, pleading with her eyes. "But I don't know if I can!"

"He said you were a Life Healer."

"I don't know what that means! I've never heard of Life Healers! Not until after he captured me!"

"You're wasting time, slave. He has less than five seconds, now."

Aya's eyes dart around the dark underbelly of the Arena, stopping on the faces of Aldur and Archer next to him. They watch her with guarded faces, but their eyes are begging her to do something, anything.

Heart pounding in her ears, she grabs Jaxon and rolls him onto his back, blood soaking into her clothes. His face is pale and his eyes half-lidded, staring at nothing.

She tentatively places her hands on his chest, over the wound. She feels his heartbeat slowing, barely keeping him alive. Closing her eyes, she concentrates. She feels warmth gathering in her chest and moving down her arms. Jaxon generates no noticeable warmth, far less than the woman she healed weeks before. She can't be sure her warmth will reach him.

After what seems like far too long, she feels her warmth enter him and reach into the chill in his body. She sees where the blade stabbed through. Jaxon's heart is nearly cut in two. She focuses all of her energy on repairing it.

The ends mend together and the blood that escaped the powerful muscle, filling his chest cavity, disappears. It's absorbed back into the body, aiding in healing. The torn skin and muscles around the heart heal, and she concentrates on finding his fading warmth. She pushes her magic beyond any point she ever has before. She finds Jaxon's warmth and grabs hold. She slowly pulls it forward, and his heartbeat grows stronger.

She must concentrate a little longer, but something strange is happening. Her warmth is escaping too far from her core. A deadly coldness fills her more than she's ever felt. If she doesn't break the connection with Jaxon soon, she'll use too much of her own life and die. She prays her magic holds on a little longer.

Relief fills her as Jaxon takes a deep breath. His breathing and heartbeat return to normal, warmth branching out through his body.

Aya tries to withdraw her magic from him, but the coldness makes her body numb. She can't find the path to bring it back, but a small amount of Jaxon's warmth shoots up her arms. It guides her magic back to her, and the deadly coldness fades.

Opening her eyes, Aya tears herself from Jaxon, falling back onto the ground. Her breath is shaky, and her eyes can't focus. The tips of her fingers are cold as ice.

Jaxon jolts upright, grabbing her hand tightly in his own. His other hand touches his chest where a hole remains in his shirt, the wound completely gone. His eyes focus on Aya and he releases her hand quickly as though touching her burned him.

"Did you...?" he catches himself, stopping the question and glances around. He glares at Seera and bares his teeth, furious. Clamoring to his feet, he grabs the woman and pulls her close. He drags her to a nearby empty animal cage and throws her against the metal bars. "You tried to kill me!"

Seera, unfazed by the sudden violent behavior, leans close to his face with a wide smile. "I did. But *she* saved you. Your rare creature is worth my time and money now." She eyes her two men and jerks her head.

One walks closer and pulls out a large bag of money. He holds it out to Jaxon, silently. The other man follows close behind with another bag. Jaxon's eyes bounce from one bag to the other.

"Since you've not only brought me a Rare Kind, but also more than the usual selection of slaves, I'll include a bonus," Seera says.

Jaxon glares at Seera, not hiding the rush of thoughts crossing his mind. Cursing, he lets go of her and grabs the bags. He crosses to Aldur and whispers angrily in his ear before the two walk away. He stops in front of the four men and meets each one's eyes. Their faces pale. Horror fills their expressions. Jaxon and Aldur leave, followed by the men of the caravan.

Jaxon leaves without a second glance at Aya. She feels a pain in her chest, though she can't explain why. Perhaps it's because he simply left without any word, no acknowledgment.

Seera appears above her and pulls Aya to her feet. "Welcome to Bloodfall Arena, Life Healer. You and the others will make for great sport."

II

THE ARENA

CHAPTER TWENTY

SEERA TAKES THE SLAVES FURTHER INTO THE DEPTHS OF THE ARENA, more darkness under the earth than Aya can fathom. The level below where they entered is filled with cages and large training grounds for animals. Brawny men lunge at a variety of strange beasts on harnessed ropes. Women with bags of food lead other beasts from cage to cage. The animals try to swipe at the passing group, and when one slave ventures too close, a beast's paw collides with her arm. She yelps in surprise, but luckily the claws missed her skin.

The next floor down, armor and weapons line the walls. Heat permeates this level, where the Arena's blacksmiths work their forges. Burning metal wafts through the air and clanging of hammer on steel echoes, loudly. Small, cunning holes fashioned into the ceiling of this level allow for the smoke to waft upward. At the center of this level are large training grounds, where slaves train with wooden weapons, parrying and blocking strikes. Seating surrounds the fenced-off training areas, providing a place for slaves and workers to sit and watch the fights.

A large, divided room built into the wall holds rows of beds. Inside, healers attend to the injured, affixing poultices to arms and legs, cleaning blood from wounds, and using their magic to close cuts and fix broken bones. Aya peers in, wondering how similar their magic is to hers, even as the others start to go down another level. Someone prods her in the back to get moving, and she scurries to catch up.

Down yet another long ramp, Aya is greeted with long hallways. There are a number of doors, and through one a few men sit at long tables, eating platefuls of food. The slaves try to peer through the other doors, but the Arena workers hurry them along.

They're now divided into two groups: men and women. The men go in a door to the left and the women through the one on the right. A few give long glances back at one another, but no harm seems imminent at the moment, so they separate willingly enough into their quarters.

Warm, moist air encompasses them, and Aya feels her lungs tighten at the heat. Other women whine at being forced into a steaming, humid room, but the workers order them to undress. With a little more encouragement—or rather, intimidation—they all strip down.

Aya is happy to remove her bloody clothes, reminders of Seera's cruelty. She throws her clothes into the basket as ordered and stands with the other women. They try to cover themselves with their hands and hair, but it's pointless. They're ushered into the next room and surprised by a large pool of hot spring water large enough for all of the women to be in at once.

Aya carefully dips her foot into the hot water and winces. It's not hot enough to burn her, but nonetheless reminds her of the long journey through the desert. She steps all the way into the water and allows it to fully cover her. She keeps her head above the water, watching the others enter the pool slowly. It's calming and she's glad to clean the muck, sweat, and sticky blood off her skin. She gently runs her hands through her hair, cleaning it, before moving to her face. Her muscles begin to unknot.

The workers order them out after a period of time and force

them to line up. They enter the next room three at a time, still naked. Aya walks in to see three women dressed in the leather of Arena workers each standing in a corner of the room. She moves to the closest one and the woman places her hands on Aya's chest.

A familiar sensation emanates from the woman's hands and Aya realizes she's a healer. It's been so long since she was on the receiving end, but she can tell it's a different magic than her own. A different healing magic than her mother and father.

The woman's eyes widen, and she stares into Aya's eyes. "Your healing magic is...strange."

"How is it strange?" Aya asks, eager to finally be speaking to another healer.

The woman shakes her head. "I shouldn't have said anything. We're not supposed to talk to any of you." She takes her hands off Aya's chest.

Aya grabs the woman's hands. "Please answer me. I haven't met another healer since my parents died."

The woman peers at the other healers finishing with their slaves. She lowers her voice so only Aya hears her. "Your magic feels alive. It sensed my magic and...mixed with it, explored it. Now go. They can't catch us speaking."

"But what do you mean? How is that different than your magic?"

"You have to move on." The woman turns her back on Aya, ending the conversation.

Aya wants to thank her but doesn't want to risk anyone overhearing. The woman hands her new clothes and motions her towards the door. Aya quickly dresses herself and follows the other two slaves out. The light clothing provides little protection and hangs loosely on their thinned bodies, and now marks them as slaves of the Arena. Now she cannot help the somewhat hopeful thought rising up inside her: perhaps she isn't wanted for combat, after all. They may want her to heal the fighters.

Once every slave is clean, given a slate of good health, and dressed in new clothes, they're taken into the room with the tables. Cheese and fruit are placed in front of them and they cautiously eat until they can't eat anymore. Some overeat and vomit, but water soothes their stomachs.

The men Aya saw earlier sit far from the group. They look over the newcomers, the fresh flesh, but make no move to greet them or acknowledge them beyond the stares. Dirt covers their hands and feet, giving Aya the impression they're not slaves, but workers. Why they were eating with the slaves, she couldn't guess. Or is there a hierarchy of slaves? She wonders.

Aya and the other slaves are ushered out of the feeding area and led back up to the training grounds where Seera waits for them. More men stand behind her, wearing the clothes of the Arena workers with light armor on their chests. They wear swords on their hips and masks cover their faces, leaving only their eyes visible.

The slaves stand in disarray, facing Seera. The weakest cower behind, while those refreshed by the food face the workers with defiant looks. Aya stands close to the front, wanting to make sure she doesn't miss a word.

Are we already to fight? So soon?

"You are all now part of Bloodfall Arena. You'll be placed into the games and be expected to entertain those above. The only way out is death. No one leaves the life of the Arena alive," Seera says.

A fearful intake of breath echoes in the room and several begin sobbing. Aya clenches her hands into fists. Games…why not simply call them what they were? Fights for survival.

Seera grabs her whip and cracks it at the noisy slaves. "Quiet! Let me finish before you devolve into whimpering children." She waits until all of them are quiet before tying her whip back onto her belt. "Now then. We will feed you and clean you. If you're popular enough or provide ample entertainment, we'll heal you to fight again. If you aren't popular or don't provide enough entertainment, you'll die from infection, or at the hands of the other slaves. Most of you will die on the floor of the Arena. Though a few of you may choose to become the master of your own fate once the sun sets tonight." She pauses to allow her words to sink in, savoring the fear crossing the faces of the new slaves. "Time to group up. Magic users on the right, non-magic users on the left."

The slaves cautiously move into two separate groups, one noticeably larger than the other. Aya finds it strange the larger group is the non-magic users. Especially since magic users are more valuable...does that mean Jaxon's usual supplies were running low? Low enough that he would venture farther than ever before simply to find one more?

"Come." Seera's voice returns Aya from her thoughts. She leads them through the catacombs. Three men position themselves behind each group, while the others stay at Seera's sides. The large group climbs the ramp to the floor where they entered.

Aya peeks at the men walking behind them. One man, standing behind the group of magic users, holds his hands in front of him, clasped together with his thumbs pointed towards his chest. None of the men behind the group of non-magic users walk with their hands in front of them. At the front, two men each stand on either side of Seera, but only the two in front of the group of magic users hold their hands in a similar position as the man behind.

Her curiosity encourages her to bring her magic out. She reaches within, but something blocks her. Neither man in front acknowledges her attempt. She angles her head to glance back at the man behind, noticing his eyes searching the crowd of slaves, and she knows he's the one stopping her magic.

A security measure to protect the workers?

Seera turns to the groups and holds her hand up to stop them. She glances up at the ceiling. "We're directly under the fighting arena."

A loud thunderous noise shakes the Arena, and the ceiling

trembles. Dust sifts downward. Several of the slaves flinch as though the ceiling were about to collapse.

"Don't worry," Seera says, laughing at the reactions. "The ceiling is sturdy and there are many layers of earth above us. There need to be, or else every earth mage would destroy the floor of the arena. But don't any of you think of trying to collapse the floor. There are a few layers of magic thrown in to keep the lower levels from ever caving in."

The roar of the crowd mixes with the sounds of the Arena workers and the beasts being transported from the lower levels.

"You saw the animals kept below? This is one of the locations from which they may enter the arena." She points to a platform next to them. "Since no animals are being used in the games until the evening, the mechanisms that would raise them up aren't in the loading position. Be aware of these mechanisms while you're moving into position for your fights. The beasts will be chained sometimes, but they can still reach out and kill you with their claws if you aren't careful. There are also entrances above where they may be released, but for the more entertaining games, we like to release them from below your feet."

She leads them to a different entrance from the one they came in and heads up a long ramp. Light grows brighter and the sounds of fighting are heard. The slaves grow anxious and whisper amongst each other.

Seera nods at the men at her sides and they rush ahead of the group. They turn a corner and two large wooden doors appear. The men open the doors and Seera takes the slaves into a long tunnel. At the opposite end is a large gate. Aya sees sunlight through the gate and a shameful excitement spreads through the group.

Are we going to watch the games?

Two shadows flash across the gate. Two men swing large, heavy blades at each other. Several of the slaves cringe back, but the arena workers shove them forward. They're level with the arena floor. This gate is one of the many entrances into the fighting area.

Aya makes her way to the front of the group and peers out into the sunlit arena. Slaves are already in the middle of fighting heavily armored men who are clearly not slaves. Blood has soaked into the sand, turning it muddy crimson.

The crowd cheers as a man in armor beheads a slave with a large double-bladed axe. Aya gasps, reminded of Elder Mircien. She fights back tears.

"Professional fighters," one slave whispers to another. "I heard they train to fight in the Arena and receive payment based on how many slaves they kill. They earn more if they kill a magic user."

Aya turns to the man speaking from the non-magic user group. His eyes are locked onto her. She reads his thoughts in the cruel expression crossing his face. If given the choice, he'd let them kill her. He'd even help, if it meant he could survive.

Seera grabs Aya by the back of the neck and forces her to watch the fights, slamming her body into the gate. "Take it all in, Life Healer," she whispers into Aya's ear. "It's going to be you out there soon enough."

CHAPTER TWENTY-ONE

AYA GRABS THE METAL AND TRIES TO PUSH AWAY, BUT SHE IS UNABLE to fight Seera's strength with her still-exhausted limbs. Dead lie on the ground, occasionally tripping other fighters or being crushed beneath their feet. A man stabs one of the slaves with a spear, but his attention is drawn to the gate Aya is being pressed against. A smile forms on his lips and he faces her.

Seera leans back to face the slaves but keeps Aya trapped against the gate. "Starting tomorrow you, fresh flesh, will be sent out to die. Though if you're lucky—"

The fighter with the spear runs towards the gate, aiming directly for Aya. She fights against Seera, but the woman's strength keeps her in place. As the spear reaches the gate, however, Seera hauls Aya clear. The tip goes through the gate between Seera and Aya. Seera grabs the wood of the spear and pulls, slamming the fighter into the gate as she thrusts her blade into the man's throat. He gurgles and blood pours from his throat and mouth.

She shoves the man away and he falls to the ground, dead. Throwing the spear back through the gate into the arena, Seera wipes the blood from her dagger on the clothes of one of the arena workers.

Aya stares at the dead man's body. The blood pooling around the man's head soaks into the ground. Not even those who voluntarily fight in the Arena are safe from its cruelty. And she will be no exception. She is not here to heal, but to die.

The armored man who beheaded a slave earlier notices the small attack and grabs the spear from the ground with his free hand. He runs the tip of the spear along the metal of the gate and waves his double-bladed weapon threateningly at the fresh flesh, laughing.

The earth shakes and rises, surrounding the man. His eyes widen and he freezes in shock. The earth slams together, crushing the man. The ground returns to flatness, dragging the man's corpse with it.

The magic user responsible appears when the ground recedes. His hair is dark brown. But his eyes are a startling light gray-silver.

He lifts his hand and the earth spits the man's mangled body into the air. It lands with a sickening thud and the crowd's cheers explode at the display of power. The magic user's eyes glare up at the crowd.

Smiling, Seera moves to the side, giving the slaves a better look at the magic user. "As I started to say, if you're lucky you'll survive and bring this Arena something exciting. Use your skills to try and defeat those who wish to kill you."

A man wearing similar armor to the dead man runs up behind the magic user with a sword. He swings it, and Aya moves closer to the gate, her heart blazing in fear for the man. The magic user raises his other hand and slaps both hands together. Water from a nearby trough rushes behind him and traps the man in armor, wrapping around him and forcing his arms to his sides. The magic user raises his clasped hands and the man in armor rises with it.

Aya's never seen magic used this way, with such ease. The only other magic users she's ever met were the other healers, the blockers, and the one bandit Jaxon killed. But this...this is completely different.

The magic user keeps one hand clenched in a fist and uses the other to pull more water from the trough. The water freezes into a spike of ice and he raises it above his head. He throws the man with his clenched fist, the water dropping to the ground once the man is free of it. The man manages to land on his feet, but the spike flies through the air and buries into his chest. Hot heart's blood blunts the icy shard; the man lies still.

The magic user lowers his arms and turns his attention to Seera. He walks towards the gate, his hands clenched into fists at his side. Gathering wind rustles his clothing and blows through the tunnel. He stops walking when he notices the new prisoners, and the wind dies as suddenly as if it had never been.

Seera moves closer to Aya, pulling her from the gate and away from the magic user. But she can't pull Aya's attention from the man. Those vivid, silver eyes pause on Aya longer than the others, a hint of curiosity in them.

"If the crowd likes you, you'll be spared. But only until the inevitable day arrives when you can no longer win. And for you magic users, I want you to play well. The people truly come for you. You're the main event." Seera aims the last part at the man in the arena.

"Why should we?" a slave asks.

Seera shrugs. "Do whatever you like. If you don't want to fight, you don't have to. But that won't stop your competitors from killing you."

A deep bell rings out from one side of the arena and the crowd's cheers increase. Aya strains, but cannot see the bell from where she stands.

"A glorious victory to those still breathing! A fine effort by our slaves! I hope those of you chose well the winners of this battle! If not, don't worry. The next game will begin soon!" a voice blares. It fills the Arena, likely enhanced with magic.

Silver looks up and to the far left at an unseen sight before he glares at the crowd one last time. He walks away from the tunnel and disappears through another entrance, following a small group of wounded and exhausted slaves.

Aya releases a breath she didn't know she was holding. Three elements. That magic user controlled three elements! She'd heard stories of magic users who could move air or water, but never both at the same time.

Chills run over her and her eyes move quickly towards a seating box built into the exact middle of the spectators. The position allows the best view of the fighting, centered perfectly where combatants would meet for combat. Although the box appears to be empty at the moment, bearing a solitary chair, she feels as though someone has been staring at her.

She hears a small gasp and turns to the man blocking her magic. His eyes are wide and face pale. His hands shake from an unseen fear, but he manages to calm himself before his fellow workers notice.

Shaking her head, Aya turns to survey the damage done during the Arena's game. Bodies are strewn about the ground. Some of the victors are still making their way off the arena floor, as workers rush out and collect bodies and body parts. They use rakes to clear as much of the blood as possible for the next event. An announcer speaks, but the magic used to amplify his voice is not as full, making it hard to understand from where the slaves stand.

Not that any of them are listening. They are taking in the carnage they are soon to be a part of.

CHAPTER TWENTY-TWO

SEERA AND HER MEN LEAD THE SLAVES BACK DOWN INTO THE catacombs.

The Arena is slowing down, the final fights of the day finishing above. A worker approaches Seera with a parchment. "We have a small issue with the payments to the fighters."

Seera stops the slaves, waving her men forward. "Wait for me, here. Keep them out of the way and quiet." She follows the worker away.

The men herd the slaves to the wall, clear of the workings of the Arena. Aya leans against the wall, watching the moving parts all around her.

Workers load large animals onto the rising platforms, brutes with thick, shaggy fur and paws the size of a man's head. Long snouts skim the floor, searching for food, long ears drooping on either side.

"Get the collars on these urso, quickly. The fightin's gettin' slow. Seera said we need to add excitement before the audience dies a' boredom," a worker barks.

Others secure chains connected to the platforms around the beasts' necks. One urso chuffs, opening its mouth to show its thick teeth. Its lips droop and drool drips to the floor. The worker scratches the animal behind its long ear, and it moves its head up and down appreciatively.

Then the workers pull levers and the platforms slowly rise. Walkways above the platforms are stationed with more workers waiting to open the floor. They raise their hands, and the earth shifts, allowing the platforms with the beasts to pass through.

After a few seconds, roars erupt from above as the urso reach their destination.

A large wagon passes the slaves loaded with bodies...and body parts. Gasps and groans rise from the slaves, and Aya feels her face growing pale. The wagon passes and enters a cordoned-off area.

Peering inside, Aya watches workers pull the bodies and parts off the wagon. Parts are thrown into large baskets marked *Feed*. Aya realizes they're for the beasts below. Bodies still in one piece are loaded onto long tables and workers dressed in black clean the bodies. They wear masks covering their faces and gloves as they scour the bodies.

Once clean, the workers grab parchment, scratching notes as other workers, dressed in similar black but without masks or gloves, take the bodies away. They wrap them in heavy cloth and load them on more wagons which are taken away.

Seera returns, her lips curled in a sneer. "Let's move." The men return to their positions around the slaves and they head off.

Many slaves break down into loud wails, finally broken by the reality of their new life. Seera's men yell at those sobbing, clouting those who are too loud. If they don't stop, the men beat them until they do or collapse to the floor. They're left behind and any who try to help them are beaten as well.

"If they're not strong enough for the underbelly of the Arena, they're better off left to die than face what waits for them above," Seera says, never once looking back at those who fall. "Of course, if they get in the way of the workers, they'll be dragged to the cells...or the animal cages."

Aya glances back at those left behind. A few manage to climb back to their feet and struggle after the group. Two remain on the ground, the fight gone from their bodies.

They return to the lowest level where they were cleaned and fed. The walls are damp, and rats scamper about, unafraid of humans, stealing food from the feeding area. Two rats fight over a strip of meat, rolling on the ground as a third runs by, grabbing the delectable morsel.

Seera leads them down one of the many hallways where the holding cells await. A large letter A is carved into the stonewall preceding a set of doors. Two men open the doors and the slaves are led in.

"Welcome to cellblock A, slaves," Seera announces.

Cellblock A is a large block with cells lining the walls and wooden stairs leading up to a second level, doubling the number of slaves that can be housed. A second set of doors is located at the opposite end of the cellblock and Aya can see more doors leading to what she can only assume is a neighboring cellblock.

She glances at the cells they pass. Many are filled with three to four slaves, men and women sharing cells. But there are still several cells empty and Aya wonders how long they've been that way. The slaves ogle the fresh flesh in silence. Occasionally, a whistle or rough comment is aimed at the group, but most of those behind the bars show little interest.

Reaching the end of the hallway, Seera turns to the group. "These are your new homes. You will be given free time to venture up to the training level or the baths if you so choose. But only for a limited time, so use your freedom strategically. If you're found out of bounds, you'll be beaten and dragged back to your cells."

A man with parchment and pen appears next to her. A second man stands next to him, holding red strips of cloth.

Motioning to the already filled cells, Seera continues. "Some of you will be sharing cells with others who've survived their fights. Others will be placed in the empty cells of those who did not. Don't get too comfortable and don't worry about claiming a bed. Most of you will die tomorrow. For those who believe you have a fighting chance, rest up. Gather your strength and pray to your gods. They're the only ones who'll show you mercy now."

The man with the parchment distributes the slaves into different cells, beginning with the non-magic users, writing their names as he goes. The second man places the red strips around the waists of the slaves as the man with parchment finishes with them.

Aya recognizes Rava, the woman she healed long ago. She requests to stay with her sister Mava. The man with the parchment waves his hand at her. Not saying yes, but not saying no.

When he moves on to sorting the magic users, he asks for their type of magic as well as their name. Aya listens intently to the different magics. There are many element users, and one who controls shadows. Another can read minds and control emotions. Another can increase the strength of his muscles for a limited time.

Fully realizing the vast span of magic, Aya is awed by those she's been travelling with. She regrets not speaking with them, but there wasn't time for niceties over the hunger, pain, and exhaustion.

She waits patiently for the man with parchment to turn his attention to her. Once all of the fresh flesh, except her, are placed in cells, he merely asks her name and magic type.

"Aya Flandeen." She hesitates before giving the title she has heard so many times in these last weeks. "Life Healer."

The second man wraps the red strip around her waist and the hairs on her arms stand. Magic is in the cloth. She touches the fabric. She tries to pull on it, but it's as though the cloth is permanently attached to her clothes.

Seera walks up behind her, grabbing her arm tightly. "The cloth will come off if you survive tomorrow's game. Think of it as a rite of passage for the fresh flesh."

"Or a target," Aya says.

A smile grows on Seera's face and she nods in agreement. "Or a target." She leads Aya towards a slightly larger cell. "You're being placed with the other Rare Kinds."

Aya wonders what makes Life Healing rarer than controlling shadows or reading minds. There is a vast world of experience and knowledge out there she had never guessed at before, but this is how she must discover it—by being placed in exactly the sort of peril the village had sought to shelter her from.

Seera opens the cell door. Inside are two men, twin brothers. They stare up at Aya in surprise, not expecting a new cellmate. There are three beds, two on the left (which the brothers are lounging on) and one on the right against the back wall.

"Be nice to her, boys. She's fresh flesh for the games tomorrow." Seera shoves Aya inside and stands in the doorway.

Aya immediately recognizes a similar feeling she had when locked in the cages of the caravan. The metal bars of the cells must have been made with the same magic. Aya walks to the back corner of the cell, away from the brothers. She sits on the third bunk and stares at Seera.

Why has she stopped calling me Life Healer? Does she want to keep it from the other slaves? Or is it too humanizing?

Loud voices sound from the end of the hallway. The bars of the holding cells are shaken or banged on with metal. The survivors of the recent game are making their way back to their cells.

Smiling, Seera peers down the hallway. "Sounds like he's on his way back."

"Who?"

"Your third cellmate, fresh flesh." Seera moves away from the door to allow the man room.

The silver-eyed magic user from the arena appears in the doorway to the cell, sneering at Seera before entering. Aya's heart jumps into her throat and she pulls her knees up to her chest. He notices Aya sitting at the back and freezes. Their eyes meet and she wants to look away, but something keeps her vision locked.

"I've already told the brothers, but this message is especially for you. This is your new cellmate. She's a Rare Kind like you, so treat her kindly. She may not be here long." Seera chuckles, closing the door and locking it.

She leaves the four alone, disappearing from view. Silence fills the cell except for the sound of footsteps moving down the hall. Slaves from other cells hiss or make rude comments. Crying erupts down the hall, but it's muffled, seemingly unable to penetrate the dense air.

The silver-eyed magic user tears his gaze from Aya and meets the eyes of the brothers, who shrug their shoulders simultaneously, before he sits at the farthest corner from her, on the floor in front of the brothers' beds. He crosses his arms, leans his head back against the damp wall of the cell, closes his eyes, and releases a long breath.

Aya lowers her view to the ground, unsure of what to do or say. The bunk sinks as the two brothers sit on either side of her. She tries to shrink into herself and lowers her head onto her knees. The following silence is more awkward than before.

Aya fears what these strangers may want from her. *These men have worse plans for you than the Arena.* Aldur's words echo in her head as the presence of the men on either side of her makes her heart pound. She understands the implication.

On occasion, when healing with Iria, they'd come across a woman in a neighboring village with injuries Aya couldn't understand. The pain was physical, yes, but the woman's mind was also deeply wounded. There was a soul pain here. She bothered Iria for an explanation for hours, until he relented and explained. "Some men only view women as useful in one way," he told her. "Whether the woman wants to or not, men with a specific mindset would force themselves on them, leading to these sorts of unusual injuries."

Were these two men with such a mindset?

129

"Who are you?" the one to her right asks, curiosity tinged with excitement like a child discovering a new toy.

She stays silent.

The one on her left leans forward, trying to see her face. "We're not going to hurt you, if that's what you're afraid of." His voice is calm, soothing.

She swallows but raises her head a fraction, so her voice isn't muffled. "Aya Flandeen."

"Where are you from, Aya Flandeen?"

"Foula Valley," she says, turning away from his pale blue eyes.

The one on her right leans forward to see her face as well, with golden eyes. She finds it strange they're twins yet have different eye colors.

He smiles gently. "You're a long way from home, Aya Flandeen."

The one on her right holds out his hand. "My name's Kylii Lakiin."

The one on her left holds out his hand. "My name's Daniil Lakiin."

Aya lifts her head up. If they had ill intentions, would they bother introducing themselves? She hesitates, staring at each brother's hand before placing her hands in theirs. They smile and move to sit in front of her, so she doesn't have to keep turning her head.

"What kind of mage are you?" Daniil asks.

She looks at him confused. "I'm not a mage."

"Of course you are. They wouldn't put you in here with us if you were anything less," Kylii says.

Daniil slaps his brother on the shoulder. "Maybe they aren't called mages in Foula Valley. What did they call you when you arrived?"

"Rare Kind."

"No, no, what did they call your magic?"

"Life Healing."

The brothers whistle, impressed. "Haven't seen one of those before. Heard stories though," Daniil says.

Kylii leans his head to the side. "Unlucky for you, though. Healers are usually the first to die."

"Easy targets."

Kylii faces his brother. "How many healers do we have left after that last big bout?"

"In this block?" Daniil crosses his arm to think. "I think there's three left...maybe four. Didn't we lose...what's his name?"

"Ferjord I think? Yeah, got his head smashed in by a mace."

"That's right. I almost forgot."

"How could you forget? It happened right in front of us."

Aya's heart drops. She doesn't have much experience fighting, but hearing the brothers' talk makes her even more nervous about tomorrow.

Daniil senses her unease. "You'll be fine. We'll take care of you. We Rare Kinds need to stick together."

"Like you took care of Ferjord?" Aya snaps. Her eyes widen and a blush fills her cheeks.

Kylii laughs loudly and nudges his brother. "I like her! Sharp tongue."

Hitting his brother hard in the side, Daniil smiles at Aya. "We'll do our best to help you, but you'll have to learn to protect yourself, too."

Aya nods. "How long have you been fighting here?"

Kylii raises an eyebrow and thinks. "Well, we've been in the Arena since we were ten ages old."

"Ten?" Aya stares at them in shock. "How?" *Seera said people usually die almost immediately. Was she just trying to scare us?*

Daniil shrugs his shoulders. "Our mother died when we were young, our father was missing most of our lives, and Arena slave traders picked us up. We learned how to survive."

"Our magic is unique. Daniil is an ice mage."

"Kylii is a fire mage. We're opposing mages who, unlike

others, *gain* power from the other instead of losing it. When we're apart, we're weak."

"When we're together, we're strong."

"I didn't know that. About opposing mages, I mean." Aya looks from one to the other. "Thank you. For being kind to me."

Kylii snorts. "Did you expect us to attack you?"

Daniil gives his brother a look, before smiling at her, comfortingly. "Like we said, we Rare Kinds have to stick together."

Aya smiles. A wave of relief flows through her, but now she peeks across the cell at the magic user with silver eyes. He's been silent this whole time. She can't make out the expression on his face.

The brothers move back to their beds and soon fall asleep, snoring lightly. Aya stays sitting on the bunk, slowly drifting off to sleep.

CHAPTER TWENTY-THREE

SCREAMING SNATCHES AYA FROM SLEEP'S SWEET RELEASE.

Fresh flesh in other cells are crying out in fear, waking from nightmares of death and violence. They call for the gods to save them or beg for the workers to release them. Some of those who've been in the Arena for years yell at them to be silent, but the cacophony continues.

Aya glances around and spies the silver-eyed magic user still sitting on the floor. He's peering through the bars of the cell, unmoving.

She wonders why he never reclaimed the bed. *Is it pity? A chance for me to have a little comfort before dying in the games in the morning?*

She hears movement from the other side of the cell and sees Daniil and Kylii are awake. Daniil is sitting up, leaning his back on the bars of the cell. Kylii remains lying down, but his eyes are open.

They all listen as the voices down the hall shred the silence. Aya wishes she could do something to calm the terrified slaves, but she doesn't know how, being trapped in a cell herself.

A solemn voice sings from one of the cells across from Aya. The resonance fills the cavern, overpowering the cries. It's an

133

older slave, his hands shaking from old age and his face covered in wrinkles and scars. He sings with his head leaning back on the wall and his eyes closed.

The words are in a foreign tongue, but even the harsh consonants don't change the soothing power of the melody. The old slave fills his voice with emotion to emphasize the message he's trying to send. Slowly, the sobs and voices calm.

As she listens, a memory rises in her mind. A time when she'd been very sick, and her parents feared the worst. Even Iria could do nothing to ease her pain. She remembers her mother singing a song similar to the one she hears now. The words are different, but the melody is the same.

A slave in the same cell with the singer joins in, no emotion on his face. They sing in duet for a while, their voices blending seamlessly. A third voice from farther down the hall joins in, followed by a fourth from the opposite end. The three new voices sing softly, allowing the older slave's voice to lead them. But all four voices echo throughout the cellblock, bringing a sense of calm.

Aya rises from the bed and moves to the bars. One of the slaves singing sits in the cell across from her. A new voice joins in with the song and her eyes move to the next cell. A man kneels against his bed and prays as he sings, tears rolling down his cheeks. Sitting behind the man is Rava, stroking her sister's hair, dried tears on her cheeks. Mava's head is on her sister's lap and she stares out into the darkness of the cellblock. They mouth the words at first, then find their voices and join in the song.

"What language is that?"

Daniil walks to Aya's left side and leans close to her ear. "They're singing for the gods to watch over them as they fight. It's a rare gift the survivors give to the fresh flesh. A chance for hope and calm before they die." His expression is grim as he stares at the elder slave. "Guvie is the oldest slave to survive the games. He's been fighting since the Blood King took the city and bastardized this Arena. He started singing for the fresh flesh many years ago. He sees it as a way to honor those who die in this place."

"He's survived this long?"

"Don't let that old bastard fool you with those shaking hands. He's brilliant with a sword and stubborn as any man I've ever met. He'd probably be able to fight death himself if he had to."

"They all know that language?" Aya asks, gesturing at the others.

Daniil shakes his head. "You'd have to ask those singing along or Guvie himself. Kylii and I aren't from these lands."

Aya presses her face to the bars enough to see the silver-eyed magic user's face. It's empty of emotion, but his eyes prove he's listening to each word of the song as much as the fresh flesh.

"Do you know what they're saying?" she calls to him.

He turns his head away. His brow furrows.

Kylii walks to Aya's right side and leans close to her ear, keeping his voice low. "You saw him fight today, didn't you?"

She nods, facing Kylii. "Who is he?"

"Yme Gurek. He's an Elemental Mage. He controls all of the elements of the world. Water, air, and earth."

"And fire?"

"He lost that magic when he was brought here," Daniil says. "The Blood King had it taken away from him."

"Part of his magic was taken away? How?"

Daniil shrugs, eyeing Yme. "Probably one of the King's few loyal mages. It was too dangerous to let him continue using it."

"Even with the bars blocking magic?" she asks.

The brothers make impressed noises.

"You sense it, too? The fear is always that a Rare Kind may be immune to the blocking magic in the metal. I don't think they took the fear seriously until he was brought here." Daniil taps the bars. "His full magic must've been amazing, to scare these workers. They increased the magic in our bars as a precaution."

"If they were so afraid of him, why didn't they just kill him?"

"They tried! But he survives everything they throw at him. Yme is the champion of the Arena, a real crowd-pleaser even without his fire. Everyone comes hoping to see him fight." Kylii walks back to his bed and lies down.

"The Blood King only comes to see him...and fresh flesh. You'll probably see him tomorrow. He likes to watch the newcomers die," Daniil says, walking to his bed.

"Why?" Aya asks, facing the brothers. Their empty stares urge her to go on. "Why does the Blood King want us dead? What's the purpose of this Arena?"

"Power, mostly," Daniil answers.

"But also fear. He likes to keep people afraid of him. Makes them easier to control," Kylii adds, yawning. "Don't worry. We'll keep you alive until you've grown used to this place."

Aya wants to talk with them more, but the brothers fall asleep as soon as their heads hit the pillows. She moves back to the third bed and lies down. She listens to the singing, letting the calm words soothe her back to sleep.

Yme stands and makes his way to the back of the cell, away from the light of the torches. He sits in the darkness, crossing his arms and legs. He struggles to conceal it, but she catches the tears rolling down his cheeks, even in the shadows of the cell.

CHAPTER TWENTY-FOUR

I STAND IN A DESERT.

The sky is black, and the wind is cold. I can't see anything in the great expanse of nothing but sand.

The ground around me trembles, slowly moving up and down. The earth rolls like waves creating vast hills. It stops, leaving me standing on top of one of the newly created hills.

The ground beneath me trembles again. A large mound rises from the earth directly in front of me. Light creeps through cracks in the mound and an orb emerges. It shoots up into the sky as the earth where it escaped heals. The orb flies higher and higher into the sky, becoming a star.

The quaking intensifies, throwing me to the ground, and more mounds rise around me. Orbs of light explode from the mounds and join the first in the sky. Some rise quickly, shooting into the sky while others rise gradually like smoke.

One orb rises from the ground before my feet. It rises to my eye level and stops. Images move inside of it. I stare deep within it and see an unknown city burning. Flames tear through the homes of dozens. Figures run through the flames, grabbing any who flee and leading them to safety. Others line up, their arms moving in tandem, magic throwing water onto the fires.

I reach out to touch the soon-to-be star, but it shoots up into the sky, joining the others rising all around me.

Inside of another star, men on a large ship sail through a terrible storm, working ferociously to keep the ship afloat. The captain of the ship stands at the front, stoically staring ahead. Next to her, a younger man laughs into the face of the storm, waving his hat over his head in excitement. A small smile forms on the captain's lips at the young man's enthusiasm. Then this star rises, and is gone.

A man's battle-worn face floats inside another, and I see he is fighting against a number of soldiers in dark red armor. Their faces are full of jeers and mockery. The man's anger is palpable, seeping from the star like a perfume.

Still another shows a woman, her skin wet with sweat, working a great forge inside the belly of an old and powerful volcano. She works the fires with a tenderness that shows respect for the power in her hands. She waves a young boy forward to help her. His eyes widen with awe at her strength. She places him in front of her and helps him hammer the metal.

Floating, the remaining stars rise from the earth. Each star is one of a million different lives at different points in time and place. They rise to the sky, filling the darkness with hope and pain, life and death. The land below is cast in a beautiful array of colors and light.

A sudden great earthquake knocks me to the ground. I manage to land on my knees and steady myself as the earth rumbles beneath me.

Hills in the distance grow into mountains, penning me in. A second earthquake splits the mountains in two and a large, dark shadow emerges from beneath the earth to stand high above the land and me.

I know this shadow. I've seen it many times in my dreams, in my nightmares. The shadow's eyes are so black they stand out against the dark of its body.

The shadow gazes up at the stars in the sky and moves

slowly towards me, but I can't tell if it's aware of me yet. A star rises in front of the shadow's eyes. The sound of laughter echoes from the orb of light. Reaching out, the shadow grabs it and pulls it close. Curious, the shadow leans its head from side to side.

Then it crushes the star in its immense hand, the sound of laughter changing to screams of pain before quieting. Opening its hand, the star falls to the earth as dust. The shadow watches it fall, then reaches out for another.

My heart drops in my chest. I felt it. I felt the lives of those inside the star disappear. So easily the life was taken, with no warning and no effort.

The shadow reaches out for more stars, crushing any unfortunate enough to rise within its reach. Its black eyes are attracted to the first star that emerged from the earth. Even after it reaches the sky, it continues to grow. What's inside is obscured from the ground.

Growing tired of trying to reach the large star, the shadow's gaze lowers to the earth below its feet…to me.

It walks towards me, each footstep shaking the land, staining the earth black.

Reaching for me, the shadow bends down to the ground. I try to run, my mind filling with images of those immense hands crushing stars. I know if I am caught, I'll be crushed into dust.

The shadow's heavy footsteps crack the earth and a familiar sound enters my ears: the sound of chains. Rising from the cracks, chains move with the shadow like serpents, slithering towards me. A chasm opens in front of me, trapping me. I turn to the shadow, its hand and the chains moving closer and closer.

An explosion of light fills the night sky as the first star falls from the sky. The shadow tries to turn as a giant fist of light smashes into its head. The shadow is thrown to the ground with such force that a great wind slams into me, knocking the breath from my lungs and throwing me into the chasm. I scream and claw the air, trying to grab onto anything, but I'm falling in a black pit of nothingness.

A warm hand catches me and lifts me gently back to the surface again. I gaze up at my savior.

The figure of light leans down to my eye level. I see the life of the star in its brilliant eyes made of white flames. This is the other figure from my dreams. The reason nothing could be seen in the first star was because it wasn't a life. It was a being of immense power.

While the being of light assures itself of my safety, the shadow attacks from behind, catching it off guard. The two titans crash into the ground. Hills are flattened beneath them. I try to gain distance, but the shaking earth keeps me off my feet.

The shadow overpowers the being of light and lifts it high above its own head. Its black eyes spot me, and it throws the being of light towards me. I know I can't escape as the glowing giant lands on top of me, the pressure crushing out my breath.

CHAPTER TWENTY-FIVE

AYA SITS UP GASPING.

I can't see! Why can't I see?

Her heart threatens to burst from her chest, her lungs tightening and her gasps turning to wheezes. She reaches in front of her, feeling nothing but air. Turning sharply, her hands hit stone and she traces the cool rock with her fingers. Her mind races, she strains to remember where she is.

The darkness is disorienting, but her sight adjusts slowly. Light from torches casts shadows on the walls, and everything rushes back to her. She's in her cell beneath Bloodfall Arena. She wasn't crushed, it was a nightmare. Wiping the sweat from her forehead, she sighs. It's the first time the two large shadows from her nightmare have been separate from the others.

What did these dreams mean? Since she'd been a small child, she dreamed about the shadows. Iria and Mircien always told her they were simply nightmares. But she can't help feeling they were more.

Daniil and Kylii's snoring echoes loudly. She stares at them, a small smile forming on her lips. Sometime during the night, they moved to the same bed, like young children sleeping close together to share warmth. She laughs softly to herself, feeling her first true sense of calm since arriving at the Arena.

Yme stands at the bars, his eyes attentive as they survey the cell block.

Standing up, she takes a few hesitant steps towards him. Wondering if he slept at all during the night, she takes a deep breath. "Thank—"

"It's time," he says, startling her.

Bells ring loudly, cutting short the silence of the holding cells. Daniil and Kylii wake and quickly jump to their feet when they realize they were sleeping in the same bed.

Arena workers file down the hall, open all the cells containing *fresh flesh*, and order the slaves out. Aya recognizes the one opening their door as the worker who blocked her magic the day before. Once the door is open, he clasps his hands together with his thumbs aimed at his chest.

Yme is the first out of the cell. Aya stares after him, realizing it's the first time she's heard him speak. Has he been avoiding her? Why?

Frustration fills her but she follows after him. Daniil and Kylii chase after.

The workers herd the slaves down the hall where Seera waits for them with her hands on her hips. Her hair is pulled back tight against her head and her whip is tied to her belt. She scrutinizes each prisoner as they approach.

"Time to wake up and face the Arena. Our first event is for the fresh flesh, a welcoming to our family. I hope you all made peace with your gods. Today, many of you are going to meet them. But don't worry, you won't be alone. This fight is open to volunteers, and some of our regulars will be joining you." Her eyes lock onto Yme and the brothers in a warning. "But don't expect them to save you. Once you enter the Arena, you're on your own."

Aya feels her body shake with nerves. A hand presses gently into her back and she glances up, expecting to see Daniil or Kylii.

She's surprised to see it's Yme's hand on her back. He keeps his attention forward to avoid Seera's notice.

"Let's get you ready. We provide you weapons and armor. Everything else is up to you. No rules. Move!" Seera unties the whip on her belt and cracks it.

The workers usher the slaves down the hall and up the stairs to the training ground and armory. The heat from the working blacksmiths' ovens rolls over Aya, sweat beading on her forehead. She eyes the forges and the caged-off holes above them that pull the smoke out.

Yme walks ahead of the group, distancing himself from the others. The workers let him wander on his own, which appears to be a common occurrence.

Weapons and armor lean along the walls of a room with long benches. The slaves rush to gather supplies for the Arena, and small shoving matches break out.

Yme disappears among the excitement and Aya is left with Kylii and Daniil. "Don't worry about what Seera said," Daniil says, leaning close to her. "She likes scaring as many as she can. Thinks it helps encourage a better performance."

"What, by scaring them to death?"

"Most of the 'regulars' would rather help the new slaves. The more of us there are, the better our chances to survive longer in the Arena."

Kylii nods. "Though there a few who would rather use the fresh flesh as shields or distractions. Stay close to us. We'll protect you."

"Why?" she asks.

"We told you. Rare Kinds have to stick together. There aren't many of us, because we're usually the main targets. The people come to see magic users fight, but also to see us die," Daniil says, bringing Aya to a wall with armor hanging on hooks.

She stops, forcing the brothers to halt. "But why don't you help the others?"

Both brothers' expressions dissolve into confusion, not

understanding. "We can't help everyone. They have to learn on their own what they're in for," Kylii says. "There're more of them than us."

"But you want to help me?"

"You're one of us," Daniil says.

"But we're all slaves here."

"Some are more valuable than others."

She shakes her head and spies Rava and Mava preparing. Each grab light armor and weapons, their expressions grim, but accepting of what they're about to do.

"You said the more slaves the better chance of survival," she speaks softly, her voice trembling with emotion.

The kindness they're showing me...is it only because I'm valuable to them? Are they no different than the slave traders?

"No one helped us when we got here, specifically because we are Rare Kinds. They saw us as distractions they could use during the games to help themselves. Those we rarely chose to help...most are no longer alive." Kylii fights to keep his emotions calm, but his eyes glow with anger. "This isn't a community or place for camaraderie. This is a place where the strong survive and the weak die."

Daniil places a hand on his brother's shoulder. "But we still try to help a few Rare Kinds. Otherwise, they will have taken everything from us, even our humanity. The core of who we are."

Aya remembers the long journey to the Arena. The lives lost...the few she saved. The spirits slowly being broken. She remembers being separated from the others once Jaxon saw her magic. The expressions on his men's faces, realizing she was worth more than the others. She remembers living in Oula Village, but never truly feeling part of it once her power appeared. The way the villagers treated her like something else, something other than human. How Iria and Mircien were the only ones who made her feel part of their lives, taking on the role of her family once her parents died.

"The weak can survive and the strong can die," Aya states. "Without freedom, we're all the same. But given the choice, I'd help as many as I could."

She doesn't wait to hear what the brothers have to say, and walks to the wall, staring at the selections of armor and weaponry. She's never worn armor. This is the first time she's even seen most of the weapons lining the walls. But going out with nothing would be a death wish.

The brothers grab a breastplate, arm guards, and two daggers each from the wall. They stand on either side of her and hold the items out to her. She looks from one to the other, trying to gauge their thoughts. Are they angry with her? Or is it still their desire to help her?

"Just take it," Kylii says, placing the breastplate in her hands, ending her mental debate. He moves further down the wall, searching for his own armor choice.

Daniil watches his brother knowingly before returning his attention to Aya. "We've been here a long time and seen different tides of slaves come and go. We've even heard the very words you spoke...a few times. Kylii is tired of having feelings for others, only to be unable to save them."

Aya attempts to get the breastplate on, struggling with the ties in the back. Daniil helps and she reaches for the arm guards. "I can't pretend to find it fair you're willing to help me and not the others."

He grabs her wrist as she takes the arm guards. "There is no *fair* in the Arena. Remember that when you think about throwing your life away to save someone. Especially when you've only staved off death until the next game." He releases her wrist, places the daggers on the bench in front of her, and follows after his brother.

She picks up the blades. His words cut her deep.

CHAPTER TWENTY-SIX

AYA ATTACHES THE ARM GUARDS BEFORE CAREFULLY PLACING THE daggers in her belt. She thinks back on the dagger her parents left her and a rush of anger fills her, knowing Jaxon has probably sold it somewhere in this cruel city. She imagines him laughing, eating and drinking and buying women with the profit.

To calm herself, she rolls her shoulders and moves her arms around, judging how much her movements are constricted. The armor is lighter than other pieces on the wall, but wearing it feels stiff and unfamiliar.

Daniil and Kylii put light armor on their shoulders, arms, and legs. The only weapons they grab are throwing knives. Murmurs fill the crowded hall. Kylii glares at his brother. Daniil's hands make large gestures and he shoves Kylii. Kylii rolls his eyes before nodding and waving his brother ahead of him.

They walk over and sit on either side of her. Kylii avoids her, but judging by the subdued glow in his eyes, he's calmer.

"Aren't you going to put on more than that?" she asks, gesturing at their minimal armor.

"Too much armor only slows the body down," Daniil says.

Kylii motions to the other slaves with his head. "First mistake newcomers make is to load up on armor and weapons. The

Arena isn't just about strength but outsmarting your opponents."

"They'll be the first targets, because they won't be able to escape. And armor can only protect against so much."

Yme sits on the end of the opposite bench alone. He hasn't grabbed any armor or weapons, and sits with his arms crossed, waiting.

"What about him? Isn't he going to put anything on?" she asks.

Kylii laughs and shakes his head. "Not Yme. There hasn't been a fighter yet to even come close to killing him."

"Believe me. His magic is the only protection he needs," Daniil adds.

Seera cracks her whip to grab everyone's attention. "Time to head for the arena. Listen. The people are already chanting for you."

Aya focuses, sorting out the buzz and noise and shrieks until she realizes what the audience is calling out.

Fresh flesh. Fresh flesh.

Her stomach tightens as the slaves line up in rows and follow Seera through the bowels of the arena. They enter a long, rising tunnel. Cheers echo as they turn a corner to where a large gate blocks the entrance into the arena.

Seera faces them. "You'll enter as a group. Those you'll be fighting will be on the other side. Before the fighting begins, both groups will face the Blood King's private box. Once he's entered and given the signal, combat will begin, and continue until the bell rings. There is no goal other than to survive. I find it helpful to think of this as your chance to show the audience your strengths."

I find it helpful... everyone else is entirely focused on the view of arena sand through the bars, but Aya catches this little slip. Was Seera once a slave here, too? Has she survived to rise through the ranks? Is that possible? How much of this squalid life is she familiar with?

147

Her thoughts slough away when drums beat loudly. The gate rises. Anxiety rumbles through the slaves, quick breaths and nervous whining giving away their unease. When the gate cranks to a stop, the Arena workers yell at the slaves to move. A few screech in surprise and fear.

The worker blocking their magic releases his hands and steps back. The reconnection to her magic fills Aya with relief. She sees Daniil and Kylii open and close their hands with excitement.

Seera relishes them with an eager smile on her face as the group leaves the tunnel. Her eyes almost glow as Aya passes her. "Good luck, Life Healer." She pats Aya on the back, hard.

Aya winces at the sting and, as they emerge from the tunnel, at the bright sun. Once her eyes adjust, she peers upward. Her mouth gapes open at the size of the Arena. Now, out in the open, she's in awe at the difference standing on the arena floor makes.

The towering walls reach into the sky, making her feel like an insect compared to those sitting above. A large bell and drums stand on a platform built beneath the highest level of the Arena. Thousands of people fill the seats of the Arena, cheering for the fresh flesh—and fresh blood.

The slaves forget their formation and mob together. Daniil and Kylii stand close to Aya. Yme appears at her side seemingly from nowhere. He meets the brothers' eyes and they move closer, forming a defensive wall of bodies behind her.

Across the arena floor, the second group enters: large men covered in spiked armor, carrying large weapons. Unlike the men who fought the day before, their armor matches in aesthetic only. And, from what Aya can make out at this distance, their weapons appear forged by multiple hands.

"Who're they? More Arena slaves?" she asks.

"These men volunteer to fight. Unlike professional fighters, who train their entire lives to fight in arenas around the world, volunteer fighters receive no payment," Kylii says.

Daniil nods. "But it's considered a great honor to fight in

148

Bloodfall Arena. It's a chance to fight before the Blood King and receive favor."

"Most of the time it's just a way to be killed," Kylii adds out of the side of his mouth.

The drums stop and the crowd becomes quiet. The silence is deafening. Everyone turns to the empty seating box Aya noticed the day before. The single, now cushioned, chair stands in the box in front of closed red curtains. On the curtains is a single symbol.

Aya's breath catches in her throat and her hands shake uncontrollably. Images from her nightmares flash through her mind. She's seen that symbol above the head of one of the shadows, wrapped in chains and dripping with blood.

A lone drum bangs once and Aya shrieks. The slaves turn to her. She throws her hands over her mouth. She feels Yme's confused eyes and Daniil and Kylii lean close, asking if she's all right. She keeps her mouth covered and shakes her head, refusing to answer. The drum sounds again.

Men in heavy, blood-red armor appear through the curtain and fill the sides of the box. One of them, with a black sash around his waist, moves through the curtain carrying his helmet under his arm. He stands behind and to the right of the chair. He signals to two others who grab the curtains and hold them open.

Aya raises her eyes as the Blood King enters. His hair is the color of coal and curls against his ears. He moves to the front of the box and raises his hand. The crowd erupts in cheers.

The blood drains from Aya's face and the shaking in her hands moves to her entire body, every inch of her embraced in terror.

This man is going to kill me. He's going to kill me if he sees me. Aya's thoughts gallop through her mind.

She sees the gates are still open as workers from the Arena check spikes and extra weapons around the wall.

She moves to run for the opening, but a hand grabs her before she can get too far. Terror shoots through her and her legs nearly give out. Strong arms pull her close to a chest and she peers up into Yme's angry face.

"Don't draw his attention. Rare Kinds are his favorite to kill. If he finds out you can heal those close to death, he'll set his sights on you."

Tears fill her eyes and she barely holds back her terrified sobs, but she slowly turns towards the Blood King.

She remembers feeling eyes on her after the fight the day before. Now she knows those eyes belonged to the Blood King.

The Blood King's smile changes to a vulpine grin.

"Too late." Yme tightens his hold on her. "He knows."

CHAPTER TWENTY-SEVEN

"WELCOME TO BLOODFALL ARENA!"

A voice fills the vast space. Above the Blood King's box, in another section blocked off from the rest of the seating area, a man stands with others sitting behind him. He waves his hands as he speaks, his voice amplified with magic.

"I am the Voice of the Arena, Dolus Otho! We have many fresh faces among our fighters today. It will be an exciting first game of the day, we can be sure. I'm excited to see which of our new competitors will be victorious and which will see their gods today. Welcome to the Arena our volunteer fighters, the Bloody Butchers!"

The audience's excited frenzy reminds Aya of a raging thunderstorm. The volume fluctuates and occasionally she hears specific words. The men in spiked armor raise their weapons above their heads and show off to the crowd. The workers finish their preparations and close the gates around the arena floor. The screeching of metal bars signals no more escape.

They must fight or die.

"Let's hope they fare better than the Screaming Skewers from yesterday, eh?" the one who called himself The Voice says with a laugh, the audience laughing and cheering in response. He eyes the King's box. The Blood King waves his hand, encouraging him to move on, and his laughter becomes nervous. "Enough talk. Let the fighting begin!"

The bell rings from above and the volunteer fighters, the Bloody Butchers, slam their weapons on their armor and shields, roaring with excitement. The slaves immediately split into two notable groups, the fighters and the cowards.

The cowards run back to the closed gate where they entered, pleading to be allowed back in. Arena workers push them back or poke weapons through the gate. Some slaves are wounded, and one frantic slave is impaled by a spear, then shaken off like a dead rat.

The audience seated above the gate call down to the frightened slaves, a few throwing anything they can get their hands on onto the sand. The slaves, realizing they have no choice but to fight, grab weapons from the walls and turn to fight.

The more experienced slaves face the opposing group and raise their weapons or slam their weapons on the ground to entice the combatants. The most eager to fight run at each other, and skirmishes flare up. Metal hitting metal, metal hitting flesh, yells and shrieks fill the air. The metallic smell of blood mixes with sweat and body odor. Magic users band together to create protective barriers against the Butchers or to defend the weaker slaves.

The chaos exploding all around her makes Aya's heart pound. Many of those dying are ones she spent so long travelling within the caravan. But she can't do anything; her feet refuse to move beneath her.

Yme hands Aya to the twins. "Watch her. Don't let anyone get close." He leans down to her and places his hands on her shoulders. "Stay with them. They'll protect you."

She furrows her brow. *Why is he suddenly interested in my well-being? What changed from last night to this morning?*

"Yme, we can't do it alone." Daniil motions to the fighting erupting all around them.

"I'll take care of them. Keep her safe. Don't use any of your magic unless you have to," he says the last to Aya, turning away.

She grabs his arm. "Wait. What's going on? You wouldn't even talk to me before now. How did you know I could heal those close to death?"

"You said they called you a Life Healer. Life Healers are the rarest Healers. That doubles the targets on your back."

Annoyance fills her quickly. "Just because I'm a healer doesn't mean I'm weak. I can fight."

"Not against *him*."

"Why do you care?"

"There's no time to talk now. Stay safe. Don't fight." Yme runs towards the flailing arms and legs, grabbing up and throwing chunks of rock at the Butchers. Great, stirred winds keep those attacking far from him.

"Come on, we need to move farther from the center." Kylii pulls Aya away.

A beefy combatant with a heavy axe appears in front of Kylii, swinging his weapon down. Daniil throws his hand at the man. A rush of cold air surrounds the fighter, freezing him. Kylii smashes the man in two with a quick kick, and the three make their way from the center of the arena. Daniil and Kylii stay to either side of Aya.

"Don't think too much about Yme's reasons for anything he does. We Rare Kinds have to stick together, that's all there is to it," Daniil says.

She glares at him, pulling herself free from Kylii's grip. "Stop saying that! You sound like you don't care about any of the others. Why do you think you can trust me?"

Another volunteer fighter runs at them, swinging his sword. Kylii turns to the man and throws a dagger covered in flames into the man's throat. His body ignites immediately. As fast as he can howl and beat at the flames, he falls to the ground, dead.

"You're a slave like us. That means you were taken from your home forcibly and someone you love was probably hurt or killed in the process. Now all you want is to go home. We're the same," Kylii says, his eyes darkening with bad memories.

"But so are they," she argues, motioning towards those around them. The fighting slaves scream as the larger volunteers overpower them. "Why don't you trust them?"

"Why do *you*?" Daniil demands.

She doesn't answer. She catches sight of Rava and Mava. They both have their weapons at the ready and fight any who approach with surprising skill. Cuts and bruises discolor their arms and legs. Aya sees the fire in their eyes—the fire of hope.

She searches the chaos for Yme. But he's lost amongst all the fighting.

A scream behind Aya makes her spin in time to see a slave stabbed in the stomach with a spear. The man holding it laughs and digs the spear deeper as the slave begs for mercy. She recognizes the slightly overweight man from the caravan cage, his nose disfigured from the quick-heal of the Arena healers after having it broken by touchy locals.

Aya turns to Daniil and Kylii. "We have to help him."

The brothers stare at her, confused. She points to the man and Kylii shakes his head. "He's a goner. We can't help all the fresh flesh."

"You either fight or you die," Daniil adds.

"This coming from men who're telling me not to fight?"

Both throw knives at attacking men who drop to the ground dead. "To be fair, only Yme told you not to fight."

"We only told you to stay close to us," Kylii adds.

Two other men manage to maneuver behind Daniil and Kylii. The brothers try to throw more knives, but the men dodge and knock the brothers away from Aya.

Ignoring her for what they assume are the larger threats, the men batter the brothers with constant attacks. Daniil and Kylii are stuck on the defensive, unable to find openings to attack. Or keep track of Aya.

She grabs a discarded spiked club from the ground. Trusting

the two can handle the men on their own, she runs towards the fighter with the spear and the screaming slave. She slams the club into the fighter's back as hard as she can, getting the weapon stuck. The volunteer drops to the ground away from the wounded slave.

Aya pulls the spear from the slave's stomach and kneels down to him. "What's your name?"

He cries and pleads, grabbing her arms. "You're the powerful healer! Please! Help me! Don't let me die!"

She nods. "I'm going to help you. Stay still." She places her hands on his stomach and closes her eyes. Hands grab her and haul her to her feet.

"What are you doing?" Daniil yells. "Yme said no magic. Besides, his wounds are too severe, and you don't have time."

The man whimpers pathetically on the ground, tears streaming from his eyes as blood spurts from his belly.

Aya rips her arm from his grasp. "I'm not leaving him. The Blood King already knows I'm a healer. If I don't have enough time, *make* time!" She kneels over the wounded slave again and places her hands on his stomach. She closes her eyes and concentrates.

Kylii walks up to them, carrying two swords. Daniil shrugs. "She did say she wasn't weak."

Each brother takes one of the swords and they brace for combat.

CHAPTER TWENTY-EIGHT

AYA FEELS THE WOUNDED SLAVE SLIPPING AWAY, HIS WHIMPERS OF pain quieting. She stretches her magic far to bring him back. She sees the muscle, fat, and skin reform, willing it into reality. She furrows her brow, sensing something new.

She feels how the blood flows through the slave's body and senses each muscle moving. Small shocks explode thousands upon thousands of times as nerves come to life. The current of information overwhelms her.

Finishing the healing, she tears her arms away and falls on her backside, gasping for air.

The large slave sits up and touches his stomach. His clothes are still torn and bloody, but his skin is clean, and no wound remains. His wide eyes peer up at her and he cries, "Thank you. Thank you!" before he stands.

"Daniil," she gasps.

Daniil jumps at his name and turns to see a combatant sneaking into Kylii's blind spot. He thrusts his hand out, and ice forms on the man's legs. With the warrior hobbled, he draws a throwing knife and hurls it. Kylii turns in time to see the man behind him drop.

Aya grabs the handle of the spiked club and pulls it from the back of the man she killed. She grabs the arm of the man she healed and twists it, forcing him take the spiked weapon into his hand.

He stares at the club and shakes his head furiously. "I can't! I've never killed anyone!"

She grabs him and pulls him close, sweat rolling down her forehead. "Neither have I. But if you don't, you're going to die. I won't heal you again if you don't at least try to fight back. We have to look out for each other, or none of us will survive in here."

A hand grabs Aya's collar and pulls her back. She falls onto her back and stares up in terror at the man she thought she'd killed. He aims a sword at her throat. She screams. The spiked club smashes into the side of the man's face. He falls to the ground dead, revealing the large slave.

His face is pale, and his eyes nearly bulge from his head with shock. He swallows and nods, making a decision. "My name is Bern. I will fight for you. I will fight to protect you."

"No." She points at his chest. "You have to fight for yourself. And for others who need protection."

After hesitating, he moves next to Daniil and Kylii, attacking combatants who come too close. Another slave trips, running from the two men chasing her. Bern runs up behind them and swings the spiked club, knocking one man away and killing the other with one of the spikes buried in his head. Before the other man can recover, Bern swings the club down onto him.

"Thank you," the woman wheezes.

Helping her to her feet, Bern's cheek flush scarlet. "Men shouldn't attack women like that."

"Well, this woman—Eka by the way—appreciates the help. I dropped my weapon once the fighting started."

"If we gave you a weapon, can you fight?" Aya asks, rising to her feet. Her legs are still shaky, and her vision blurred.

Eka nods her head. The brothers each hand her a throwing knife, and she and Bern face oncoming fighters.

Aya squeezes the bridge of her nose with her fingers. She still feels everything that was happening inside of Bern's body in addition to her own body's workings. The world spins and she falls forward into the sand.

Kylii grabs her, helping her stand. "Whoa there! This isn't the place to pass out."

"I'm fine," she mumbles, shaking her head to clear her vision.

Daniil freezes a group of three. Bern and Eka move behind them to protect them as they move away from the combat. They set her down against the wall of the arena.

"Sit there and rest up. The fighting doesn't look like it's going to end soon," Daniil says, cleaning the blood from throwing knives he recollected from those who died at their hands.

Nodding her head, Aya gazes across the arena. Bodies lie on the ground, those still fighting stumbling as they step on the soft masses.

No time to mourn. She holds her head in her hands, forcing herself to recover, to concentrate.

FOUR COMBATANTS SURROUND YME. They attack him from all sides, and Yme uses his air magic to keep them back, but they've clearly fought magic users before. They maneuver closer to him without a single hit.

He's forced to use his earth magic. He stomps, and the ground crumbles beneath their feet. All but one manages to move to solid ground; the fourth disappears into the earth. Yme then creates hard rock spears from the ground to attack from beneath, but the men avoid them.

He searches the walls of the arena for troughs of water, but none are placed in reach of this fight. He groans, then spies spectators sitting along the wall with glasses of water. He takes a deep breath and pulls the water from the stands to him. The crowd cheers at his maneuver and all focus goes to him.

He uses some of the water to moisten the earth and agitates it using his magic, making a pool of deep, wet sand. He shoots another spear out of the earth at one of the combatants, throws him into the deep mud, then hardens the earth, making it impossible for the man to escape. The two others move away to avoid the same trap.

Yme takes the remaining water and throws it at one of the men, who dodges and laughs. Yme pulls the water back, twirls it and ices it, honing it to a sharp point. It stabs through the man's back and explodes through his chest. He falls to the ground dead.

The third man grabs Yme from behind and tries to crush him with brute strength, keeping his arms pinned to his sides. Yme releases a blast of air magic, sending both flying into the air. They land with Yme on top, but the man tightens his grip. Yme kicks hard at the ground, and the earth crumbles. The man rolls away as soon as he feels the earth loosening, throwing Yme off of him.

They stand and face each other, other fighters milling around. The man pulls a hidden blade out of his arm cuff. Yme rolls his eyes and throws his hands up into the air. Pillars of earth surround the man and crush him. Those fighting nearby stumble at the sudden lurch of the earth.

The man still trapped in the muddy quicksand trap pleads for mercy. Yme turns to him, walks over and raises a boulder over his head. When he drops it on the embedded man, the crowd explodes with excitement. They thrust their arms up in rhythm and chant:

Yme! Yme! Yme!

Yme faces the central box and throws the bloody boulder at the Blood King. He only smiles and crosses his legs. One of his guards moves in front of him, pulling a long chain from his belt. He throws it at the boulder, and the chain comes to life. Magic fills the metal and it wraps around the boulder. The guard changes its course to hit a group of slaves huddled against the wall of the arena.

The slaves scream, but Yme stops boulder in midair and redirects it to the ground, harmless. Two combatants attack the group while they're distracted, easily killing the entire group quickly.

Yme yells furiously and punches the closest combatant, powered by air magic. The force sends the fighter flying into the wall of the arena, crushing the man upon impact.

CHAPTER TWENTY-NINE

Aya feels her strength returning and uses the wall of the arena to stand. Daniil and Kylii keep fighters back with walls of ice and fire. Bern and Eka join Mava and Rava holding off more of the volunteer fighters. Everyone able to is fighting. Wounded slaves trying to run are eventually swept back into the fray.

The few slaves who can provide healing magic are trying to help as many with minor wounds as possible. But those with more severe wounds lie barely conscious, forgotten.

Aya feels a strong urge to help, the brothers' words repeating through her mind. *Some are more valuable than others.* She can't sit and watch as others die.

Those fighting focus on the more dangerous slaves, so Aya carefully makes her way to those injured. She stumbles and steadies herself with the wall. The sounds of her body fill her mind and she closes her eyes.

"Breathe," a voice says to her.

She looks up. A cloaked figure stares down at her. She tries to see his face, but he leans back, out of her sight. She returns her attention to the injured slaves and takes a deep, calming breath. The noise in her mind softens and a small surge of strength fills her.

She uses the wall to propel herself forward. She's thankful for the tall seating that towers above, blocking the morning sun from showering heat and casting a shadow over her corner of the arena.

Reaching the group of wounded, she moves to a woman with blood-crusted hair. She's trying to heal a man who legs are broken, when she stares up at Aya. "You're the new Healer they brought yesterday, aren't you?"

"Yes. I can help with the more serious wounds."

"We have people dying here. I can only stop the bleeding."

Aya points to another Healer. "How about you?"

The man looks up from the slave he's tending. "I can fix broken bones, but if they've lost too much blood, I can't do anything."

She eyes the third Healer.

"I can only heal cuts and bruises." The young girl's voice is high and shrill.

"All right, I need names."

"Skara," the woman with blood-crusted hair says.

"Tristan," the man answers.

"B-Bon," the girl squeaks.

Trailing over the wounded, Aya takes a breath to organize her thoughts. She remembers several years ago when a storm tore through Foula Valley. Many in her village were injured and Iria needed help when too many wounded flooded his home. Aya's magic was still new to her, but Elder Mircien requested her help. Aya helped identifying internal injuries, Iria did his best to heal, and Mircien cleaned the injuries and helped with recovery. It's what led the two men to determine that Aya should study healing. Now, she divvied up the duties similarly.

"Skara and Tristan, fix those with broken bones and internal bleeding. Bon, once they've finished, clean up the cuts and bruises." Aya points to each as she speaks. "Have you already separated the ones with more life-threatening injuries?"

Skara nods and points to a small group lined up against the wall. "Some of them are too close to death for us to help."

"Don't worry about that. Make sure you move together and communicate clearly. Whoever isn't working, keep an eye out for attackers."

"And what do we do if someone does attack us?" Tristan asks.

"We'll take care of them." Rava, Mava, Bern, and Eka surround the group, weapons at the ready.

The three Healers leap to their posts while Aya brings those closest to death back. Unfortunately, one is too far gone for her to help. She reluctantly moves on, after using her magic to keep the pain as minimal as possible.

She moves from one body to the next, absorbing an overflow of stimuli, but she manages to focus on the areas she needs to heal. She gains more and more control as she works, though her energy levels are quickly depleting. The tips of her fingers and toes tingle, numbing as she pushes her magic. Her head feels disconnected from her body, light and floaty. Before long her eyelids droop and she struggles to fight the exhaustion.

Those she and the others heal take up discarded weapons to help screen the healers from the fighting. When Aya finishes, she takes a few minutes to regain some of the strength she's lost before more freshly wounded approach.

Aya ignores the fighting until she needs another few minutes of reprieve.

Daniil and Kylii stand at the forefront, protecting the healers and ordering the growing group. A slave strangling a combatant with a chain is unaware of two men readying to stab him in the back. Daniil freezes one and Kylii sets fire to the other. The slave remains none the wiser and continues fighting.

Fighters not focusing on the gathered slaves are picked off by Yme. Wind sends a number crashing into the walls of the arena, earth buries others, and water covers one man's head, drowning him where he stands.

With her strength back, Aya returns to healing, working on a man whose arm is held together by only a strip of muscle. The number of wounded brought to them slows, but Tristan, Bon, and Skara still listen to every direction she gives. The four function cohesively as a group. Soon, they don't need to vocally communicate anymore. They simply exchange looks and motions.

The loud bell rings out across the Arena, but it isn't until the drums start again that Aya realizes the fighting is over. She finishes healing the last of the wounded and looks up. Standing with effort, she gently pushes her way to view the Arena, gripping the shoulders of those she passes to keep her balance. Blood stains the ground and bodies of slaves and opponents alike litter it.

Even with all the frantic healing, the slaves lost a third of their numbers. The Bloody Butchers lost fewer, the last of the volunteer fighters grab their wounded and exit the arena floor.

"Aya!"

Daniil and Kylii make their way to her and each grab a hold of her. Cuts on their arms are shallow, but mostly they're intact. Their gazes bounce from her to the wall of people behind her, their expressions a mixture of awe and sadness.

Above them the audience cheers, filling the Arena with thunderous noise. Those who are left join in the cheering. Those behind Aya chant her name.

"I thought I told you not to draw attention." Yme gives her a stern look and glares at the brothers.

Aya pulls away from the brothers and grabs him by the chin, forcing him to look into her defiant eyes. "I can handle myself. I'm not going to let these people die if I can stop it."

He sighs, grabbing her arm and lowering it from his chin. "At least you didn't bring anyone back from the dead. You *didn't* bring anyone back from the dead, did you?"

"No."

He smiles, a reaction she doesn't expect.

"The fight is over!" The booming voice silences the Arena and the slaves all turn to the Blood King's private box. The Voice places his hands on the stone balcony. "It would appear the newest fighters to our beloved Arena have more fight in them than previous groups."

The audience cheers, stomping their feet in agreement.

"But let us not forget the bravery and skill of the Bloody Butchers! Show them your respect."

The cheering increases. Workers of the Arena open the gate the slaves entered through, preparing to lead them back to the depths. Seera stands inside the open gate, her whip in her hand.

Then everything stops.

The audience is silent, the workers stop what they're doing. The strange silence and stillness overtake the Arena. Even Dolus Otho is silent and frozen with his eyes wide, staring below him.

The Blood King stands and walks to the edge of his box, scanning the slaves curiously. He smiles and opens his arms wide.

"Congratulations, victors," his voice thunders through the air. "I hadn't expected to be so thoroughly entertained. I applaud your strength and look forward to seeing you in future games. I decree these fighters be given the rest of the day as a reprieve to relax and enjoy their victory. And for those of us who were here to witness this...*inspiring* show of abilities, a celebration is in order."

The Arena explodes in applause and cheers. The slaves rejoice and hug each other. Tears roll down many cheeks and some fall to the ground weeping. They survived their first fight. The red cloths on the waists of the fresh flesh fall to the ground, the magic gone from the fabric.

Rava, Mava, Bern, Eka, Tristan, Bon, and Skara pull Aya away from the brothers and Yme into a group hug. She's surprised to see tears in their eyes.

She turns back to her cellmates with a smile, but it quickly fades. The worried expressions on Yme and the brothers' faces

165

sends a chill up her spine. She glances towards the Blood King to find him speaking quickly to the man with a black sash and The Voice of the Arena, Dolus Otho.

He turns his head so his eyes meet hers, and smiles. His smile is cold. One corner higher than the other, almost a smirk.

A smile of pure evil.

CHAPTER THIRTY

THE SLAVES RETURN TO THEIR CELLBLOCK DEEP BELOW THE ARENA. Slaves requiring additional treatment are taken to the Arena Healers but beg to be healed by Aya's little group.

"Let them help," Aya argues. "We have no energy left and can't guarantee full recovery."

Defiance greets her, but ultimately, the slaves allow the workers to take them away.

Those not requiring healing are taken to the dining hall, where a large meal awaits. The slaves stuff a cornucopia of meats and vegetables into their hungry mouths, limiting conversation. Arena workers, who had been unable to witness the fight, ask for details as they liberally pass out drinks. Slaves from other cellblocks join the victors, introducing themselves, eager to spread word through the rest of the cellblocks of the fresh flesh's victory.

After the first wave of gorging passes, the cellblocks fill with jovial conversations. Cellblock A is abuzz with excitement. The experienced slaves who didn't volunteer to fight cheer as Aya and the others walk to their cells. The veterans of the Arena treat the surviving fresh flesh as friends and pray with those who lost close friends in the fight.

167

Many stories about past games and great fighters move through the cell block. Guvie, the oldest surviving Arena slave, tells a particularly funny story including an embarrassing moment for one of the Blood King's personal favorites.

"The fighter was so confident in his victory, he showed up drunk and pissing his pants as he saluted his King. The fight didn't even last through the end of the starting bell's ring. He passed out at half salute." To emphasize his point, Guvie holds his arm suggestively. The slaves' laughter fills the dark underground caverns.

Then the talk of today's fight centers on Aya's healing magic. Word spreads quickly through Cellblock A about her healing during the journey as well as the fight.

"You're very popular," Kylii comments as he sits down on his bed.

Daniil nods from the floor, leaning against his brother's bed. "You'll be getting a lot of attention after today."

Frowning, Aya sits on her bed, her feet resting on the floor. "All I did was help. There were other Healers; why do I get all the attention?"

"For one, you healed injured folk who would've been left to die otherwise," Kylii says.

"Two, you rallied the slaves together...including us. That never happens," Daniil adds.

"You mean it wasn't the usual free-for-all." She crosses her legs underneath her on the bed. "The slaves actually fought together."

"We go until the bell tells us to stop. Sometimes you fight together in order to secure your own survival. Say, against a highly skilled fighter that hasn't been killed by Yme."

Yme glares at Daniil from his spot at the back of the cell. "If we fought together, we'd never lose."

"Why haven't the slaves fought together before now, then?" she asks.

"They'd punish us," Kylii answers. "Take away our food,

send smaller groups to fight against impossible numbers, things like that."

"They can't afford a revolt in the Arena. Haven't you wondered why, with so many slaves, non-magic and magic alike, we haven't taken over the Arena and gained our freedom?" Daniil asks.

"I thought it was because there are others like you two who think your lives are more valuable than others," she says, meeting their gazes with an eyebrow raised.

A stifled laugh comes from the back of the cell and Yme turns his head away from the brothers' glares.

"Besides that," Daniil says, turning back to Aya.

"They have contingencies in place in case such a thing occurs." Kylii sits up on his bed. "Some of the Arena workers, if you hadn't noticed, have the ability to block magic. Magic to negate magic, as it were. There aren't many of them and only a few are known, but force would never gain any of us freedom."

Aya remembers the worker who opened their cell door that morning. She also remembers the workers on the upper levels using magic to work the large machinery of the Arena. A number of magic users are employed here. They'd have to fight through them, too, possibly with their own magic negated.

The joviality that filled the air moments before is fading. Aya and the brothers peer out of the cell, trying to see the cause.

Seera walks to the center of the cellblock to ensure all cells hear her. Two men follow. "Excellent fighting today, but don't be fooled by kind words or extra food. You're all still slaves of the Arena and tomorrow many of you will once again fight for your lives."

Crossing to the door of Aya, Yme, Daniil, and Kylii's cell, she continues, "Oh, and we have a special surprise for the stars of the fight. You have a visitor."

Opening the cell door, Seera quickly steps back, leaving a wide opening between her and the cell. The two men move to either side of the open door and clasp their hands, their thumbs pointed at their chests.

The slaves fall silent as the sounds of heavily armored footsteps fills the cellblock. The soldiers from the private box appear, invade the cell, and force the four occupants to their feet. They surround them, ushering them towards the center of the cell. They leave a path to the door for the coming visitor.

The silence of the cellblock amplifies the next set of footsteps, which echo down the hall. Slaves retreat, away from the sight of the owners of the footsteps.

Aya's heartbeat pounds in her ears and she shakes uncontrollably. She moves behind Daniil and Kylii, who close ranks to block her from view. Yme tenses, a frown darkening his face.

The man with the black sash walks into the cell holding an ornate helmet under his right arm. He steps to the side of the entrance and straightens. He taps his helmet with two fingers and the men in armor draw their swords. They grab the hilt with both hands and touch the blade tips to the ground.

A feeling of dread fills the cell as the Blood King enters, his strange eyes landing on the brothers and moving to Yme. One eye is reddish brown, and the other is an intense green. He smiles, while Aya cringes behind the brothers.

"I wanted to personally congratulate the stars of today's fight. I see one here, a very familiar face," he says, stepping close to Yme. "But what about the other? The girl?"

The Blood King raises an eyebrow towards Daniil and Kylii, who eye each other, but refuse to move. The Blood King turns to the man with the black sash who immediately steps forward and, handing his helmet to the closest soldier, shoves Daniil and Kylii apart. He yanks Aya forward, directly in front of the Blood King. She tries to hold back, but a tiny yelp passes her lips.

Yme grabs for Aya, but the man shoves him away and threatens to unsheathe his blade before Yme recedes. Sneering, the man with the black sash retrieves his helmet and returns to his position by the door.

"It's nice to see you caring for another life instead of taking one," the Blood King says to Yme. He turns his attention to Aya. "Don't be afraid. You can look me in the eye."

Aya raises her head to stare the Blood King in the eyes.

"And what is your name, Rare Kind?"

She answers with silence.

"Your king has asked you a question, slave!" Black Sash yells. Aya flinches at the raised voice, her eyes falling to the floor, but remains silent.

With the raise of a hand the Blood King regains control. "I apologize for Teron's rudeness. Perhaps I should properly introduce myself first. I am Klaeon Vacuda. Blood King, they call me. Now what is your name?"

She swallows the lump in her throat but can't bring herself to answer. She doesn't want him to have her name. She doesn't want to hear it spoken from his lips.

"Maybe a little encouragement will loosen your tongue." Klaeon nods at Teron.

Black Sash jumps to life and grabs Kylii's hand. In one swift motion, he takes one of Kylii's fingers and bends it back. Too far back. Kylii shrieks as his finger nears breaking.

"Aya Flandeen! Just stop!"

Klaeon raises his hand and Teron releases Kylii and steps back to his post. Kylii grabs his hand and curses under his breath as Daniil grabs his brother.

Klaeon moves his hand to Aya's cheek. She wants to flinch but manages to stay as still as possible. "A Western name. Where do you call home?"

"Foula Valley."

"An Eastern home. Interesting." He turns his head to the right. "What games are scheduled next?"

Seera appears with her head bowed. "My lord, the chariot races are finishing as we speak. After, will be the lottery tournament. Immediately following will be a brief animal fight, then awards for the tournament. Your presence is anticipated for the awards ceremony."

Waving his hand at her, Klaeon nods his head. "Of course. Teron." Black Sash steps forward. "Escort our young Rare Kind to my private box. I'd like her to join me for the rest of the tournament." He turns and leaves the cell without another word.

Aya's blood runs cold and she feels movement behind her as Yme and the brothers try to grab for her. But Klaeon's men raise their swords to block their path, separating her from them.

"Yes, my lord." Teron steps forward and grabs her arm tightly. He drags her from the cell, followed by the armored men. She stares at the magic blocker, who meets her eyes before turning away.

Seera quickly locks the cell door behind the last guard before Yme, Daniil, and Kylii can escape. She hits the bars with the handle of her whip and laughs as she walks away.

The three grip the bars of their cell tightly, watching Aya as she disappears.

CHAPTER THIRTY-ONE

AYA IS HANDED OFF TO TWO OF THE BLOOD KING'S MEN AS TERON stops to speak with Dolus Otho. The announcer listens intently, his face slowly losing color.

She's taken through empty hallways, passing few workers. As the men in armor pass, the workers avoid their eyes and flatten themselves against the walls. The sound of the audience echoes down the hallway and Aya's heart races.

The excitement has only grown since the first game of the day. The chariot races have finished and Arena workers efficiently clear damaged chariots, dead men, and few dead animals from the arena floor.

The men lead Aya into the private box as one of the Arena's workers places a stool next to the lone chair. Blood King Klaeon is already seated, a small smile on his lips.

Inside the Arena, workers begin to set up a platform at the far end for Dolus Otho to perform the lottery drawing. The floor opens, and animals are brought up on chains.

Klaeon waves his hand at the men holding Aya. They release her and move to their posts around the private box. Teron, the man with the black sash, enters and, barely glancing at her, stands against the wall, closest to Klaeon's left.

173

Hesitating, Aya peeks behind her at the men guarding the entrance. Their eyes are focused ahead, but their hands grip their weapons, expectantly. If she attempts an escape, they won't hesitate to stop her with force.

"Have a seat, Aya Flandeen," Klaeon says, holding his hand towards the stool at his right.

Her heart flutters in her chest. Hearing her name from his lips only makes her feelings of dread grow. The longer she's near this man, the more dangerous for her. The friendliness in his voice cannot hide the underlying menace. She knows something is hiding beneath the surface, something wanting to swallow her whole.

"You don't have to be so nervous. While in the public's eye I won't do anything to you. It wouldn't sit well with the crowd if I killed you after the big show. Sit and enjoy the festivities."

"Festivities? Festivities are things of happiness and celebration, not death." Aya curses herself in her head for speaking this aloud. She has to remember she's a slave now and speaking out of turn could get her killed more easily than any fight in the Arena.

Klaeon laughs and turns to face her, his green eye glistening. "The Rare Kind has spunk in her after all. I was worried when I saw you cowering behind your cellmates. Sit."

Taking a nervous breath in, she cautiously steps forward. As she sits, she feels the eyes of thousands land on her and an excited muttering fills the air. She can almost hear the questions being asked.

Why is she sitting with the Blood King? Is the Blood King showing favor to her because she's a Rare Kind or because he's taken a fancy to this young woman?

"Idle talk is harmless unless you provoke it," Klaeon says, his voice close to her ear.

She faces him, meeting his strange eyes for a moment before lowering her gaze to the arena floor. She avoids the rapt gaze of the audience, concentrating on the workers' preparations.

An amused laugh fills the private box. "I take it you're not used to being the center of attention for thousands. It is a bit unnerving at first. Though it didn't seem to distract you on the arena floor."

"I had other things on my mind," Aya says softly.

"You certainly did. I particularly enjoyed your reckless rescue of the skewered fat slave." Klaeon waves to the entering combatants.

They salute, and Dolus Otho rattles off the names of the participants and the rules of the tournament. "This will be an exciting lottery tournament. We have an unprecedented number of participants today. But as you all know, only a handful will be given the opportunity to fight for the prize. We also have a very special surprise for those who are chosen to compete today. Be sure to cheer on your favorite."

"I can't help but wonder...what you are, Aya Flandeen from Foula Valley," Klaeon says.

Her face fills with confusion.

"We have several Healers in the Arena, workers and slaves, but you healed fatal wounds. People who should have died long before any Healer could've reached them." Leaning on the arm of his chair, he lowers his voice so only she can hear. "So, I ask again...what are you?"

The air around her grows heavy and she feels another presence moving around her. A soft touch on her arm makes her jump, but when she looks for the culprit there's nothing there.

"I'm merely a Healer," she answers, her voice trembling; trying to allay further probing suspicion, she adds, "my lord."

"A Healer placed with Rare Kinds is far more than a Healer. What did they call you when you arrived?"

The other presence surrounds her, making it hard to breathe. Fear turns to terror and she leaps from her seat, shrinking as far from the Blood King as possible. The soldiers step close together, creating a wall to block her from exiting the box. She presses her back against the wall, her eyes locked on Klaeon's smiling, calm face.

"Life Healer," Aya says, regaining her voice.

A LOUD CHEER from the audience signals the end of the lottery drawing, and Klaeon returns his attention to the Arena. The guards surrounding her shift minutely, and she can sense the tension beginning to ebb. Down on the sand, two thirds of the combatants leave, their heads hanging low. Those still left wave their weapons in anticipation of the tournament to begin.

The air in the private box feels more usual as Klaeon stands to acknowledge the lucky fighters chosen to compete. He eyes Dolus Otho, who knowingly nods his head. He resumes his seat, and motions for her to do same.

"Life Healer. A true Rare Kind. I've heard many stories about Life Healers…haven't seen one in many, *many* years. Or heard of any that still lived. Tell me, Aya," he takes her hand as she sits, pulling her close. "Have you ever brought someone back from the dead?"

She shakes her head.

"Have you used your magic to give immortality?"

A confused shake at his words. "Th-those are only stories, my lord."

His eyes search her face for any sign of deceit. Seeing none, he smiles and releases her hand. "But all stories stem from some truth."

Immortality? Is it even possible? I've just learned what my magic truly is. I'm still learning. Every time I heal someone, I discover something new.

The arena floor is ready for the tournament to begin. Platforms now cover the floor, surrounding a larger one raised slightly higher than the others. Several of the platforms have ferocious beasts chained at the center. Others have fire pits built at their bases. Many of them have other hazards to make the competition more difficult: traps, spikes, weapons, nets.

At the center of the largest one is a golden cloth. Each fighter chosen from the lottery is placed at different points around the edge of the platforms. They wave to the excited audience, increasing the anticipation in the air. When they're ready and in position, Dolus Otho holds his hands up for silence.

"The rules are simple. The fighters must make their way to the center platform. Whoever claims the golden cloth will be declared the winner and will receive a great reward. However, they are free to interfere with their competitors in any way they see fit. They may choose to ignore everyone, hunt each other down, or team up to ensure survival. But there will only be one winner. No exceptions." Dolus Otho glances at Klaeon once before lowering his hands. "I wish all of you luck. Now begin the tournament!"

The bell rings loudly and the fighters spring into action, rushing towards the center. Some have a clearer path than others, but it doesn't mean it will be easy.

A female fighter is the first to fall, thrown into the fire pits below. The cheering crowd drowns out her screams, but Aya winces. She can almost feel her own flesh burning.

The man who threw the female fighter celebrates prematurely as another fighter sneaks up and stabs him in the back. They tussle, but the backstabber manages to toss the other from the platform into spikes protruding from a nearby platform.

Beasts maul two of the competitors, their screams again covered by the audience. Their blood coats the platform as fangs rip meat from bone.

A pair of men fighting together climb toward the large platform at the center, but just as they scramble up, the platform they stand on collapses beneath them, revealing a pit of spikes beneath. One manages to grab the edge of the wall, and his partner grabs his leg, climbing his partner's body, reaching for the edge of the wall. The man yells, "Stop!" but the partner ignores him, and he loses his grip. Slipping, flailing, both fall into the spikes. Their screams linger a moment then stop abruptly.

Tearing her eyes from the gruesome fighting, Aya realizes Klaeon has been staring at her since the match began, his eyes dancing hungrily over her. Aya's nerves tense with fear.

"It's a shame," he says, returning his gaze to the fighting. Aya stares at him a moment longer, wondering what he means.

The bell rings loudly. Aya jumps at the loud noise. In the arena, a man stands holding the gold cloth, a wide smile on his face. The others, still alive, stop what they are doing and stare at the victor in anger.

Dolus Otho again looks to Blood King Klaeon, uncertain. Klaeon gives a nod, and the announcer swallows a large lump in his throat.

"Congratulations to our victor! And to those who survived! As I said, today we have a special prize for all who were chosen to fight."

Dolus Otho falls silent and steps off his platform, climbing stairs into the crowd. Confusion fills the audience and those still on the arena floor. The workers of the arena leave through the large gates, shutting them.

"I was hoping the stories about immortality were true," Klaeon says. "I would've been inclined to spare your life."

The blood drains from Aya's face.

He stands, moving to the edge of his private box. "We can't have you healing every injured slave. It doesn't provide much of a show for the crowd. Part of the fun is watching slaves be killed. Fighters, beasts, or other slaves; it doesn't matter to them." He gestures to the audience.

The confusion in the Arena increases. The fighters notice their escape is blocked off, and gather on the center platform. The winner holds the gold cloth tightly, unsure what to do.

"But if you take the death away…personally, I find it boring. How about you, Teron?"

"Very boring, my lord," Teron answers, crossing to Aya and pulling her to her feet. He drags her to stand beside Klaeon, not bothering to do it gently.

"So, you did bring me here to kill me?" she asks, fear clear in her voice. She winces at the pain in her arm, and struggles against Teron.

"I already told you, Life Healer, while in the public's eyes, you're safe…"

Screams from the arena floor pull all attention to the large platform. The gold cloth wraps around the victor, covering him from head to toe. He screams, but it only makes it easier for the cloth to enter his mouth.

The other fighters step away from him, but the gold cloth grows and shoots out towards them. It grabs them by the arm or leg and slowly covers them. Soon all bodies are entombed in the gold cloth, creating golden statues in differing throes of death.

The audience sits in stunned silence, unsure of what they witnessed.

"It isn't fun to kill you here when there are far more creative and entertaining ways," Klaeon finishes, turning to her. His reddish-brown eye gleams with excitement. He waves his hand at Teron. "Take her back to her cell and inform Seera and Dolus Otho I'd like a small change to tomorrow's games. I'll send them more information tonight."

Teron bows to his king before dragging her away. She steals a look back at the arena floor, twisting against Teron's grip.

The gold statues are disintegrating into dust, blowing away in the wind. Klaeon raises his hand to the crowd and an eruption of thunderous applause greets him.

CHAPTER THIRTY-TWO

"HE DIDN'T DO ANYTHING TO YOU?" KYLII SEARCHES HER FACE IN disbelief.

Aya sits on her bed with her knees held tight against her chest. She shakes her head, fear filling every part of her body. "No. But he wants me dead."

"Klaeon told Dolus Otho to kill all of those fighters. They weren't even slaves. And he killed them all," Aya says. *Killed them all to show me his power.*

"He wants all of us dead," Daniil points out. "Otherwise we wouldn't be here."

Raising her eyes to the brothers, she squeezes her knees. "But why? I don't understand."

"Because he can, because he's afraid of us, because he hates magic users…take your pick," Kylii says, leaning back on his bed. "No one leaves the Arena alive."

Her eyes narrow and she thinks back at her experience with the Blood King. "How can he hate magic users…?" She trails off, unsure what she's even thinking.

Yme stares at her from his habitual spot in the back of the cell. His expression is one of curiosity, but he quickly changes it to a more neutral one. "He saw how you coerced the others into working together. The audience wants bloodshed, not teamwork."

Aya glares at him. "I didn't coerce anyone! Even if I had, he can't punish everyone for something he *believes* I did."

"He can do whatever he wants," Kylii points out.

"You didn't have a proper teacher, did you?" Yme's voice is a dark rumble.

Her anger turns to confusion. "What?"

"For your healing magic," Yme clarifies. "You don't heal the same way as the others."

Still confused, but relieved at the change of subject, she nods. "I was the only one in my village who had magic. But our village healer taught me a lot about the human body and how it works. He taught me how to heal without magic, but I practiced my magic on animals for a while before I ever attempted using it on people."

"You demonstrated advanced healing techniques on some of the wounded, according to those three Healers. That's impressive," he says, his eyes shining with approval. "Natural talent in magic is hard to find. But from what you say, you learned without magic as well."

"I apply what I learned, and use that before I go in with my magic. If I didn't have my village's healer, I don't think I would've been able to do anything I did out there." Her voice is ragged, tinged with sadness, remembering.

"But what about your parents? Surely, they helped you, too?" Daniil asks.

Her eyes lower and she shakes her head. "My parents died before my magic appeared."

"Oh, I'm sorry."

"Stories say Life Healers are able to bring the dead back to life and the most powerful can grant immortality," Kylii says. His brother punches him in the shoulder. "Ow! *What?*"

"Learn to read a room, Brother," Daniil says, angrily.

The words of the Blood King ring through her thoughts. He'd mentioned stories everyone seemed to know, except for her.

Sensing her mood, Yme shrugs his shoulders. "Not all stories should be believed. That only leads to ignorance and paranoia."

"The King said all stories rise from a grain of truth."

"There are tall tales associated with all Rare Kinds. That's what makes us appear more than we are," Daniil says.

"We still bleed and die like everyone else," Kylii adds. "We're just a little tougher."

"And we have to protect each other." She echoes his words with a small glimmer.

She hears a banging on metal rings out in the block. Everyone walks to their cell doors. Seera walks in with her guards. A wide smile is on her face, but annoyance fills her eyes.

"Hello, victors, and the rest of you. I hope you're relaxing and gaining your strength, because there've been some changes to tomorrow's events. Some not surprising, but others very exciting." Seera's eyes scan the faces of the slaves eagerly. "The afternoon's animal fights have been moved to the morning, before the main event."

Murmurs rumble through the cellblock. Two guards slam metal poles on the nearest cells, silencing the crowd. Aya looks to the brothers for help, but they appear as confused as she.

"The afternoon fights are generally the main events. Moving them to the morning doesn't mean good things for us," Yme says.

Waiting for all attention to return to her, Seera clears her throat loudly before continuing. "As for the main event...it will be a first for the Arena. A tournament—"

Aya's presses the palms of her hands to her eyes to blot out the sight of the gold cloth wrapping around the screaming fighters.

"—of one-on-one fighting, open to the public and professional fighters of all levels."

The cells fill with voices. Most reflect fear, and the rest a mixture of confusion and excitement. Seera allows the conversations to go on for nearly a full minute before signaling her guards to silence the cellblock.

"I know what most of you are thinking." Her smile widens. "How will the fighters be determined? Well, don't worry about that. Our King has picked random fighters from our extensive lists. And to make the tournament more entertaining and interesting for our crowds, he picked a small number of you to fight. Two from each cellblock."

Relief rushes through the cellblock, masked by the screams of terror of those who truly realize what Seera's words mean.

Yme slams his hand against the cell door, the clanging echoing loudly in the small cell. Noticing his reaction, Seera walks to the cell.

"Your cellblock shall be represented by Yme, the top fighter of the Arena," Seera looks at Aya, "and the Life Healer."

A few voices call out, but Seera waves them off. "Our King gave specific instructions. No changes. Fight well tomorrow." Seera lowers her voice so only Aya and Yme hear her parting shot. "It may be your last."

The guards unlock the cell door. One grabs Aya and drags her out roughly. Yme grabs the other guard's hand and bends two of the man's fingers back. There is a sickening crack and the man shrieks in pain. Yme releases the man's disfigured hand and walks out of the cell, a frown darkening his expression.

The third guard, the magic blocker, takes a step back from the angered mage. He knows that, even with Yme's magic blocked, he is still dangerous.

"Where are you taking us?" Yme demands.

Seera taps the end of her whip against the side of her neck. "To the other fighters. You're to be kept separate from your cell until after the tournament. If you survive until then."

Glaring at her, Yme walks to Aya's side. He grabs the guard's wrist, tightening his hand. "Tell him to let her go." The guard stares at Seera. She nods, and he releases Aya.

Letting go of the guard's wrist, Yme moves close to Aya. Seera leads Aya and Yme out of the cellblock, the guards following.

CHAPTER THIRTY-THREE

AYA AND YME MOVE THROUGH THE BOWELS OF THE ARENA, PASSING workers frantically preparing for the next day's change in events. They avoid the chaos of animals being moved and the last of the day's fighters heading back to their cells. Seera halts at a room filled with beds. Some bear wounded fighters on them, and in the back corner six men and six women huddle together.

"Head over to your fellow combatants. Guards will be posted at the doorway. I'll return in the morning to fetch the lot of you when it's time," Seera says, leaving the two to wander back to the group. Twelve pairs of eyes turn on them, no surprise in a single one.

"The one he hates and the one who caused this. Should've just been you two," one of the combatants, an older woman, snarls. "I'm not even a magic user."

"Shut your mouth, Yvette. The Bastard King doesn't care if you have magic or not. You're here for the same reason as the rest of us, a false king leading people to a false future," one of the men says. A large scar covering his neck bounces with his speech.

"And what future would that be, Chaput? The way he throws anyone in here, there won't be people left to rule soon."

"Oh, there will. People who are too afraid to defy him. People who will choose to fight for him to protect themselves."

"Or else they end up in here," Yvette spits, "forced to fight when some stupid, young girl can't play by the rules."

"She's right," Aya says, glaring at those around her. "It is my fault, but I don't understand why. I can't change who I am, how I was born. Fighting one another won't help solve the problem."

Yvette snorts and glances at Yme. "What do you think, Top Fighter? You agree with the little brat?"

"What did you call me?" Aya's hands ball into fists.

"I do agree with her," Yme steps in. "Fighting amongst ourselves isn't helping. If anything, it causes more of us to die and encourages them to keep hunting for more slaves. This tournament was bound to happen sooner or later. Klaeon gets bored easily. Be glad this is the only change...for now." Yme walks a few beds away and sits on the floor, only the top of his head visible to Aya.

The group falls silent, trying to think of things besides the coming fight the next day. Feeling Yvette's angry eyes on her, Aya sits on the bed next to Yme, leaning her back on the wall.

"Thanks for agreeing with me. Here and with the brothers."

A soft grunt comes from him as he leans his head back. His eyes are closed and his breathing slow and methodical.

"You must be used to people blaming you for Klaeon's mood swings, huh?"

He doesn't answer.

So she prods. "Before I got here and became his new favorite toy to torture, you probably had to deal with a lot of unfair fighting, right?"

He opens one eye and stares at her. "You're asking me a lot of questions. Why?"

"Because I'm trying to get to know you."

"Why?"

"We're comrades, we're both fighting for our lives, one of us might be dead tomorrow, I'm scared...pick one."

"Yes."

"Yes?" She raises a brow. "Yes, to what?"

"Yes, I'm used to being blamed for Klaeon's mood swings and yes, I had to deal with a lot of unfair fighting...on and off the arena floor. There's a reason Daniil and Kylii said they'd protect you when you first arrived."

"They said it was because I'm a Rare Kind like them."

He nods. "There are some in the cellblocks that wouldn't think twice about killing you."

"But why?"

"Because Rare Kinds are treated differently."

"Not in a good way," she grumbles. "Unless they're jealous of constantly being targeted."

"They're jealous of how others treat us, the constant idolization."

Her eyes widen. Memories of the villagers and the journey to the Arena flash before her. Each eye filled with hope and veneration made her uncomfortable and hate herself. She wished only to be normal and treated like everyone else.

Yme clenches his hands. "They feel jealous that we have magic at all."

She moves to sit on the edge of her bed, closer to him. "Do you hate them for thinking that?"

Opening his eyes, he stares at her with his haunted silver eyes. "Only the ones who think killing us means they'll escape these walls. The Arena doesn't work that way."

Sensing he doesn't want to talk any longer, she crawls under her bed's scratchy, woven blanket. Healers she's never met before walk from patient to patient. She's tempted to ask them about their magic, but they probably won't talk to her.

The magic blocker stands against the wall, his clasped hands shaking slightly. *He's blocking our magic without affecting the Healers. There's still so much I don't understand.*

"How long have you been fighting in the Arena?" Aya asks Yme.

The other fighters are already asleep, leaving them the only ones awake besides the Healers and the workers assigned to guard them. Most of the torches have been removed to allow the fighters to sleep, and only low amber light dances along the dirt floors.

"Nine years. I was taken from my home when I was sixteen," Yme answers from the floor.

He refuses to sleep on the beds, but she wraps her blanket around him. "Was it hard?"

"What?"

"Your first fight?"

"I nearly got my head caved in." He takes a deep breath, pulling the blanket tighter. "The only reason I survived in the beginning was because of Daniil and Kylii."

A small laugh escapes her lips before she can stop it. His silver eyes catch the low light in the darkness as he glares at her.

"What's so funny?"

Aya lifts her head from the bed. "Not funny. Sweet. Those two seem kind, but at the same time, they don't get along with... well, anyone."

Realizing she isn't laughing at him, he relaxes a little. "They don't. Before I was thrown in here, they never thought to talk to any of the other slaves. They kept to themselves and rarely volunteered to fight when given the choice."

"You changed them."

"I disagreed with how they chose to live in here. Though, as you probably realized, I didn't change everything."

She hesitates, gripping her blanket tightly. "They mentioned those they've tried to help in the past. Kylii said most are dead. And I hadn't realized...they've been here longer than you."

He nods. "There were a few others they became close to besides me. They weren't Rare Kinds, but the brothers protected them like they were. But it only takes a moment in this place for something irreparable to happen. After a while, they stopped letting themselves feel anything for the other slaves. It's easier that way."

A strained silence passes while the sound of patrolling guards checking the Arena's security soon fades. Aya's eyelids grow heavy.

"You should get some rest," Yme says softly. "Tomorrow is going to be a long day and I'm sure Klaeon has more surprises in store."

She yawns, then smiles. "I should be saying that to you, mister I-won't-sleep-on-a-bed. It's not like there aren't any vacant ones."

"I don't deserve comfort."

She sits up slightly. "Why do you say that?"

"You haven't been here long. This arena destroys people. Makes us do terrible things. After a while you stop caring about the horrible things you're doing and about the others around you."

"Don't start sounding like those two downstairs. To me, it seems like you still care a lot. If you're punishing yourself for what you've done here, then your spirit and heart haven't been destroyed yet." She stretches her arms out to the side and yawns again. "I may not have been here long, but I can see through the little act you put on."

"What act is that?"

"You know exactly. *I don't need any help. I can take on fifty men all on my own. Splash, whoosh, thump...*" She waves her hands in the air.

"Thump?" he laughs, quietly.

"I don't know what other sound to use for earth slamming into a person." She hits the wall made of stone, making a dull thud. "There. See? Splash, whoosh, thud."

"You're really strange." He chuckles. Then his eyes close and his head lowers. His breathing calms as he falls asleep.

"No. Just tired." Her eyelids grow heavy and she rolls onto her back.

Movement catches her eye and a Healer walks towards them with an Arena worker behind her, carrying something metallic in his hand.

CHAPTER THIRTY-FOUR

"TIME TO WAKE UP, SLAVES!" SEERA'S VOICE BOOMS.

Aya jumps at the sudden noise and raises her right arm to her head. She feels a strange weight and opens her eyes. A metal shackle is on her wrist. She follows the and sees it's connected to a shackle on Yme's left arm. She spots another shackle on his left ankle with a chain disappearing beneath her blanket. She throws the blanket off her and sees the chain connecting to a shackle on her right ankle. She touches the metal with her free hand, and she remembers the Healer and worker walking towards them right before she fell asleep. They must have used magic, for everyone to sleep so soundly through the metal and the locks.

The clanking of the chains wakes Yme and he blinks lazily. He glances down at his arm and leg and his eyes widen. He moves his arm roughly, judging the strength of the metal. His sudden movement nearly pulls Aya from the bed and she yelps in surprise. He stops, noticing the chains connecting them.

"Shit." Sudden understanding fills his face. An odd mixture of fear, anger, and shock.

The other slaves wake up and, finding themselves in similar positions, aim angry questions at Seera. Watching their reactions, excitement glistens in her eyes.

191

"A special addition our King has requested for the main event," she says.

"I thought it was a one-on-one tournament. How can we do that chained to another fighter?" one of the other twelve says, angrily.

"Blood King Klaeon realized a simple one-on-one match up wasn't thrilling enough. So, now you will be chained to each other and you both will be fighting two fighters...who are not chained together." A sly grin crosses her blunt features.

The slaves talk all at once.

"There's no decided order you'll be fighting in," she blares over them. "Like our lottery tournament, we will draw each fighter before every fight. Your names are in multiple times, and whoever we draw will fight along with their chained partner."

"So we might be forced to fight more than one round," Yme says, glaring at Seera. "Based on our luck."

She nods. "Each of your names will be placed in the lottery based on our audience. They were each given sticks with your names on them. They will put in the names of the fighters they wish most to see. The collection will soon be finished, and Dolus Otho will draw one name for each pair of fighters."

Aya feels the chains between her and Yme shake with his rage. The other slaves stare at him with hope and relief in their eyes. He is the top fighter, the one the audience adores. It will be a miracle if any of the other fighters' names are drawn in the lottery.

"Don't get comfortable." Seera chides them, clenching the whip at her hip. "Dolus Otho is a professional. If the audience begins to bore, he'll find a way to reawaken their spirit. He also enjoys building tension, so don't count yourselves safe simply because of who else is in the lottery."

With that, the slaves' calm evaporates. Seera has a talent for eviscerating hope. Now, they eye their own partners with concern and suspicion. Is it worth the risk to fight together? Or should they sabotage the other to get the handicap removed?

"Now you head to the waiting pen. No stops at the armory or for weapons. Everything you'll need is waiting for you in the arena. Move." Seera cracks the whip.

Arena workers surround them, and they file out of the Healing Room.

The bowels of the Arena are alive with motion. The change in the day's schedule means a lot of projects put off can be finished. Men work on strange contraptions, new obstacles for the games. Others make repairs to old machinery needed for future games.

A new caravan, smaller than Jaxon's Black Caravan, has arrived with yet more fresh slaves. Their cargo is limited, only ten still living. A man with parchment inspects the slaves and offers money for each, ignoring arguments by the caravan leader. Two of the large men she recognizes as the ones who attacked Jaxon. Now they stand eager to silence the caravan leader.

The workers occasionally glance at the passing slaves, but with Seera in the lead, their gazes don't linger. A wagon passes, animal corpses piled on top. Blood flows from deep gash wounds. Broken claws and horns lie strewn and bloody foam dribbles from their mouths. Their bodies still twitch uncontrollably.

Aya recognizes the signs of deadly poisoning. She'd only seen it once in her village. Iria specifically took her to a neighboring village to teach her about poisons. They witnessed a small rodent force-fed poisoned food. Within seconds the animal collapsed, its body twitching and foam filling its mouth. She hated Iria for many days after, not understanding the need to see the poison in effect when he could've just told her.

"Stay sharp," Yme whispers in her ear.

She looks at him, memories fading away.

"Daydreaming is dangerous here."

"I wasn't daydreaming. And what should I be worried about, chained to the Arena's top fighter?" She ensures the sarcasm is thick in her voice, aiming it as a particularly dark joke.

His expression doesn't make it clear whether he understood

her to be sarcastic or accusatory. "There are a lot of things that will kill you if you're not paying attention."

They arrive at the large gate and are commanded to stand against the wall. Workers walk up and down the line, cleaning any who appear dirty, a strange courtesy to those about to fight.

The low rumbles of the crowd beyond the gate echo down the corridor. The fighters shift uncomfortably, the chains binding them together clinking softly. Eyes shift towards Yme and Aya.

Seera taps her whip against her thigh, a strange expression crosses her usually strong face. Nervousness. Her usual enjoyment of the oncoming fighting seems to be far from her mind. Aya wonders if it is due to the sudden change in schedule, or something else?

"Seera!" A familiar voice bellows down the hallway from behind. Everyone turns to see Dolus Otho storming towards the gate. He ignores the line of slaves standing against the wall, his focus on the woman in charge of the Arena's bowels. "Is everything prepared? He's getting antsy."

Seera gives a bouncy, cheeky wink. "Are you speaking of our King, or of yourself?"

"No. Not today. This is serious."

Seera darkens, and pulls him away from the line of slaves. They lower their voices so none can hear them. But Aya recognizes the body language and frantic gestures. They're arguing, anxious.

Aya turns to the gate leading into the arena. She sees workers pass by a raised platform at the center of the grounds, but it reaches above the top of the gate.

Gripping the manacle around her wrist, she feels the weight of the chains. The cold metal wants to pull her down. Maybe it will be heavy enough to bury her in the earth, escaping the Arena, she thinks. She feels weight on her shoulders, the weight of the words of the other fighters from the night before. This is her fault, and people are going to die.

A gentle tug pulls her attention from the sun-filled arena to the man standing beside her. Yme leans against the wall, his eyes on the two speaking in hushed voices.

"Can you make out what they're saying?" she asks, leaning next to him.

"I'm observing," he says. "They're upset. Nervous. They don't seem to like the change." Yme's silver eyes lock onto her. "Judging from the sweat stains, Otho's clothes don't like change, either. And if Seera taps her leg much longer, she's going to bruise."

Staring at him in surprise, Aya places her hands behind her back. "Were those attempts at jokes?"

"My humor only kicks in when I'm terrified."

"Well, I know *that's* a joke," she says, looking away. "Or else I would've seen this so-called humor sooner." She stares at the gate leading into the arena.

She hears the clanking of metal and feels a hand on her arm. It moves down and takes her hand, and she looks at Yme. He avoids her eyes, but gives her hand a comforting squeeze.

CHAPTER THIRTY-FIVE

THE ARENA HAS BEEN TRANSFORMED.

A large section of the floor has been raised up to eye level of the seating area, encased in a cage the top of which reaches many heads high. Stairs made of stone lead up to a fenced-in waiting area outside of the cage closest to the slaves. Benches are placed along the railing, enough for the fourteen fighters.

The slaves are led up the stairs and ordered to sit on the benches. Aya peers through the bars. Weapons and shields are attached by hooks and straps to the metal of the cage.

A second waiting area, for the fighters the slaves will be facing, is larger and built on the floor of the arena. Shades provide cover from the sun and so the audience can't see the opponents until they climb the stairs up to the fighting arena. Aya can see that there is also food and water set out for the fighters while they wait.

The excited murmurs of the crowd die out as Blood King Klaeon walks through the curtains and stands at the edge of his private box. His strange eyes hesitate on Yme and Aya. He smiles and sits, signaling for Otho to begin.

Dolus Otho, in his spot above Klaeon's private box, clears his throat and magic fills the air. "Welcome to the main event. A first for our Bloodfall Arena, a tournament with such excitement we had to let you, our most esteemed fans, participate." Otho waves his hand at a large bowl filled with sticks. "With your votes, you will determine the order of our fights today. Nineteen pairs of fighters will be fighting our most talented and fiercest slaves in the Cage of Conquest."

Aya stares at the bowl, noting it clearly isn't big enough to hold the votes of every single audience member. She doubts the audience cares, as long as the fights are exciting.

The crowd cheers and chants of Yme's name with their cacophony of voices. The slaves sitting next to Yme and Aya eye the pair with a mixture of relief and fear. Of course, the audience would vote for the top fighter more than them, but Seera's warning of Dolus Otho's ability to build tension stifles them with caution.

Otho holds his hands up, silencing the crowd. It takes a moment, but soon they quiet enough so he can continue. "Nineteen fights...not a round number, is it? And so, as a special treat, the twentieth fight will be a special surprise not to be missed. Now, to the rules. The fights will continue until either side is dead, or the professional combatants cede the match. Any and all weapons are allowed, any and all magic is allowed, and there is no time limit. Fight well, fight proud, and fight for your life!"

The crowd erupts, feet stomping the stone floor of the seating area. Aya's heart pounds and she checks the arena workers standing around them. The magic blocker is at his usual post. Others stand at the top of the stairs. At the bottom an empty cart waits.

Awaiting their dead bodies.

"Our first challengers are anxious for their chance at glory. Welcome to the arena... Granger and Hugh!" Dolus Otho throws his arms in the air.

A small laugh escapes Aya's lips. *It's hard to feel threatened by a fighter named Hugh.*

Two men emerge onto the stairs from beneath the shaded

cover. They wear little armor. Broadswords strapped on their backs reveal another truth of the day's fight: the challengers are allowed their own weaponry, while the slaves must choose from the motley selection ranged across the Arena.

The gates on both sides of the cage are opened. The two men enter. They wave at the audience, smug smiles on both faces. The slaves warily wait. Who will be the ones chosen to fight them? Who will be first?

"And now their match-up," Dolus Otho says, reaching into the bowl of sticks. Pulling out the first of nineteen draws, the announcer's eyes narrow to read the name. "Surprises begin early. Our first pair of slaves will be from Cellblock B. Yvette and Chaput."

The crowd, in a mixture of excitement and disappointment, cheers and mutters.

Yvette stands quickly, the chains connecting her to Chaput rattling. She glares at Aya. "It should've been you two." She and Chaput head for the open door and enter the Cage of Conquest.

I was going to wish you good luck.

The cage doors slam shut.

Yvette and Chaput grab swords from the walls. The bell rings, beginning the fight.

Hugh and Granger draw their broadswords. They separate, moving to either side of the cage. Yvette and Chaput walk forward, placing their backs together to keep eyes on the two men. The chain connecting their legs drags in the dirt, but they keep the metal from tangling their feet. Hugh and Granger stop moving and hold their swords in front of them, mirroring each other. All four combatants freeze.

The tension in the air is short-lived. The two men rush forward, thrusting their swords at Yvette and Chaput. The slaves hold their ground until it seems like they're simply waiting for the broadswords to run them through. Then both step to the side as one, splitting apart. Hugh and Granger can't change direction, but manage to keep from stabbing each other. The moment of confusion is enough, though. Yvette and Chaput whirl about to stab the two men in the chests. The broadswords fall harmlessly to the ground. The blades are followed by their owners as Hugh and Granger collapse.

The audience takes a moment to understand what happened before loud cheers fill the air. The fight was quick, but thrillingly smart.

The bell rings, ending the fight. Yvette and Chaput walk towards the door of the cage, beaming at one another. The door opens and they exit, returning to their seats.

The other slaves congratulate them. Aya watches the workers running to clear the bodies. They pull the swords from the bodies and kick the weapons away. The broadswords that belonged to Hugh and Granger are left in the cage, to her surprise. This could prove to be an advantage.

"Victory to the slaves! Our next challengers are first-time fighters in our Arena. Hailing from the Karrion Desert, welcome the Dongo Brothers, Zid and Kaj!"

The next fighters are already climbing the stairs. Their skin is dark, and masks cover their faces. The weapons on their backs are more elegant...and well-used. They wear letters on their armored chests: Z for Zid and K for Kaj.

"The ones chosen to fight them are," Dolus draws another stick. "Cellblock D. Leid and his partner, Quin!"

Aya looks to the two slowly rising from the benches. Quin's pale expression reflects her dread, but Leid's face is empty. The two walk into the Cage of Conquest and wait. Neither goes for weapons, only standing and facing the two men across from them. The gates are closed, and the arena falls quiet.

Quin, visibly shaking, pulls away from her partner. The chains connecting the two stretch to their full length.

The bell rings and the audience comes alive with excitement. The Dongo Brothers draw their weapons and wait for the slaves to make the first move.

Leid turns to Quin and walks towards her. But Quin walks

backwards, trying to stay far from her partner, and the audience's murmurs change to confusion.

"Doesn't look good for Quin," one of the other slaves says.

Her partner hits her arm. "Shut up, Lili."

"What do you mean?" Yvette's voice draws everyone's attention.

"Géroux doesn't want me to say it," Lili says, glaring at her partner. "But it's true. Quin got the worst person to be chained to of all of us."

"Why?" Aya asks, peering at the two slaves inside the cage.

Quin is at the wall of the cage, her back pressing into the metal. Leid grabs a large axe and weighs it in his hands. He swings it lazily left and right. As the chains stiffen, Leid continues moving. Quin is slowly dragged from the wall. In terror and humiliation, her bladder lets go.

"Is he....is he attacking his own partner?" Aya cries in disbelief.

"Leid isn't like the rest of us. He wasn't sold as a slave to the Arena," Géroux says.

Lili leans in. "He's a killer. Mad, a criminal. He murdered his family and most of an entire village before he was captured and thrown in here."

Leid stops holds the axe in one hand, looking at Quin with his crazed yet empty expression. He grabs the chain on his wrist and yanks her roughly forward.

Quin grabs the chain and pulls against it. "No! Gods, no! Let me out!" Her screams fill the air, the sound of her feet dragging on the stone floor and the chains the only other sounds as the audience collectively holds its breath.

The Dongo Brothers lower their weapons, unsure of what to do.

Leid pulls Quin closer and closer with one hand, as the axe in the other rises above his head. With one swift motion, he brings the axe down, aiming for where Quin's neck and shoulder connect. With surprising strength, the axe buries deep, stopping only when it hits resistance from bone.

Quin's screams are replaced with gargling as blood fills her lungs and mouth. Leid forcibly pulls the axe free and, with the same swinging motion, brings it down on the same spot. With less resistance, the axe passes through, splitting her.

The audience screams, a raucous mix of horror and pure elation. The slaves in the waiting area stare at Quin's corpse in shock.

Leid uses the axe to free the shackles off Quin's arm and leg before he throws the overbearing weapon away. His attention turns to the two men who waited for him to finish.

Leid spins the now-free metal chain above his head and holds his other hand out to the brothers. "I'm ready." His voice is cold, unaffected by what he's done. To him, Quin had been nothing but a disadvantage.

The brothers hesitate, but then raise their weapons and charge the solitary slave. As the first brother reaches Leid, Leid throws the spinning chain towards the man. The men split, avoiding the chain easily, but Kaj, to Leid's right, is slower than Zid. Leid's right leg kicks the chain attached to it and entangles Kaj's legs, tripping him. With him stunned on the ground, Leid changes the direction of the chain on his arm. He slams the heavy shackle into Kaj's head repeatedly, killing the man in quick spurts of blood and bone.

"Kaj!" Zid grows furious, and sloppy. He swings his weapon, but Leid squats as Zid swings and the blade only hits air. Kicking his left leg out, Leid knocks Zid onto his back. He leaps atop his chest and wraps the chain around his throat. He kicks the weapon out of Zid's struggling reach and tightens the chain. The frantic movements slow, then stop.

The bell signaling the end of the fight rings out to a bewildered audience. Aya stares at Quin's mutilated body. Leid slowly stands and walks to the gate of the cage, waiting for the arena workers to open it. They do, and step back from the man as he walks to his seat. The chains drag on the ground behind him and when he sits, he pulls them to rest underneath him. He crosses his arms and stares straight ahead, the empty expression still on his face.

CHAPTER THIRTY-SIX

"ANOTHER VICTORY FOR THE SLAVES!" DOLUS OTHO'S VOICE BREAKS the silence. "Leid is the victor!"

The audience returns to life and thunderous applause and whoops of approval fill the Arena. Workers rush the area and clear the three bodies, carrying them to the carts at the bottom of the stairs and throwing them on top of Hugh and Granger. Water mages wash the blood away, and soon the arena is ready for the next fight.

"What an exciting fight. How can we possibly top that? We're going to give it a try," Dolus Otho calls out.

Aya stares at Leid, fear growing at this man who felt nothing for the woman he so easily dispatched for his own gain. A hand grabs hers, and she turns to look at Yme.

"Don't think about it. He won't do anything on this side of the cage." But Yme's cautious stare at the man betrays his words.

The next match is called, a pair of amateur fighters versus Cellblock C, Ziv and Pangur. The match isn't as quick as the first, and both pairs put up enough of a fight to keep the audience enthralled. Ziv and Pangur defeat their opponents, but the professionals yield and are allowed to leave with their lives.

Dolus Otho goes right to calling the next match. A father and son duo versus Cellblock F's Sanna and Darin. This fight lasts longer, but when Darin is cornered by the father and son, Sanna uses their lack of focus on her to kill the son from behind. The father capitulates immediately, then carries his son's body out of the arena himself.

"Our challengers for fight number five are former workers of Bloodfall, but loved the fights so much, they decided to become professional fighters themselves. Welcome Serg and Klas! As to who they shall be facing…" He reaches into the bowl of sticks and smiles broadly at the result, "Cellblock A, Yme and Aya!"

The audience erupts into roars of approval. Finally, Yme will fight, and with the newest flesh of the Arena.

Yme and Aya stand and walk to the gate. As it closes behind them, Aya peers back at Leid's blank expression. *Is Yme thinking it would be easier to get rid of me? Is he thinking I'm a burden?*

"Focus." Yme gently pulls on their chain. "Worry after we win."

Aya faces forward. Their opponents wait at the center of the cage. They both carry dual knives and scars cover their skin. She spies a small shield close to her, grabs it and pulls it close.

"Yme Gurek," one of the fighters says. "Long time no see, little puke."

The other fighter laughs and lifts his shirt, showing a large scar on his abdomen. "Remember this? Got it when your sorry ass tried to escape when you were fresh flesh."

Yme cracks his knuckles and stretches his arms over his head. "Sorry. You're going to have to be more specific."

"He's playing dumb, Serg!"

"We'll have to give him a little reminder, Klas."

"Been a lot of grodun dungs who used to work here and who I may have nearly killed. But you're the first two to come back to finish the job," Yme says.

Aya yells, "Do you really think pissing them off is helpful?"

"They're going to try to kill us either way. Might as well have some fun." Yme holds his hands out in front of him. He points, and the floor in front of him cracks and rises. A large boulder rises to eye height and Yme smiles.

The starting bell rings and the two fighters split, Serg running for Aya and Klas running for Yme. Yme throws the boulder at Serg, as Klas slams into him. The two men collapse to the ground, the chain dragging Aya back a few steps. She winces as her arm wrenches behind her.

Yme uses his legs and Klas's momentum to throw the man into the cage wall, but not before Klas buries his knives into the chain links of Yme's wrist shackle. Yme tries to sit up, but the blades are buried deep and he can't free his hand.

Aya is pulled down to her knee. She sees movement out of the corner of her eye and raises the almost forgotten shield in her other hand. Serg's knives hit the metal of her shield and bounce off, one flying into the middle of the cage.

A trail of blood rolls down the side of Serg's head, dust spattered in his hair from the stone Yme threw at him. Serg recovers from the shield block and swipes his remaining knife at Aya's legs. She moves out of the way but the chain on her right leg tightens. She's unable to completely clear the distance. The sharp blade slices her skin.

Arms wrap around Aya from behind and she drops the shield. Klas grunts, pinning her tightly as Serg moves in for a killing blow.

A blast of wind slams into Serg and throws the surprised man into the cage wall. He hits the metal hard enough to shake some of the weapons off the walls. He groans on the ground, trying to regain his footing. Yme, having freed himself, runs forward and punches Serg in the back of the head, using his air magic to increase his hit. Serg falls and goes still, and Yme turns his attention to Klas.

Klas pulls Aya away, trying to gain distance from Yme, but the chains connecting Yme and Aya don't allow much separation. Yme hesitates to use his magic against Klas, afraid of hitting Aya.

Aya struggles against the arms around her. She raises her leg and aims at Klas's shin. As her foot makes contact, she feels her magic rise sharply inside of her. It shoots down her leg and into Klas's muscle and bone. Klas screams and falls to the ground, gripping his leg. Aya grabs her shield and turns to the large man on the ground. His lower leg is angled in a painful way. Bone sticks out of his skin and his hands are covered in blood. Aya freezes. This is the sort of wound she was born to heal, not cause.

Yme rushes forward and grabs Klas's throat, pulling him close. "Give up. You can't keep fighting with that injury and your partner is unconscious. End this fight or I *will* kill both of you."

Klas shoves Yme away, but the move sends fresh pain through him. He screams, grabbing his wounded leg. "All right, all right! We concede!"

The bell rings, ending the match and the audience cheers at the victory.

Yme and Aya walk to the gate and wait for the workers to open it. Once they do, they make their way back to their seats. Serg and Klas are helped out of the cage and disappear down the stairs.

Aya winces at the sharp pain in her leg. She looks at the cut and is relieved to see it's not deep. The bleeding is already clotting.

"I don't like this," Yme says almost to himself.

"You're going to have to be more specific. There's too much shit around here to know what you mean."

"They focused on you. They got me out of the way almost long enough to kill you."

"Not sensing a lot of faith in my abilities. I don't need you to worry about me if it's going to be a distraction for you," Aya says, resting her back on the railing.

Yme leans his arms on his knees and looks away from her. "They all think you're the weaker fighter. They're going to try to take you out first before focusing on me. I'm sure you can handle yourself against one fighter, but I don't know your abilities enough to safely assume you'd be able to handle two."

Aya doesn't answer. She can't. She doesn't honestly know, herself, and she doesn't want to admit she had no plan to free herself from Klas as Serg nearly stabbed her. If Yme hadn't intervened...

"Thank you for not abandoning me," she says.

Yme turns his head sharply to look at her. "I would never abandon you."

A smile forms on her lips, sensing the truth in his words.

CHAPTER THIRTY-SEVEN

"Our next match up is our first repeat performance," Dolus Otho announces, holding up two sticks. "Cellblock B, Chaput and Yvette!"

Yvette's aimed glare chills Aya. Then Yvette storms for the cage door, nearly dragging Chaput. He bustles to catch up to her. Their opponents are already in the Cage of Conquest, sisters and first-time fighters in the Arena. One carries a sword while the other holds a crossbow.

Yvette grabs an axe and Chaput grabs a mace. They walk to the center of the fighting floor, standing across from the two sisters. Yvette's head keeps turning to Chaput and her lips move as she whispers to her partner. Shock appears on Chaput's face. He shakes his head and lowers the mace in his hand, as though whatever Yvette said has drawn the strength from him.

The bell rings. The crossbow sister moves away, loading her weapon. The other sister raises her blade, preparing for whatever attack Chaput and Yvette use.

Yvette raises her axe and quickly brings it down on Chaput's arm. The man screams as blood drips to the ground. In the stunned moment where both sisters stare at the two slaves, Chaput throws his mace with deadly accuracy at the crossbow sister. Unfortunately, in his blinding pain he misjudges the distance and it lands at her feet.

"Damn it, Chaput!" Yvette screams. She raises the axe again, this time bringing it down on his ankle. A crossbow bolt shoots into her side, knocking her off balance, and the axe buries into Chaput's thigh. The swing isn't strong enough to cut through his muscle and he collapses to the ground, dragging Yvette with him.

The sister with the sword moves forward, swinging at Yvette. Yvette quickly rolls off of Chaput as the blade swings down. Chaput screams; the sword stabs into his chest. The sister pulls the blade free, but Yvette already has her axe free of Chaput's thigh. She swings it at the sister, forcing her to jump back. Changing the trajectory of the axe, Yvette cuts through Chaput's ankle, freeing her from his twitching body and grabs the shield Aya left from the previous match.

Yvette raises the shield as a crossbow bolt flies towards her. It bounces off the metal and falls harmlessly to the ground. Yvette uses the shield to break the bolt still in her side, so it won't get in her way.

The sister with the sword lunges for Yvette, but now able to freely move, Yvette bashes the young woman with her shield. The wind is knocked from the sister and Yvette uses her hesitation to bring the axe down on her head. The sword falls and she collapses to the ground. Yvette uses her foot to free the axe from the girl's skull.

By now the other sister has reloaded her crossbow. Another bolt fires at her, but she deflects them with the shield. She charges, using the shield to protect her head and upper body. The sister changes her aim and a bolt buries into Yvette's thigh. She yells in anger and pain as she slams the shield into the sister's weapon, knocking it from her hands. Yvette swings the axe under the girl, knocking her from her feet.

The girl gasps for air, but Yvette doesn't give her a chance to concede the fight. She buries the axe into the young girl's chest.

Blood fills the girl's mouth and spatters over her startled eyes. Yvette pulls the axe free and buries it into the girl's head. She kicks the air, then stills.

The bell rings, ending the fight, Yvette stands and throws her weapon and shield to the ground. She wipes the blood of those she killed from her cheek. She pulls the bolt from her thigh and limps to the gate. After it opens, she walks up to Aya and glares down at her. "Weak links should accept their fate and get out of the way of the strong."

The other slaves gawp at the two in silence. Even Yme doesn't interfere, curious to see how Aya reacts. Yvette grabs the broken bolt in her side.

Aya grabs Yvette's hand, stopping her from pulling the bolt out. "Don't remove it. You might bleed out." She stands, meeting the woman's eyes. "Even strong links rust and break one day."

Yvette sneers and sits as far from Aya as she can, panting. Aya waits until the other woman is seated before sitting back down. Yvette tears strips from her clothes and ties the make-shift bandages around her thigh. She winces and grabs the broken bolt, preparing to pull it free, but freezes. Her eyes flicker to Aya for a moment. She scoffs and crosses her arms, leaving the metal in her side.

Workers clean the fighting area, and clear the bodies for the next match. Dolus Otho calls the next fighters, another repeat: Cellblock C. Ziv and Pangur rise and head into the arena. Their opponents are mercenaries and prove tougher than their previous match. One of the mercenaries dies to a blade in his throat but not without seriously injuring Pangur in the leg. The still-living mercenary gives up, banging the gate to be released.

As Ziv and Pangur return to their seats, Aya eyes the open wound on Pangur's leg. The blood from his wound drips to the floor, pooling beneath him. His skin pales and his eyes droop. Aya fears the wound may be fatal.

Standing, she walks up to the magic blocker, the chains connecting her to Yme straining. "Let me help him."

"You're not allowed to use your magic outside of the cage."

"That leg wound is bleeding too much to be anything other than an arterial cut. He's bleeding out, fast. He has only minutes left."

The magic blocker shakes his head. "You're not allowed to use your magic outside of the cage."

Dolus Otho calls the next fight. Cellblock E.

"Sit down, slave," a second arena worker yells, holding a small club in his hand.

Aya returns to her seat, biting her tongue in anger.

Lili and Géroux stand and enter the cage. Their opponents are first-time fighters in the arena but have fought as mercenaries for years.

The bell rings and Lili and Géroux each grab a weapon and move close together. Their opponents go on the offensive and attack the two.

"You're confusing." Yme keeps his voice low.

"Confusing?" Aya asks. "How am I confusing?"

Lili and Géroux fight in perfect tandem. They understand the best chance of survival is working together and they do so beautifully. Their opponents have trouble finding openings in their defenses but are able to keep their own defenses high as well.

"*If given the choice, I'd help as many as I could.* Isn't that what you were spouting to Daniil and Kylii before your first fight?" Yme asks.

"So?" Aya is slightly surprised he overheard the conversation between her and the twin brothers.

Stifling a laugh, Yme leans close to her. "How is pissing off Yvette helping her?"

"I think it was smart," Sanna from Cellblock F says. Her brown hair is ratty and encompasses her face like a mane.

The man attached to her, Darin, crosses his arms and tugs gently on the chains connecting them. "Sanna, let them be."

"Think about it. Yvette's mad, but now she's considering what you said. She killed her partner, and who knows how many more times she's going to have to fight? Our opponents aren't going to get any easier. She'll soon wish she still had Chaput with her. This is all a show." Sanna waves her arms above her head, her bones long and thin. "All of this is a show for the false king. And we are nothing but kindling to ignite the fire. Yvette tossed in a stick. It was stupid."

"Let them be," Darin says angrily.

"Everyone calls the King false," Aya echoes, and Sanna abruptly turns, her fingers going to her mouth. She chews on her already short nails, her wide eyes moving erratically as she follows the fight.

"I get it," Yme says, understanding dawning. "You purposefully angered Yvette by insinuating she's weak so she would consider why you think that. You want her to realize that killing her partner was a mistake."

"She's right, you know. Yvette won't survive without Chaput," Sanna whispers loudly, then falls silent as her partner tugs roughly on the chains.

Aya shrugs. "Sometimes people need to hear the truth, but most times they need to be smacked over the head with it."

"Pangur? Pangur!" Ziv's terrified voice echoes over the continuing fight.

Pangur has slumped on the bench. Blood drips onto the ground, a large pool spreading around his leg. His face holds an expression Aya knows all too well. The pale face with blue lips and the dark circles under the half-lidded eyes...she's seen it too many times.

The closest Arena worker shakes Pangur by the shoulder, but it's too late. He doesn't move. Aya watches his chest. It does not rise and fall.

"Oh, Gods, Pangur!" It's unclear whether Ziv's terror-filled voice is because of her partner's death or the fact she'll now have to fight alone.

The bell rings and Aya looks out to see that Lili and Géroux stand triumphant. The Arena workers open the cage and remove

Pangur's body from the waiting area to throw it with the remnants of Quin and Chaput. Three dead on the side of the slaves. Seven dead on the side of the fighters.

She wants to believe no more will die. But she knows it's a false belief. *This is all a show. All of this is a show for the false king. And we are nothing but kindling to ignite the fire.*

CHAPTER THIRTY-EIGHT

"It would appear," Dolus Otho's voice interrupts, "one of our slaves took more damage than we realized. Pangur of Cellblock C has died from his injuries. But don't count the Arena slaves out! Lili and Géroux of Cellblock E performed valiantly and overcame their challengers. Who shall face our next challengers, Bruter and Minna? I feel another repeat performance is coming, eager audience!"

The air tenses among the slaves, recalling that their fates were in the hand of chance.

Dolus Otho reaches into the bowl and pulls a stick out enthusiastically, a true showman. "And here it is! Our next match will see the return to the cage of...Cellblock A, Yme and Aya!"

The audience cheers loudly, excitement thundering through the air. The other slaves relax, relief filling them.

Aya is the first to stand, desperate to move away from Pangur's pool of blood. Yme walks next to her, his expression calm.

"You're not upset?" he asks as the gate to the fighting arena is opened.

"Was there any doubt we'd have to fight twice?"

214

Yme grabs her arm and stops her from entering the cage. "I was talking about Pangur. Your expression was…"

"I knew, as soon as he sat down, he was going to die from that leg wound. There was nothing I could do, with our magic blocked. What were the chances they'd let a Healer help him? They don't want us healed. They want us worn down." Arena workers head for them, to force them into the cage.

"No, I mean, your expression was like everyone else's," Yme says. He moves her into the cage before the workers can get too close. "Everyone else's in this place."

She stares at him. "So it bothers you when I appear to show the same indifference to death as those who've been here longer? Like you?"

His calm expression flickers, and she regrets her words.

"No, what you saw was helplessness. I wore the same expression the day my parents died; I assure you." She pulls her arm free of him and grabs a sword from the wall.

She feels his eyes on her, but she refuses to look at him. Instead she focuses on the two men across the cage. One is a large man, Bruter, with muscles bursting beneath his skin. He wears metal on his hands to increase the damage of his hits. The other man is smaller and wears no visible weapon, though the gloves on his hands are missing the thumbs.

The gates clang shut behind the them and Yme stretches his hands out, preparing. Aya feels a tingle of magic in the air and gasps rise from the audience.

Water sluices up from troughs placed around the walls of the arena and enters the cage. It gathers around Yme, circling him.

Aya sizes up the two men as they wait for the bell. Bruter smiles eagerly and nods to the smaller Minna. Minna raises his hands in front of him, clasps his hands together, his thumbs touching, and Aya's eyes widen. She yells, "No!" but her voice is a tiny, ineffective buzz against the beast that is the Arena.

The bell rings. Minna presses his thumbs to his chest and the magic filling the air stops.

The water surrounding Yme falls to the ground. He curses. He tries to summon his other magics, earth or air, but nothing happens.

Grabbing a spear from the cage wall, Yme readies for the large man now running towards him.

Bruter moves much faster than Yme or Aya expect. He reaches Yme quickly and raises his fist, ready to bring it down on Yme. Aya feels a rush of energy inside of her. The air around him is vibrating with magic, and she knows Yme can't even sense it.

Yme raises the spear to stop the blow, but Aya tugs on the chains, moving Yme out of the way of Bruter's punch. As the man's fist misses and hits the ground, the floor cracks, magic filling the space Yme previously occupied.

Yme glances at Aya in surprise. "His magic isn't blocked. How did you know?"

Shaking her head, Aya eyes Minna. "I'm not sure. You *can* fight without your magic, can't you? Or would you like me to take the big guy?" She smiles briefly.

He grips the spear in his hands. "I think I can handle him."

Bruter attacks Yme, forcing him and Aya to move apart. The chains on their arms and legs strain at the distance, and Bruter stomps on the metal links. The sudden jolt throws both Yme and Aya to the ground. Bruter throws his fist at Yme, but Yme is able to roll clear of another magic-powered punch.

Bruter throws another punch with his other hand, but Yme again rolls out of the way, clambering to his feet to clout the large man in the side of the head with the handle of the spear, knocking him back. Yme uses the moment of confusion to kick the legs out from under Bruter. The large man slams into the ground onto his back. Yme stabs the spear at Bruter's chest, but the large man blocks with his metal-covered fists. The tip of Yme's spear hits the metal and breaks off from the pole.

Yme doesn't hesitate and pulls a knife from Bruter's belt. He buries the blade into the larger man's side before moving away from Bruter's flailing fists.

Aya does her best to make sure the chains connecting her and Yme don't interfere with his fighting, but her eyes constantly return to Minna, the magic blocker. He focuses on the fight between Yme and Bruter carefully. His hands shake slightly at the strain of blocking Yme and Aya's magic but letting Bruter's run free. It must take a lot of concentration and focus to block two out of three magic users.

Aya reaches down to where her magic lives. The familiar feeling of a block stops her from reaching too deep, but it's different than when the Arena workers block her magic. It's far weaker. She pushes a little and feels her magic turning beneath the block. She studies Minna's face, expecting to see him reacting to her push.

But Minna is utterly focused on Yme and Bruter.

Bruter is back on his feet, keeping Yme on the move. Yme uses the spear pole to keep Bruter's fists far from him, using the wood to knock at the wrists. But then Yme steps on the broken tip of his spear and stumbles. Bruter takes advantage and punches low. Yme manages to dodge most of the hit, but a corner of Bruter's fist swipes his side.

The magic behind the punch makes it feel like a landed blow, and Yme grabs his side with one hand and gasps. Aya can't tell if any serious damage was done, but judging from the pained expression on his face, the chances are high.

Yme recovers and grabs a new spear from the wall, this one made completely of metal. He dodges Bruter's punches and circles the man. Aya does her best to follow him, keeping the chains loose enough so Yme can fight.

Bruter lunges forward, catching Yme off guard and lands a punch in his gut. Yme gasps and kneels on the ground. He grabs his side but screams as soon as he touches it. Before he can recover, Bruter grabs the chain connecting Yme and Aya's arms. He smiles and Aya feels his dark magic thrum in the air.

Bruter takes a deep breath and turns, rearing his arm back. He yells and throws with magic-enhanced strength at both Yme and Aya across the fighting arena. They slam into each other, hitting the ground and dropping their weapons.

Loud sounds of shock and surprise make their way from the stands to the fighting floor. Klaeon leaps to his feet, a large smile on his face. He applauds with excitement and laughs loudly before shouting something to his second in command, Teron.

Aya tries to sit up, but a shooting pain in her right arm stops her. She rolls onto her side and uses her good arm to drag herself towards Yme, who is sitting up, holding his left arm. A large lump disfigures his shoulder, and now she understands the pain in her right arm. The force of Bruter's throw pulled the chains hard enough to dislocate both Yme and Aya's shoulders. Yme's gasps are short and quick. He tries to move his arm, but a pained yelp escapes him.

While Bruter and Minna gloat, she stops crawling, places her hand on her right arm, and closes her eyes. She reaches deep down to her magic, feeling it pounding against the block. She emboldens it, and it leaks through. She pushes it to numb the pain shooting through her. Slowly the pain fades, and she finds the strength to sit upright. She grabs Yme's left arm, ignoring his cries of protest. Sweat beads up on her forehead as she forces her magic into his arm. She sees the dislocation and her magic numbs the area. With a deep breath she pops the bone back into place, something she's done hundreds of times without her magic, but never one-handed. She quickly checks for damage caused by the injury, but nothing is torn.

Then she sends her magic to where Bruter's hit landed. She sees it, broken ribs tearing into skin and muscles. She draws more of her magic from behind the block and heals Yme quickly. She knows the price of going this fast will be great, but she can't let him fight in such a condition.

Aya opens her eyes and sees the look of surprise on Yme's face. He moves his arm around cautiously before shoving her away, hard. The shock of the sudden push knocks the wind from her lungs, but she realizes why he pushed her away as Bruter's fist slams into the ground between them, creating a small crater. Then he goes in for another punch, aiming for Aya. She rolls away, narrowly avoiding the hit.

As she rolls, she angles herself to push against the ground, popping her own arm back into place. With her shoulder no longer dislocated, she uses her magic to heal the small wounds caused by the injury. She climbs to her feet and moves away from the large man. She spies Minna, the magic blocker. Aya grabs a knife from the sand and throws it at him.

Minna flinches as the knife flies towards him, and he tries to clasp his hands together to stop the blade. As soon as his thumbs leave his chest, the ground beneath him opens up and he is swallowed up to his shoulders. He can no longer block the magic.

With a triumphant yelp, Yme grabs the metal spear and swings it at Bruter. The large man grabs the spear in his hands and laughs. Aya grabs the sword she dropped and stabs him in the back with the blade. He yells and releases the spear. Yme steps, running the spear into Bruter's chest. The man falls back, burying Aya's sword further into his back. Blood pools on the ground beneath him.

"I concede!" Minna yells from his encrusted spot, over the audience's roar of approval.

Aya's knees shake beneath her and she falls to the ground. Yme walks to her side and touches where the ribs had been broken. He stares down at her.

She smiles up at him. "I thought you could handle him?"

He laughs as the bell rings. "Your magic wasn't blocked?" Yme asks as he and Aya return to their seats. "Just mine?"

Shaking her head, Aya motions towards the Arena worker. "He wasn't as good at it as the Arena workers. I think it was because he still needed to let Bruter's magic through. It took too much concentration."

"But how did you know Bruter's magic wasn't blocked?"

Earth magic users free Minna and fix the ground enough for the next fight.

"Some magic vibrates the air." Aya looks at Yme. "You can't sense it, can you?" She knows the answer but wonders how aware of it Yme is.

"No. But Daniil and Kylii have spoken about it before. They say magic fills the air around me. Not just my air magic, all of it. They described it like that sense before lightning strikes." He stares at his hand. "I've tried to sense the magic of others, but I've only felt it once."

"When was that?" Aya asks.

Yme hesitates. "When my fire was taken away from me." His eyes darken and he clenches his hand into a fist.

As much as her curiosity wants her to ask more questions, she feels a stronger urge to give him time.

CHAPTER THIRTY-NINE

DOLUS OTHO ANNOUNCES THE NEXT FIGHT: CELLBLOCK F, SANNA and Darin, facing more members of the Bloody Butchers. The combatants appear evenly matched. Sanna's odd movements make it easy for her to dodge attacks. Strange balls of light form in Darin's hands and he throws them at the fighters. Aya has never seen this magic before. One of the balls hits the arm of one of the Bloody Butchers. His sleeve catches fire, but he's able to rip the cloth off before the flames reach his skin.

The fight goes on much longer than any of the previous fights. Despite herself, Aya feels her eyelids droop, sleep threatening to overpower her. She leans back against the railing, her head resting on the top wooden beam. She closes her eyes and listens to the sounds of the audience and those fighting.

What are Daniil and Kylii doing? Are they worried for Yme and Aya? What about those others who arrived with her?

Then her mind wanders far from the Arena. What's happening back in her home? Has Oula Village recovered from Jaxon's attack? Is Iria all right? So many questions flood her mind, an oddly welcoming distraction from her current predicament. But as she thinks about her old home, other memories come to her—painful ones of her parents.

221

The few times her parents used their magic in front of her were rare, and only due to true emergencies. The reason became clear when her father became ill. Aya's mother never used the term Life Healer, but she told Aya the magic inside of her was special. And the price of being special was steep.

After her parents' deaths, Aya feared the magic that had yet to appear within her. Would the same illness that took her parents from her lead to her own death? Then Elder Mircien suggested she learn natural healing from Iria. Accompanying Iria on many of his calls to heal encouraged her to rethink her fear. Her parents knew the consequences of using their magic, but it never stopped them from helping those in need.

Someone leans against Aya, and she opens her eyes. Yme has fallen asleep. His head is resting on her shoulder and his breath dances on her skin. His arms cross his chest even in sleep.

Aya glances around at the other slaves and notices a number have also taken the time to catch some sleep. Her eyes move to the fighting arena. Sanna and Darin are still fighting, small cuts the only sign of struggle. The two Bloody Butchers are breathing heavily, blood from their own injuries covering their arms, legs, and faces.

Even the audience has lost most of its energy. Aya sees many walking around the seating areas, taking the time to find food and drink. Many yawn, stretching their arms over their heads. A few even huddle together, seeming to play a game to pass the time. The sun is high in the sky, ready to soon begin its descent.

Aya spies Dolus Otho sitting above Blood King Klaeon's private box, his head resting on his hand. He eats fruit from a gold bowl, but his attention seems to be more on the man below him.

Blood King Klaeon scrutinizes the fight with a boredom similar to many in the audience. His second in command, Teron, is nowhere to be seen; instead one of Klaeon's other guards is standing in the other man's usual position. Klaeon angles his head so he can speak to Dolus Otho, and the announcer immediately perks up. They speak only for a moment before Dolus Otho nods vigorously and the two return their attention to the fighting.

Aya's arm tingles uncomfortably but fears moving it would wake Yme. She shifts slightly, attempting a little relief.

"Concede! Gods, we concede!" One of the Bloody Butchers walks to the gate on the opposing side and bangs the hilt of his sword on the metal.

The bell rings louder than previously. The slaves jump at the sudden noise. Yme, realizing he's using Aya as a pillow, sits up quickly.

Dolus Otho stands and, with a brief glance at Klaeon, says, "Another victory for the slaves!"

The audience cheers, but not at the usual volume. The Arena workers quickly open the gate to let the Bloody Butchers out, but before the workers can open the gate for the slaves, Dolus Otho stops them.

"Loyal audience! It would appear surprises never cease." Dolus Otho holds up the next drawn stick. "A repeat performance for Cellblock F."

Sanna and Darin sag, their bodies rolling with sweat, but they turn to face the Arena once more.

"Though I do believe these new challengers won't be as eager for a drawn-out fight as the Bloody Butchers. Welcome to the Arena our own...Seera and Banger!"

If any were still dozing, the announcement of the first challenger wakes them up. The head of the Arena workers walks up the stairs and into the cage. Following her is a large man covered in sweat and soot. He carries the largest hammer Aya has ever seen.

"What's the head blacksmith doing fighting with Seera?" Yvette asks to no one in particular.

"What's Seera doing fighting at all?" Géroux asks. The other slaves nod and murmur.

Sanna and Darin watch the two familiar opponents enter the

223

cage. Exhaustion weighs the slaves' bodies down and their movements are slow. They face the woman who runs the entire Arena and one of the men who forges the many weapons on the walls of the cage.

The bell rings. Sanna and Darin grab fresh weapons and run at their opponents. Seera doesn't move, watching the approaching slaves with her eternal cold smirk.

Yme leaps to his feet, surprising Aya. "Don't attack from the front! Banger is a magma mage!"

His words reach the two drained slaves too late. Banger swings his large hammer down in front of him. Where he strikes the ground the earth heats. As though alive, lava races across the arena floor. Sanna and Darin can't stop or dodge in time. The lave reaches them and their bodies burst into flame. Their screams echo through the Arena but die quickly as they disappear in the molten lava.

Lifting his hammer, Banger rests the large weapon across his shoulders. The lava cools as soon as the hammer is off the ground, leaving behind only black–charred earth. Nothing remains of Sanna and Darin, not even their chains.

The bell cracks the silence and the audience erupts back into life.

Aya's heart pounds loudly in her ears as Seera slaps the back of the large man next to her. The laughter escaping from the head of the Arena's mouth sends a chill through her. She'd suspected the magic users working in the Arena were powerful, and now those suspicions are confirmed.

Escaping the Arena is entirely impossible.

CHAPTER FORTY

"A SPECTACULAR PERFORMANCE! YOU CAN ALWAYS DEPEND ON OUR Lady of the Arena and the Magma Blacksmith to give us a show! How could we possibly top that?" Dolus Otho leans forward as though he were whispering in confidence, but his voice remains magically at full volume. "Let's try."

Cellblock D, Leid, is called next. The emotionless man stands and walks into the cage. The chains still connected to his arm and leg drag behind him. He doesn't seem to notice them as he faces his opponents.

Aya's hands shake. She can still see Sanna and Darin disappearing in flames. She can still hear their screams. She tries to keep the nerves hidden, but fails to do so.

"What's wrong?" Yme asks.

"It happened so quickly. Sanna and Darin couldn't do anything," Aya says.

"They fought that first match to give the rest of us a chance to rest. They could've ended their fight much sooner, but they gave us a brief moment of respite. They were punished for it. That's all."

"What do you mean?"

225

"Seera and Banger don't fight. They execute," Yme says, returning to the fight in front of them.

The two chosen to fight Leid don't fare any better than the first two who faced him. Leid manages to catch one with his chain and buries the man's own weapon into his head. The second fighter manages to avoid the chains, but not the body of his fallen comrade. Once he hits the ground, the fight is over. Leid pulls the weapon from the corpse and kills the remaining fighter.

The next match is Cellblock C, Ziv alone, since Pangur died of his wounds. She faces two women. Both are water mages and, without her partner, Ziv is killed. It's the quickest match, but Aya remembers Ziv's eyes when she walked into the arena. She knew she wasn't going to make it out alive.

"Our next challengers are on special loan from our own King, two of his own guards eager to show their strength. And who will they be facing?" Dolus Otho reaches into the bowl of names and eagerly pulls out the next stick. "Cellblock A, Yme and Aya! Will their third fight be their last?"

Yme stands, glowering. "Special loan, my ass. Klaeon is up to something."

Aya follows Yme into the cage. Their opponents enter the fighting arena and already Aya sees a difference in their carriage compared to other fighters. The two men draw their weapons before saluting Klaeon. The Blood King's smile widens, and he waves his hand at his men.

Aya grabs a large shield from the wall, then a dagger. She glances down at the cart holding the dead bodies of Quin, Chaput, Pangur, and Ziv. There weren't even bones left of Sanna and Darin.

Her breathing quickens and she steps behind Yme. It takes everything in her power to not collapse to the ground and cry. *How can the audience enjoy this? We're dying in here, and they cheer.*

Yme eyes the two soldiers in front of them before turning to face Aya. He takes her head in his hands and forces her to look at him. She knows he can see the fear in her eyes.

"Forget about all the previous matches and focus on this one," he tells her, his voice low and calming.

"Can you read minds on top of elemental magic?" Aya jokes, but her voice shakes.

A small smile appears on his lips. "Only when I need to. Are you ready?"

She nods.

The bell rings and the two soldiers immediately sprint towards Aya. They move so fast that she barely manages to block the first blade with her shield. A second blade arcs in a blur towards her and she knows she can't stop it.

The earth rises between her and the soldier's attack. It knocks the sword upward, but the soldier keeps his grip and dodges back from the wall of earth. Yme tries to attack with a fist covered in rock. The soldier uses the butt of his sword to hit Yme in his torso. He gasps and grabs his belly, stepping back.

The soldier swings his sword at the wall of earth, breaking it. The other soldier presses down on Aya's shield with his sword. She grips the shield with both hands, being careful with the dagger in her right hand. She hears the wall of earth breaking next to her and sees the sword moving closer to her.

She needs to move. Bracing herself, she angles her shield down to the right, turning her body with the force. The soldier's sword slides across the smooth metal and the soldier falls. Aya follows through with her turn and stabs her dagger at the soldier's back.

The second soldier's sword blocks Aya's dagger, and he raises his other hand and punches her hard across the face. She stumbles back, the pain in her cheek making her see stars. A knee to her stomach catches her and she doubles over. The air is forced from her lungs and she feels what little is in her stomach threaten to rise out of her mouth. She falls to her knees, her dagger and shield falling to the ground.

A rush of wind moves around her, slamming into the two soldiers standing over her with their weapons drawn. They're sent flying back, hitting the walls of the cage with loud bangs.

The audience cheers and Aya glances up at Yme. His hands are outstretched in front of him, his breathing is ragged. Lowering his arms, he places a hand on his side. He inhales sharply and winces.

"What's wrong?" Aya asks, grabbing her shield and dagger.

Yme takes a shaky breath. "That bastard broke my ribs."

Moving close to him, Aya moves her dagger to her left hand and places her right hand gently on his arm. "It didn't look like he hit you that hard and I didn't feel any magic strengthening him." Still, she concentrates on Yme's abdomen and sees he's speaking the truth. The bottom two ribs on his left side are broken.

"The impact...I think he's a force mage," Yme says.

"Force mage?"

"The force of his hit is more powerful at the point of impact."

"Then why did it take him so long to clear that wall of earth?" Aya asks, remembering the man struggling to reach her.

"It might only work when striking something alive."

Aya heals Yme while the two soldiers climb back to their feet and adjust their shoulders, checking for injuries.

Aya starts eyes the two men. "Are they focusing their attacks on me?"

Yme rubs the area where his ribs healed. "Special orders from Klaeon, I'd wager."

"Fantastic." Aya finishes and smiles at him. "Were there any rules about breaking the chains?"

Yme raises his left arm and stares at the chains connecting them. "No rules at all, that I recall. Why? Are the chains infused with magic?"

Shaking her head, Aya grabs the dagger with her right hand and steps away from him. "Just iron. Can you break it?"

The soldiers run towards Aya, ready to strike. A sharp tug on the chains nearly pulls her off her feet. She looks at Yme in surprise.

"Never know 'til we try." Yme pulls both chains on their wrists and ankles taut. He stomps the ground with his free foot and a thick wall of earth rises between the soldiers and Aya. The wall completely blocks the soldiers from the half of the arena Aya and Yme are in.

Yme grabs a rock from the ground and slams it down on the chain. It crumbles in his hand and he curses. Breathing deeply, he raises a hand and a large boulder emerges from the ground. He flicks his wrist and the boulder slams down on the metal.

Aya eyes the wall of earth in front of her. "How long is it going to take?"

"Almost done with the first one," Yme says. The metal chain bends at a strange angle, the link straining to hold on.

Loud pounding echoes in the arena. Small pieces of earth crumble and fall from the wall in front of them. Aya grips her dagger tightly in her hand, the chain still pulling on her wrist as Yme's boulder slams down again.

The first chain breaks and their arms are able to move freely, though with half a chain still hanging to the ground. Yme raises the boulder over the chain connecting their feet.

A hole appears in the wall in front of Aya. Through it, she sees the soldiers doing their best to tear the wall down. "They're getting through."

"Almost finished." Yme keeps his focus on the boulder cutting through the chain.

A second hole breaks through the wall close to the first. The earth between the holes crumbles as the two soldiers break it down. They work to widen the opening enough to climb through.

The pull on Aya's ankle disappears and she looks down. Chains are still connected to her wrist and ankle, but now she and Yme have the freedom to move around the arena independent of each other.

Yme raises his free hand, and water flies through the bars of the cage. The audience murmurs with excitement as the water gathers around Yme and forms a disk shape, spinning faster and faster. He holds the boulder with one hand and the water disk with the other.

"You ready?" he asks.

She raises her weapons. "Guess we'll find out."

CHAPTER FORTY-ONE

THE WALL OF EARTH CRUMBLES APART, AND AYA PREPARES FOR THE attacks. The force mage runs at her first, the hammer he used to break through the wall above his head. He swings it down, but she dodges, feeling lighter, freer, without having to watch Yme's position as well as her own. But then the force mage grabs the chain still attached to Aya's wrist and pulls her towards him.

He swings the hammer as she stumbles close, but before the heavy metal hits her, water slams into the force mage's head. The strike stuns him enough to loosen his grip on the hammer and it falls to the ground. He releases Aya's chain and she jumps away.

The second soldier is right behind the first, his hammer hanging low as he reaches for Aya. Earth rises and tries to catch his hand, but he swings the hammer up, breaking the earth. He dodges around a second attempt and closes the distance.

There is no fair fight in the Arena.

The soldier swings his hammer, and Aya dodges. But he easily changes direction and slams it down on the loose chain. She's jerked to a stop. A fist rushes at her face.

You either learn to fight or you die.

The punch sends a wave of shock through her. Aya's knees

give out beneath her, but she tugs at her magic and kicks at the soldier's leg. At the moment of contact, her magic surges into the man. She feels the bone give beneath her foot and the soldier yells out in pain. He struggles to shift his weight to his good leg. He's able to remain standing, but Aya is free to take her chain from beneath his hammer.

She scurries to the wall of the cage and grabs an axe. The weight of the weapon is heavy, but there are no smaller weapons close by. The soldier limps towards her, wounded fury in his eyes. A roar from the crowd freezes both Aya and the wounded soldier; they realize what Yme has done.

The ground is wet with water and blood from the spinning disk, floating at neck height. Aya's eyes move to where the mage's head should be, but there's nothing. Yme's breathing is ragged, and blood covers his face and chest. He lowers his hand and the water disk falls, harmless as rain, to the ground. His other hand releases and the mage's body is allowed to fall.

The audience's cheers fill the arena, even the slaves rising to their feet and pumping their fists in joyous awe.

Aya and the wounded soldier lock eyes. She sees panic. Not fear, but a rush of thoughts. She can tell he's thinking about how to handle both her and Yme. His eyes return to Yme, wanting to keep the more dangerous one in his sights.

Yme steps over the force mage's body and moves towards the wounded soldier. He raises his hand, the chain still dangling from his wrist, and a wind blows around the three.

Aya lifts the axe in her hands, holding it in front of her defensively. She watches the soldier, ready for his next move, but praying for him to concede. His broken leg drags on the ground as he hops to back away.

A sharp whistle cuts through the air. The soldier stops, eyes widening. He turns and stares at the private box. Aya sees Klaeon standing at the edge. As she notices the barest of nods from the man, a chill moves up her spine. He returns to his seat, his smile growing.

The wounded soldier stands straight, balancing his weight on his good leg. He closes his eyes and takes a deep breath.

Aya feels magic filling the air around him. Yme approaches the soldier, oblivious to the building magic. "Wait!" she yells. "Stay back!"

The soldier opens his eyes and a blinding white light erupts from him.

Aya raises one arm to block the light, lowering the axe. The light fades away and she realizes the sounds of the arena are gone. All she hears is wind and the rustling of leaves.

Lowering her arm, shock fills Aya. She's home. Her house is in front of her, the surrounding forest of Foula Valley almost glowing green with the sunlight. She glances around, turning in circles. The axe falls from her hand and she fights the tears threatening to form.

Standing on the path leading to Oula Village are Elder Mircien and Iria, their hands clasped together. Their other hands are in front of them, reaching for Aya. She takes a tentative step towards them, her breath coming in gasps.

"Mircien," she whispers.

Two figures step out from behind the two elders and the tears she's been fighting flow.

"Mom, Dad."

Her parents smile at her, embracing the way she always remembered. They raise their hands, too, waiting for her. She reaches out, but something feels wrong. The wind is blowing harder and harder, making the trees sway. The gusts hit her in waves, knocking her back.

She looks from her parents to Iria and Mircien, their faces never changing, the wind seeming not to touch them. The ground shakes beneath her feet and the sound of water hitting metal fills her ears.

This is wrong.

Aya remembers the flash of light, the wounded soldier. She's not home, she's still in the arena. This magic is forcing her to see something not actually in front of her.

The forest disappears. Mircien and Iria disappear. The arena surrounds her, and she sees the crowd enthralled in the match. Aya spies the wounded soldier standing across from her, his eyes now white. Realizing she's broken from his magic, the soldier awkwardly shuffles farther from her and shifts his focus entirely to Yme.

The wind Aya felt, the earth shaking, and the water against metal...those are real. Turning, she sees him...her partner.

Yme stands with his back to the wounded soldier, but she can see his face. His eyes are the same white as the soldier's, but it's the rage darkening his expression that terrifies her. His magic electrifies the air. Wind blows, knocking into Aya and escaping the caged arena. The audience is both excited and fearful of the rushes of wind hitting them. The ground around Yme cracks, shaking the arena. Water attacks an invisible foe, slamming into the wall of the caged fighting area.

He stops attacking the wall, turns slowly as though hearing a sound, and faces Aya. The rage changes to heartbreaking pain as his eyes lower to an unseen figure on the ground.

"Niya," Yme whispers, horror in his voice. Emotions move quickly across his face, a hideous mosaic of pain and rage. His eyes rise, seeing Aya but not really seeing her.

Seeing whoever he believes is standing in her place.

The pain and sadness are gone, replaced exclusively with rage. The earth shakes beneath Aya and wind surrounds her. Yme holds his hands up, water gathering above his right.

Aya understands. The wounded soldier has somehow conjured up in Yma a memory from before he came to the arena...before he lost his fire. A terrifying thing, driving Yme into an uncontrollable rage.

Rage that is now aimed at her.

The ground rises beneath her, the sudden movement

throwing her off balance. Wind slams into her, throwing her to the rising ground. She gasps in shock but knows she can't stay still. She rolls onto her stomach before scrambling to her feet. She feels a change in the air and dodges to her right. A line of water slams into the ground where she'd been lying.

Locking eyes on Yme, Aya sees he's thrown his left hand towards her, but nothing happens. Confusion causes Yme to hesitate. In his memory, he has not yet lost his fire. She uses his stunned moment to grab her discarded axe.

She hears the crowd murmuring with excitement as the wind dies down. She imagines the shock of seeing two slaves who had worked together now fighting each other. As one of the two slaves, however, she finds it terrifying. Especially with the other being Yme.

The moment of confusion passes and Yme runs at Aya. He swings a fist at her, wind magic curving the air around it.

She holds the axe up, the flat side making contact with the fist, but the blast of wind sends her a few steps back. A second fist, covered in earth, zooms to uppercut her. She leans back; his second hit misses her. She uses the handle of the axe to hit him in the back of the knee, dropping him to the ground.

She knows it will only be for a short time, and moves away from him. Yme is back to his feet quickly and stomps one foot onto the ground. The earth around her feet softens to fine sand and she struggles to find footing. Her ankle rolls. She falls onto the softened ground.

Again, he thrusts out his left hand, expecting fire, and again nothing happens. Frustration fills his face as he stares at his hand.

Aya crawls out of the sand. The confusion in his eyes reminds her of how she realized she was inside of an illusion. She sees the white filling his eyes fade slightly, the magic weakening. But then the white takes over again, the confusion fades, and the rage returns.

The wounded soldier's focus is entirely on Yme. Without her splitting his magic, the soldier's full force keeps Yme trapped in the illusion.

He can't break free on his own. And if I don't free him soon, he's going to kill me.

CHAPTER FORTY-TWO

The Arena isn't just about strength but outsmarting your opponents.

Kylii's words echo in Aya's head. She's barely keeping up with Yme; how, she doesn't know. His fighting is more instinctual than skillful, and she wonders if being trapped in the illusion might mean he's forgotten his skills from the arena.

Would it be better to go for the wounded soldier? Or try to snap Yme out of the illusion?

She doesn't know enough about this kind of magic. She feels it in the air but doesn't understand how it affects them. This magic doesn't require contact of any kind, doesn't need the user to perform any movement. All he needs is concentration, and yet he can still watch Aya while his magic focuses on Yme. Even his broken leg doesn't waver him.

Which means he's aware of me. But with Yme blind...

Aya bolts straight at the soldier, but Yme creates a wall of earth between them. She turns to the right, running along the wall. Water splashes the ground in front of her, freezing. She slips on the ice, but slams the axe into the ground, breaking the ice. The shards cut her ankles, but she keeps moving.

Following around the wall of earth, she again aims for the wounded soldier. He takes a step back, his broken leg dragging.

The wall of earth explodes, turning to fine sand and filling the air. Wind blows it, creating a small sandstorm. The grains get into Aya and the wounded soldier's eyes. The soldier winces, struggling to move away from Aya. She closes the distance between them, throwing the axe at him. The weight is too heavy, and it lands harmlessly in front of him.

Pick it up, pick it up, Aya chants in her head.

The wounded soldier awkwardly leans down and picks up the axe. He stares at her and raises the blade, readying to throw. She knows he won't have trouble with the weight.

His body jerks and his eyes widen, the white fading away. He drops the axe and falls forward. A sharpened spear of earth sticks out of the wounded soldier's back.

Standing behind him is Yme, his eyes fading from the white to silver and filling with confusion. "What...?"

The sandstorm stops. The arena is eerily quiet as the sand falls to the ground.

Aya gives a shaky breath. "You were stuck in an illusion."

The bell rings loudly, igniting screams of approval in the crowd.

Yme's eyes move from the dead soldier to her. "*He caused the...illusion?*" Anger vibrates through his voice.

The spear of earth from the soldier's back rises, blood covering its pointed end. Aya watches the spear, nerves causing her to take a step back. "He wanted us to attack each other. You thought I was somebody else and...you thought you still had your fire magic."

His attention lowers to the cuts on her ankles and the burns on her skin from the sand. "I did that to you?"

She shrugs. "You didn't know it was me."

"Did I...did I say anything?"

Should I tell him? Should I ask him who he saw? Aya hesitates, the pause seeming to last forever. "You said Niya."

The expression Yme aims at the dead man is the most terrifying Aya's ever seen. Yme grabs the spear of earth and slams it into the soldier's head over and over. Aya turns away from the bloody sight, gasping in shock.

The door to the cage opens and workers of the arena enter, including the magic blocker. He meets her eyes before cutting off her and Yme's magic.

"What a treat!" Dolus Otho's voice booms. "The first to ever survive against our star fighter! Looks like we'll need to keep our eyes on the Healer."

The workers try to usher Yme and Aya out, but Yme refuses to move, threatening the workers with the spear of earth in his hands.

"Shall I draw the next name?" Dolus asks to stall for time, but this draws an excited murmur of cheers from the crowd.

"Enough of this!" Yme throws the earth spear into the wall of the cage. The force causes the spear to break apart. He turns to the private box. "If you want us dead, fight us yourself!"

The audience soon grows silent at Yme's bold words. The workers stop attempting to drag Aya out and wait to see the Blood King's response. Aya watches the still man sitting patiently in the private box. By now the sun is lower, her stomach growls, and everyone must be terribly thirsty. When will this end?

Klaeon stands and walks to the edge of his box. His eyes never leave Yme, showing no interest in his two dead soldiers. "Our star fighter seems to be bored with the Arena. Perhaps he needs something to remind him who is the slave and who is king." He motions to Dolus Otho above him. The other man leans over to hear what the Blood King has to say.

"Remove Yme from the cage," Dolus announces. "The next fight will be the Healer alone!"

CHAPTER FORTY-THREE

BEFORE THEY CAN PROCESS DOLUS OTHO'S WORDS, THE ARENA workers drag Yme from the caged arena and Aya is locked in, alone. She stares behind her at the slaves, confused.

The door across from her opens and two women enter. Aya faces them, her heart pounding in her chest.

"Welcome to the Arena the Bowton Sisters. Perhaps you know them better as TrueStrike Faye and Jera Ironwind?" Dolus Otho's voice is drowned out by the excited cheers of the crowd.

Clanging on the door behind Aya grabs her attention. She turns and sees Yme holding onto the metal bars. "You can do this."

"If I die, it's your fault." Aya means it as a joke, but the fear inside of her fills the warning with truth. "Any tips, partner?"

"They've fought many battles in the arena, but rarely two on one. Don't get stuck between them...unless that's part of your strategy."

"Not helpful."

He glances behind her at the two fighters. "They're both using weapons to keep you away. Get in close to limit their attacks."

The bell rings and Aya grabs a dagger from the wall. "That's helpful."

She watches the women. They curiously meet her gaze. Neither appear particularly threatened by Aya. One carries a spiked ball on a chain, which she lazily swings in slow circles. The other has a spear, leaning on it as she stares at Aya.

"We get stuck with the easy kill. How is that fair?" the one with the spear says. *She must be TrueStrike Faye,* Aya thinks.

"At least she's a Rare Kind. We'll get more gold for her," ball-and-chain, Jera Ironwind, answers. "Just keep her from healing herself. You gonna try to break our legs, too, healer?"

Aya bites her lower lip. These two had been watching the previous matches.

But so have I.

Aya raises her knife in front of her, defensively. She reaches deep inside, the warmth of her magic gathering in her chest.

"Not gonna talk, huh?" Jera asks, spinning the chain in her hand faster. The spiked ball blurs as it moves faster and faster.

"That's fine," Faye says. "We ain't ones for talking either." She lowers the tip of the spear to the ground in one hand, her other hand in front of her defensively.

Jera slowly walks to Aya's right. Aya counters the move, keeping both women in front of her. It's difficult, but she doesn't want to get stuck between them. Not yet.

Which one will attack first? I thought ball and chain might, but I can't lower my guard to the spear holder. Tension fills Aya's muscles, her magic responding with flutters in her chest. *If they won't attack, that leaves it to me.*

Aya runs towards Faye, surprising the woman. But not enough. The spear rises quickly, almost a blur. Aya dodges the point, but not the pole swinging into her side. The wood hits her rib, sending a vibration of pain through her chest. The flutters of her magic spring to life, soothing the pain away. She tries to grab the pole, but Faye spins away, pulling clear of Aya's hand.

Movement in the corner of Aya's eye catches her attention. She falls to the ground and rolls as the spiked ball flies overhead. If she hadn't moved, the ball would've collided with her head. She manages to get back on her feet and uses the chain on her arm to tangle around the chain.

"Bad move," Jera says, smirking. She wraps the chain around her arm and turns sharply. The sudden tug drags Aya towards Jera.

But Aya expected it and uses the momentum to increase her speed. She slams into Jera, knocking the wind out of the woman in a loud whoosh. She buries her dagger into Jera's inner thigh, then lets her go. The time Jera spends pulling the weapon free allows Aya to detangle her chain and grab a spiked club from the cage walls. She moves away from the wall, her eyes on the wounded fighter.

Jera jerks the blade out and glares at Faye. "Why didn't you stop her?"

"You're the one who made the leg comment. I thought it was ironic," Faye's face moves in a twisted smile as she circles behind Aya.

The blood rolls down Jera's leg thick and dark, rolling to the sandy earth. Taking a step, Jera's face pales and she collapses to the ground.

"Jera!" Faye yells to her sister.

Now Aya rushes at Faye, swinging the spiked club into her side. She grabs the spear pole and pulls the woman close. "I can save her if you concede right now."

Faye looks into Aya's eyes, gasping for air and wincing at the spikes in her side. She tugs on her spear, trying to free it.

"She's got maybe one minute before she's beyond saving. You might have less. *Concede*," Aya demands.

Faye's eyes glance to her sister then to Aya. Her eyebrows lower and her lips curl down into a frown. "This is a trick."

"You can wait and find out or you can concede right now,

and I'll heal her and you." Aya tightens her grip on the spear, feeling Faye pulling. "You're both running out of time."

Faye's foot kicks Aya in the stomach. Aya gasps and releases the spear, falling back. The spiked club falls from her hand as she wraps her arms around her stomach. Faye places a hand on her bleeding side, then grips her spear with both hands and attacks.

The spear jabs toward Aya and she dodges as best she can, but the tip stabs into her left arm, making her scream. Faye pulls the spear free and aims for Aya's middle. When Aya dodges, Faye turns and slams her elbow into Aya's tender stomach. Before Aya can catch her breath, Faye uses the bottom of the spear to sweep the feet out from under Aya. Aya falls onto her back and the last of her air is forced out of her lungs. She feels something hard lying in the sand against the back of her head.

Faye slams on top of Aya, her knees on either side of Aya's torso. She lowers the butt of the spear to Aya's throat, but Aya is able to catch the pole with both hands to keep the wood from cutting off her air. Faye pushes with all her strength to force the spear pole lower.

Reaching with one hand, Aya feels the hard thing under her head. She grips the wooden handle and with one motion, pulls the axe up from where it was buried in the sand. She feels her magic fill her arm and give her muscles the strength to drive the axe into Faye's neck. The spear pole at Aya's throat stops pushing down. Faye's eyes widen and her mouth opens in shock. Blood drips from the neck wound onto Aya's face. Faye's eyes glaze over and she falls to the side.

Gasping for air, Aya stares at the roof of the cage. She turns her head to the side and sees Jera still lying motionless on the ground. Behind the body she sees movement beyond the cage. The slaves are on their feet, cheering for her. The realization brings the sound of the Arena back to her.

Aya slowly sits up, shoving the rest of Faye's body off her. She climbs to her feet and spots Yme, knuckles white on the bars of the cage. A smile breaks out over his face, he nods at her.

She walks towards him, her legs shaking as the adrenaline and her magic fades. She grabs the bars. "I did it. I guess my death isn't your fault...yet."

"Not today," Yme says.

The guards open the door to the cage and enter the arena to clear the bodies. They pull the axe from Faye's neck and lift Jera from the large puddle of her blood. Aya walks toward the door of the cage, using the bars to keep her legs from giving out. Yme follows along the cage to meet her at the door.

"Congratulations to the Life Healer," Blood King Klaeon's voice booms through the air.

Aya freezes, her eyes widening. She turns to the royal box and sees him watching her. Beneath the smirk she can see fury sparking.

Klaeon stands at the edge of the royal box, his mismatched eyes never looking away from Aya. "An impressive display. Deserving of a reward."

Aya feels a hand on her arm and Yme pulls her quickly from the cage and back to the seating area before the king can say anything more. She sits down next to Leid, not caring how frightening the other slaves find him. He stares at her in silence, his eyes not betraying his thoughts.

"You're bleeding," Leid says, his eyes lowering to the injury on Aya's arm.

Aya places her hand over the wound. She heals it before the magic blocker cuts her off. Revealing the healed arm, she raises her eyes to Leid. He leans his head to the side and raises his hand. He pokes the healed skin and makes an interested noise before turning away from her. He crosses his arms and watches the workers inside the cage.

The cage workers finish clearing the arena and await orders. The audience murmurs with anticipation and excitement for the next twist of the fights.

Dolus Otho silences the crowd with the raise of his hands.

"Our King was so impressed with that last fight he has decided to reward the slaves. The fights are over." He pauses.

The audience erupts in shock and disagreement, but Aya watches Dolus Otho. She sees through the theatrics to the lie. *But what does it mean?* Aya wonders.

CHAPTER FORTY-FOUR

"THE FIGHTS ARE OVER...BUT THE SPECTACLE IS ABOUT TO BEGIN!" Dolus Otho announces. "Our King has decided for the final four fights, you, our loyal audience, will be rewarded! Our King knows what you want to see."

The audience roars from disappointment to excitement. The other slaves physically relax, but Aya notices the tension in Yme's shoulders grow.

"Bastard," he curses.

"The final four fights will be fought by Yme. Alone!" Dolus Otho announces. "Take the other slaves back to their cells!"

Klaeon shoots a look to Dolus Otho, his lips moving quickly.

"Leave the Healer to watch," Dolus adds quietly and hastily, speaking to the workers.

The rest of the slaves are forced to their feet and led away. The only one who doesn't move is Leid. The workers eye Dolus Otho, who checks with Klaeon. Klaeon nods, and the men leave the silent man sitting next to Aya. Aya watches Yvette limp away and wonders if she will be taken to the healers.

The workers inside the cage leave to grab Yme and shove him into the arena. Yme glares at them.

Aya leaps to her feet and runs to the door as the workers close it. "Can you fight four more fights?"

Yme turns to her. "I don't have a choice. Guess you did too good a job of not dying."

"This isn't the time for jokes. Even bad ones," Aya says.

"Bring on the next fighters!" Dolus Otho yells.

Yme turns to face the incoming fighters. Aya reaches through the bars and grabs the back of his shirt. She sees him tense, but he doesn't turn around.

"Don't abandon us," Aya says softly.

"Us?" Yme asks.

"Me, Kylii, Daniil, the other slaves…us." Aya pushes him forward. "Now get fighting, crowd favorite."

The bell rings and Yme faces the two fighters waiting for him. Aya walks back to the seating area and sits down next to Leid. The two fighters facing Yme are large men carrying spears with blades on both ends. Yme's magic fills the air as he walks forward.

"Interesting day," Leid says.

Aya jumps at the man's voice, almost forgetting he was still there. "Do you ever speak more than two words?"

"Sometimes." He turns to her, his cold eyes meeting hers. "I don't usually get to come out of my cell. They didn't like how short my fights were."

"I'm sure it got boring to watch you kill without a conscience. This audience seems to like watching people with emotions," Aya says, remembering Quin's screams for help before Leid killed her.

"You're probably right. There's no *spectacle* when I fight. I don't see the need. If you're going to kill someone, do it."

The crowd cheers and Aya returns her attention to the arena. One man is using his double-bladed spear to break away chunks of the earth engulfing his feet. The other man is struggling to free his spear from a tower of ice. Yme runs up to the man with his feet caught, and wraps the chain still attached to his left wrist around the man's throat.

"The others said you were put in here after you killed your family and a village," Aya says.

Leid takes a deep breath, the smallest crack in his emotionless façade. "My family was dying. I released them from their pain. But the village…" he fades off. "That was for fun." She cannot tell whether he is serious or hiding something.

The man Yme strangled falls to the ground, unconscious. Yme grabs the double spear before it hits the ground and stabs the other man in the back. The bell rings, ending the fight.

It doesn't take long for the arena workers to clear the floor, and the next fighters to enter the arena. Aya stares at the metal in the skin of a man and woman fighter: studded silver piercings cover their arms, legs, and torsos. The woman holds a sword in each hand. The man carries a metal whip with spikes.

"If I fought Yme, perhaps I would give the spectacle the audience wants," Leid says.

Chills run through her. *I think I liked him better when he didn't talk.*

Yme struggles with the two fighters. Something about how they move seems to give him trouble. Aya watches the man with the whip carefully and realizes why. He and the woman are blind, but they easily dodge Yme's attacks, sometimes with barely a move. The woman manages to slice Yme's side. The man uses the whip to keep Yme's attention away from the woman.

Are they using magic? How else can they dodge his moves so easily? Aya finds herself wishing she were inside the cage.

The whip wraps around Yme's right arm and the man pulls, forcing Yme to counterbalance. He pulls against the whip, but the woman moves behind him and prepares to stab him in the back with both swords. Yme takes a deep breath and releases it forcefully, sending a whoosh of air in front of him. The force of the wind sends him into the woman behind him. The man with the whip is yanked to his knees but keeps the whip tight on Yme's arm.

The woman tries to avoid Yme's body, but Yme slams into her and pulls one of the larger piercings in her side free from her skin. She screams and swings both swords towards him, but he quickly pulls on the whip. The man pulls back with a surge of strength, clearing Yme of the blades.

Yme turns and throws the metal piercing at the woman, hitting her in the face. The sharp metal cuts her cheek. Yme uses the distraction to kick a block of earth at her. The earth hits her in the stomach and knocks her onto her back. A wind gathers around Yme, kicking sand up into the air. The sand circles around him and the man with the whip.

"Have you figured it out yet?" Leid asks.

Aya shakes her head. "Figured out what?"

"Why they're pierced?"

That's the trick. "The metal piercing allows them to see."

"It allows them to sense everything around them. It's a common trick used in the south eastern villages. It helps them hunt."

"So, it's not magic?" Aya asks.

His eyes move quickly, easily following the fighters in the sandstorm. "I didn't say that," he says. "You don't seem familiar with magic users, Rare Kind." He turns to her, his emotionless eyes sending another chill down her spine.

"I was the only one with magic in my village," she tells him.

"Most magic users come from the homes where their magic is common. They've learned to use it without thought. Like an extra limb or sense." Leid returns his attention to the fight. "Or to fill in for a sense, in the case of these two."

Their magic is common... Yme must already know of it, then. Has he fought these two before, in his nine long years here?

The sand stops and the man is on the ground, blood on his skin from where Yme tore many of the piercings free. Yme stands above him, holding the whip around the man's throat,

249

but loose enough the spikes don't cause serious damage to his skin.

The woman stands, her blank eyes filled with panic. "Nero?" She moves her head from side to side as though searching for her partner.

Is it because Yme pulled out the piercings? She can't see anymore? Aya wonders.

"We concede!" the man, Nero, yells.

The bell rings. The woman rushes towards the man, nearly crashing into Yme as he releases the whip and stands. The man quickly gets to his feet and grabs her. She touches him where the piercings were and releases a relieved sigh. They're escorted out by the arena workers and the next fighters enter.

Aya stares at Yme's back. His breathing is heavy and blood drips from his hand. The spikes on the whip dug deep into his arm. He pulls water from a nearby trough and washes it from his arm, tearing his shirt to create a make-shift bandage. He glances behind him to Aya.

Two down. Two to go.

The next fight drags on for longer than Aya thought it might. She can tell Yme's energy is draining. But even with his slower reactions, he manages to defeat the third pair of fighters. As he waits for the bodies to be cleared, he walks to the bars of the cage.

Aya rushes to him, wondering if he needs something. "One more to go."

Laughing, Yme shakes his head. "That's only nineteen fights. Not a round number, remember?"

"What do you think they have planned?" Leid asks, appearing next to Aya.

Yme glares at him, but Aya sees his will to argue fade. "I don't know. But you two shouldn't get comfortable."

Fear fills Aya. "Do you think they'll have us fight each other?"

"No. The others would still be here if that was it."

The bell rings, ending their conversation. Yme turns to face the two fighters and immediately fills the air with his magic. Wind blows around him and earth rises in front of him. He walks towards the two fighters and attacks.

"We should sit, then. Reserve our energy," Leid says, walking back to his seat.

Aya doesn't move. She watches the final fight with her hands squeezing the bars of the cage. The two fighting Yme are skilled. One uses magic to make weapons appear from thin air, but there's a limit to where he can make them appear. The other is able to teleport short distances. Together they make it a difficult fight for Yme. The two fighters work well together. When the one teleports, the other makes sure a weapon is waiting for him wherever he appears.

Yme is kept on the defensive, unable to attack the fighter who teleports. But when he tries to attack the conjurer, the teleporter appears behind him with a knife. Yme gathers earth on his back, creating a thick shield, but the conjurer adjusts with blunt weapons the teleporter can use to crack through the earth.

The sun disappears behind the wall of the arena as Yme finally defeats the two fighters. Workers light torches throughout the arena, fighting back the darkness.

Yme spits blood from his mouth, his bottom lip cut from a sneaky back-fisted punch from the teleporter. But that had been the teleporter's mistake. He attacked from the front, and Yme was able to stab him with one of the weapons the conjurer left on the ground. The conjurer fell easily after Yme took out the teleporter.

But the bell doesn't ring to end the fight. No workers enter the cage to clear the bodies. Confusion fills Aya and the audience.

CHAPTER FORTY-FIVE

"My dear audience," Dolus Otho's voice rings out over the confusion. "Nineteen fights we have presented to you in honor of our Great King. But twenty will create our finale."

A breeze moves through the evening air, blowing Aya's hair around her. The familiar tingling of magic in the air makes her skin crawl and she turns. Something isn't right.

"Our most gracious King has brought a special treat for you, our most enthusiastic of audiences. A treat from across the Great Sea."

A sound echoes in the arena and the audience grows anxious. Aya tries to feel where the magic is coming from but sees nothing. Her eyes move to Leid, who is staring upwards. She follows his gaze and gasps. A shadow is circling the arena high in the sky. She turns to see Yme has noticed the shadow, too.

Workers surround the cage in tandem, more magic filling the air. Raising their arms, the workers close their hands into fists and pull back, as though pulling on invisible ropes. The cage shudders and the top opens. The spectacle entices the audience and they cheer excitedly.

"From lands beyond the Great Sea, I present to you a beast of legend, a monster of magic." Dolus Otho pauses, the excitement of the audience growing with each word. "The final challenger to face our Champion: The Deadly Volacerta!"

The shadow in the sky drops to the ground, sending a large cloud of sand in the air. The ground shakes, Aya holding tight to the bars of the cage. Wincing against the cloud of sand, she can make out Yme backing towards the wall of the cage. His back touches the bars and his shoulders shake slightly.

A low rumbling fills the air and the magic tingling over Aya's skin increases. The cloud of sand settles and Aya's breath catches in her throat.

A massive, scaled beast stands in the center of the Cage of Conquest. A long, split tail hits the bars of the cage, sending shudders through the metal. Thick legs carry a lean, muscular body rippling with energy. Massive wings take the place of front legs, easily holding up the torso. Curved, sharp talons dig into the earth beneath the creature's feet, thicker than a man's arm. A triangular head sits at the end of a long neck, displaying massive spear-like teeth every time the large mouth opens. Eyes the color of fire sit deep within the head of the Volacerta, exhibiting an eerie intelligence as they scan Yme.

Yme's hands grip the bars behind him tightly.

He's afraid, Aya realizes. *He can't fight that thing alone.* Aya pulls against the bars. She doesn't think she'll be able to open the heavy door, but she has to try. She bangs on the metal with her hands.

The noise draws the attention of the Volacerta, and the beast growls loudly. Its eyes glow and the magic tingle in the air grows even louder. A glow fills the Volacerta's throat and Aya's eyes widen.

Hands grab Aya and pull her away as flames erupt from the beast's mouth. The fire blasts the spot Aya had been standing in, melting the metal of the cage. The flames catch surprised arena workers, who run screaming as the flames cover their bodies and they fall off the seating platform to the arena floor below. As the flames subside, the audience roars with approval.

Aya stares at the hole where the door had been, glowing metal dripping to the ground. She turns to see Yme scooting away from the damage.

"Not very smart to draw the attention of an angry Volacerta," Leid says.

Aya realizes he's the one who pulled her clear of the flames. "We have to help him."

"What?"

"Yme. He can't fight that monster alone." Aya scrambles to her feet, pulling free of Leid's grip.

Leid stands with her. "But it's not my fight."

"Some fights start that way. But we decide when it's time to make it our fight." She doesn't wait for his response. She hops through the melted hole into the cage and stays close to the wall, hurrying to Yme.

The screeches of the Volacerta send fear through her, making her heart pound loudly in her ears. But she pushes to reach Yme. Kneeling down, she grabs his arm. He jumps at the sudden touch and stares at her with wide eyes.

"What are you doing?"

"Helping." She pulls him to his feet. "You're shaking."

Yme presses his back to the bars of the cage. He can only manage one word. "Fire."

Nodding, Aya turns her attention to the beast in front of them. "I gathered that after it nearly burned me alive."

"I can't fight fire," Yme says.

"I've seen you fight worse things."

Yme's eyes glance at her briefly before returning to the monster in front of them. "I can't control fire."

"Neither can I, but the sharp claws and teeth frighten me more." Aya takes his hand in hers. "Come on, champion. You going to let this be the end of your winning streak?"

Yme squeezes her hand. "Daniil and Kylii would laugh me to the grave if I let that happen."

Leid appears on Aya's other side. "Fine. This will be my fight, too." He looks at Aya. "Only because I want to fight Yme another day."

CHAPTER FORTY-SIX

"CAN THESE DO ANYTHING TO THAT THING?" AYA ASKS, INDICATING the weapons remaining in the cage.

"If I may," Leid says, curiously polite for someone rumored to be a crazed killer. "I can take those things off your arms and legs."

Confusion fills Aya, but Leid grabs her right arm and takes off the chain still hanging from her wrist. He bends down and does the same to the one around her ankle.

"How did you—" Aya starts.

Leid waves his hand at Yme and the chains fall from his wrist and ankle. "I'm a metal mage. How did you think I killed an entire village?"

Aya looks at Yme for an explanation, but he shakes his head. "I had no idea. He's never used it before," he says.

Leid lifts his hand and Yme's chains rise from the ground, floating to Leid's hand. "I'll make an exception today."

"But not before now?" Aya says.

Leid stares at her. "I assume you're speaking of the woman I killed earlier."

"*Quin.*"

"Why put the target on my back for someone who was going to die anyway?"

"Now isn't the time for this," Yme interjects, angrily.

"Fine. Do you have any tips for fighting a...volatera?" Aya asks.

"Volacerta. Don't stand in front of it. Watch out for the tail. Watch out for the fire," Leid says. He combines the chains into two long ones after detaching the ones on his ankle and wrist.

"And the claws...?"

"If you're close enough to worry about the claws..." He leaves the sentence unfinished.

Arena workers standing behind the Volacerta cautiously move forward and poke the beast with long poles. The Volacerta roars and swipes the bars of the cage with its tail, scaring the men back. But soon its attention turns to the three in front of it.

Magic fills the air like a song, and its mouth glows. Leid runs clear and Aya grabs Yme's arm, dragging him in the opposite direction. Flames erupt from the Volacerta's mouth, and this time, it turns its head to follow Leid. He stays ahead of the flames and throws one of the long chains at the beast's eye. The metal hits the fire-colored orb and the Volacerta roars, rearing back and swatting at the chain. Leid releases the chain and it snakes its way around the Volacerta's throat. He squeezes his hand and the chain tightens.

The Volacerta panics, scratching at its throat with the talons on its wings. Using the distraction, Aya moves behind Yme as he gathers earth and water. She places both hands on his back and brings her magic forward. She heals the wounds Yme received during the last four fights. His body shivers at the feeling of her magic healing him, but Aya can feel his magic growing as his body heals.

Yme mixes the earth and water, creating thick mud. He throws the mud at the Volacerta, hitting it in both eyes. He quickly releases a breath and pulls one hand back. The water is

257

pulled from the mud, leaving dry, hard earth in the beast's eyes. It roars again, this time in pain.

The Volacerta slams its wings on the ground and turns quickly. Its split tail swings towards Leid, but he easily avoids it. Then it suddenly reverses direction and the tail slams into his arm and side. The chain around the Volacerta's throat loosens and it manages to claw it from its long neck.

Leid slams into the cage wall and falls to the ground. He sits up, but Aya can see his arm is twisted, broken. "We have to keep that thing away from Leid."

Yme turns his head to look at the fallen man. "For someone who wouldn't do the same for us?"

"He's in here, isn't he?"

Lowering his arms, Yme clenches his fists and bends his knees. He sucks in a deep breath before jumping. He releases his breath as his feet hit the ground and the earth beneath the Volacerta's wings rises quickly. The beast is thrown back before it can balance on its rear legs. Its back hits the cage wall, bending the metal and sending the Volacerta out of the Cage of Conquest, hitting the earth below with an earth-shaking thud. Audience members nearby scramble for cover.

Leid uses his second chain to pull himself to his feet. He moves away from the new hole in the cage, his right arm hanging limp.

Wind rushes towards Aya and Yme. Wings stretch and the Volacerta is soon rising from the ground.

"Tear the wing skin," Leid yells over the rushing wind.

"How are we supposed to do that?" Yme asks.

Aya glances around and spots a circular blade on the ground. She leans down and grabs it. The handle is at the center encircled by the blade.

Yme takes the weapon and inspects the blade.

"You're the elemental mage," Aya says.

Furrowing his brow, Yme uses his left hand to raise earth in front of him. "Distract it."

"What?"

"Distract it, so it doesn't shoot fire at me."

Aya grabs a sword remaining on the wall and runs away from Yme. She bangs the sword on the bars as she runs, keeping her eyes on the Volacerta. The creature moves its head, following the noise. Rearing back, magic tingles through the air. It exhales a rush of fire towards Aya, but she deftly avoids it.

Yme runs up the earth rising in front of him, creating steps to the Volacerta. He vaults from the top towards the right wing, raises his weapon, and buries it in the leathery skin. His weight pulls him down, tearing through the scaled flesh. The Volacerta roars in agony and tries to fly higher, but with its wing torn it can't stay airborne.

Falling, Yme uses wind to slow his descent. He lands inside the cage and backs away from the flailing Volacerta. It lands halfway in the cage, half-perched atop the bars. It roars and snaps at where it thinks Yme is, but he backs away. Water rushes towards him, freezing into a spear, and he stabs it into the bleeding eyes.

Fire rushes from the Volacerta's mouth and Yme falls to the ground. The flames pass over him, and he uses his magic to push the earth beneath him lower to keep him clear.

Aya bangs her sword on the bars again, screaming loudly to get the monstrous beast's attention. It works, and more fire races towards her. She drops the sword and runs away from the path of flames. She sees Yme stand and climb onto the back of the Volacerta. He raises the circular blade above his head and slams it into the thick, scaled neck, but it shatters in his hand.

A chain wraps around the neck and Aya looks over at Leid. His left arm is raised in front of him and he squeezes. Yme grabs the chain and pulls tightly. The Volacerta thrashes its head from side to side, forcing Yme to release the chain and hold onto the creature's neck to keep from being thrown to the arena floor.

The Volacerta's tail tries to whip Yme off, but it can't reach him. It tries to claw him off with its wings, but its right wing is too injured.

Aya searches the arena for a weapon that can possibly cut through the thick, scaled skin.

A black dagger drops to the ground in front of her. Aya stares at it and then at the direction it came from. In the lowering sun and confusion, she cannot see who threw it.

Leid returns his attention to the Volacerta and removes the chain from its throat. It wraps around the uninjured wing to keep it from clawing at Yme.

Aya picks up the dagger and takes a deep breath. She runs towards the Volacerta. *It's a living thing. It must have blood flow like other living things.*

She avoids the thrashing head and finds her way to the base of the Volacerta's neck where it joins its torso. She feels the magic building in the air, and heat emanates from the Volacerta's body. It roars, breathing fire all around as it flails.

She hears Yme's grunts and yells as he hangs on to the creature's neck. Aya sucks in a deep breath and stabs the dagger into the side of the Volacerta's throat. The blade easily cuts through the scales, a loud sizzling sound and smell of burning flesh surrounding Aya. She screams and pulls the blade across the throat, opening a deep gash from one side to the other. Blood pours to the ground in steaming gouts.

Aya runs from beneath the Volacerta, blood dripping onto her hand from the blade. She feels the heat, drops the dagger, and wipes her hands on her ragged clothes. She sees the ground beneath the Volacerta smoking as the blood pools.

The thrashing slows and it gives a final gurgling roar before its head falls to the earth. Yme falls from the neck, clear of the blood. He scrambles to his feet and backs away from the dying creature.

He turns to Aya with wide eyes. "You killed it."

The audience's reaction drowns out anything Yme is saying. Aya notices arena workers gathering outside the cage preparing to enter. She recognizes the magic blocker and realizes her time to help Leid is limited.

She reaches Leid as he collapses to the ground. If he feels pain from his injuries, he hides it. "Impressive. Maybe you're the one I should be interested in fighting."

"Stop talking," Aya orders. "I don't have much time." She places her hands on his side and concentrates. Broken ribs, torn organs, internal bleeding. She pushes her magic to work quickly, feeling it drain her energy. Once she's sure she's taken care of his internal organs, she moves to his arm, which took the full brunt of the tail. Shattered bone, torn muscles, so much blood. It's amazing the skin didn't break, with all the damage beneath.

Aya concentrates on the arm, but as she does, she feels her magic fading. She shakes her head, forcing her magic to keep working. Then a magic wall slams down, cutting off her magic completely.

"No. No, no, no!" She screams in frustration and stands, turning to the magic blockers. "I wasn't done! Let me heal him!" She runs towards the workers, not sure what she's going to do once she reaches them.

Yme grabs her before she gets too far and pulls her into a tight embrace. "Calm down. There's nothing you can do."

"It's completely shattered. I barely did anything," Aya yells angrily. Tears squeeze from her eyes as she pulls against him.

A sickening thud sends a shock through Aya. She turns in Yme's embrace and sees Leid hacking at his own arm with a sword, halfway down the humerus. Then he manages to stumble to the corpse of the Volacerta. He buries his stump into the gaping wound. When he pulls it free, the skin is burned over, stopping the bleeding.

Leid staggers back to her and Yme. "The healers here can't handle anything that severe."

Aya forces herself from Yme and storms up to Leid, tears blurring her vision. "So, you just disfigure yourself?"

Smiling, Leid waves the stump in front of her and Yme. "Consider this your handicap."

"Well-done, well-done, little Healer," Klaeon's voice booms in the arena. The audience immediately falls silent. Aya, Yme, and Leid face the private box.

Blood King Klaeon stands at the edge. Aya notices his hands are clenched tightly into fists. His strange eyes stare at her, the reddish-brown one almost glowing the same red as the dead Volacerta's eyes.

"Who knew the healer would find the strength to not only survive her two-on-one fight," Klaeon's eyes move to the Volacerta. "But also kill a beast as vicious as a Volacerta?"

"The victory goes to the slaves!" Dolus Otho announces. "Their reward is a break from the fights. Humble audience, I hope we've lived up to our promises! And to our honorable and most forgiving King!"

Klaeon stands straight and glares at Yme and Aya one last time before turning around and walking out of the private box.

"He's leaving," Yme says.

Aya looks at him. "So?"

"After a failed attempt to kill his toys, he leaves. But when he comes back..." Yme trails off, his eyes moving to the Volacerta.

"He comes back with something worse," Aya finishes Yme's sentence.

The arena workers gather and take them out of the cage. They're led back into the depths of the arena, but Aya glances behind one last time at the pile of bodies of those who fell this day.

III

THE BRÜDEL

CHAPTER FORTY-SEVEN

POUNDING. LOUD POUNDING.

Inside her head it echoes, and the weight of Aya's eyelids makes it difficult to open her eyes. She struggles, only managing to open one eye. Even the dim light of the few torches hurts.

Closing her eye, Aya takes a deep breath and rolls onto her back. She tries to sit up, but her muscles freeze in agony. She raises her right arm and feels the wall with her hand, trying to find anything she can use to pull herself upright. Finding nothing but wall, Aya groans and flops back onto her side. She uses her arm to push herself into a sitting position.

She can't remember the last time she felt this sore. All of her muscles ache and her head feels heavy on her neck. She barely remembers how she got to her bed.

She remembers being led from the fighting arena and down into the catacombs. A vague impression of being healed by the arena Healers. She remembers Leid taken away, returning to his cellblock with one last empty smile and a wave with the stump that used to be his arm. But the moment she returned to her bed is lost in a haze.

The pounding returns and now that Aya is awake she realizes

it's actually bells ringing from another cellblock. As the bells fade, Aya hears soft voices from a nearby cell.

"The King wants the Rare Kind dead. If we take them out, we'll be spared." The first voice sounds like an older man.

"Seera said *all* magic users will die," the voice of a boy replies.

"They just want the Life Healer dead."

Aya's breath catches in her throat. *They're talking about me. Why?*

"Shut your traitorous mouth!" a familiar voice silences the two whispering slaves. Aya recognizes it as Mava. "She wouldn't hesitate to save your sorry hide. You may be slaves, but you're still human beings! Now, act like it."

A moan rises from the bed across from Aya. Yme lifts his head and glares towards the loud voices. He rolls over, pulling the blanket over his head.

Aya forces her legs over the edge of the bed and stands. Her body protests, but she manages to keep from shaking too badly. She walks to bars of the cell and peers out into the cellblock.

She sees Mava and her sister, Rava, standing at the bars of their cell and trying to see into the cell next to them, which holds four people. Two are curled on the floor, either asleep or ignoring their cellmates. The other two are an older man and, Aya assumes, his son. The boy, barely in his teens, spies Aya and looks away in shame.

"Not all of us are fighters," the older man yells.

"None of us *started* as fighters," Mava replies.

"At least we aren't cowards who stab others in the back," Rava adds. "Or were you planning to do it in her sleep?"

"Shut it! Some of us are trying to sleep!" a voice from farther down in the cellblock yells. Others agree, voices rising. The boy drags his father from the front of the cell, but the older man gives Aya an angry sneer.

"What did I do to piss him off?" Aya asks, more to herself than anyone in particular.

"He's afraid of how everyone is going to be punished because of you."

"Because of me?"

"Your actions in the arena," Daniil says from behind Aya.

Aya turns to him and Kylii, who is sitting on the third bed in the cell. She walks back to her bed and sits. "What was I supposed to do? *Not* fight?"

Kylii smiles and shrugs his shoulders. "Logic isn't the strength of those who feel afraid."

"How long have I been sleeping?" Aya asks, rubbing her sore arm muscles.

"A day and a half. Probably would've been two if they didn't wake you."

"A day and a half? They let us sleep?"

"When Klaeon isn't here, the games calm down. The other cellblocks are used, and we get a break," Daniil says.

"Until he comes back. Then it's all Cellblock A until he leaves again," Kylii says.

Aya looks at the bars of the cell. "And we stay here."

"You missed recreation times, meals, and Seera's visits," Daniil says.

"Seera's visits are a scheduled part of our day?" Aya asks, not feeling bad for missing the head of the Arena's visits.

Kylii scoffs. "They are when she has 'good' news. In case you're wondering, that means *bad* news for us."

"We'll fill you both in after you've finished resting. Tomorrow is our free day," Daniil says.

"Free day?" Aya wonders how loose the term is when it's applied to slaves.

"Each cellblock gets one free day out of every seven when the games are light. They even let us use our magic," Daniil adds. "But only in the training grounds."

Aya's eyelids lower. The excitement passes and exhaustion fills her. *If only Leid had waited. Perhaps I could have healed him after all.*

"Get some sleep," Daniil says.

Aya lies down. Her head barely touches the pillow before she's back asleep.

CHAPTER FORTY-EIGHT

"Is it just me, or is everyone staring at us? More than usual, I mean?" Aya asks.

"You and Yme were asleep when Seera announced the 'good' news," Kylii says from his reclaimed bed.

"What news?"

Daniil swings his legs over the edge of his bed. "Our *noble* king has announced his return."

Aya's chest tightens. "Already?"

"Two cycles of the moon," Kylii says. He lifts himself up onto his elbows. "But rumor has it he's bringing something a bit worse than the monster you and Yme fought."

Something worse than the Volacerta? Aya's heart pounds in her chest. "What is he bringing?"

"The Brüdel. Klaeon's personal assassins."

Brüdel. Like the stories? Flashes of Jaxon cross her thoughts. People thought the same of him. The cruel, unkillable men with black blood. Were they more than stories? Did Klaeon actually have true Brüdel as his assassins?

The crack of Seera's whip silences the cellblock. "Time to wake up. Today is Cellblock A's free day. You may eat, bathe,

269

train, or do nothing if you so desire. Your cells will remain unlocked until after the evening meal. If you do not return to your cells by then you will be punished severely." She eyes Aya with a cruel smile. "If you're caught above ground, you'll be punished. Or executed, depending on who catches you."

The Arena workers open the cells and leave, but Seera walks to Aya's cell. "Life Healer."

So I am no longer fresh flesh, Aya thinks.

"I never got the opportunity to congratulate you on your fight against the Volacerta. Very brave and very stupid. But I commend your bravery. Too bad it encouraged our great king to declare the end of magic users."

"*What?*" Aya throws her hands before her mouth.

"That's right, you and our champion missed the announcement." Seera moves quickly to grab Aya's chin in her hand. "Rare Kinds are filth that must be eliminated. Your powers are too dangerous to be allowed to go unchecked. When our king returns, the largest game ever will be displayed. All magic users will fight not only the king's personal assassins, but also those slaves in cellblock A who have no magic. Any who refuse to fight will be killed."

Aya tries to pry the woman's hand off. "You can't do that!"

Smiling wide, Seera laughs. "Oh, but our king has ordered it. And he especially wanted you to know it was your actions during the tournament that convinced him it was high time to cleanse these cells of troublesome vermin." She releases Aya's chin and steps back, placing a hand on her hip. "The one who brings our king your head will receive the highest prize, of course."

Turning to leave, Seera stops and feigns an expression of sadness. "It's a shame, really. We'll have to start collecting magic users all over again." She laughs with honest glee and walks away. "Enjoy your final days alive, little Healer."

Aya backs away from the open cell door and sits on her bed,

staring at the dirt floor in shock. Her magic has sentenced all the other magic users to death.

Daniil and Kylii walk over to her. "You should get some food. You haven't eaten in days," Daniil says, sitting next to her.

"I can't go out there. I can't face anyone. They'll blame me," Aya says. The argument from this morning makes more sense. She doesn't blame the father of the boy for wanting to kill her. "And they're right to. Everyone is being punished because of me. Why? I can't help having this power. None of us can."

"That bastard king's been looking for an excuse to wipe us out for some time," Kylii says, crossing his arms. Kylii kneels beside the bed. "The others? They're scared, but you can't let that get to you."

"Why?"

"Why what?"

"Why does he want us all dead?"

"If I knew that… Well, Kylii and I are going upstairs to train. Some of the others who arrived with you have been asking us to teach them. If you feel up to it, I think they'd appreciate seeing you there…supporting them." They rise together and leave.

Aya watches them walk out of the cell and sees many she's healed following, Rava, Mava, and Bern among them. The boy whose father argued with Mava follows with his head hanging low. He peeks at Aya before blushing and moving closer to Rava.

"The brothers are right," Yme's voice comes from the floor.

Aya leans over the foot of the bed and sees him lying close by.

"If these people are going to fight for you, you should show them some respect."

Furrowing her brow, Aya shifts onto her stomach, avoiding strain on her back and neck. "What are you talking about?"

"Those you healed will protect you."

"How do you know that?"

"I see it in their eyes when they look at you."

"I never asked them to fight for me."

"You didn't have to," Yme says. "The only way we're all going to survive when the Brüdel get here is if we unite and show Klaeon we won't fight against each other."

Aya stares at him. "There've been other Rare Kinds you, Daniil, and Kylii haven't helped in the past. Why did you decide to help me?"

Yme is silent for a moment and takes a deep breath. "You give us hope."

She waits for him to elaborate, but he remains silent. "What do you mean?"

Yme angles his head to stare up at her. "I saw something in the eyes of those with you when they arrived. Fresh flesh usually arrive with their spirits already broken. But your group had a fire in their eyes that couldn't be explained—until I saw you. Whatever you did to give them such hope is something the Arena has never seen before."

Aya's mind flashes to the escaped slave who died in the desert. The expression of victory on his face, even in death, as her carriage passed him. Bern saving her life. The new strength she helped them find...is that the hope Yme claims to see?

"All I've done is show kindness." The kindness Elder Mircien and Iria taught her in Foula Village. The kindness Iria told her a healer needed to show. *Can that really be what filled them with hope? Mere kindness?* And how had she repaid their hope? She allowed her fear to cow her. She had nearly allowed Seera and Klaeon to make her forget kindness.

Aya walks to the open door of the cell. She takes a deep, calming breath before stepping out. She feels the eyes of those who stayed in their cells on her, but she ignores them and turns to Yme. He flashes a rare smile.

"Let's go watch the training."

He stands, uncoiling to his full height. "You want me to go with you?"

"I'm not the only one who gives the people hope." Aya holds out her hand.

He walks to her side but does not take the offered hand.

A loud grumble rises from Aya's stomach. She places a hand on her belly and fights the blush rising to her cheeks. "Maybe some food first?"

CHAPTER FORTY-NINE

THEY HEAD FOR THE DINING HALL AT THE CENTER OF THE LEVEL. The kitchens keep the hall at a comfortably warm temperature. The food is, as always, surprisingly fresh. Aya had expected gruel or something even worse when she first arrived—perhaps economically trimmed bits of those fallen in the sands.

"Since many don't survive long in the Arena, any meal could be a slave's last. Small comfort before a fight to the death," Yme explains.

They sit against the wall, eating separate from the few in the hall. Tables of varying lengths fill the room. An opening in the wall emits delicious scents: cooking meats, freshly cut fruits and vegetables, and potent spices.

Two men sit at the opposite end of the hall. Their hands are dirty, and they sit with the ease of those who are not slaves. "Who are they?" She points with her spoon between bites of food.

Yme motions towards the doors leading into the kitchen. "Cooks. Since there are a lot of bodies to keep fed, there are a lot of them. They don't get long breaks, so they stay close."

Nodding her head, Aya swallows her mouthful. "Where does the food come from?"

"Most is grown on farms between the city's outer walls and the Arena. You wouldn't have seen them if you entered from the South. And some food is given by the citizens of Bloodfall to curry favor with Klaeon."

Aya stares at her bowl, moving pieces of meat with her spoon. "I never even knew there was a king. And here I am, his slave."

"He's not a real king," Yme spits angrily. "He only rules these lands because no other took hold south of the Great Mountains."

"The mountains behind the arena?"

"Mm-hm." Yme takes another bite of food before locking eyes with Aya. "You really never heard anything about Klaeon?"

Embarrassment flushes Aya's cheeks, but she forces the feeling down. "My village is very far from here. When I was taken by the slave caravan, it was the first time they'd ever been to my village." Memories of the fires consuming her home fill her. "The head of the caravan told me my village hadn't been worth the risk before."

"Then they heard about you," Yme says.

Nodding, Aya leans on the table. "My parents weren't from Foula Village. They chose to live there and used their magic to help the villagers. They didn't like talking about anything that happened before they moved there. But now I have to wonder..." she swallows a lump. "I wonder if they knew about Klaeon."

"They were Life Healers, too?"

"They died when I was seven. My magic hadn't even begun to show yet." She smiles. "The elders of my village took me in and raised me, taught me about healing without magic. It helped when my magic started appearing. It wasn't as scary."

"But you had no one to teach you about magic."

Aya shakes her head. "What about you?"

Yme leans back in his chair. "There were other magic users in my village. I learned some things from them, but not long after

275

my magic appeared, I was brought here." His expression darkens and a silence falls between them.

Sensing he doesn't want to talk further, Aya stands. "We should probably go. We don't want to miss the training."

They leave the dining hall and head for the stairs to the next level. Arena workers walk down a hallway to one of the other cellblocks. Aya wonders how the others from the tournament are...the ones who survived. She wonders how Leid's arm is, but quickly catches up to Yme when she realizes he's already halfway up the stairs.

The training level is the most open area besides the actual Arena itself. The ceiling is high, with hanging lanterns to provide plenty of light. The forges where weapons and armor are made and repaired line the walls on one side. On the other side are healing rooms. She recalls being taken here to the healing rooms on the second level before the tournament.

At the center of the level are the fenced-in areas of sand and dirt she remembers seeing on her first day here.

Daniil and Kylii mill in different areas. Daniil focuses on defensive moves while Kylii teaches offensive maneuvers. The slaves focus on the brothers with eager eyes and pick up on the moves quickly.

Aya and Yme sit on a bench next to those awaiting their turn at practice or gaining the confidence to enter the training grounds. Turning to the two new arrivals, the slaves' expressions brighten.

Bern manages to keep Kylii on the defensive until he trips over his feet trying to dodge a thrust. Bern falls to the ground and Kylii prepares to deliver the final blow with his wooden sword. Tristan, one of the healers from cellblock A, appears at Bern's side and blocks Kylii's slice. He pushes him back and helps Bern up. The two men tag team attacking Kylii, bringing an unexpected laugh from his belly.

Daniil is sparring against Rava and Mava, testing their defensive stances. Standing to the side, watching with a worried expression, is the teen boy. He kicks the wooden sword in his hand absentmindedly.

Noticing the boy's reluctance, Daniil ends his match with Rava and Mava. He calls to the boy. "What's your name?"

The boy almost drops his sword. "Cal."

"Well, Cal, get over here and show me what you've learned from watching."

Cal cautiously steps forward, raising his sword. Daniil smiles and invites the boy to attack. Cal swings his sword and Daniil knocks the wooden blade away with his own. "Again." Thrusting the sword at Daniil's stomach, Cal is again thwarted by the taller man's sword. He tries the thrust again, but this time Daniil disarms the boy. In a panic, Cal kicks Daniil's leg.

"Well, that is some quick thinking. But always keep your eyes on the blades." To emphasize his point, he places both wooden swords at Cal's throat. Cal nods and Daniil hands over the sword. "Again."

Aya watches intently as each slave takes a turn. Many improve or learn new tricks to escape. Flashes of her fights during the tournament remind her she has a lot to learn.

Daniil and Kylii tell everyone to practice with each other. They hurry over to the fence, to Aya and Yme. "You two gonna sit there all day?" Kylii asks.

Daniil motions to the slaves sparring each other. "They keep asking for you two. They want to see what you both can do."

Yme laughs. "Then they should've paid for seats at the tournament. We're both a bit tired of fighting."

Aya watches many of the slaves who journeyed to the arena with her. *They're working hard to survive here. I won't survive long if every fight I'm in is based on luck.*

She squares her shoulders. "Teach me how to fight."

Startled, Yme shakes his head. "You handled yourself pretty well during the tournament. Just keep doing that."

"That was luck. I need to know how to fight."

"I don't teach."

"Show me, then." Aya stands and walks towards the training ground.

With a great sigh, Yme lopes after her. The groups practicing stop and make room for the two new trainees. Aya faces Yme as Daniil and Kylii hand each a wooden sword.

"Fine. Attack me," Yme says, sword raised.

Aya raises her sword with both hands, noticing Yme holds his sword in his left hand. "I didn't realize you were left-handed."

Yme shrugs. "I don't use weapons often enough for anyone to notice."

Aya slowly moves to the right and Yme mirrors the movement. Moving closer as they circle, her eyes watch the sword in Yme's hand.

Taking in a quick breath, she swings the sword towards Yme's right side. He blocks. Aya tries to hit him from the other side. He blocks again.

Then Yme swings at her left arm. Trying to block, she turns her sword at an odd angle. Yme's wooden blade hits her sword hard. Her hands ache from the strike and Yme hits again, knocking the sword from Aya's hands.

Quickly retrieving the weapon, Aya adjusts her hold. Yme attacks the right arm this time, but Aya blocks successfully. When he goes back for her left, she adjusts the angle and manages to stop him, but the wooden blade still touches her arm.

Adjusting her hold again, she attacks, aiming for Yme's left leg, but he blocks. Using the force of the hit, Aya swings the blade up to the right side of his head.

He easily raises his weapon to stop her. She moves away.

Aya slices diagonally from right to left, but Yme raises his weapon at the attack and the force knocks Aya back a step. She tries going the opposite direction and her eyes widen as she watches Yme block again. But this time, it doesn't surprise her. Feinting another diagonal slice, Aya watches carefully. As Yme moves to block, she thrusts the blade forward and the force of the block sends her blade into the area where his neck and shoulder connect. Yme immediately uses air magic to knock her blade away.

Now his eyes are wide. "How did you do that?"

"I don't know."

Raising his sword, he lowers his stance. "Do it again."

Aya reverses her diagonal slice, attempting to cut from lower right to upper left. Yme tries to block again, but Aya sees what she saw before. Thrusting her sword forward, Yme changes the trajectory of her sword. He uses his air magic to blow the wooden sword away before it makes contact with his skin.

Aya mimics Yme's stance. "When you move to block, I can see your muscles instinctively pull back towards your body."

Yme practices a block and nods. "How did you see that?"

"I saw your muscles tense before they contracted."

"That happens in an instant. Only highly trained swordsmen could make a move in that amount of time," Daniil says from the side.

"Or Life Healers," Kylii puts in.

"How does being a Life Healer help?" Aya asks.

Yme's admiration is evident in his expression.

"You can predict how someone is going to move," Kylii continues. "Your magic puts you in tune with every minute indication the body gives that your opponent isn't even aware of. Every bad habit a fighter has, you can pick up on and exploit."

"Like my tendency to pull my arms closer to my body when I block." Yme shrugs inward with a comic demonstration.

Those watching make impressed sounds.

Yme raises his sword at Aya. "Ready for more?"

A smile grows on Aya's lips and she raises her sword. "Ready, teacher."

CHAPTER FIFTY

THE SLAVES TRAIN UNTIL THEIR ARMS ARE TOO TIRED TO LIFT THEIR wooden swords. Still, when Daniil and Kylii announce training is over, the slaves protest. Aya understands their feelings. The training focused mainly on fighting without magic. Those without magic were hoping to learn more useful tricks against magic users.

"There will be time for more training on our next free day."

As everyone returns to the bottom level, Aya hesitates at the bottom of the stairs. She stares at the hallway leading to Cellblock D. *How is Leid doing?* She wonders. He was taken to the healers after the tournament ended, while she and Yme were returned to their cells.

Aya grabs Yme's arm. "Are we allowed to go to the other cellblocks?"

Confusion fills his eyes. "The other cellblocks? I...I don't know."

"In nine years, you haven't once seen anyone try?" Shame angles his face to the floor. "I'm going to find out." She eyes workers standing nearby, and walks towards the hallway. They make no move to stop her. Yme stays where he is while she walks down the hallway to the doors leading into Cellblock D.

Peering through the small window, she sees an identical room to Cellblock A. The only difference is the number of slaves. Unlike Cellblock A, the cells in D are filled to bursting.

Opening the door, Aya steps inside. Arena workers standing on either side of the door jump at her appearance, but don't stop her. "Where is Leid?" Aya asks.

Two workers ogle her, confused. The taller one points up the stairs. Aya nods and climbs the wooden stairs quickly. One cell appears empty, but she can hear heavy breathing inside. She walks to the bars and peers into the darkened cell. Sitting on his bed, back against the wall, waits Leid.

A bandage covers his right arm, or what's left of it. His chest rises and lowers with each breath he takes. His eyes are closed. Aya taps the metal gently with her finger.

"I'm still alive," he says, opening his eyes. "If that's why you came. The Healers were able to heal the burns and enough of the bruising." He lifts the stub of his right arm.

"I wanted to see how well they healed you."

He slides his feet to the ground and stands. He comes to the cell bars and takes the bandages off to show the healed flesh beneath. But Aya notices the pale scar from where the skin knit together to cover the broken bone.

Why did the Healers leave a scar? Aya wonders. She remembers Leid's interest when she healed her arm. He'd poked the freshly healed skin as though it were an odd thing. *Can the Healers here not fully heal skin?*

Leid places the stub on the bar of the cell so Aya can see it clearer. She touches his skin, wanting to use her magic to see how well the healers did beneath his flesh, but only feels the wall blocking her magic.

Aya prods the arm, feeling the muscles and bone beneath. "How did you know that knife would cut the Volacerta's scales?"

"Volacertas are not rare on this side of the Great Sea. They don't grow as big, but they're rampant where I'm from," Leid says.

"How big do they usually grow?"

"The size of a small child. A brave one will try to steal babies from their beds. But once in a fire moon one the size of a grown man causes trouble. The men of my village would gather to hunt it. Blades made of obsidian are the only things that can cut a Volacerta's flesh, other than another Volacerta's teeth and claws." Shrugging, Leid leans on the bars. "I noticed the knife during my first fight. That's why I ran in the direction I did when the fight started."

Smiling, Aya took a step back from the bars of the cell. "Honestly, I thought you were abandoning us to the fire."

Leaning his head to the side, Leid returns the smile. "It clearly didn't work. The fire chased *me*."

"A risky wager," a voice says behind Aya. Turning, Aya sees Yme coming up the stairs, evaluating Leid carefully.

"It paid off. You live another few days, champion," Leid says, eyes widening slightly at the surprise visitor. "I understand why she came to see me. But why have you?"

Yme stands next to Aya. "I was wondering how long you've been in the Arena."

"Longer than you, but you knew that. What do you really want to know?"

"Tell us about Klaeon's assassins."

Boredom fills Leid's face. "Which ones?"

"The Brüdel."

Leid's eyes turn to Aya. "Did you know Cellblock A has the highest number of magic users? In this cellblock and all the others there are only a handful. There used to be more in the other cellblocks. Until about fifteen ages ago."

"What does that have to do with the Brüdel?" Aya asks, afraid to look away from Leid's cold, emotionless eyes.

"Fifteen ages ago, magic users from the south tried to overthrow the Blood King. They lost. They were all gathered and brought here. For their crimes, the Blood King made them fight against his Brüdel. As punishment to all who believed they could one day overpower their new king, magic users from the Arena—ones who were already slaves before the attempted overthrow—were forced to fight alongside those from the south." Leid bangs his hand on the bar of the cell, causing Aya and Yme to jump. "The Brüdel slew all of them within five minutes. Hundreds of magic users against a dozen of the Blood King's assassins and they couldn't even kill one of the Brüdel."

"That can't be true," Aya says. "That's impossible."

Leid raises an eyebrow. "The truth remains. Every person who fought the Brüdel died. The only magic users who survived didn't fight. We were children and hid our magic very well."

"So, you didn't actually see them?" Yme asks.

"I'm still here, aren't I?"

Yme turns to leave, hesitating only to glance back at Aya. "Our Free Day will be over soon. We shouldn't be caught outside of our cell."

Nodding, Aya follows Yme, but stops and looks back at Leid. "They're going to force you to fight the Brüdel this time."

"Or I could give the Blood King your head. I'm sure that would end the festivities quickly," Leid says.

Yme scowls. "It won't end until all magic users are dead. You know that."

Leid's lips curl. "I also know how much he hates you. Perhaps he'll be more forgiving if I bring him both of your heads."

CHAPTER FIFTY-ONE

FREE DAYS COME QUICKLY AND ARE SPENT TRAINING INTENSIVELY. Many from Cellblock A join in. Daniil and Kylii prove to be eager teachers, happily guiding those with or without magic on defensive and offensive maneuvers. Though Aya still occasionally has to remind the twin brothers to be gentle with the younger slaves when their rhetoric turns pessimistic.

Aya longs to visit the other cellblocks to see how the other fighters are doing, but Yme convinces her to focus on training. "They're alive. That means they're fine. The other cellblocks don't fight the most dangerous fighters. Except when Seera buys new beasts."

"She uses them to test which beasts are worth setting on us," Kylii adds.

Each Free Day, Aya notices more and more slaves hanging around her cell. Even a few of the Arena workers spend their breaks close by rather than in the dining hall. Aya doesn't mind, but she can sense growing tension with Yme and the brothers. They're not used to having others so interested in spending time with them.

Talkative Yme slowly fades away as the day draws closer.

The day when loud, thunderous bells signal Klaeon's return.

Aya senses the tension building in the cellblock as all slaves stop what they're doing to listen.

"His royal highness is back," Kylii announces, spitting on the ground. Daniil hits his brother. "What?"

"I've told you not to spit inside the cell."

"Sorry."

"That means the Brüdel are here, too." Aya tries to keep her voice steady but fails.

Yme walks to the bars of the cell. "Yes, it does."

Gripping the bed beneath her, Aya takes a breath. *Time's up.* Are they ready? Can they win?

"This is our chance," Yme says, his voice low.

"Chance for what?" Daniil asks.

"After the fight, we're going to escape this place."

The silence following Yme's statement is heavy. Aya stares at his back. "Escape? Is that even possible?"

Kylii scoffs with a confused look. "Are you insane?"

"Even if we survive the fight, Klaeon is here with a small army," Daniil adds.

"A dozen men, give or take a few," Yme clarifies.

"Right, a dozen men with weapons and the city guard with weapons and the arena workers with weapons. Oh, and magic blockers. With weapons."

"We would have to get through the Brüdel."

Yme turns to face them. "And we will."

"How?" Daniil, Kylii, and Aya ask in unison.

"The slaves with no magic. We have to convince them to fight with us. We have to show Klaeon we won't fight against each other." Yme meets Aya's eyes. "And I think we've already got that covered."

Daniil and Kylii stare at Aya and nod.

Aya furrows her brow. "Why are you staring at me like that?"

"Those who came here with you already pledged their protection. Those you've fought alongside and healed have as

285

well. If we use that to our advantage and rally the others together, that leaves only the Brüdel to fight."

"And how does that help us escape?" Aya asks.

"With his best fighters dead, Klaeon's men will have to focus on protecting him. With the slaves united, we can overpower the arena workers." Yme smiles. "And if we win, we may not have to worry about the workers."

CHAPTER FIFTY-TWO

ARENA WORKERS BANG ON THE BARS OF CELLS, FILLING THE cellblock with loud clanging. Aya sits up quickly at the noise, the yells of others torn from their sleep echoing her thoughts.

At the center of the cellblock, Seera addresses them "Today is the day. As you know, our King has declared non-magic users, assisted by our King's men, will fight magic users. But you won't be the first show. Such an event requires several preliminary games to work the crowd up before you make your entrance.

"The magic users from other cellblocks are ready and waiting, whom you'll soon meet. You will all be cleaned, fed, and may use this extra time for rest or practice if you so desire. When you hear the bells ring three times, return to your cells." Seera aims her final words at Aya. "Enjoy your last few hours in this world."

The workers open the cells and return to their posts as Seera leaves the cellblock. Slaves are hesitant to leave their cells. Nerves are high and a new feeling fills the air.

Suspicion.

Magic users watch those without magic, wondering if they will be enemies. Aya notices several eyeing her. Cal's father has kept quiet since his argument with Mava, but Aya catches him angrily mumbling.

"Ooh boy, those are some nasty looks you're getting," Daniil says.

"They're scared. I'm an easy target to focus on before the fight. I'm not naïve. I know what they're thinking."

"Kill her and it might be over sooner," Kylii says.

"Kylii!" Daniil throws a pillow at his brother's face.

Catching the pillow, Kylii throws it back at Daniil. "What? She said she knew what they were thinking."

"Doesn't mean you have to say it out loud." Daniil dodges the pillow and grabs Kylii, wrapping an arm around his brother's neck. "C'mon. Let's get some food and head to the training grounds."

Kylii struggles against Daniil, angling to face Aya. "Will you be joining us?"

"Go ahead. I need a minute," Aya says.

The brothers shrug and leave the cell. Other slaves follow the brothers as they head off.

Aya leans against the bars of the cell, raising her shaking hands in front of her. She clenches her fists and sighs. *Klaeon's assassins, the Brüdel.* What kind of fighters are they? How many will they be facing? Would the other slaves join them to fight?

"You need to eat." Yme sits next to Aya. "We don't know how long we have before they call us to the Arena. The last thing you want to do is go into a fight starving."

"How long did it take you to stop being afraid before every fight?"

"I never stopped being afraid."

Aya eyes Yme with a smirk. "You're just trying to make me feel better."

Shaking his head, Yme holds up his left hand so she can see the shakes. "I'm afraid every fight. No matter what it is. If you stop being afraid, you start making mistakes."

"You hide it very well."

"I'm not hiding anything. Everyone chooses not to see it. It wouldn't fit their image of the Arena's top champion if they realized I was shaking like a child."

Aya smiles at him. "Knowing you feel fear like the rest of us makes me feel better."

"Should I take that as a compliment?" Yme asks.

"Yes."

Aya eats more than she expected. Then they arrive at the crowded training grounds. Exhausted trainees rest with their elbows on the seats behind them, their faces flushed. Blacksmiths stand outside of the forges, watching the overly excited exercises.

Aya and Yme find a spot to sit and watch Daniil and Kylii training the usual group; Mava, Rava, Bern, and Cal. The timid, fresh flesh are gone. They're slaves of the Arena, but now, a fire burns in their eyes.

Mava and Rava work together, learning from the brothers how to watch each other's back as they fight. Rava's weapon of choice is a spear, while Mava excels with double blades. Cal has shown the most improvement, finding his own in swordplay. Though when his father makes the trek up to the training grounds, Cal keeps to the bench, afraid to disobey.

After training, Mava and Rava grab Aya to go to the baths. They're joined by a few others, but still the baths are empty enough for the three to be relatively secluded. The water is hot, steam filling the air. Aya lowers up to her shoulders in the hot water. Mava and Rava sit back against the stone wall and stare at Aya.

"There are rumors spreading about an escape," Rava says.

Aya is taken aback at Rava's bluntness. "An escape? Where did you hear that?" *We just talked about it yesterday. Are Daniil and Kylii spreading it to others?*

"Small rumblings of what may happen should we be successful in defeating the Blood King's assassins. Not sure who started it. Are they true?" Mava asks, moving closer to Aya.

"I wouldn't know."

Rava moves to the other side of Aya. "The only ones who would even *think* about escaping would be from your cell."

"If I said yes? What would that mean to you?"

Mava and Rava eye each other before moving in front of Aya. Each take one of her hands. "We never told you this, but we come from a village just outside Oula Valley. But no matter where you were from, we would follow you wherever you go."

CHAPTER FIFTY-THREE

THE BELL RINGS THREE TIMES.

The focus found in the training grounds is replaced with nerves and hushed whispers. Arena workers separate magic users from the other slaves. Then those without magic are ushered out.

"They don't want us working together," Aya observes.

"They're too late," Yme says.

Aya watches Bern, Mava, and Rava follow the rest of those without magic. The three glance at her before they walk out of sight. She knows what Yme means. There may be a few who won't stand together, but most of the non-magic users are willing.

"Do you think it's going to be enough?" Aya asks. "Do we have a chance if we unite?"

"Strength isn't necessarily measured by the size of muscle or the power of a sword," Daniil says from Aya's side.

Kylii moves to her other side. "The strongest are those with hope. They can win even against the worst odds."

She nods as a memory flashes: Jaxon facing the bandits in the canyon alone, armed with only a sword. She remembers how she thought the odds impossible for him, but he defeated the entire

291

bandit group alone. Even when she decided to help Yme against the Volacerta...she had no doubt that, if she helped him, they would win against the beast.

The Arena workers return to take the magic users to the armory. The recent training affects their selections, as many have found preferred fighting styles and know what they need to protect themselves. Armor that allows greater mobility, and less cumbersome weapons.

Aya grabs a long knife and hides two smaller knives in her arm cuff. Without knowing what kind of combatants the Brüdel are, she needs to be ready for anything. She finds armor to cover her chest and upper thighs, focusing on protecting areas she knows could be fatal strikes.

Magic users from other cellblocks are led into the armory. Aya spies Leid meandering past the wall of weapons. His eyes search the selections, never landing on anything. The number of magic users from other cellblocks surprises her. The impression from other slaves had been there weren't many in the other cellblocks, but the number of magic users nearly doubles.

Some try to disguise hostility when they meet her eyes, straining to keep the frowns hidden. Others smile with excitement to meet the one they've heard about for months. They all know who she is.

They're led to the same long tunnel leading to the arena floor as the non-magic users. The two groups are kept separate, against opposite walls from one another. The final sounds of a game echoes through the tunnel: the roars of beasts, then human screams.

The crowd cheering above sounds much larger than even the tournament audience. The walls shake with yells and stomping feet. The ending bell strikes and the tunnel fills with nervous energy. Workers enter the Arena to clean the ring and clear the animals.

Aya looks down the line of magic users. Tristan, Skara, and Bon stand on the other side of Daniil and Kylii. Cal stands next to them, his eyes on his father across the way, who is glaring at her. She is startled; the way in which the twins had asked about her parents when she first arrived led her to assume magic always ran in families. But here Cal and his father stand, separated by the empty space down the middle of the aisle. It might as well be an ocean, a universe, between them.

Bern, Rava, and Mava smile and nod at her. Others nearby do the same.

Yme leans close. "You've already recruited most of them without even trying. We only need to convince the rest." Aya feels the hand on her back. Yme pushes her forward and she barely catches herself from falling. Out of the corner of her eye she sees an Arena worker approaching. Yme steps between her and the worker, slamming the man into the wall with air magic. The two groups murmur with confusion.

Yme murmurs, "Now. Convince the rest."

Aya eyes the worker who always blocks their magic. His hands are at his sides and he nods to her. She takes a deep, exhilarated breath. The other workers freeze, unsure.

Aya seizes the opportunity. "We're being pitted against each other for one man's enjoyment." All attention moves to her. "A man who makes others search the lands for slaves. A man who destroys our homes without thought. Now, this Blood King wants you to fight and die for his amusement. Why? Because we threaten him. The ones you should be fighting are the ones waiting for us out there. I'm not going to lie to you. I'm afraid. I'm afraid of whatever is beyond that gate. But we can defeat it if we stand together."

The slaves mumble, some avoiding Aya's gaze.

"But if we fight for the Blood King, then we won't be killed," a man protests from the end of the non-magic user line.

"Maybe not today," Yme steps next to Aya. "But what about tomorrow when you go back into the Arena and there are no magic users for the fighters to spend their energy on?"

"If you want to survive, then we must fight together," Aya repeats. "Who's with me?"

"I will fight for the Life Healer," Bern shouts.

"We will fight for the Life Healer," Rava says, and Mava fervently nods her head.

"The Blood King doesn't control us," a voice calls from the non-magic user group.

"Today," Aya says, "we can prove we're more than slaves."

"This is madness!" Cal's father throws out his arms to those around him. "You would risk your life for magic users?"

Cal steps forward, before his father. "I believe in Aya and Yme. The Blood King wants to control us. I'm *tired* of being controlled." He meets his father's eyes. "I still have a choice, and I choose to believe in people I trust. People who have proven they care about others, no matter who they are."

The slaves echo the boy's words, and soon murmurs of agreement outweigh the dissenters. Cal's father shuns the defiance in his son's face. Aya takes the boy's shaking hand in hers and squeezes.

The workers try to regain control, but the slaves ignore them. Seera cracks her whip at the end of the tunnel. "What is happening here? Back in line, all of you!"

All eyes move to Aya, waiting to see what she will do. Taking a breath, she moves back into the line, pulling Cal with her. Yme does the same and the other slaves follow.

"There will be no more of that behavior!" Seera walks down the lines, taking in every face. "You are about to be moved into the Arena. Magic users will take their places in the normal starting position. Non-magic users, you will cross to the opposing side. You will wait for the signal, then begin fighting. Your goal is simple. Kill each other. Our King has spoken." She stops in front of Aya and Yme, gloating.

The gate at the end of the tunnel opens as the last of the workers finish cleaning the ring. The roar of the crowd grows, filling the tunnel.

"Fight well and give the audience a good show." Seera cracks her whip, and the workers yell at the slaves to move.

Passing Seera, Aya focuses on the magic blocker, now held by two other workers. Seera walks up to him and grabs his hand. Turning to Aya, she waves the magic blocker's hand at her, laughing shrilly.

CHAPTER FIFTY-FOUR

BLOODFALL ARENA IS COMPLETELY FULL. EVERY SEAT IS TAKEN, hordes of people standing wherever there is room. Even the top level, reserved for the wealthy, mills with pressing crowds. Stomping feet shake the ground. Aya almost feels as if the stamping might cause the Arena to crumble down around them.

The slaves move to their starting positions, magic users on one side and the non-magic on the other. Weapons line the walls of the Arena, additional options should the weapons the slaves chose not prove sufficient.

Already seated, Klaeon surveys the two lines of slaves with a smirk. His second in command, Teron stands to his right with a sour look on his face. She wonders if the man always wears that expression, or if today is a special occasion.

"Our beloved audience! Welcome to Bloodfall Arena!" Dolus Otho's voice fills the space, quieting the crowd. Aya sees Dolus is standing on a platform opposite the private box, his usually theatrical appearance noticeably toned down. "Today we present a unique game our most generous King wishes to share with all of you."

The audience turns its attention as Klaeon stands and raises his hand, creating another wave of stamping feet.

296

Dolus Otho continues. "Today, we have already witnessed several magnificent games, but those were only a small taste of what we've planned for you today. Magic users, non-magic users, Rare Kinds. You've seen these slaves fight together. Now, watch them fight each other." He pauses for cheers as the anticipation grows.

Aya moves closer to Daniil and Kylii. The two stand close together, their eyes locked on the one gate still open. It's the largest of the gates, its opening much higher than the others. She feels anxious staring into the dark maw. Strange sounds emerge from the dark tunnel and the others shift uncomfortably.

"Though to pit normal slaves against magic users is unfair," Dolus Otho continues. "Therefore, these slaves won't be fighting alone. Our beloved king has given them a gift."

The audience begins a chant, starting soft and growing exponentially.

"Brüdel! Brüdel! Brüdel!"

The chant fills the arena, drowning out all other sound. Aya stares at the dark tunnel, wishing whatever was hiding inside would stay there.

A high-pitched scream rises from the tunnel and the non-magic slaves jump, moving away from the tunnel. The audience goes mute when an Arena worker runs from the tunnel.

Shock shoots through Aya. It's the magic blocker. But what fills her with fear is the sensation of magic filling the air, emanating from the tunnel.

The magic blocker reaches the center of the arena before a blade attached to a chain erupts from the darkness of the tunnel, racing after him.

Before she realizes what she's doing, Aya's feet are already moving. She doesn't know what she can do to stop what is happening, but she can't stand idly by. Daniil and Kylii yell her name, but her focus is on the magic blocker.

His expression fills with hope when he sees her running towards him, but it is cut short. The blade explodes from his chest, stopping his forward motion. Blood gushes into the sand beneath him.

As he reaches towards Aya, his eyes fill with tears. "Help...me."

She reaches out, but as their fingers touch, the chain grows taut and he's yanked back. He's dragged across the Arena floor. He disappears into the dark tunnel, his screams echoing.

Then the screams stop.

In the moment of silence, laughter reaches Aya's ears. She spies Klaeon, amused in his private box. He claps his hands and says something to Teron before more chuckling.

A hand grabs Aya's arm. She spins around, ready to attack. But it's Yme. He gently leads her back to the other magic users as shapes file into the sunlight from the dark tunnel. The crowd goes wild. They are monstrous beasts of men. Scars and piercings deform their bodies and faces. Some stand nearly twice Aya's height. Some appear more animal than man, bodies hunched over in contorted shapes. All carry twisted weapons. Three hold terrifying beasts on chains, that roar and claw the air.

One of the Brüdel drags the dead magic blocker behind him. A trail of blood follows the corpse. Aya stares at the one dragging the body. She memorizes his face, the scar across his nose, the metal chains pierced through the top of his ears. Then he drops the body to the sand. All behind him step on the body, crushing it to pulp, never slowing their pace.

The non-magic users move away from the approaching men in fear, making a large space. The Brüdel stop and face Klaeon. They salute their king and Klaeon lowers to his seat.

Dolus Otho says, "I introduce to you our King's personal fighters, the Brüdel! Let the fighting begin!"

The starting bell rings and the Brüdel slam their weapons on the ground. The animals roar and pull against their chains towards the slaves. All but five of the non-magic slaves run away from the men and join the magic users. The crowd murmurs in confusion before cheering for the unexpected change. The Brüdel look to the Blood King's private box, confused.

Klaeon's smile disappears and he stands. "Slaves! You are to fight each other!"

The slaves draw closer together, moving behind Aya and Yme. Daniil, Kylii, Mava, Rava, Bern, and Cal stand on either side of Aya and Yme, staring at the private box.

Klaeon's rage fills his face. Waving his hand, he sits back down. "Very well, then. No mercy shall be shown to any. Kill them all!"

The Brüdel shriek excitedly and kill the five slaves who stayed behind. Screams and pleas for mercy are unheard by the Brüdel as they rend and smash the slaves to unrecognizable lumps with dull weapons and bare hands. Once the last slave is killed the Brüdel turn to the rest and run at full speed with weapons raised.

Several slaves run to meet them. Yme pulls Aya back. "Stay away from the fighting. We'll bring the wounded to you. Tristan, Skara, and Bon, stay and help her. If you get into trouble, call for me or the twins."

Aya nods and moves away with the other healers. Two new healers join them from the other cellblocks, both older. They assist Tristan and Skara in clearing a place by the wall of the arena. Several non-magic slaves follow the group, their weapons raised, ready to defend the healers.

Aya watches the slaves who've already engaged the Brüdel. Bodies are already falling to the Arena floor. The Brüdel are far more skilled fighters than anyone the slaves have fought before.

Can we actually survive this? she wonders. *And what will happen to us if we do?*

CHAPTER FIFTY-FIVE

"WELL, FEARLESS LEADER?" DANIIL ASKS.

Yme motions at the Brüdel who dragged the dead magic blocker. "I'll start with Chains, there."

"And you really think we can win?" Kylii asks.

Yme shrugs. "It'll be fun finding out."

Daniil laughs. "You're a real motivator, Yme."

"Shut up and fight."

Yme splits to the left from Daniil and Kylii who move to the right. The chains hanging from the piercings in the assassin's ears swing wildly, mimicking his weapon of choice.

It burns Yme that the death of the magic blocker is his fault. He noticed the young man's attraction to Aya and used it for his own goals. It had been easy to convince him to slowly lower the guard of the other magic blockers. But it paid off. Their chances of survival are higher now. But they still have to defeat the Brüdel.

"Chains" keeps his distance and throws his weapon. Yme uses his wind magic to throw the weapon away from him. The Brüdel uses both hands to pull the chain taut, redirecting the sword and swinging it towards Yme again.

Yme barely dodges in time and throws a boulder at Chains,

who easily moves, reeling his weapon back in. He throws the blade again, embedding it in another of Yme's boulders. Yme tosses the boulder to the side, as a second blade shoots from behind the first blade. He tries to dodge, but the blade slices his leg. Blood flows down his leg, dirt stinging the wound.

The crowd gasps and cheers. *"Brüdel! Brüdel!"*

Chains pulls his first weapon free from the boulder and spins the two chains. The spinning blades produce a piercing whine. Chains smiles, showing rotting teeth and festering gums, then throws one weapon followed immediately by the other.

Yme dodges the blades, unable to find an opening to use his magic. Cursing, he tries to grab one of the spears hanging on the wall of the Arena. Chains aims one of his blades at the spear. Yme releases a rush of air at the sword, blowing it clear so he can grab the spear. He faces the Brüdel with the spear in front of him. As the second blade flies past, he maneuvers the spear against the chain, snagging the metal.

The chain goes taut and the Brüdel tries to pull free. But Yme tightens his grip on the spear. Using the time he's gained, Yme gathers his magic and stomps his foot, sending a shock through the ground towards Chains. A crack opens beneath him and he falls into the hole. The taut chain pulls against Yme as he rushes to close the hole.

The second blade stabs his arm from behind, interrupting his concentration on his magic. He yells and turns. The second blade had been thrown with the first with such precise timing he hadn't seen it. When he caught the first weapon, he was too distracted to see the second blade land behind him.

The Brüdel pulls himself from the hole, pulling on both chains to help him. Yme yelps in pain as the second blade slices deeper into his arm from the Brüdel's weight. As Chains appears over the edge of the hole, the blade rips from Yme's arm and returns to the Brüdel. Yme drops his spear, clutching his wounded arm.

Chains pulls his first sword back, untangling it from the

spear and then throws both weapons at Yme to strike him from either side.

Yme tries to pull up a shield of earth, but distracted from the pain in his arm, he raises the earth only to his knees. He tenses and lowers his stance.

Shadows fall over him and he hears the clang of metal. Bern and Cal stand to his right. Mava and Rava stand to his left. They blocked the blades with their weapons. The roar from the crowd at the surprise rescue fills the air.

"The great champion of the Arena becomes a weakling after only two scratches? Hardly the legend everyone makes you out to be," Bern says.

Ripping a piece of cloth from his shirt, Yme wraps it around his arm. "Pain can be distracting. That's why I try not to get hit."

"Try harder," Mava urges.

Laughing, Yme gathers air between his hands. He throws a gust of wind towards Chains and stretches his arms wide. The gust turns into a wall of wind, but Chains buries his blades into the earth and sustains his position. Yme throws up the earth beneath Chains, tossing the man and his weapons into the air. Before he hits the ground, Yme throws the raised earth into the Brüdel's side, hitting him with such force it knocks him across the Arena.

"Get the wounded to Aya," he commands. "We have to keep as many alive as possible. Fight only if you have to."

Mava and Rava run off to find the injured.

Yme turns to Bern and Cal. "Keep them safe. They'll need help if any of the Brüdel spot them carrying the wounded."

They nod and chase after the sisters, but Cal stops and turns to Yme. "We're going to win, right?"

Yme glances across the Arena. The slaves are managing to hold their own against the Brüdel, but none of Klaeon's men have fallen. Yme returns his attention to Cal. "What's your full name, Cal?"

"Calston Lito."

"Thank you for helping us in the tunnel."

Cal's expression lightens and he smiles. "It was the truth. I'm sorry for my father. He was never very good at standing up for himself."

Cal's father had been one of the five slaves to stay on the Brüdel's side. He had also been the first to plead for mercy as he died. "I'm sorry too," Yme says.

Cal raises his weapon. "He made his choice."

A warning shoots across the Arena and Yme moves out of the way of the two blades on chains. They're thrown wildly, with no focus, and strike another of the Brüdel in the back. He roars and tries to pull the swords from his back. The chains go taut. He turns and charges Yme, mistaking him for the culprit. He raises a giant, bloody club above his head. The blades stab into his neck and chest. He drops his club and grabs at the chains but cannot pull the swords free.

Chains spins the chain attached to the sword in the other Brüdel's neck and pulls. The chain pulls the sword around, nearly beheading the man. The large body collapses to the ground, dead. Yme steps clear and turns to Chains.

"The Rare Kind is mine!" Chains shrieks, blood rolling down the side of his head.

"I didn't know you could speak."

"I'll kill you! I'll slice your limbs off one by one and use your head as a pissing bowl!"

"We'll see who does the pissing." Yme smiles and raises a hand to Chains. "You won't touch me with your blades again."

CHAPTER FIFTY-SIX

"DANIIL?"

"Yeah, Kylii?"

"Why are we the only ones fighting the terrifying beasts that can tear us apart with their sharp teeth and claws?"

Daniil sighs and the air cools around him. "Because Yme can't be bothered to share the load. Are you ready Kylii-li?"

Kylii claps his hands, creating sparks. "Always, Daniil-li."

One of the beast men sneers. "We only get to kill these two? What a fucking bore!"

Two of the beasts strain against their chains, eager to attack. The men hold them back and beat them with whips made of spiked chains. The beasts become more aggressive and the men laugh.

The third beast lies calmly on the ground staring at nothing in particular. A single horn curves back over its scaled head. When it yawns, razor-sharp teeth flash. The body is covered in dark-red scales, with a brown mane running down its back and chest. The mane continues all the way down to the end of a long tail. The back paws are larger than the front paws, but both bare sharp claws.

"Who should go first, Scorch, Ears?" the one with a large

tattoo across his face banters. The other two men, one with severe burns on his body and the other missing an ear, snarl at him.

"Let your dujian tear 'em apart, Face. My rotrauk will be too quick," Scorch shouts.

Face laughs, his large belly jiggling. "Don't come crying to me when there's nothing left for your beasties to kill." He releases his dujian with a quick motion.

It leaps towards Kylii and Daniil, roaring. It's a huge creature with a great mane stretching down its back. Two tails whip wildly back and forth, cracking the earth, as razor sharp claws dig into the ground. The horns on its nose and forehead bear dark stains and pieces of meat hang from its long, sabre-sized teeth.

Kylii bows his head with hands stretched towards the beast. "This one's all yours."

"Too damn lazy to help, huh?" Daniil groans and steps towards the dujian.

The three Brüdel laugh and stomp. "What? Are you going to fight one at a time? This'll be nice and quick."

The dujian swipes at Daniil, who moves out of its way and pulls a knife from his belt. He throws the knife at the dujian's face. The hilt bounces off the dujian's face and falls harmlessly to the ground.

Daniil looks at his brother. "Oh. I see what you mean."

Kylii leans his head and smiles, devilishly.

The dujian leaps at Daniil's turned back. But Daniil raises a hand and encases the beast in ice. It falls to the ground. Long icicles extend inward from the frozen shell, piercing the animal at specific points on its body. A wave of Daniil's hand melts the ice and releases the dujian to fall to the earth, dead. Blood pools around its still body.

The three Brüdel stare in shock. Face walks forward and places a hand on his dujian's head. His face twists in rage and he draws a large, curved sword from his belt. He rushes Daniil, swinging wildly. Daniil tries to freeze Face, but the wild man manages to dodge.

Daniil forms ice on the ground in front of and behind Face, struggling to keep away from his angered foe. Fueled by rage, Face leaps over the ice and brings his blade down at Daniil.

Face erupts into flames. He screeches and drops his sword, slapping his arms and legs to put out the flames. No matter how much he rolls, the flames grow stronger. Daniil looks at Kylii, who stands with his hand raised at the burning man.

"I was fine."

"Yeah, keep thinking that. Meanwhile, I'll deal with reality for you."

The flames covering Face's body go out. He turns to Kylii, and grabs for his sword. Before he can reach it, Daniil retrieves it and cuts Face's arm. Blood spurts from a severed artery. Face stares in silence before the pain hits him. He howls and falls to the ground.

Scorch releases his rotrauk, but it leaps onto his burned, bleeding comrade. The wails abruptly stop. Raising its head to Daniil and Kylii, the rotrauk opens and closes its long snout full of sharp teeth. It hops on its long legs as its spindly tail wraps around the remains of Face like an inquisitive arm. Thin, wiry hairs cover its body, revealing pale flesh beneath.

Daniil motions to Kylii. "Would you like to take care of this, or should I?"

Kylii shrugs, walking towards the new beast. "I can't let you have all the easy ones."

"*Easy?*"

The rotrauk leaps, but Kylii drops and rolls under the animal. Daniil freezes over the ground where the animal lands. It slips with no traction for its claws. Falling forward, it rolls in the dirt, tail slapping the ground. It clambers up and skitters towards Daniil, who is now closer. Kylii raises his hand and a wall of fire divides his brother from the rotrauk. Skidding, the rotrauk spins to face Kylii. This time it's Daniil who throws up a wall in front of it—a wall of ice. With no time to change direction or slow down, the rotrauk crashes into the wall headfirst. When it tries to stand, its legs tremble.

"I can take care of myself, Daniil-li."

"Fine, I'll leave you to it."

The wall of ice disappears. The rotrauk shakes its head and regains its feet. The spindles on its tail shake and vibrate, making a horrid rattling sound. It takes a deep breath and spews a dark gush of liquid towards Kylii. Kylii leaps to land behind the body of the dujian. The liquid hits the body and dissolves it.

Daniil shakes his head. "You said you could take care of yourself. So, handle this *easy* one. Don't look to me to help you."

CHAPTER FIFTY-SEVEN

THE ROTRAUK INHALES AGAIN AND SPEWS THE LIQUID AT KYLII. HE tries to hide behind the mauled body of Face, but the acid dissolves the flesh and bones. Kylii desperately tries to devise a defense, but the rotrauk leaps onto what's left of Face's body, digs its claws into the acid-soaked flesh, and inhales again. At such close range, Kylii can't dodge.

He raises both hands. The rotrauk spews acid as flames appear from Kylii's palms. When the acid and fire meet, an explosion knocks man and beast apart.

"Kylii-li!" Daniil shouts.

Kylii sits up and coughs. He shakes his head. "Great, it not only melts flesh and bone, it's also explosive."

The rotrauk rolls to its feet, shakes the dust from its mangy hair, and runs for Kylii, who rolls, but the beast slams into him. Kylii struggles to keep the large jaws from his face as the two roll across the Arena floor.

The rotrauk's tail wraps around Kylii's throat and claws dig into his sides. He yelps, but the tail tightens. Kylii feels the air becoming cold around them and glares at Daniil. "Don't you dare!" he manages to croak.

Daniil pauses to throw his magic at the two Brüdel. With the ground frozen, Scorch slips and falls, landing on the tail of the third animal. The beast goes gives a crazed roar. Scorch scrambles to his feet. He and Ears struggle to keep the animal under control. The beast swipes Scorch across the stomach with a large claw on its left paw. Shock mixes with terror and Scorch punches Ears in the face. Ears kicks Scorch's leg. The two men lock arms and try to throw each other to the ground.

Ears shoves Scorch away, knocking him to the ground. Scorch stiffens, convulsions shaking his body. Foam fills his mouth, white at first before turning red. Blood pours from his eyes, ears, and nose. He jerks several times before stilling, his life gone.

Kylii wishes to get a hand free to use his magic, but one is wedged against the pressure of the tail wrapped around his throat, and the other staves off the slavering jaws. He sees the spindles of the rotrauk's tail shiver, and curses. He rolls so he will be on top if the animal does not let go. Sure enough, the rotrauk keeps its grip and prepares to spew acid. At the last second Kylii raises a hand and a fireball rises and spins in his hand. The fire hits the acid and the animal roars in pain. The tail whips away, and Kylii groans and rolls onto his side. He pushes himself up and looks at the rotrauk writhing on the ground. Its head is smoking. The flesh around its jaws bubbles and uncovers the bone. With great effort the rotrauk rolls onto its feet and glares at Kylii, who struggles to his own feet, holding his wounded side.

"Didn't like that, did you? It's dangerous to keep all that explosive acid inside you. Especially around a guy like me."

The rotrauk roars and runs towards him. Kylii leans forward and stretches his hands out in front of him. He yells loudly, mimicking the rotrauk's roar, further infuriating the beast. It increases its speed, its spindles shining brightly.

Kylii runs forward to meet the rotrauk. The beast opens its mouth to take a deep breath, preparing to spew its acid. Kylii rams his right arm down its throat. Grabbing the back of the beast's head, he moves his right arm as far as he can.

The rotrauk freezes, trying to close its jaws.

Kylii winces as teeth dig into his arm. He feels the acid inside the rotrauk burning his hand. Smiling, he looks into the eyes of the animal. "Bye-bye." He releases his magic, fire mixing with the acid inside of the rotrauk. The explosion throws Kylii into the air. But as he lands, gobbets of singed rotrauk flesh rain down. Acid hits slaves and Brüdel alike, screams echoing through the air.

Daniil runs to his brother and stares at where Kylii's right arm should be. Everything below the elbow is gone. Skin is still melting from the scorched, black bones and muscle.

"Should've let you blast your own damned arm off." Kylii howls as one last hunk of the rotrauk hits him. "Fucking bastard had to get the last word in, didn't he?"

Daniil stares at the remaining Brüdel and beast. "I don't think we can win."

Kylii grabs his brother with his good arm, glaring at him. "What the hell kind of talk is that, after your brave brother sacrifices his arm to get us this far?"

"It's a Khorgoi."

Kylii looks at the animal. White eyes study the two brothers. "A Khorgoi? I thought those were just stories to frighten children."

"It killed that Brüdel with one scratch." Daniil nods to the body of Scorch.

"What do we do?"

Daniil glances across the Arena at those fighting. He spies a small group running from one wounded slave to another. Recognizing Rava and Mava, he waves them over. When they see Kylii's arm they both gasp, Mava turning away from the grave sight.

"Take him to Aya. She has to be the one to help him."

"Daniil-li! What are you doing?"

"It's my turn."

"You can't fight alone. Let me help." Kylii tries to stand but yelps at the small movements. The sisters lead him away, able to overpower him due to his wounds.

Daniil stands and walks towards the Khorgoi and Ears.

The Khorgoi perks up and stands, pulling against its chain. Ears laughs. "Going to fight alone? Your partner didn't fare so well."

"Kylii-li thinks more with his heart than I do. And I don't think you understand who's actually controlling whom."

"What're you going on about?"

"No one controls a Khorgoi. They're intelligent creatures that choose when to be seen. They can kill a man with a single scratch. Or they can fight by your side to victory. They're to be respected, not treated as common animals."

"What the hell are you talking about?"

Daniil laughs. "You don't even know what you have. You think you're a great beast master because of how easy this animal was to tame, am I right? The thought probably never crossed your mind that this animal *allowed* you to capture it and only acts as though you're in control."

The Brüdel sneers. "You think you're fucking clever." He whips the Khorgoi. "Kill him!"

The Khorgoi doesn't move, staring at Daniil. Ears whips it again. "Go on. Kill him, you stupid beast!"

The Khorgoi moves faster than Daniil can see. Ears screams as his flesh is carved from his bones. When the Khorgoi is finished it turns back to Daniil. It breaks the chain around its throat easily with its front claws and shakes. It walks towards Daniil, staring with its emotionless, white eyes.

Daniil takes a deep breath and raises his hands.

CHAPTER FIFTY-EIGHT

AYA DIRECTS THOSE CARRYING THE FRESHLY WOUNDED. "MAKE SURE to keep those with minor injuries separate from the severely wounded. If they can wait to be healed, ask if they can keep guard. Mark the severely wounded with an X on their forehead and move them closer to me."

"Mark with what?" Bon asks.

"Mud, blood, whatever you can."

Bon nods and spreads Aya's orders to the other healers and injured. Aya finishes healing the man in front of her and moves on to the next one, a woman with a broken arm. But a woman with her stomach torn open is quickly brought over and Aya hands the broken arm off to Tristan. Aya holds the woman's abdomen together to prevent her insides from spilling out. Crying softly, the woman's eyes fade in and out of focus, her face deathly pale, and her breathing staggered. Aya takes a deep breath to keep nausea from the smell at bay.

She heals the woman but tells her to rest to allow her body to recover from the severe repairs. The woman nods and moves to sit against the wall of the arena next to others in similar need.

Sagging back on her heels, Aya wipes the sweat from her forehead. Although many she's healed multiple times are fighting bravely, more and more slaves lie dead on the ground—while the opposing side seems hardly reduced in numbers.

Glancing behind her, Aya spots the slowly growing pile of those she could not save. There are even more left on the battlefield where they fell, but there are still too many in the pile.

"Aya!"

She turns and sees Rava and Mava carrying Kylii between them. He smiles at her, then winces in great pain. His face is pale and his eyes sunken.

"Kylii! What's wrong—?" she stops, staring at Kylii's right arm in horror.

"Got a little too close to a beastie," he jokes.

Mava and her sister lower him to the ground. Aya leans down to assess the damage. "Gods! How did this happen?"

Kylii laughs. "Reached my arm down the gullet of a sweet little guy that spat explosive acid, and received this little memento."

Aya slaps his forehead. "That could've killed you!"

"Hey! It was the only way to win. I knew you could heal me." He smiles and leans his head to the side.

"If you died, I couldn't. What would Daniil have done then?"

Kylii's smile fades as he turns his head away. "It worked out."

Aya sighs and pushes him down onto his back. "Hold still. I've never restored this much bone before. It's going to hurt."

"Not as much as getting it, I bet."

"That's what you think," she says, to make him smile. Then she places her hands on the remnants of Kylii's right arm and concentrates. She feels her magic fill her and moves it into Kylii. Warmth fills his arm and his body responds. Bone grows. Muscle stretches into place. Veins, arteries, and nerves recreate their networks. Aya's head fills with the sound of the repairs and the shocks of nerves reconnecting.

Kylii takes a sharp breath and grips the earth. Rava grabs his left hand and, judging by her face, he squeezes hard.

Skin grows from existing cells to cover the new arm. Aya feels the blood enter the remade arteries, veins, and muscles. Once she finishes, she falls on top of Kylii, gasping.

He lifts her up. "You okay?"

Aya shakes her head. She hears Kylii's body, Rava's body, the sound of flesh tearing and blood rates increasing, decreasing. She focuses on her own body and the warmth inside of her, silent until the overwhelming flow of information fades.

Taking a deep breath, she stares back at the anxious faces around her. "I'm fine. It took more effort than I expected."

"You weren't kidding." He smirks and tweaks her cheek with his new hand. "That hurt a lot more than getting it."

A cheer from the crowd causes them to look across the Arena to where Yme has trapped the Brüdel with chains in earth and strangled him with the very weapon he'd used to kill the magic blocker.

I hope he suffered. Aya wishes she didn't enjoy the thought, but if she denied it... that would make her a liar, and untruthfulness bruised the soul.

Immediately, more Brüdel attack Yme. He kicks the encased body at those approaching and continues fighting, with no evidence of fatigue.

Kylii gazes at his new arm, rotating it. "Thanks. I have to get back to Daniil. He's fighting something no man should ever face alone."

"Then maybe a *man* should go help him," Rava says, smirking.

Kylii shrugs. "He'll just have to be satisfied with me." He runs back out into the fighting.

Aya watches him disappear into the chaos. Even injured, he exudes optimism. A vast change from the taciturn fighter she met on her first day.

Rava and Mava head off to gather more wounded. Aya returns her attention to those desperately needing her help, quickly moving from one to another—healing and speaking words of encouragement. Until...

"Guvie!"

The oldest of the Arena slaves lies on the ground, clutching deep wounds in his abdomen and chest. His face is ghostly white, making the blood X mark stand out nearly black on his forehead. He smiles at her. "Life Healer, it is an honor to have fought at your side today."

Even before touching him, she knows he's too far gone for her magic. Tears threatening to fall. "I'm sorry."

"There's no need for an apology, Life Healer. It's my time to die. Don't waste time on me. Heal those you can."

Aya leans down and kisses him on the forehead. His eyes flutter closed. She puts her hand to her heart for a brief moment before moving to the next wounded slave.

The wounded slave wears a helmet covering his face. Aya sees a large dent in the metal and blood running down from underneath. She struggles to remove the helmet, wondering if swelling kept the metal on. The helmet comes off and Aya surveys the damage. The face beneath is heavily scarred, blood covering the man's entire face.

But she sees no wound and as her magic explores the body, there's nothing unusual.

The man grabs her throat. Sitting up, he smiles and wipes blood from his face. "You're the little healer who has caused so much trouble?"

Aya struggles to breathe. "Brüdel..." she gasps.

He pulls her close and his yellowed eyes take her face in. "The Blood King has a lovely prize waiting for the one to bring him your head." He pulls a jagged knife from his belt. "That will be me."

Aya tries to scream, but he tightens his hold on her throat and thrusts her to the ground and straddles her, placing the blade at her throat and his hand on her chest.

"My favorites are the healers. They try so hard to help everyone, save everyone. So easy to trick, so easy to sway. My favorite was a high-level bone grower. Convinced her to heal me and I would save her from my brethren. Once I had my leg back, I sliced her into so many pieces no healer could put her back together." The blade presses harder at Aya's throat as he leans in. "But I only need one piece from you, little healer. Your tiny head."

A shout catches both the Brüdel and Aya by surprise. Guvie slams into the Brüdel, freeing Aya, but then he collapses. The Brüdel slices Guvie's throat quickly, and grabs Aya's leg before she can escape. He pulls her towards him, raising his blade.

A spear stabs into the Brüdel's chest, the wielder pushing him off Aya. He tries to turn, but a sword comes down on his neck.

"Are you all right?" Bern asks, pulling his spear from the dead man.

Aya nods. "Thank you."

"You need to be more careful." Leid wipes the blood from his sword onto the dead Brüdel's clothes and kicks the decapitated head away. "These assassins are far more deceitful than regular fighters."

Bern helps Aya to her feet.

"Do I need to be careful of *you*?" Aya asks Leid.

Leid turns his emotionless gaze on her. Bern tenses, his hands squeezing the wood of his spear tightly.

"I haven't decided yet," he answers.

CHAPTER FIFTY-NINE

A POINTED ROCK PIERCING HIS SKULL SIGNALS THE END OF A BRÜDEL with sharpened teeth. He falls on top of his brethren. Yme takes a moment to catch his breath. The number of Klaeon's assassins has decreased. But the number of slaves has decreased far more. It seems the fighting will never end.

Two Brüdel try to trap Yme by attacking from both sides. He raises his arms at the elbow and earth rises in front of them. Once he's stopped their forward motion, Yme pushes outward, causing the walls of the earth to drag the men back, smashing them against opposite walls of the Arena.

"These are Klaeon's greatest assassins?" he shouts.

He runs towards a group of slaves fighting off two large Brüdel and three smaller, quicker men. The smaller men move in for quick slashes, taunting while the large Brüdel keep the slaves from escaping. Yme pulls water from buckets around the walls of the Arena and freezes the feet of the smaller men.

While they're distracted, Yme sends gusts of wind to separate the two large Brüdel, creating an opening for the slaves to escape. They surround the Brüdel and Yme leads them in a counterattack. Earth flies as earth magic users finally have use of their magic. A magic user kneels, placing his hands on his shadow. He slowly stands, raising his hands. Dark smoke rises, swirling as though alive. The shadows form into human shape and the slave throws them about, confusing the Brüdel, who attack the shadows, unsure what is real. Yme crushes the three smaller men and soon the group of five is dead. The slaves thank Yme with a wave and rush to help others. The slaves are finally taking control of the fight.

A horn sounds and echoes through the Arena. He turns his attention to Klaeon's private box and sees him whispering into Teron's ear. Teron bows and disappears through the red curtains at the back of the box.

The large cranks opens. A giant emerges out of the darkness. Towering over all the Brüdel, he looks around the Arena with large, empty eyes. Long, greasy-black hair hangs to his shoulders. Two Brüdel enter the Arena after him, yelling words at the giant in a strange language.

The giant turns his head as though it's too heavy for his neck. He sees the slaves fighting the Brüdel and an expression flashes across his face that reminds Yme of an overexcited child. The giant yells loudly, swings his long arms around, and stomps his feet before tromping over to the nearest fighting group. Raising his monstrous feet, he crushes slave and Brüdel alike, like a child squashing bugs. Any who try to fight him are smashed by a fist or sent flying into the audience. Slaves run in terror from the monster. Brüdel move out of the giant's path and cheer him as he passes, using the same guttural language.

The excitement shooting through the audience at the giant's arrival is palpable and increases with each kill—until he crashes into a wall at full speed. The size of the giant destroys not only the wall, but also a large section of seating, killing many audience members and dropping a number of them into the Arena. They scramble to find an escape, but workers keep them away from the gates, unwilling to risk any escapes just for these few citizens. Brüdel who come across the frightened people kill them without a second thought. Others scamper to climb back up into the seats, but only trample each other.

A few, friends or family of those who were killed, break down in shrill cries. Even so, most of the remaining audience remains at high energy and the Arena overflows with roars of excitement. Those sitting near the damaged area climb into other sections.

The giant bellows and moves around the Arena at random, attacking any who wander into his line of sight. He moves to attack the audience directly, but a voice in his harsh language from below stops the giant cold. He turns his large head and Yme notices a strange motion from the giant's lips.

Is it trying to smile?

Yme follows the giant's gaze and his heart turns to ice. The giant charges the area where Aya and the healers are treating the wounded. And the giant's attention is locked on Aya. She and the other healers are too busy working to see the immense man heading for them.

Yme curses and runs for the group. Other Brüdel, seeing Yme, chase after him or try to block his path. He crushes them with his earth magic, knocks them away with his air magic, or drowns them with his water magic. He shouts to Aya, but the noise of the fighting and roar of the audience drowns him out.

Kylii runs forward, and Yme changes his path and grabs the twin's arm. "Have you seen that monster? Aya is in danger!"

"Have you seen Daniil? I can't find him or the beast he was fighting."

"Later! Right now, we have to stop that thing from reaching the healers!"

Kylii sees the destination of the giant's rampage, bites his lower lip, and nods. "All right."

The two race after the giant.

CHAPTER SIXTY

AYA FINISHES HEALING ANOTHER SEVERELY INJURED MAN AND stands. All are running out of energy. Aya experiences more strain each time she heals. If the fighting doesn't end soon, they won't have anything left.

An enormous hand grabs her around the waist and lifts her. Aya screams as she stares into the face of a giant. His expression is empty, his mouth hanging open. But the lips are twisted into a deranged smile. He touches Aya's hair with his other hand, breathing heavily. She slaps the hand away and tries to wriggle free.

The giant grimaces and squeezes. Aya gasps, her chest tightening to a narrow passage, and she claws at the hand holding her. Small tracks of blood appear, but the giant only squeezes tighter. Concentrating, she attempts to use her magic to strengthen her body against the pressure. She screams as she feels a rib crack, but she pushes her magic harder to keep any more from breaking.

She reaches for one of the knives hidden in her wrist cuffs and aims for a large vein visible under the taut skin. The giant yells in pain and grabs his fist with his other hand, only squeezing her harder.

Her vision darkens around the edges. She tries to raise her arm to stab at the vein again, but her limbs have gone limp. Her knife falls from her hand and her head rolls forward. Her magic fades and she feels the darkness grow stronger.

The giant releases her, air rushing past as she falls. Then a strong updraft slows her descent. She lands in warm arms and hears the grunt of the one catching her. She inhales deeply and coughs, nearly choking. When her vision returns, she sees Yme's face. He lowers her legs to the ground, keeping an arm around her waist for support. He leads her away from the giant.

As a large foot stomps the ground nearby, Aya spies Kylii dashing between the thick legs. He throws up a wall of fire whenever the giant's hands get too close. The giant cringes from the burning light and tries to step on Kylii.

Yme takes Aya clear of the fight. "Stay here. Kylii and I will take care of this."

"Where's Daniil?"

Yme shakes his head.

The giant growls and kicks. Kylii is too fast and dodges the attempts to crush him. The giant's tattered and filthy pants burst into flames, bringing screams from the wearer, who smashes into the nearby Arena walls to smother the flames. The murder of audience members continues to grow.

The healers scramble to move the wounded away from the battle, but there are too many bodies for five people. "If he keeps going, he's going to crush the injured," Aya says.

"Stay here." She starts to argue, but he barks, "Just this once, do as I say."

Aya nods. "I need to do some healing on myself before I go anywhere."

Yme sprints across the Arena. He joins Kylii in steering the giant away from the wounded. Aya slumps to the ground, stirring up her magic.

∼

YME PULLS a boulder from the earth and throws it at the giant's head, drawing its attention from the slaves and healers transporting the wounded. One enormous hand reaches for Yme, but a fireball slams into its neck. It bellows and grabs at its throat. Turning, it chases after Kylii who runs out of reach. Yme pulls another boulder and smashes it into the giant's back. The impact knocks the enormous man forward, landing on his belly.

Kylii pops up, glaring at Yme. "Can you please *not* almost crush me with a giant?"

"You're quick enough."

The giant grabs a large slab of stone from a crushed wall of the Arena and uses it to try and smash Yme and Kylii. He slams it down over and over again, missing each time. Frustrated, the giant growls and throws the slab into the audience. They try to scramble out of the way, but the crowd is too large and much of the Arena is already damaged. Dozens more die in the stands. Now, the audience sounds begin to change.

"This bastard isn't going down!" Kylii throws his fireballs high up into the air, aiming for the giant's eyes.

Yme throws earth up, trying to trip the giant who merely crashes through with his huge feet. "Daniil's freezing would be useful right now!"

A howling roar rises from behind them with the click of running claws. The Khorgoi leaps over them, zig-zags towards the giant, avoiding his attacks, and claws the giant's feet, cutting deep enough to show bone.

The giant raises his fist high above his head, ready to bring it down on the Khorgoi. Ice covers his hand and lower arm, throwing his balance off and causing him to fall to the ground onto his back. The Khorgoi leaps onto the giant's chest and digs into the flesh. The giant raises his free hand and slaps at the beast. The Khorgoi jumps to the ground, avoiding the large hand. The giant slaps one hand against his raw, bloody chest and bellows in pain. Pink ice freezes the hand to his chest. He struggles to raise his other arm, frozen fist and all, but he can't. The giant stops struggling, his body jerking violently from side to side, as scarlet foam erupts from his mouth.

Daniil walks over to his brother. "Hey."

"Where the hell have *you* been?" Kylii demands.

The Khorgoi moves to Daniil's side and sits. It looks up at him, expectantly.

"What is that?" Yme asks.

Daniil places a hand on the animal's head and smiles. "This is Tanith. She's a Khorgoi."

Kylii stares at his brother, confused. "How do you know it's a she? For that matter... how do you know its name?"

"What's a Khorgoi?" Aya asks, surprising them.

Tanith huffs and Daniil holds his hand out as though calming her. "Khorgois are legendary beasts in our part of the world. They're said to be spirits that watch over the earth. I know her name because while we fought, I...I heard her voice."

Kylii grabs Daniil's shoulders. "You're delirious. Run that by me again?"

Yme turns to scan the Arena for the remaining Brüdel.

"I heard her voice in my head and she told me her name," Daniil insists.

"What does that even *mean*?"

The healers sag, near exhaustion. Those protecting them drop their weapons to the floor. Yme scans but there don't seem to be any more Brüdel.

"It means she wants something."

"What did she ask for?"

Daniil regards his brother cautiously. "She wants to be returned to her home."

"Quiet!" Yme shouts. The group falls silent and turn to him. He waves his hand around them at the still arena. "Listen."

A strange silence fills the Arena. Shock fills every face.

They are victorious.

CHAPTER SIXTY-ONE

THE BRÜDEL ALL LIE DEAD ON THE ARENA FLOOR. DESPITE MANY dead and still more wounded, the slaves stand victorious.

Applause starts somewhere in the audience. A low cheer follows, slowly growing to fill the Arena. A chant blocks out all sounds.

Aya, Yme, Daniil, Kylii, and those around them stare up at the excited crowd. The audience's chant continues on and on.

"Freedom! Freedom! Freedom!"

The surviving slaves hug each other in surprised relief. They survived the Blood King's deadly game. And the audience is declaring its desired reward for them.

Aya takes in the thousands of faces. Some are yelling, "Aya!" Those who don't know her name yell, "Healer!" Some shout for Yme, their champion. But she spies a figure standing in one of the many openings leading outside of the Arena, wearing a hooded cloak that casts his face in shadow. But she remembers him. He was there during her first fight. Something about him brings mixed feelings of fear and familiarity.

A bell rings out over the sound of the cheers, but it still takes a long time for anyone to notice it. Dolus Otho holds his hands up in an attempt to catch the attention of the crowd. Calming, the crowd focuses not on Dolus Otho, but on the Blood King's private box.

Standing still as a statue at the edge, Blood King Klaeon's eyes are flush with rage. He glances around the Arena at the crowd before returning his focus to Aya. He turns away. Waving at his men, Klaeon disappears through the red curtain, followed by Teron.

Only once the last of the Blood King's men is out of sight does the audience turn to Dolus Otho. The Arena announcer's face is pale, but he manages to keep the smile on his face. "A victory for the slaves! The Gods have chosen their champions!"

The audience's cheers return full force. Hearing the official declaration, many of the slaves pick their weapons up and raise them above their heads. They strut to the edges of the Arena to encourage the audience's cheers.

The relief overtaking Aya drains the last of her energy. Her legs collapse beneath her and she laughs while tears roll down her cheeks.

Arena workers open the gates to usher the slaves back into the bowels of the Arena—this time with smiles and praise instead of jeers and threats. Soon the underbelly of the Arena is filled with the echoes of cheers and laughter.

Two workers attempt to capture Tanith, but the Khorgoi easily leaps over them to remain close to Daniil. Their second attempt goes just as poorly. Tanith swings her tail into the head of one, knocking him out. She huffs her breath at the second worker, nodding up and down, threatening him with her horn. He backs away, dragging the first worker by the wrists to safety.

The rush of their victory transitions into exhaustion. Their legs drag down the stairs and a few lean on others to continue forward. Wounded slaves branch off to the arena healers as the rest continue to the cellblock level.

Many of the slaves head for the baths, eager to relieve the soreness in their muscles or wash the blood from their skin. All

Aya wants is her bed. Her head aches from the adrenaline rush of the battle and her stomach grumbles.

The workers leave the cell doors open, showing each survivor newfound respect and sitting with them as equals. Workers sit inside the cells listening to stories of the fight. A small group circles together, praying for those who fell. Praying for Velan to lead the dead safely to Moirai, the realm after life where those who died will one day see their loved ones again.

Food is brought directly to the cellblock. Seera is nowhere to be seen, so the workers must have decided among themselves to lay out this feast. The air fills with light-hearted laughter as the many skirmishes are told from numerous points of view.

The only ones missing from the feast are Aya, Yme, Daniil, and Kylii. Tanith is allowed to remain with Daniil after biting three workers who prevented her from entering the cell.

Bern, Cal, Bon, Tristan, Skara, Rava, and Mava stay close to Aya's cell, bringing food to the four Rare Kinds. Bon even brings food and drink for Tanith, carefully placing the plate and bowl in front of the animal.

Aya picks at the food in front of her, knowing she needs to eat. *I need to recharge. But all I really want is to sleep.* She notices Yme and the twins are similarly slow in consuming the large quantities of food. Tanith is already asleep underneath one of the beds, her tail curled around her body. The plate of food Bon brought for the Khorgoi has been licked clean.

Aya gazes through the bars of the cell. Even with the crowd of workers and slaves from other cellblocks, there are a noticeable number of slaves missing. Cells that were filled beyond capacity are empty now, or only have one occupant.

"You saved a lot of lives today," Yme says. "But you look defeated."

"For every life I saved, two more were lost." Aya turns to him. "If victories cost huge casualties, are they still victories?"

"You aren't responsible for their deaths. They fought hard and valiantly."

"For us."

"For themselves. We gave them the strength to fight for what they truly wanted."

"Which was?" Aya asks.

"Freedom to choose. All we can do now is honor their sacrifice and keep living."

"Seems unfair to those who died."

The familiar whip crack announces Seera's arrival. The mirth silences and everyone turns to her. Parting the slaves and workers, she stops at the entrance to the Rare Kinds' cell. She places a hand on her hip and squeezes the handle of her whip tightly.

Yme walks forward to meet her.

Tension rises around the two figures as the slaves make ready for whatever Seera plans to do.

Seera holds her free hand out in front of her. Yme slowly accepts it with his own hand. They shake and the tension eases.

"This Arena has seen thousands of fighters, witnessed thousands of games, and held hundreds of thousands of spectators. This day, this fight, and *all* of these brave fighters..." Seera indicates the slaves with her other arm, "will be spoken of for ages. You, for today, have discarded the title of slaves. You are all true warriors."

The slaves are struck dumb by her words and her attitude. Cheers ignite the celebration back to life as workers bring out more food and drinks, even some grainy, amber sort of alcohol. Singing arises from the long tables at the center of the cellblock.

Seera steps into the cell and pulls Yme close. "The cell doors will be kept open in honor of your victory. Feel free to enjoy the fresh night air."

Yme pulls away with surprise. Seera winks, pats him on the back, then runs a hand through Aya's hair.

The gentle touch brings tension to Aya's shoulders.

"You surprised us all, Life Healer." Seera leans down. "Be wary of those you trust. We all choose wrong on occasion."

Aya jerks away from the woman and stares at her. The cruelness she's come to expect is still there, but as Seera leaves the cell, she wears a kinder smile. She pats the shoulders of those she passes and disappears into the celebrating crowd.

"What did she say to you?" Kylii asks Aya.

"Just congratulations." Yme returns to his seat beside Aya, his thoughts distant. Aya places a hand on his leg, breaking him from his thoughts. "But what did she mean about the fresh night air?"

Yme motions for Daniil and Kylii to lean in close. "She meant it's time. Tonight, we escape this place."

IV

THE FIRES OF HOPE

CHAPTER SIXTY-TWO

The celebration continues into the night. The slaves enjoy themselves for the first time in many months—many years for some. Word of the escape passes quickly, encouraging them to share their rare alcoholic drinks with the workers until they leave for their own beds or pass out at the tables or in the many now-vacant cells.

After the final worker leaves, a low whistle echoes down the block. The slaves venture out of their cells to the center. Aya and Yme step from their cell, followed by the twins and Tanith. Many watch them for instruction, and Aya nudges Yme forward.

"This is our chance." He speaks loudly, but not enough to fill the entire block. Slaves from the upper levels climb down to join the gathering crowd around Yme. "It's time to escape this arena of blood. Those who wish to escape, follow us. Those of you who choose to stay...may the Gods watch over you."

Aya moves next to Yme and watches the crowd. To her surprise, a third of the slaves return to their cells. But she spots Leid approaching her.

"You're staying?" she asks, gaze lingering on his missing arm.

He glances into her cell. "Someone will need to keep the

audiences entertained to cover for your sorry hides." His cold eyes move to her face. "I was placed here for a reason. Perhaps, now, I may make amends."

"You saved many today. Come with us. We could use your strength."

"My strength is not for saving. We'll meet again in the after-life, Aya." A smile forms on his lips. Hearing him speak her name sends chills through her body, but she returns the smile. Leid walks into the cell and lies down on her bed. "May the Gods watch over you, too," he murmurs.

Taking a deep breath, Aya looks at Yme. "Let's go."

He nods and they both head out, followed by Kylii, Daniil, Tanith, Bern, Mava, Rava, Cal, Bon, and Tristan. After a moment, the rest follow. Hearts in their mouths, they head for the stairway.

The group moves carefully through the catacombs, avoiding workers who didn't join the celebration. They're scattered, distracted, preparing for the next day's events, making it easy for the group to slip through unseen. Still, the slaves keep to the shadows. They traverse the training grounds to the floor with the animal pens. They navigate through the cages, avoiding any animals still awake.

Yme stops the group and points ahead. "Those aren't Arena workers." He indicates a group standing at the stairway leading up to the staging floor.

"Klaeon's men?" Daniil asks.

Two dozen soldiers stand in ranks, holding torches. One barks orders and points back towards the stairway leading down to the training grounds. The slaves disperse to hide amongst the cages as the men pass by.

"Looks like the Blood King wasn't happy about out victory," Kylii whispers as the slaves regroup.

"We were supposed to die. I don't suppose he was thrilled when we didn't," Daniil replies.

More soldiers walk down and move off in a different direction. *Another set of stairs*? Aya thinks. A third group of soldiers appears, waiting.

"But what are they doing here?" Aya asks. "I thought Klaeon left?"

Yme chuckles, low. "They're here to kill us in our sleep."

"I still don't understand. Why does he want to kill us?"

"We threaten his power, especially his power over the people. Think of all those in the audience who will spread the story of our victory today against his strongest fighters. He's afraid we'll rally them against him."

"*Is* that what you've been doing?"

"Trying to," Yme shrugs his shoulders and nods his head at her. "But it hasn't worked until recently."

Kylii leans between the two. "Enough talking. How're we going to get past them?"

"Too many to take on without weapons," Bern says, walking up next to Yme. "We didn't grab anything from the armory."

"Is there no other way?" Mava asks.

"If you don't mind digging your way out of here," Daniil says.

"There is another way," a familiar, stern voice says.

The group jumps and prepares to fight. Seera walks around the corner of a cage and leans against the metal bars. "I can show you, but you have to take me with you."

"And me." Dolus Otho appears next to Seera, drawing a soft gasp from the slaves. Hushes move down the group.

Daniil glares at Seera. "Why would you want to come with us? Your lives are comfortable here."

"They were," Dolus Otho clears his throat. "Until you won the fight today. Who do you think the Blood King is going to blame?"

"Our fates were decided the same as yours when you won," Seera spits. She throws two severed heads at Yme and Aya's feet. "He didn't send his best soldiers for this little mission. I killed these two before they even knew Dolus or I were awake."

Aya glances at the heads. The faces have been slashed beyond recognition. Horrified, she wonders if she should accept these brutes into their company.

But Yme doesn't seem to notice. "Where is this other way out?"

Kylii steps close to Yme. "Hold on, you can't honestly be thinking of letting her come with us?"

Others in the group voice agreement and Yme holds his hands up to silence them. "We need a way out. We can't go this way, and if she's speaking the truth, then we have to trust her."

"I don't trust her," Aya says flatly. Seera smiles back at her and laughs. "But I believe her. Klaeon wouldn't leave those who failed him alive. Their heads are on the line as much as ours."

"What if they're lying? What if they want to make sure the Blood King's men find us?" Daniil asks.

"Daniil, your pet—" Yme starts.

The Khorgoi stares at Yme with her white eyes, indignant.

"Her name is Tanith and she's not a pet," Daniil corrects.

"*Tanith*," Yme corrects himself. "You claim you can hear her voice."

"And she understands human speech. What's your point?"

"We'll have her watch Seera and Dolus as they lead us out. If it starts looking or feeling like a trap, have her kill them. Will that ease your minds?"

Dolus Otho shrinks, visibly uncomfortable, but Seera grips his arm tightly to keep him quiet. "We agree to the terms."

Daniil confirms with Tanith that she understands the plan.

Yme nods to Seera. "Show us the way."

"And you'll take us with you?" Dolus Otho asks.

"Yes."

"Well then, follow me," Seera says, heading back the way the group came.

334

CHAPTER SIXTY-THREE

DANIIL, TANITH, AND KYLII STAY DIRECTLY BEHIND SEERA AND Dolus. Aya and Yme follow next and then the rest of the group. They walk through the animal pens, where most of the beasts are asleep, but those who hunt at night are alert to the strange group.

A small cadre of Klaeon's men walk through the pens. Seera signals towards the shadows and the group moves, avoiding the light of the soldiers' torches. Seera whistles and shadows across from the group begin moving. The group realizes, to their relief, they are Arena workers, faithful to Seera. The workers sneak behind the soldiers, killing them quietly and pulling the bodies into the shadows.

Seera leads the group to the far end of the animal pens. She grabs a torch from the wall and motions the group to follow closely. Aya peeks at the Arena workers now following close behind. None of them are workers she's ever seen before. She bumps into Dolus Otho. The Arena announcer's pace slowed. Up close, the lines on his face appear deeper and the dark circles under his eyes show exhaustion.

"Have you always been the 'voice of the arena?'" Aya asks.

"It is a position that has been filled by the Otho family for

335

generations. Even before the Blood King's rule, we were the Voice of the Games. Though after this transgression, I feel that may no longer be the case."

"How can he punish you for our victory? You can't control that."

Dolus Otho leans close to Aya. "You don't understand. It is our duty to *ensure* the slaves do not win when they're not meant to. Seera did not plan for her workers to turn on her."

Aya remembers the magic blocker who was brutally murdered in front of them by the Brüdel. "She rigged the fight?"

"Her workers were told to aid the Brüdel. Instead, they disobeyed. A small number even aided your group. They thought Seera didn't notice...but she knows everything that happens in the walls of this Arena." Dolus Otho gasps and turns away as though he spoke words he shouldn't have.

Aya thinks back on the two heads of the soldiers Seera killed. Something about how the faces were carved beyond recognition bothers her. The lack of severe bleeding from the scarring suggested it had been done after the soldiers died. But why bother scarring the faces beyond recognition after decapitation, unless...

Aya grabs Dolus Otho's arm. "Those weren't soldiers, were they?"

Ahead of the group, Seera signals for the workers at the back of the group to move quickly to two large, stone doors at the end of the hallway. They strain at the immense weight of the stone.

Seera urges the group. "Hurry!"

Then cool wind blows from the opening doorway. The slaves press forward, eager to see the outside world.

Dolus Otho pulls against Aya's grip. "Let me go."

"The men Seera killed! They weren't soldiers?" Aya repeats, squeezing his arm tighter.

The group pushes forward, moving Aya and Dolus Otho with them. As they walk through the doors, they're greeted by Blood King Klaeon's soldiers. Spears aim at the group. Dolus

336

Otho shoves Aya to the ground and tries to fight through the group back through the doors.

The doors slam shut before any others in the group realize what's happening. Otho pounds the stone with his fists. "Seera! Open the doors!" Those closest to the doors try their best to force them open. Earth magic users try to force the stone to move, but carvings in the stone prevent the magic from taking effect.

"It's a trap!" Kylii yells, scrabbling at the door.

Mava and Rava help Aya to her feet as Klaeon's men move in. "By order of his majesty, Blood King Klaeon Vacuda first of his name and Lord of Myldea, you are all sentenced to death," a soldier yells.

Yme, stomps his foot on the ground and spreads his arms wide. A crack races towards the men and encircles them. The circle beneath the soldier's feet crumbles and the men scream as they fall through to the floor below.

"Daniil!" Yme points to Otho.

Daniil looks at Tanith, and the Khorgoi leaps towards Dolus Otho. The voice of the arena screams and falls to the earth, his arms covering his face. Aya steps between Tanith and Dolus Otho. Tanith stops, glancing back at Daniil.

"We're taking him with us!" Aya yells.

"He betrayed us! He and Seera planned this trap!" Kylii storms towards Dolus Otho, the air heating around him.

Aya places a hand on his chest, stopping him. "Klaeon will kill him if we don't take him with us."

"That was a lie to trick us into trusting him!"

"He didn't know Seera was going to shut him in with us! Klaeon has killed for less. If we escape, then Dolus will be murdered in our stead."

"Enough! We're wasting time arguing. Let the coward choose to come with us or stay here. We have to run! Now, before more soldiers come!"

The group dashes around the hole in the ground. Aya grabs Dolus Otho and pulls him with the group. She glances into the hole, where men mix with earth and weapons below. More soldiers appear, blocking them.

Magic fills the air and the ground shakes. Roots burst from the earth and grab two soldiers, dragging them down into the soil. Wind mages wave their arms, slamming soldiers into the walls and ceiling.

Those without magic gather up the weapons and join the fray. Aya kicks those who get too close to her, her magic flaring up to cause injury. Mava and Rava stay close to her, finishing those she incapacitates. Dolus Otho huddles at the center of the group, but when a soldier gets too close, he pulls a knife from his belt and stabs the man in the neck. Workers awakened by the fighting don't hesitate to join the battle. Most fight alongside Klaeon's men, several fight with the slaves.

Yme, Daniil, and Kylii clear a path through the soldiers to a stairway leading up to the floor above. Bodies are left in the group's wake, but the number of soldier's is diminishing. The blocked exit is their final obstacle.

Yme pulls a large chunk of stone from the stairwell, causing the path to collapse. He throws the stone at the blocked exit, creating a large hole. Night air pours through the hole.

"This way! Everyone out!" Yme yells.

The slaves run through the hole as more soldiers appear. Some Arena workers stay behind to buy the exhausted slaves time. Dolus Otho and the others escaping with them crawl through the hole quickly. Then they help the slaves through. Aya sees Bern, Mava, Rava, and Cal assist the healers and workers in helping others through before following themselves. She turns to see if the workers need help, but Daniil and Kylii grab her. They drag her through the opening followed by Tanith. As soon as they clear the hole, earth rises, blocking the opening.

The cool, night air blows over their skin and whoops of victory fill the sky. Relief flows through Aya. "We're out!"

CHAPTER SIXTY-FOUR

DANIIL WAVES MAVA AND RAVA OVER. "HEAD FOR THE MOUNTAINS. There are places to hide in the thick woods. We will find you."

The two sisters nod and hurry ahead of the group, spreading the word of their destination. The slaves follow quickly, eager to be far from their former prison. Even Dolus Otho rushes to move as far from the Arena as possible.

Aya, Daniil, and Kylii follow at a slower pace, wanting a moment of privacy. "I can't believe your plan worked, Yme," Kylii pants, gasping for air.

He's answered with silence. Aya turns and realizes Yme is nowhere to be seen. She turns to the brothers as they search the group ahead of them. Yme isn't with them.

"Where's Yme?" Aya's blood runs cold.

"He was right behind us, wasn't he?" Daniil asks.

Kylii gives his brother an odd look. "I thought he was ahead of us."

Aya shakes her head in disbelief. "But he closed the wall. He didn't close it from the other side, did he? Why would he do that?"

Daniil turns to Tanith. "Go. Find Yme." Tanith lowers her

339

head before leaping into a run back to the Arena. "She'll lead him to the mountains."

"What if he needs help?"

"He'll be fine, Aya. He took care of a dozen Brüdel on his own. He can handle a few soldiers," Kylii says.

"He's not going to fight soldiers," says a voice from the shadows.

Daniil and Kylii instinctively move in front of Aya and raise their hands, magic filling the air. A cloaked figure walks out of the shadows and stands in front of them. "He is heading for Klaeon."

"Who are you?" Kylii demands.

"I need to take Aya to Yme. He's in danger."

Daniil asks, "Who are you?"

The cloaked figure walks towards Aya.

Daniil and Kylii step forward to stop him. "If he didn't answer me, why did you think he was going to answer you?" Kylii asks, elbowing Daniil back. He glares at the figure. "And what's to say you aren't here to give Aya over?"

The cloaked figure's head lowers.

Aya forces her way between the brothers. "Why do you think he's headed to confront the Blood King?"

The cloaked figure looks over his shoulder as though expecting someone to be there. "I can take you there, but only you."

He's alone. Fighting that man. That monster! Aya remembers the strange presence that surrounded her in the Blood King's private box. And Klaeon's second in command, Teron...Can he handle both?

"Daniil, Kylii, go with the group. I'm going to get Yme," Aya says, turning to the brothers.

"We can't leave you alone with this guy. We don't know if we can trust him!" Kylii yells.

"I'll be all right. Go."

Kylii tries to grab her, but Daniil stops him. He leads his brother away. Kylii protests, but eventually stops fighting and the two run off after the escaped slaves.

Facing the figure again, Aya takes a deep, calming breath. "Take me to Yme."

CHAPTER SIXTY-FIVE

YME GASPS FOR AIR AS HE RACES THROUGH THE HALLS OF THE Arena. He knows Daniil and Kylii will be furious with him, but he had to stay.

He's here. I know he is. He wouldn't want to leave without witnessing his handiwork, Yme thinks as he finds the gate leading onto the arena floor. He raises the gate with earth pillars and runs outside. Soldiers follow him, but he uses his earth magic to drop the gate and lift himself to the broken seating area.

He climbs the steps and nearly collides with another group of soldiers. They charge with weapons raised, but Yme uses his air magic to knock them to the ground. He searches for the stairs to the higher levels and skips every other step to stay ahead of any soldiers still following.

Reaching the third floor, he realizes the stairs leading further up are on the opposite side of the Arena. Yme takes off down the long, curved hallway, hearing dozens of footsteps following behind. Past the curve, soldiers wait ahead of Yme, trying to cut him off. Pulling large sections of the Arena's walls inwards, Yme uses the stones as a shield as spears are thrown towards him.

When more soldiers gather in front of him, potted plants provide water to assault the legs. They try to cut at the liquid,

342

but their weapons only go through the stream. Yme uses air magic to throw them out the large windows. The men scream as they plummet toward the distant ground. Yme turns to the group of soldiers chasing behind. He leaps forward, slamming his fists onto the floor. The floor drops, sending them down two floors. Yme raises his hands and the floor returns, clear of the enemy. Yme reaches the stairs leading up to the fourth level, relieved to find them clear. He climbs, only to discover the stairs to the top floor blocked by more soldiers.

Yme grabs two potted plants and throws them at the soldiers. He pulls the water from them as they fly. They smash into two of the soldiers, who manage to stay standing, but shards draw blood from their arms. Yme throws the water beneath their feet and uses his air magic to freeze it. One soldier slips and knocks several around him down. They scramble to stand, but only manage to knock more of their comrades down.

Yme uses the moment of confusion to grab a large shard from the floor. He jabs it into the throat of one of the last soldiers then runs up the stairs, using earth magic to raise the stairs to keep the soldiers from following.

The fifth floor, usually reserved only for the wealthiest of audience members as a place to eat, drink, and socialize while they watch the fights in the Arena below, stands empty. Yme walks through the carpeted halls, sneering at the marble pillars and statues displaying the wealth of the Arena.

There won't be any soldiers here. Klaeon doesn't need their protection.

Lit torches ahead cause him to slow his pace. His heart races when he sees the figure standing at a large window staring down at the Arena floor.

"Those you convinced into escaping have already left the city." Blood King Klaeon turns. His reddish-brown eye and green one glisten in the torchlight. "But you stayed. Do you want me to kill you that badly?"

Yme glares at him, rage filling his body. "I haven't come to kill you—yet. I came to take back what is rightfully mine."

Klaeon smiles. "If you want it back, try and take it."

Yme throws the pot shard at Klaeon, but he easily bats it away. Using his earth magic, Yme knocks a statue towering behind Klaeon over, attempting to crush him. Klaeon calmly steps out of the way and the statue shatter against the floor. Yme forcibly pulls the water from pots. He circles the water around Klaeon and splits it into many lines. Yme blows cold air and the water transforms into sharp, thick icicles. Yme brings his hands together and the icicles fly towards Klaeon.

Klaeon throws out his arms, and two thick shields fly to him from their spots on the walls. He kneels, protecting his body with the metal. The icicles shatter harmlessly.

A knife flies at Yme's leg, but he turns in time to avoid it. Yme spies Teron behind another statue. Cursing, Yme quickly turns his attention back to Klaeon in time to see one of the shields flying at him. He doesn't have time to dodge and the thick metal hits Yme in the gut. Gasping, he stumbles back.

Klaeon runs at him with the second shield raised above his head. He slams it down on Yme's back. Yme falls to the floor and Klaeon raises the shield to strike again.

Yme rolls onto his back and protects himself with the first shield. Klaeon tosses his shield to the floor and kicks Yme in the side. Screaming in pain, Yme rolls clear and scrambles to his feet. The pain in his stomach and side force him to gasp for air.

Klaeon draws his sword and knocks Yme in the head with the hilt. Yme falls to the floor, his vision covered in stars and darkness. Klaeon raises the blade above his head. The sharp blade rushes towards Yme's face and he quickly raises his hand. Dirt from a nearby plant spatters into the Blood King's eyes.

Klaeon shouts in pain and anger. Yme crawls away, wincing at the ache in his head. Teron appears behind him with his sword drawn. Yme raises the stone floor, lifting Teron off the ground and throwing him backward into a marble pillar and nearly out the window. Yme forces the floor to rise high enough to block the entire hallway, keeping Teron from getting involved again. Yme curses when soldiers appear at the other end of the hallway behind Klaeon.

Looking up, Yme punches the air. A hole explodes in the ceiling, and as the dust settles, Yme raises the section of floor he and Klaeon are standing on. The floor merges with the roof, blocking any from reaching the two men.

The movement of the ground beneath him causes Klaeon to stumble as he wipes the dirt from his face. The sword falls from his hands, slipping over the edge of the roof. "You truly have improved, fighting in the Arena. But I've been getting stronger as well." Klaeon runs at Yme. Yme tries to knock him down with wind, but Klaeon avoids each blast as though he knows where Yme will attack from next.

Changing to earth magic, Yme throws sections of the stone roof into the air, dropping them randomly. Yet Klaeon avoids the sudden changes easily and kicks with such force Yme is thrown back and lands on the roof hard. Before he can react, Klaeon kicks him again, the force throwing him off the roof.

Yme scrabbles for the edge with his hands, but it's out of reach. He uses wind to move him till he manages to grab onto a broken piece of stone. He feels his grip slipping as he tries to pull himself up. The harder he tries, the more pain shoots through his body.

Klaeon walks to the edge and stares down at Yme. "Before I kill you, I'm going to take the rest of your magic away. I want you to feel completely helpless before your heart stops."

"Yme!" Aya's voice echoes across the roof. Both Yme and Klaeon see her being helped onto the roof by a cloaked stranger.

"How lucky for me. After I kill you, I'll finally get to kill the Life Healer with my own hand," Klaeon says.

Yme tries to pull himself up again. "Don't touch her!"

"Or what? You'll stop me? I'm afraid it's too late for that." Klaeon kneels down and grabs Yme by the throat. Yme grabs the hand around his throat and tries to loosen it. Klaeon pulls him onto the roof and forces him to his knees.

Dark magic fills the air, blacking out the night sky around them. Yme struggles, but the power surrounding them feeds into Klaeon's strength.

Aya takes a step back. "He's a magic user!" She has felt it, deep inside, all along, yet till now hadn't allowed herself to believe it.

The cloaked man nods. "He's called Blood King because he's able to use the forbidden Blood Magic. He can take away another's magic and kill with a single touch to the heart."

CHAPTER SIXTY-SIX

YME STRUGGLES TO BE FREE OF KLAEON BUT HIS STRENGTH EBBS away. The feeling triggers a memory of the last time they fought. He remembers his rage blinding him, making it easy for Klaeon to overpower him. He remembers Klaeon's hand closing on his throat and his strength fading. He remembers his magic fading.

Having his magic pulled from his body terrifies him every bit as much now as it had then.

The alien presence fills him, searching inside for where his magic is hidden. Even his most secret places, places he can't access on his own, are invaded. The presence finds what it's seeking and withdraws, taking magic and strength with it. In a panic, Yme strikes out at Klaeon, but his blows are weak.

Klaeon laughs. "You can't fight me anymore." His reddish-brown eye glows red and his hand tightens around Yme's throat.

A roar surprises Klaeon. He turns; Tanith plunges sharp fangs into his thigh. Screaming, Klaeon tries to kick the beast away. But her fangs are embedded deep in his flesh and muscle. Tanith drags him away from the edge of the roof before releasing him with a hiss. The cloaked man uses the moment to move next to Klaeon and stab him in the shoulder. Klaeon glares but manages to keep his grip on Yme's throat.

347

Yme's vision darkens as less and less oxygen enters his lungs. A shadow appears behind Klaeon and grabs the Blood King's arm. Klaeon's hand releases, and Yme gasps in deep lungfuls of air. Yme's magic flees from Klaeon, returning to its place inside of Yme. The force of it knocks him to the ground. Simultaneously, his strength returns, and he scrambles back to his feet. Tanith stands beside him, growling at Klaeon.

Yme is shocked to see that Aya is the one holding the Blood King's arm. Klaeon's hand hangs limply at the wrist, but his attention is on Aya. A wide smile forms on his face, and Yme sees the terror filling Aya. Klaeon whispers something to her and she releases his arm. Klaeon grabs her with his other hand.

The cloaked man kicks the back of Klaeon's knee. The Blood King falls to the ground, blood pouring out of his wound. The cloaked man brings the knife down, aiming for Klaeon's hand holding Aya. Klaeon releases her. The cloaked man changes course, grabbing Aya and pulling her clear. The knife stabs again into the same spot on Klaeon's shoulder and the Blood King yells in pain.

Running towards Yme and Tanith, the cloaked man motions his hand ahead of him. "Move!"

Yme stares at Klaeon. *My fire didn't return yet. I have to get it back. I can't let him slip away.* Yme takes a step, but Tanith bites on his clothes and tugs him back.

The cloaked man stops in front of Yme, handing Aya off to him. "You can fight him another day."

Yme stares at Aya. Her body trembles. She rubs her shoulder where Klaeon had grabbed her and Yme understands. She felt it, too. She felt the other presence try to force itself inside of her.

Aya grabs his hand in hers. "Daniil and Kylii are waiting. I would never abandon you."

The anger in Yme's heart disappears, as the words he spoke to Aya are said back to him. Had she truly thought he was abandoning them?

The cloaked man leans close. "There is strength in knowing

when to retreat." The stranger hurries past Yme, followed by Tanith. Yme hesitates before he and Aya follow the group across the roof.

Yme creates a flight of stairs from the roof and they hurry down. He spies Klaeon struggling to his feet. The Blood King's furious wails fill the night. Dark red fire erupts from his hands and flies towards the group, chasing them down the stairs. Yme forces the dark magic away using his wind, but a small ball of flame hits him in the still tender side. The flames burn his skin, causing Yme to yelp in pain. He feels something else move across his skin, draining his strength. Yme uses the last of his energy to close the roof access before he collapses. The cloaked man grabs him, and, with Aya, helps the exhausted Yme hobble, with Tanith leading the way.

Outside the Arena, they run as fast as they can, considering Yme's injuries. They slow only when Tanith needs to sniff the air, searching for the scent of those who escaped before them. The Khorgoi leads them out of the city towards the mountains.

Yme turns his head to watch Bloodfall Arena disappear behind them, a sight he's dreamed of for ages. The pain in his side fades as his strength leaves him. His eyelids droop and soon the world around him goes dark.

CHAPTER SIXTY-SEVEN

AYA READJUSTS HER GRIP ON THE LIMP YME, TAKING IN THE cloaked man helping her hold him between them. The hood of the cloak casts a dark shadow, and his mouth is covered by a cloth, making it impossible to see the man's face. But the man's voice is so familiar to her. She can't be sure, but her heart tells her she knows this man.

The rough terrain challenges their ability to balance the limp Yme. Tanith navigates, her snout low to the ground. She stops suddenly and her ears perk up. Tanith inhales as she smells the air. The Khorgoi leaps into a sprint, catching both Aya and the man off guard.

They try to catch up, but soon the beast is gone. Voices and a light ahead quicken their pace. Praying it's the rest of the group, Aya understands Tanith's excitement. The escaped slaves and former Arena workers wait for them, sitting on boulders, and treating any who were wounded during the escape.

Daniil and Kylii leap from a boulder and take Yme, now completely unconscious, from Aya and the cloaked man.

Aya grabs Daniil's arm. "Take him to Skara. He may have internal bleeding."

Daniil nods and the brothers quickly take Yme to the healer. Aya collapses to the ground and tries to calm her breathing. Blood King Klaeon's whispered words echo in her mind. *"We haven't tasted Life Healer in so long."* The words chilled her to the bone. Aya could hear another voice in Klaeon's own. And the presence she felt when she sat in the private box… trying to force itself inside her, trying to find her magic. If the cloaked man hadn't saved her, would her magic have been taken away, like Yme's fire?

The cloaked man sits on a nearby boulder and watches the group celebrate their escape. Aya stares at him, noticing a second dagger on his belt. She recognizes it.

The man pulls the dagger, with hilt, free from his belt.

"This is yours." He doesn't ask. He knows it to be true.

"Who are you?" Aya asks.

The man raises his hands and pulls the hood and cloth covering his mouth away, revealing the familiar black hair and blue eyes. Aya chokes back a sob.

"Jaxon?"

The leader of the Black Caravan nods and holds out her dagger. "You thought I forgot about you, didn't you?"

Aya nods, taking the dagger from him. As she grabs it, she spots a bracelet on Jaxon's wrist. She recognizes the beautiful silk and her mouth opens in shock. Grabbing his arm, she moves his wrist closer to make sure she's not seeing things. But there it is. The woven bracelet made of four colored silks.

"My bracelet." She stares into Jaxon's eyes. "I thought you sold it?"

Jaxon shrugs. "I never intended to sell it. I knew if any of the other men in the caravan saw you wearing it, they'd steal it for themselves." He carefully unties the bracelet and hands it to Aya.

"Thank you." Aya holds the last treasures from her parents close to her chest. "I never forgot you."

Laughing, Jaxon sits down beside her. "I'm glad to hear that. After Seera nearly killed me, I realized my heart wasn't in slave trading anymore. Truth is, it'd never really had been."

Aya reaches up and touches Jaxon's cheek.

He flinches at her touch, but doesn't pull away, confusion filling his expression.

"How are you here? How did you know where to find us?"

Gently taking her hand in his, he lowers it back to her dagger. "I saw your first fight. I was truly impressed. I watched you fight for survival and kill that beast. I watched your victory against the Brüdel, and that's when I heard rumors of a possible escape. I knew I needed to help."

"Why?"

"An attempt to make up for some of the things I've done to you and the others I brought to that awful place."

"What about your caravan? Your men? Aldur?"

"I'd never let him go off on his own," Aldur says from behind Aya. She looks up into his familiar face and at the group gathered behind him.

"*You* led them here?" Aya asks.

"I did, missy. Spotted 'em running for the mountains. The Blood King may've claimed this city, but he doesn't know the land as well as those of us who grew up here."

Jaxon nods at Aldur and he walks away. "I disbanded my caravan. To be more exact, I gave it to those who wanted it for themselves. Aldur and Fleance were the only ones who decided to stay with me."

"Fleance?"

"Ah, you probably never knew his name. He was the young man who brought your food and water every day."

"The Archer."

Skara interrupts them, grabbing Aya's hands tightly. "Something serious is wrong with Yme."

Aya's heart drops as she stands. "What?"

"I can't heal him. Something is blocking my magic!"

"Lingering effects of the Blood King's power," Jaxon says. "He was hit by that dark fire."

Aldur and the Archer—Fleance—return with Yme and lay him on the ground in front of Aya. Daniil, Kylii, and a few others follow. Meanwhile, Rava, Mava, Bern, and others who traveled with Aya gawk at Jaxon in shock. Some expressions are filled with terror, others with rage.

Aya catches Dolus Otho staring at Jaxon. *He didn't expect to see his best slaver here.*

"You should heal Yme first. Then we can all talk," Jaxon says.

Aya looks down at Yme. "But my magic is blocked."

"You're a Life Healer."

The certainty in his voice keeps her silent. She kneels down and places her hands on Yme's chest. She feels it, the block. It reminds her of the presence surrounding Klaeon, but weaker. It covers Yme like a second skin. Aya feels it draining his strength.

She hesitates, then tests her magic, gently urging it down her arms to where her hands touch Yme's skin. As soon as her magic touches the dark magic, it evaporates. Relaxing, Aya reaches deep into her magic. Some she sends across Yme's body to rid him of the dark magic. With the rest, she heals him.

There isn't the old sensation of energy draining, or the cold building within her. Aya realizes how much stronger her magic has become while she was in the Arena. Was it truly only a few months ago she could barely heal a broken leg? But even as she ponders this, exhaustion fills her. A strange noise tickles at the back of her mind, so faint Aya wonders if she's truly hearing it.

Yme opens his eyes, gazing up at Aya. He carefully sits up. "We escaped?"

Aya nods and places a hand on his shoulder. Her magic returns to her as the last of his wounds heal. "You still have all of your magic? Klaeon didn't take any of it?"

Yme lifts his hand and a stone rises. He uses wind to throw it and pulls water from Aldur's water jug. He puts the water back in the jug and shakes his head. "He didn't take anything." He holds his hand palm up and concentrates. His expression becomes grim. "But I didn't get my fire back."

"You're lucky he didn't steal all of it. Fighting the Blood King without all of your magic is dangerous and reckless," Jaxon scolds.

Yme turns his attention to Jaxon still sitting on the boulder behind Aya. "Good thing you showed up when you did, then."

"Jaxon Parth."

"I know who you are. People say the leader of the Black Caravan bleeds blood black as the death that follows him. You sold many slaves to the Arena."

Jaxon smiles and bows his head. "I'm honored you've heard of me, Yme Gurek. The stories are spread far and wide of the Rare Kind with four elemental magics. Well...*three*."

Yme frowns and stands. "Why did you help us?"

"For her."

"A lot of people are interested in her. Many want to kill her. What makes you any different?"

Aya stands between Yme and Jaxon, placing a hand on the former's chest. "Excuse me. Don't talk about me like I'm not here. If you need a reason to trust Jaxon how about two? He helped me find you and his men helped our friends get away from the Arena? We can trust him."

She sees the struggle in Yme's eyes. She knows he's trying to think of an argument, a reason for distrust. She makes sure the expression on her face erases those thoughts from his mind.

Taking a calming breath, Yme crosses his arms over his chest. "So, how are you going to help us?"

Jaxon stands, a smile growing. "I know a place we can go for a little while. There's an oasis town at the end of this canyon that the Blood King doesn't know about. Or if he does, he doesn't care enough about it to station any of his soldiers nearby. The town will give us shelter, food, maybe clothes."

"How far?" Aya asks.

"Two days on foot."

"And after that?" Yme asks.

Jaxon's smile widens. "We'll talk about that after we get there."

EPILOGUE

BLOOD KING KLAEON SLUMPS IN HIS PRIVATE CARRIAGE IN SILENCE. He rubs his chin with one hand and reads from a parchment in his other. The writing on the report is nearly illegible, having been written quickly.

An attack in the south has taken out another of his scouting groups. Opinions are circulating that Klaeon is wasting men sending groups that far south. *They don't understand why I need men down there. It couldn't matter less to me what they think.*

He crumples the report, which immediately bursts into flames. He throws the residual ash out the window. He winces and curses as the shoulder wound the cloaked man gave him stings. He glares at the dagger responsible for the pain, sitting in a glass box across from him. When he finds out who that cloaked man is, he will personally execute the bastard along with that traitorous beast that bit him.

Knocking on the door of the carriage, Teron calls, "My Lord."

"Enter."

Once Teron climbs in, he kneels on the floor before standing. "My Lord, we're almost ready to depart."

"Very good. Make sure everything is finished quickly and thoroughly. I don't want to have to clean up another mess."

"Yes, My Lord." Teron holds out a black envelope. "This was on the carriage."

Klaeon raises his eyebrows. "Well, I haven't seen one of these in a while. Did you see who delivered it?"

"No, it was affixed to the door with wax when I approached. I checked with all the guards and no one saw anyone approach. Should I punish them for their failure?" Teron's hand tightens on the hilt of his sword.

Shaking his head, Klaeon takes the letter. "No need." He turns it over, but there's no writing, only a small, symbol-shaped indent on the front. He opens the envelope and scans the letter inside.

A smile spreads across his face. "Get several of your best men together, Teron. It seems our favorite Shadow Watcher has some interesting information for us. He's infiltrated the escaped group of slaves containing the Rare Kinds and knows where they're going. I want you to follow them, and kill them all."

"All, My Lord?"

"Except for the Life Healer and the cloaked man who wounded me. I want you to bring them to me alive. I want the pleasure of killing them myself."

"And the beast that attacked you?"

"I want its head."

"Yes, My Lord." Teron bows and leaves the carriage.

Klaeon rereads the letter and looks at the envelope closely. He tries to burn it, but the material doesn't burn. It changes from black to red and writing appears on the envelope. He reads the writing and lifts his head.

"Teron!"

Teron appears at the door of the carriage. "My Lord?"

"Before you leave, I've got something to give to you. Once you've gathered your men, return to me."

Teron bows his head and leaves, closing the door behind him. Klaeon places the envelope next to him. A sharp headache causes him to gasp and grab his head.

357

"Not now," he growls. The pain increases, but eventually fades. He opens his eyes and leans his head back. "We'll have the Life Healer soon. You can feast on her magic all you want."

His reddish-brown eye glows a deep scarlet, the color of coagulating blood.

ABOUT THE AUTHOR

J.A. Ludwig received a BA in Theater Technology and has been fortunate to work for two theaters in Southern California. She is a proud techie who feels more comfortable behind the scenes dressed in black than on the stage. Since she was young, she's been lost in her imagination or in books. If you want an insight into her mind, you can check out her blog, A Joy on the Updays.

Babylon Books is an imprint of Bernhardt Books, Inc.

Editor-in-Chief: Alice Bernhardt

Chief Financial Officer: Harrison Bernhardt

Marketing Director: Ralph Bernhardt